THE PATH TO REDEMPTION

BY

PHILLIP TUCKER

www.philliptucker.com.au

ACKNOWLEDGEMENT

I'd like to thank the many friends, who encouraged me to write, especially Mary, Fiona, Nigel, Gayle and Michelle, my editor, who showed me that even a person with appalling grammar could write. All it takes is imagination and a computer with spell check and good friends. But most of all I thank my family, especially my wife, Michelle, for putting up with me during this time.

This book is dedicated to my grandson Bailey who makes me feel both young and old at the same time.

CONTENTS

THE PATH TO REDEMPTION
FOREWORD

Steve Roberts belongs to a five-man unit, formed in the Eighties by the CIA. Their brief was to complete missions that for political reasons, America could not be seen to be involved in. The unit carried out many successful missions, until their enemies became aware of their existence, making them a liability. Worried, the CIA decided to terminate the unit; the first attempt failed.

In the Nineties, changes in the CIA's Directorship initiated another attempt; this too failed but resulted in the death of Steve Roberts' wife. Going underground after the murder, they became a mercenary unit for hire. Working out of Singapore, for a gunrunner named Mr Lou they stayed off the radar avoiding the CIA. This continued till roughly 1996 when by mistake, they destroyed an Israeli Bioweapons plant in Turkey. The Israelis, with Intel from the CIA, eliminated Mr Lou's organisation along with Japanese unit member Sukai.

Following this, the unit disbanded going into hiding until 2010. After meeting and falling in love with a young woman named Justine, Steve sought to clear his name and stop running. Contacting Ali, his unit leader, they put together a dangerous plan to stop the Americans and the Israelis hunting them. With the help of the surviving unit members Cody and Aaron, they seized the White House. After negotiations with the Vice President, the siege was covered up, and they were allowed to retire in peace.

As the unit separated for their journey home, Steve, ever cautious, stayed in America for a short time to make sure that they kept their part of the deal.

Feeling finally in the clear, Steve went to the airport for his flight home. It was here that he read that Justine, his girlfriend had been murdered.

GOING HOME

Are you alright Sir?" Holly, the Qantas stewardess, asked, sounding out of breath, after her dash across the room. She'd only been working at Los Angeles Airport for the last two months, without any problems. Sure she'd had the occasional lecherous drunk, but nothing major until now. She remembered serving the man one drink only and giving him a paper. Curious if there was a link, so she glanced down at the paper seeing it opened on page three. It showed the photo of a murdered girl.

"Did you know her Sir?" She asked softly, getting a brief nod of acknowledgement from the man in return. Sitting down, Holly hugged the man as she would a hurt child, trying to give him reassurance. "I know it's not much of help at the moment, but I heard they caught the man responsible," Holly informed him, having heard it from a pilot that very morning. The man, who seconds before had seemed to be on the verge of a total breakdown, suddenly bolted upright, looking intently into her eyes.

"Are you sure?" He stammered out as if waking from a bad dream.

"Yes, it doesn't mention it there, but he's been linked to two other murders in that area. He escaped from jail a few weeks ago, always targeting women in high-rise units. A pilot from Australia told me about it this morning," she said hesitantly, a little afraid of the man's reaction.

"Thank you," he groaned, before slowly getting to his feet and wiping his eyes. Pulling himself together, he took a couple of tentative steps, stumbling, as Holly jumped up to steady him.

"Would you like me to walk you to your plane Sir, it's about to board?" both worried and somehow drawn to this man.

"That would be good, thank you. I'm not sure I can make it on my own," Steve replied softly.

"It's no trouble, and there's no one else here anyway." Holly smiled, taking his arm, supporting him.

Strolling through the terminal, Holly tried to engage the man in conversation, pointing out different things she'd learned about the airport while working there. He seemed to listen to her, though apart from answering when necessary, he contributed little. Approaching the boarding area, Holly noticed two plainclothes FBI agents assigned to the airport. The agents looked towards her smiling, as their eyes shifted to the man beside her. He must have noticed them as well, as tension flowed through his body, into the arm she was holding. She could feel his muscles flex involuntarily, becoming like a compressed spring.

As if electricity was flowing between the man and the agents, the two agents tensed as well, reacting like two small sharks, detecting a much more substantial predator. Visually they became more alert, their eyes glued to Holly's partner, as he stopped at the barrier. Handing his boarding pass to the air hostess on the gate, the man turned to Holly, his eyes looking past her to the agents, who stood watching him.

"Thank you for your help, I'll be right from here," he informed her, giving a warm smile, his eyes returning to hers. Placing some money in her hand, he kissed her lightly on the cheek, before turning and walking confidently through the gate.

"What a strange man!" She whispered to herself, catching her breath. A feeling as if she'd been in the presence of a dangerous creature, filled her with both fear and arousal, as she watched him move away from her. Feeling a little scared of her attraction to him; she wondered what type of life he led, as he walked down the boarding ramp, to catch his flight. Once he was out of sight, Holly looked at the tip the man had given her. Shocked, she found ten one hundred dollar notes. Smiling at the generous and much-needed money, she put the notes in her pocket, hoping the man would find some happiness.

"Excuse me miss, who was that man you were with?" One of the FBI agents asked Holly, distracting her from her thoughts.

"Just a Business Class traveller, he had some bad news while in the lounge. I accompanied him to his flight, to make sure he was okay," Holly replied.

"What was the bad news?" the Agent enquired.

"A woman he knew in Australia was murdered. He saw it in the paper. He seemed pretty upset," she answered sadly; before walking back to the business class lounge, her thoughts still with the mystery man.

The agents took in this information, both coming to the same conclusion. The look in his eyes was not a threat, but a show of anger at his loss. He wanted to hit out at someone in authority they wrongly concluded. Relaxing, the threat gone, the agents resumed their surveillance, as the other passengers boarded.

Sitting in business class, Steve tried to contain his mixed emotions, at the loss of Justine. He'd nearly blown it with the agents back there he admitted angrily. When the hostess had offered to walk him to the plane, he had accepted out of fear, more than his physical condition. Knowing he was shaken up by Justine's death and unsure if it was connected to his past; he'd used the woman as a shield, to get him to the plane. Ashamed of himself for putting the girl at risk, he knew he had no other choice, for he had to get on that plane, no matter the risk.

With the young woman walking by his side, he knew he was less of a target to any potential assassin waiting for him in the terminal. Then the agents had appeared and forgetting his training he had angrily looked them in the eye, challenging them. Luckily for him, they hadn't reacted. Instead, they'd held their position, watching him or by now he'd most probably be in a cell.

He'd loved Justine, and even though it felt wrong, he was hoping that her death wasn't connected to his past. This meant he wouldn't have to ring the other unit members and warn them off before they all started running again.

"What do I do now?" Steve groaned, making several passengers turn his way suspiciously, before going back to what they were doing. 'Settle down and think before you speak,' he told himself, knowing how badly her death had affected him.

Once the plane took off, and the flight got underway, Steve drifted between semi-wakefulness and sleep. He tried desperately to pull himself together, as vivid scenes of his past missions, mixed with the memories of the people he loved came one on top of the other, so randomly and broken up, that after a while he couldn't tell reality from fiction. One memory however always surfaced, and that one, he always recognised. On his first mission in Vietnam, he'd killed his first man. The poor bastard had come walking out of the dense scrub, as Steve was preparing to kill a sniper in a tree.

Steve reacted more out of fear than training, burying his knife deep into the man's chest, piercing his heart. He died instantly, leaving him free to kill the sniper. Steve knew he would never forget the look in the man's eyes, as his life left his body.

Snapping fully awake bathed in sweat; Steve opted not to sleep for the rest of the flight. Downing mugs of coffee, and pacing the aisles endlessly, Steve fought to stay awake, scared to dream. During this time, he remained deep in thought, avoiding contact with the other passengers, wondering what to do once he reached Brisbane.

He'd planned to pick up Justine at Ballina and drive south to Sydney. There he was going to introduce her to his girls or young women, as they were now. With her death, that was all over now he thought sadly. Time was what he needed, time to sort out his problems and pull his shit together before it got him killed. He had already waited in America for nearly a month, watching for any sign of treachery from the yanks, before travelling home. Now, this had happened he wondered how safe going home really would be. Deep down he still believed Justine's death was connected to him and that made him afraid.

'Best thing to do is wait a week, and then head for Ballina. Once there, I'll visit Justine and pay my respects,' Steve thought. Then I'll find the bastard responsible, he promised himself as the plane continued on.

BRISBANE AUSTRALIA

When the plane touched down in Brisbane, Steve was only half awake, from lack of sleep. Still, on edge, he quickly grabbed his bags and hired a four-wheel drive, telling the man at the hire desk, he was going out west. Leaving the airport, he drove through a series of back streets and freeways, ever watching for tails. Confident he wasn't being followed; he turned north following the coast, disappearing into the floating tourist population that swarmed up and down this part of Queensland.

After spending eight days lying low, Steve arrived back at Brisbane Airport. Although he felt both anguish and guilt at the loss of Justine, he felt replenished. He'd spent a lot of time fishing and just relaxing, something for the past twenty years that had been at most, fleeting. His life had been a series of gut-wrenching moves, always keeping one step ahead of his enemies, and never letting his guard down. Only on two occasions had his enemies come close to getting him.

THE TOP END

When Steve had first arrived back in Australia after travelling from Singapore, he'd taken a job in the 'Top End'. There he guided adventure tours around the Gulf country, in the Northern Territory. He'd been there over a year when unknown to him his cover had been blown. An American tourist, impressed with the tour, had taken a photo of him. Returning to the States, he had entered it in a tourism contest, for the best holiday. The CIA's hunting dogs controlled by its Director; Don Brooks must have got wind of it, informing the Israelis.

Desperate to capture or eliminate any of Steve's unit members, the Israelis, had sent a four-man squad to investigate the sighting. Steve was leading a tour when the four had arrived in Darwin.

Although their booking office was in Darwin, all the tours started and finished in Alice Springs several hundred miles to the south. When the men arrived at the office, they immediately booked the next available tour. Skye, one of the office team, became suspicious. The men were asking a great deal more about Steve, than about the tour. They also had a photo of Steve taken by an American tourist. This they continually showed to staff, making sure he was the one still guiding the tour.

Contacting Steve by radio, she told him about the four men, thinking they might be cops. Steve, at first wasn't too worried, thinking the men might just be on holidays, looking for the excitement the American tourist story had implied. The tours they operated ran through the Gulf country, taking ten days, from start to finish. This included an overland section, followed by a boat trip into the swampy upper reaches of Alligator River. Here the tourists come face to face with the deadly man-eating crocodiles, which infested the river.

At the end of the river trip, the guests were taken back to Alice Springs by plane. No more than ten tourists at a time could partake of the tour, as along with two guides, the vehicles and the boat could hold a maximum of twelve people. Once the tourists had departed, the two guides would then travel back down the river to their vehicles, then back to Alice Springs, for the next group of tourists.

At the time Skye radioed Steve, they were loading the tourists onto their waiting plane. Steve with Adrian, the other guide, then started back down the river.

The twin-engine flat bottom boat, minus the 10 tourists, positively flew along the mirror-like surface of the river. Going up river pausing periodically for photo snaps by the amazed holidaymakers, took four days. Coming back down took only one. Adrian and Steve loved this part of the trip, as with no tourists they could relax and just take in the sights.

Around a kilometre from their vehicles, both men noticed a change in the engine's noise followed by a vibration. Slowing down, knowing stopping here to look at the engine was too dangerous, they nursed the boat to their tour's departure point. Using one of the four-wheel drives, they carefully pulled the boat from the river. During this process, Adrian was forced to fire several warning shots at some nosey crocs, who thought the two men look like a tasty meal. An hour after they'd beached the boat Steve found the problem.

The gearbox on the left rear engine had shot a bearing. The problem was common on this type of motor, and they carried spares for it. Unfortunately, someone would have to stay and repair it, while the other drove to Alice Springs to meet the next group of tourists. There he could arrange an additional driver to bring the tourists and supplies back here to the river part of the tour, in three days time.

Adrian readily volunteered to go, having a hot date that night in town, leaving Steve to fix the boat. In a cloud of dust and honking of horns, Adrian's smiling face disappeared into the dense scrub.

It was close to 6pm when Steve called it a night. Most of the job was complete. To finish, he only had to reassemble the driveshaft, and that could wait until daylight tomorrow. Working near the river on your own, in the failing light, was a recipe for disaster. Steve knew the crocs were watching him, so he decided to turn in early, sleeping in his jeep.

Early next day rifle held ready, Steve alighted from the vehicle having had a careful look around. There were two sets of drag marks near the boat, meaning a couple of the river's reptilian friends had come looking for him. Not taking any chances, Steve kept the rifle close at hand, as he continued working on the engine. By ten that morning, the work was complete and with the help of the jeep, he quickly relaunched the boat.

Moving it slowly along the river, using a long rope, Steve secured the craft to an improvised jetty they used for the trips. Taking it for a quick spin along the river, Steve satisfied the gearbox was sound, returned to the dock. Filling up the fuel tanks and having another day before the clients arrived, he decided to move to higher ground away from the river. Putting up his tent, making himself comfortable he decided on a catnap, sleeping through the hottest part of the day.

Awaking around three in the afternoon feeling dehydrated, Steve went to his jeep, gulping down half a canteen of water, before deciding to radio Adrian. For over half an hour Steve tried to raise his friend, but the only reply was static. A bad feeling settled over Steve at the lack of response. Changing frequency, he radioed his head office in Darwin, hoping someone was still there.

"Steve! It's Skye! Can you hear me?" answered a garbled voice.

"Yes Skye, you're faint, but I can hear you." He was happy he'd made contact.

"Come back to Alice Springs, something has happened." She asked her voice sounding strained.

"What's wrong?"

"Adrian's missing! His girlfriend told the police she'd seen him being dragged into his jeep by some men. The police have cancelled the tour, till they find out what's going on." Steve sat silently for several seconds unable to reply before a dark thought came to him.

"What about the four men who wanted to go on the tour, have you heard from them?" As in the pit of his stomach fear started to grow.

"No one's been able to contact them, Steve. The boss thinks they may have heard it on the news and went elsewhere." Skye replied sensing Steve's concern. "Do you think they're involved?" She asked.

"I'm not sure Skye but just in case, leave town for awhile and tell the boss to do the same."

"Okay, I'll pass it on. Be careful Steve," she added, as the transmission ceased.

Turning off his radio, Steve slowly took in his surroundings, listening for anything out of the ordinary. He hadn't used the road to come to this spot, meaning no one would happen by. The problem was anyone coming to the river would spot his tyre tracks. 'They could already be here,' Steve realised, as he grabbed the 303 rifle from the passenger seat and walked silently into the scrub.

After spending an hour looking around, including walking back to the river, Steve returned to the vehicle. 'I could just drive away' he thought, knowing there were many tracks out of this area. Of course, that would mean abandoning Adrian, who could be already dead or would be if Steve ran. 'No best to wait' he told himself, as the sound of a vehicle could be heard in the distance approaching.

"Well, that ends that debate!" Steve smiled. Grabbing his pack from the jeep, he swiftly loaded it with supplies, before slipping away into the surrounding scrub.

"He's got to be here somewhere?" Jed, the leader of the four-man team, pointed out, as his men checked over Steve's abandoned vehicle.

"Well, he isn't going anywhere without his vehicle!" Clef smiled, seeing the vehicle parked in the scrub up ahead.

When given this assignment, Jed, short for Jedadia, had been told to pick his own team. He'd picked Clef, Jose and Damian, mostly for their ability as soldiers, plus their good American accents. Their cover was that they were American tourists here for some excitement. In reality, they were Israeli paratroops, working for Mossad, Israel's security organization.

They'd been sent to track down Roberts and if possible bring him back alive. Their government wanted him for some horrendous crimes, carried out against Israel. Why he hadn't been told exactly what Roberts had done worried Jed. It made it difficult to plan his capture knowing only a little of his background. Unfortunately, orders were orders, so here they were.

Upon arriving at the river, they'd spread out on foot, following Steve's jeep tracks up into the hills, dragging Adrian along with them. They weren't murderers and had no intention of killing Adrian, but he knew where Roberts was and for now, they kept him out front as bait.

"You're making a mistake!" Adrian smiled, as he led the group up the hill towards Steve's campsite.

"Just keep moving and shut up," Jed whispered pushing the barrel of his Uzi into Adrian's back.

"He'll eat you four for breakfast," Adrian laughed, this time getting thumped across the back of his head, knocking him to the ground. "Did I mention he's an expert shot with that rifle he's got!" Adrian taunted, rubbing his head and laughing, as the four men watched the surrounding light scrub.

Having had enough of the taunting, Jed taped Adrian's mouth shut, leaving Clef to watch him. With the other two men, he formed a rough skirmish line, moving forward and securing Steve's campsite. After a thorough search of the area, the four men and their prisoner took a break while Clef started Steve's jeep.

"Back to the river men, let's make sure that boat's going nowhere," Jed ordered, as they jumped aboard Steve's jeep, slowly retracing their steps. They'd nearly reached the river camp, when the front tyre suddenly exploded with a loud bang, forcing Clef to grip the wheel, while he slammed on the brakes. All of Jed's team jumped clear of the vehicle, expecting trouble, leaving Adrian behind. Laughing hysterically behind his gag, he sat there with tears in his eyes, as the four paratroopers rolled to the ground fanning out. Jed felt like shooting Adrian, as he stared at the tyre seeing a bullet hole.

"Watch the prisoner Clef! We'll look for Roberts!" Jed ordered, as with the other two men he charged off in the direction that the shot had come from. After an exhaustive search of the area, the three men returned finding both Clef and Adrian gone.

"Fuck!" Jed shouted angrily, startling the others, as he ran forward looking for prints, finding nothing. "Let's get back to the other jeep," he ordered, a feeling of frustration settling over them all.

The walk to the river was slow and terrifying, as it occurred to the three men that now there were two men out there armed. Jed felt a fool, thinking one of their men was most probably dead, at the hands of an enemy of their country. Coming up to the clearing where their jeep sat, the three men waited silently knowing at any moment a well-aimed shot, could take one of them out.

Emerging from the thick scrub, Jed walked forward leaving his men to cover him. His heart rate increased, as he slowly crossed the open ground to the jeep expecting not to make it. Approaching Adrian's jeep and seeing the hood of the engine ajar, he quickly lifted it to find the distributor cap missing.

"That's just great!" Jed said out loud, signalling the others to come forward. "He must have been here when we first arrived," Damian put forward, Jed nodding.

"Check the boat, Damian. Let's see if we can use it as a backup," Jed suggested, knowing they wouldn't leave without finding Clef first.

Damian, having never been to Australia before, walked to the rear of the boat, at the river's edge. Thinking it quicker, he walked out into the water, preparing to climb over the rear of the boat, rather than walk along the jetty. Twenty metres out in the murky water, a four-metre crocodile flapped its tail, accelerating towards the prey that it had watched for the last two days. Breaching the water the jaws of the mighty croc flew open, closing swiftly on Damian's legs.

Jed and Jose watched helplessly, as Damian disappeared under the water, as a shot rang out above them. Seeing the water spurt into the air where the croc was, Jed and Jose raced forward. The croc had been hit right between the eyes. Both men still sprayed the beast with well-aimed shots just in case. Damian breaking the surface, suddenly free, scrambled up the bank. Both his legs were badly lacerated and bleeding, as he collapsed onto the riverbank.

Dropping his weapon, Jed ripped open his first aid kit, wrapping field dressings around the deep puncture wounds in Damian's legs. This stopped the bleeding enough to allow Jed to inject him with morphine, before starting to stitch up his wounds. While Jed worked on Damian, Jose kept watch on the surrounding bushland. Another shot echoed above them, making Jed and Jose flinch. On the river, a spurt of water jumped into the air as the bullet impacted. Momentarily, a crocodile broke the surface, before disappearing below the mud coloured surface.

Jose startled, frantically sent a full clip into the water as Jed dragged Damian away from the bank, towards the jeep. It took over an hour for Damian's wounds to be stitched up by Jed before the men relaxed.

"That was close!" Damian muttered weakly, coming around, still shocked by how close he'd come to death. "Who fired that first shot, you saved my life!" He asked close to tears, thinking it was one of them.

"It wasn't us. It must have been Roberts or Adrian," Jed admitted utterly baffled.

"He's supposed to be some type of mad killer, why he'd save Damian?" Jose asked angrily, wanting answers.

"I don't know Jose, it's a mystery," Jed replied confused.

"Maybe he's hoping we'll leave him alone, by saving Damian," Jose put forward.

"He could have killed us all just then, why bother saving one of us?" Jed answered, wondering exactly what Roberts had done against his country.

"I'm for bugging out," Jose admitted, hating this place and the assignment.

"We've got orders, my friend. We stay till the mission's done. There's also Clef, I'm not leaving without him!" Jed informed him.

Looking at Jose, he saw his eyes shift from him to behind him. Grabbing for his weapon Jed spun around, as a knife came to rest across his throat.

"Don't do anything stupid!" A voice commanded, as Jed defeated, lowered his weapon. Disarmed the three men waited, as the piece of vegetation gathered up their weapons, tossing them in the river.

Jed silently watched as the man stripped off his camouflage while keeping a constant watch on the three men. The shame Jed felt at the three of them being so easily taken prisoner, by one man, was unbearable. Once Roberts had his knife around Jed's throat, the others had no choice but to surrender, making it his fault. That hurt a lot more, than the knife cut on his neck from the razor sharp blade.

"Where's my other man?" Jed demanded, breaking the silence.

"Adrian's bringing him here now, he's okay just a little upset at being captured." Steve smiled, checking Damian's legs. "You're a lucky man, not many can say they survived a croc attack." He told him, before moving away. Sitting down opposite them, Steve leaned his rifle against the jeep still holding his knife. Jose looked to Jed seeing a chance to escape.

"Don't even think about it, gentlemen. I was trained by the best, I can assure you," Steve said softly, but with a hint of steel.

"So what's your story, Roberts? Why does our government want you?" Jose asked as he settled back onto the ground, showing Jed he didn't want to try to take this man.

"It's a long story, but to summarise, we neutralised a Bio lab in Turkey your government was running. Mind you at the time we thought it was being run by the Iranians, a guise your government put in place," Roberts replied.

"That's bullshit! We never had a Bio lab in Turkey," Jed spat out angrily.

"A couple of years back, by mistake; my unit destroyed the lab, killing six guards, who we gather were paratroops. Your government then sent twenty men after us in Singapore. That cost them another eight dead plus two wounded. Surely in a small army like your country has, you would have heard of the loss of elite soldiers?" Steve suggested, seeing recognition in their eyes.

"I don't know if you're telling the truth, but I heard we lost those men in two different raids. The circumstances were never released," Jed admitted, knowing why Roberts was targeted. Jed was just about to ask what happens now, when Clef and Adrian appeared out of the scrub, walking across to them.

"Hate to say I told you so," Adrian said to Jed smiling, as he instructed Clef to sit, holding Clef's Uzi casually.

"Give me that before it goes off!" Steve ordered, as Adrian not understanding, tossed it to Steve. The four men on the ground cringed, as the weapon flew through the air. The Uzi's they knew was a great little weapon, but with the safety off, as it was now, the weapon could easily discharge. Catching it smoothly, seeing their alarm, Steve flicked on the safety switch, giving Adrian an angry look.

"That was stupid! My CO would have given you a shitload of trouble for doing that!" Steve exploded, seeing Adrian get the message.

"I'm sorry, I was only kidding around. And anyway what about them, they kidnapped me!" Adrian replied, realising he'd been stupid, trying to pass the blame.

"That was their fault. I should give you back to them." Steve smiled, letting the incident pass. "So, its Jed isn't it, what do we do now?" Steve continued.

"We've got orders to bring you back," Jed mumbled, finding himself off guard by this man's confidence.

"Look that's not going to happen. They'll just torture me while trying to find out what happened and then get rid of me. No, I'd rather just disappear again. When you get back, tell your bosses that next time I won't be so forgiving." Steve warned them. Standing he walked towards the jeep.

"What happens to us?" Jed asked surprised by him walking away.

"The other jeep tyre needs changing, other than that you've just got to avoid the police. Mind you, I wouldn't stay here near the river too long," Steve smiled. Adrian, ahead of him quickly replaced the distributor cap, before jumping behind the wheel and starting the engine. Throwing it into gear, they both drove away, Adrian waving happily at the four men.

"What do you make of that?" Jose asked Jed.

"I not sure, but I think we should take his advice," Jed answered, as they all looked towards the river, spotting several crocs looking their way.

"I can't believe how easily he captured me!' Clef exclaimed as they headed towards where they'd left the other jeep.

"Yeah, when we get back I'll have something to say about the lack of Intel on Roberts. We'd have been ready for him," Jed replied.

"I think no matter how we come for him, he'll be ready. For me there'll be no next time, I can assure you," Damian declared knowing how lucky he was to be alive.

That was the last time Steve saw the Israelis. Only one other time had his enemies got close, and that was far more painful to think about. A car honking behind him brought Steve back to the present, as putting his car into gear, he moved off.

BALLINA

Driving into Brisbane international airport, he returned his rental car, telling the girl at the counter that he was travelling to Perth, leaving in two hours. Saying goodbye, he walked around the corner to another car rental stand. Hiring another car, he arranged to drop this car in month's time in Sydney. Leaving the airport, again making sure no one was following, he drove south towards Ballina. Wanting no trouble, he observed the speed limit as he tried to work out what to do when he reached there.

Crossing the border into New South Wales, Steve checked his rearview mirror for any tails. 'Old habits die hard', he told himself smiling, as a blue coloured sports car overtook a white van travelling a couple of hundred metres behind him. With a puff of smoke, the blue convertible roar passed him, its two female occupants giving him a seductive wave. Laughing Steve waved as the two girls who broke into laughter. Continuing on, sticking to the speed limit, Steve watched the blue convertible overtake another two cars about half a kilometre in front of him.

'To be young again' Steve smiled to himself, as in the rear vision mirror the van stayed at the same distance. The van's continuing presence for some reason started to unnerve him. He became aware that since leaving Brisbane airport, at one time or another, a white van had been in the traffic behind him. Of course, white was a favourite colour with vans he reassured himself, unsure if it was even the same van he noticed earlier. Still, he found his eyes were now drawn continuously to the vehicle.

Sick of being tormented by his suspicions about it, he slowed down below the speed limit, Steve watched the van, noticing it didn't get any closer.

"It could be nothing. The driver might be tired and just travelling behind me for the company," he said out loud, getting angry with himself, for overreacting. Still, the voice inside his head told him he had to do something. Looking ahead in the distance, Steve saw a blue light flashing. Approaching the light, he saw the two girls in the sporty convertible, had run afoul of the law. Closing swiftly on the highway patrol vehicle, an idea came to him.

Putting on his indicator, he pulled over behind the police car coming to a stop. The van moments later cruised by, continuing on, leaving the police officer looking back at Steve. Getting out of his car, Steve casually approached the officer, who was writing out a ticket for the lead-footed young lady.

"Sorry to disturb you Officer, but is Ballina in this direction?" He asked.

"Another hour Sir, just stay on this road." the Officer informed him with an amused smile, before continuing with issuing the ticket to the young girl.

"Thank you, officer, it's the first time I've driven down here, thought I'd just check," Steve then turned, walking back to his car.

"How could the silly old bugger get lost on this road?" the young lady driver asked the cop flippantly.

"Who knows, but at least he isn't getting a ticket, is he?" the Officer shot back, handing the girl her ticket, who prudently decided to shut up.

The Officer had finished with the young lady, walked slowly back to his vehicle. He'd watched Steve drive pass, waving to him. He in return nodded, studying Steve.

"The ladies are right, if you get lost on this road you shouldn't be driving!" the Officer mumbled to himself. What bothered him was the driver just didn't look like the type of guy who would get lost. As he entered his vehicle, he decided to run Steve's plate. It came up as a hire car, rented at the International Airport, by a man returning from overseas. This allayed the officer's suspicions as he drove off, looking for another speeder.

Continuing on, driving cautiously, Steve was passed by the highway patrol car, which turned up a side ramp, turning back onto the highway heading in the opposite direction. Moments later the two young ladies roared past. This time they didn't wave. Scanning every off ramp and entry point, Steve watched for the white van, in the end shrugging it off as nerves, continued on to Ballina.

Arriving late in the afternoon, Steve booked into a motel, off the highway, in the town centre. He then hesitantly went to the Ballina Police station. At first, he'd thought of waiting until the following morning, but he knew after waiting over a week, he desperately needed answers. Parking right outside the front door, Steve got out of his car and entered the station. Walking up to the front counter, he asked a young police officer, if he could see someone in charge of the case.

"Are you related to the deceased?" The young officer replied, not even looking up.

"She was my girlfriend and the unit she was living in, belongs to me."

"I suppose we got to take your word for that."

"Why don't you do your job and get someone in charge of the case, out here!" Steve growled dangerously.

The officer picking up the change in the voice looked up. He was just about to put the man in his place when his eyes locked on Steve's. For a split second, he saw something dangerous lurking there, making him step back away from the perceived threat.

"I'll get someone," the officer stuttered before he retreated into a back office.

"Can I help you Sir?" came a familiar voice, as Detective Boulton walked from the same rear office, coming to a halt when he saw Steve.

"Good afternoon Detective can you tell me what happened to Justine?" Steve asked, his eyes studying the detective. He'd given Steve a hard time when he'd lived near over a year ago, causing him to leave town. Steve had been involved in a fight at a pub, where several locals had been severely beaten. At the time Boulton couldn't prove anything but had heavied Steve into leaving town.

"Mr Roberts if you could come into my office, I'll bring you up to date," Boulton replied, leading Steve down a corridor to a small office overflowing with paperwork. Once inside the detective moved some documents off a spare seat for Steve.

"Do you want a coffee or something?" Boulton asked remembering Steve's threat to bring his army unit back here if anything happened to Justine.

"No, I'm okay detective. I just want to know what happened."

"I'd like to say she died without pain, but you know I'd be lying. She put up a good fight and scratched the offender's face badly; it allowed us to catch him later that night," Boulton showed he respected her courage, before continuing. "The man involved had escaped from a prison at Grafton, a couple of hundred kilometres south of Ballina. He'd killed two other women, both living alone in high rise units, posing as a repairman. His tactic was to convince someone in the building to give him access and then wait for the woman to return home," He explained, his voice sounding]genuinely sad.

"Who found her?" Steve asked.

"Since the trouble at the pub, I've been keeping an eye on Justine, and we became good friends. I found her that night after a neighbour reported hearing screams. We cordoned off the area, and one of our patrols spotted the guy with his face bleeding." Steve noticed the detective's eyes were misty.

"What happened to him?" Steve asked his voice cold.

"He hung himself in the cell out back!" Boulton replied, his voice just as cold as Steve's, as they both sat in silence.

"Thank you, detective. I know we didn't part well last time, but I'm glad you were her friend, call me Steve," he said putting out his hand, which Boulton shook.

"The name's Dave," Boulton appeared embarrassed by nearly crying, as he wiped his eyes.

"Where is she buried?" Steve asked sadly, needing to visit her and say his goodbyes. After getting the location and directions, Dave walked Steve out to his car, handing him a card to contact him if he needed anything, getting grateful thanks from Steve.

The detective stood silently for several seconds, watching Steve drive away. Roberts looked different to Dave somehow, as if Justine's death had taken the life out of him. 'Death of a loved one does that to you,' Dave contemplated, hoping the guy would find peace, before re-entering the station.

"Who was that guy, he was scary," the young officer asked Dave, as he came in the front door.

"Someone who deserves more respect than you gave him Constable Simon! Like everyone else who comes in that door!" Boulton spat out, having heard the way the officer had talked to Roberts when he had first entered.

"I was busy!"

"Bullshit you were Constable. Next time you talk like that, I'll kick your arse back to the academy!" Dave shouted menacingly, before going back to his office, leaving Simon bewildered.

Sitting there Dave thought back to the night when he'd found Justine. The bastard had cut her up viciously, after she'd scratched him, leaving an absolute horror scene for him to find. Dave had broken down, crying like a baby, only pulling himself together when backup arrived. He had ordered every available police vehicle to blanket the area, hoping to spot the killer.

In the early hours of the morning, one of the general duties patrol cars had by luck, spotted the offender in an alley. He'd given them the slip at first, but Dave wasn't letting the bastard go, ordering every car available to surround the area and search on foot. After a painstakingly thorough search, they'd cornered him in a disused factory. Even with the backup, he still managed during the arrest, to slice one of the arresting officers with a hidden knife. Not fatally, but enough to put him in the hospital for several days.

When he'd been finally thrown into a cell, he'd laughed in their faces saying how much fun it had been killing and torturing those three women. He told them how easy it was to escape from a prison, and how next time he'd go after a policeman's wife.

"Well, he isn't laughing now!" Dave said out loud, a cruel smile on his lips, remembering how he'd struggled when they'd hoisted him up with that rope.

SAYING GOODBYE

Steve stood quietly looking out over the ocean from the cemetery. It was a strange spot for a graveyard, with its sweeping view of the coast. Someone in the past had put their community ahead of profit and giving the deceased a beautiful spot to be buried. Steve found it peaceful; as he walked through the well-maintained gardens, listening to the surf breaking on the shoreline in the distance. Calming his emotions, Steve sat down beside the young woman who had saved him from himself and loved him.

Knowing they were her favourites, Steve had brought a bouquet of roses to place on her grave. They were not the only flowers there, meaning Justine had other friends who missed her. Sitting there silently Steve's life flashed before him. This was the second time he'd buried a woman who'd loved him. Looking at her grave, Steve realised how lonely he felt without her.

"I wish I'd know you better my love, we didn't get much time to enjoy life," Steve whispered sadly, wiping his eyes, as he cried for a woman who had loved him even after finding out about his dark past. "If it weren't for you, I'd still be running. Thank Justine, you gave me back my life." Collapsing onto the ground next to Justine's grave, Steve wondered if he'd ever find someone again and was it worth the pain.

Seeing the light start to fade, Steve looked around feeling drained, having no idea how long he been there. Remembering he'd arrived early in the morning, he sat up realising he'd stayed there all day. Getting slowly to his feet and pulling himself together, he walked away knowing he was leaving a part of his himself here forever.

Arriving back at his motel, Steve climbed slowly out of his car and entered his motel unit, for the last time. Looking out his window onto the river, Steve watched a fishing trawler slowly push its way upriver against the tide, its crew lounging on the deck enjoying the homecoming, as people along the riverfront waved.

'God I wish I could stay here longer,' he said lying down. Ballina was a peaceful seaside town with a laid-back lifestyle. This suited Steve. It was far removed from the hustle and bustle of the cities, yet big enough for a man like Steve to blend in. However, he missed his family and knew he must move on, hoping to start a new life. 'Maybe someday I'll return,' he told himself softly, looking forward to seeing his girls.

Outside across from the motel, a white van took up station, watching Steve's room.

"Sleep well Captain Roberts; it's your last one," the driver grinned, before driving off confidently, to rest until tomorrow.

THE HIT

Up early, Steve packed up his belongings, before driving down to the unit. He had several things to do to before leaving, including clearing out the unit he'd bought for Justine. Parking out front, he decided to take care of all the other jobs leaving the unit til last. At around lunchtime, Steve entered their unit, a feeling of great sadness settling on him. It was the first time since arriving in Ballina that he had been in the unit, preferring to stay at a motel rather than stay where Justine had met her end.

Inspecting the apartment, Steve found no damage, as her friends, out of respect for her, had painstakingly cleaned up the place after the attack. There wasn't much of his here to take with him he realised, only a couple of photos and a few books, which he quickly pack into a suitcase. He'd decided to sell the unit, telling the local homeless charity, that they could have the rest of the contents after he'd left.

Stacking the books carefully in a bag, Steve came across an old army manual and realised it was the one he had helped publish years ago while in the SAS. He had just returned from America and was training a group of SAS soldiers in the same way the Yanks had trained him. They had then outperformed the other units of the Regiment; showing a need for an instruction manual on this new form of training. 'God those were good days' Steve smiled to himself, before suddenly freezing. With his heart labouring in his chest, Steve's breathing slowed. 'He'd never had a copy, how did it get here?' Steve's mind screamed.

Becoming instantly alert; his dark pasted flashed in front of his eyes, as Steve carefully examined his surroundings. Finding no danger, he tentatively opened the book, finding a picture of himself and his friend John.

John had been his Regimental Sergeant Major and co-author of the manual. What made Steve stare at the photos, was across had been drawn across both pictures. Picking up the phone he dialled the police station asking for Detective Boulton, and after identifying himself, he was put straight through.

"What's the trouble, Steve?"

"Look I'm sure it's nothing, but are you sure the killer was working alone?"

"I'll come over, are you at the unit?"

"No, better I meet you somewhere else, I don't feel comfortable here."

"I'll meet you across the road at the pub in ten minutes," Dave suggested, Steve, agreeing.

Arriving five minutes early, Steve bought a drink and grabbed a booth in the corner, from where he could watch the whole room. He sat quietly watching the people around him, his survival instincts heightened by the discovery of the journal. On time, Detective Boulton walked into the pub and seeing Steve had a drink, headed over via the bar, where he gathered a glass of liquid courage.

"I judge you found the book?" Dave asked downing half of his beer.

"Yes I did, what's going on?" Steve asked as he watched the comings and goings of people in the pub.

"Relax Steve; it's not connected to her murder I can assure you. The book arrived in her letterbox a week before her death. Justine showed it to me, as she was a bit concerned that someone might be after you. When she was murdered, I checked her killer out from his escape from prison to here, including the two other murders and I can tell you it was just him, no one else!"

"Did you get anything on who sent it?" Steve asked, watching as a well-dressed man seated himself in the booth next to theirs.

"No. All we know is it was posted in Sydney."

"Why didn't you tell me?" Steve asked suspiciously, watching as the businessman got up and left, not finishing his drink.

"She said when you got back she didn't want you to worry, so she wasn't going to tell you," seeing Steve's attention was elsewhere. "What's wrong?" Dave asked, as Steve got up and looked in the booth next to theirs, before turning swiftly.

"Get everybody out now!" Steve yelled, as he grabbed a briefcase from the booth beside theirs and carefully carried it out the back of the pub. Dave, flourishing his badge, ordered everyone to leave the area, as he radioed for assistance. The customers, sensing danger in Dave's voice, needed no prompting as they swiftly fled outside.

"You think it's a bomb?" Dave asked softly, making sure everyone was out, as Steve joined him near the front door.

"I'm not sure Dave, but do you have a bomb squad up here?"

"We never had a use for one before!" Dave replied a slight smile on his lips, thinking Steve was overreacting when the blast came. Even though Steve had moved the case out the back of the pub, the explosion was spectacular, as panic broke out in the crowded street.

Evacuated patrons ran in every direction, trying to get away, as Dave and Steve found themselves lying flat on the ground.

Half blinded by debris, and their ears ringing from the blast, they groggily got to their feet, staggering towards the curb away from the pub. Looking up, they saw a fire engine screech to a halt, as firemen raced past them, into the pub. Battling smoke and flame, they fought desperately to extinguish spot fires that had erupted all over the building, trying desperately to smother them, before they took hold.

Two paramedics seeing Dave and Steve's appearance dutifully escorted them to the back of an ambulance, double parked behind the fire truck. Quickly examining them for injuries and finding none, the paramedics poured the saline solution into their eyes, clearing out the grit. As their hearing returned Dave and Steve, slowly got to their feet. Thanking the departing medics, they then took in their surroundings. By this time, a large number of police had arrived, and after getting the crowds back, they rushed up to Dave to find out what had happened.

"Tell the media and the crowds, that it was a gas explosion," Dave ordered getting surprised looks from his fellow officers who knew a bomb alert had gone out.

"But detective," One officer started to say, as Dave exploded.

"Don't give me any shit, just get moving!" Dave yelled this time, as the police officers hastily moved away from their angry superior. Pulling out his notebook Dave wrote rapidly on a piece of paper, before handing it to Steve.

"That's where I live," Dave said, handing Steve a key. "Go there now, I'll clean this mess up and meet you there," Dave stammered out, still dazed from the explosion, as Steve, having a quick last look around, turned and left.

Watching from the barricade erected by the police, Bruce Hall, a local reporter snapped off another photo of Detective Boulton and his mysterious friend.

'Who are you?' Bruce asked himself, as the stranger walked off into the crowd like a hunting tiger, eyes constantly scanning the crowd. At one stage they even came to rest on Bruce, making him look away nervously. He'd been listening to the police radio when the bomb alert had gone out, but now the story was, that it was a gas leak. Looking at the pub and the crater at the rear, it didn't look like a gas explosion to Bruce, especially after talking to the owner of the pub.

He had seemed confused, admitting he didn't even know of a gas pipe in the area let alone running through the back of his pub. Sensing he was onto something Bruce decided to send the information onto his papers head office in Sydney, maybe they could find out who this guy was Bruce thought, as he snapped off another photo.

When Steve entered Dave's unit, he knew straight away that Dave was single. The walls were covered with either football posters or very attractive cheerleaders; something a wife or girlfriend would have trouble with. It was surprisingly clean as well, with all the plates gleaming in the drying rack next to the sink. This was something Steve had never managed to be able to do on his own. Changing out of his suit that was covered in dust, Steve used Dave's shower, before putting on a pair of jeans and a plain shirt.

"And so it starts again!" Steve said out loud, making a decision. Reaching into his pocket Steve reluctantly grabbed his mobile phone out, dialling Ali's number. Ringing four times then hanging up, Steve rang again as a female voice came on the phone.

"Hello, who is it?" a familiar voice asked.

"Hello Julie its Steve, how are you?"

"Steve it's so good to hear your voice, it's been years!" Julie answered excitedly.

"How are the kids?"

"Getting big, Peter is in the army of all things, and Michelle is at university," her voice changing as she spoke about her daughter, who she had named after Steve's dead wife.

"I'm happy for you Julie."

"Ali said you met someone." as Steve stood there unable to continue. "Is everything okay Steve?" Julie asked suspiciously, worried by his silence.

"Is Ali there Julie, I need to talk to him?" Steve answered; trying to keep the emotion out of his voice, as Julie called out to Ali. Her voice told Steve she knew something was wrong.

"Come visit when you can Steve, we miss you," was all Julie got out before she broke down crying dropping the phone, leaving an apprehensive Ali to pick it up.

"Steve, what's the problem?" Ali asked trying to sound happy, but Steve sensed he knew the truth.

"Someone tried to kill me today!"

"Tell me the whole story," Ali requested all business, as Steve filled him in on what had happened.

"And your sure Justine's death wasn't connected?"

"Yes, I'm positive. The local detective is a good guy and liked Justine. He's sure."

"Look, Steve, I'm not sure what's going on, but I'll make a few calls, then ring you back tomorrow night at the same time okay?" a little angry that the Americans may have gone back on the deal.

"Thanks, Ali, I'll do some digging here. See what I can find out," praying it wasn't the Americans, as Dave entered the unit.

"You okay?" Dave asked his voice showing a little fear and concern.

"Yeah, I'm glad no one was seriously hurt."

"You're a dangerous person to have as a friend," Dave exclaimed, a slight smile on his lips.

"Yes, it would appear my problems follow me wherever I go."

"If that was meant for you my friend, your enemies don't care about the innocent bystanders or publicity, do they?" Dave replied his mind working.

"You're right Dave, I never thought of it that way. Whoever did this doesn't care about the fallout, and that doesn't sound like the people who I thought may have done it."

"Who'd you think it was?"

"I thought it was the Yankee government," Steve answered evasively, not wanting Dave to get involved.

"Bloody hell! Why would they be after you Steve?"

"Have you been watching the news?"

"What, that siege thing at the White House, where they killed those terrorists!" Dave answered, wondering where this was going.

"They didn't kill those terrorists Dave, I was one of them," Steve confessed, as Dave without a word, slowly rose and went to the fridge. Getting out a bottle of bourbon, and grabbing two glasses, he sat down reluctantly, handing Steve a drink.

Steve spent the next two hours giving Dave a rough outline of his life. Being a police officer for more than twenty years, Dave who thought he'd heard it all, downed several glasses of bourbon while listening quietly.

"So after all the shit you've done for the CIA, killing whoever they thought needed killing, they betrayed you. So you decide to get even, by grabbing their President and forcing them to back off. God! I don't know what you're worried about Steve!" Dave said bursting into laughter.

"I don't think it's a joke, Dave."

"Fuck you're not kidding! It could be anyone Steve, you and your team seem to have pissed off everyone!" Dave exploded, with a mixture of anger and fear in his voice, wondering who he'd given a key to his front door too.

"Look it might be best if I go?"

"Forget it, Steve, it's just a lot to take in, after nearly getting blown up, that's all," Dave answered, settling down.

"Getting back to that, any chance we could get the pub's surveillance camera footage."

"Shit, you never stop do you?" Dave smiled, as he reached into his suit pocket and pulled out a disc. Watching several different camera shots of the pub, they finally got a good shot of the businessman.

"He's not local, but I've seen him around town lately," Dave admitted, deep in thought.

"I've never seen him before, but there something about him that's familiar."

"Of course there is. Look in the mirror, he walks and acts just like you do," Dave replied, seeing the connection straight away.

"So he's probably ex-military?"

"And by now, almost home I'd say, after botching the hit," Dave chuckled.

"No, he won't go until the jobs done. He knows if I leave here he won't get another chance, I'd say he followed me back here," Steve suggested, as Dave got out his pistol watching the front door.

"You're a real fun date, Steve!"

"He won't try yet, not while we're alert. He'll wait till we go to bed."

"In the back bathroom, there's a small window we could get out that way. Once out we could go across the road to the park opposite, and wait for him."

"Good idea, you do that. I'll stay here and wait."

"Are you sure Steve, he could still get you, even with me across the road and I've only got the one gun."

"I'll be alright Dave; you've got plenty of knives. Now get going, before it's too late," Dave, without another word, climbed out the back window.

Kneeling silently behind a hedge in the park, Dave sat motionlessly, gun drawn waiting for the killer. Steve was right Dave thought, this guy not going till he gets his pay packet, and that was Steve. When Steve had told him about grabbing the President, he'd nearly wet himself with fear, wondering what was about to happen to his small town. But this guy was a murderer of innocent people, the bomb had proven that and Dave wanted him stopped.

"Come on hitman, I'm waiting," Dave said softly, a slight smile touching his lips, as he watched his front door across the road.

Several hours passed, and Dave started to doubt if he was coming at all, thinking he'd moved on. The metallic touch of a gun barrel, against the back of his head, proved he was wrong. A feeling of complete failure touched Dave, as his own gun was taken from him.

"It amazes me how little they teach you local cops!" A smug English accent whispered in his ear, as a gag was pushed into his mouth. Roughly searched, Dave was then forced to lie on the ground, his hands tied behind him. "Is Roberts in the house?" The voice asked pleasantly, receiving no response. "Look you can die slowly in great pain, or quickly. Answer the question," the voice spat out, as Dave was kicked viciously in the kidneys. Through a sea of pain, Dave was just about to give him the finger, when a second silhouette appeared behind the man.

"They didn't teach you much either did they?" Steve whispered, his voice barely human, as he chopped the assassin down, clearly breaking something in the process.

Releasing Dave, Steve professionally tied up the unconscious man, as Dave put a few good kicks into their sleepy friend. Breathing heavily and looking angrily at Steve, he then called for backup.

After their badly beaten friend was safely locked away in a cell, Dave, who had been quiet since the attack, exploded.

"You bastard, you set me up as bait!" Dave bellowed his face right up next to Steve's. The two police officers on duty froze.

"Like you said, Dave he was like me, I had to think what I would do if the positions were reversed," Steve explained, expecting a punch any second. Dave stood toe to toe with Steve for several seconds until he suddenly backed away, visually shaking. Saying goodnight to the two officers, who just nodded, Dave hurried outside before throwing up in the gutter.

"That was close Steve, he could have killed me!" Dave admitted, his hands shaking, as shock settled in.

"I'm sorry, but it wouldn't have worked if you had known what I was going to do."

"Shit Steve, having you as a friend is a full-time job!" repeatedly spitting, before wiping his mouth.

"Come on I'll drive, let's get you home," Steve suggested, grabbing the keys. Dave agreeing let Steve walk him to the car, fearing he might collapse completely. Once home, Dave showered and got himself a sizable drink of bourbon, before sitting down quietly. Steve sat across from him watching a local football match on TV.

"What are you going to do now?"

"I'm not sure, depends on what our friend tells us," Steve replied distantly, still watching the football, something he hadn't done for a long time.

"You know we don't use torture here!"

"Yeah that's going to make it a little harder," Steve answered grinning, before turning serious. "Why are you doing all this for me Dave, you hardly know me?" Dave looking at Steve appeared to hesitate as if he embarrassed by Steve's question.

"Look I know how much you loved Justine Steve, but while you were gone, we'd got close, and I have to admit, I'd fallen for her," Dave confessed his eyes misting up, as Steve took in this information.

"It happens, my friend. We were both lucky to have known her," Steve replied, before returning to the football match lost in thought. Dave wiping his eyes headed for bed, realising Justine would have been lucky whoever she'd picked.

THE REACTION

On the other side of the world, Ali dialled a number not knowing what reception he would get.

"Hello Agent Chandler here," answered the familiar voice of the FBI agent who'd captured Ali nearly six months ago.

"Good morning Nigel, how are you?" Ali replied in a normal voice, waiting for an answer.

"Is that you Ali?"

"Yes Nigel, it's me and I can assure you, ringing you again was the last thing I thought I'd be doing."

"What do you want?"

"Has your government gone back on their deal with us?" Ali asked dangerously.

"How the hell would I know?"

"Someone tried to kill Roberts in Australia using a bomb, something that wasn't just an accident."

"I know nothing about it Ali, but I'll call John Wilson, and see if he knows anything.

"I'd do it fast Nigel, or we'll hit back. Ring me on this number when you find out!" Ali threatened hanging up abruptly. At the other end, Nigel sat looking at his phone, a bad feeling in his stomach. He wondered what hitting back would entail. Redialling, he called the Director of the FBI's private number.

"John Wilson here, what is it, Nigel?" Wilson asked in a friendly voice, after seeing it was Nigel calling. The two men had become good friends since the attack on the White House, keeping in touch.

"We've got a problem Boss, and it's big!"

"Give me a rough idea."

"Someone tried to kill the Ghost with a bomb," Nigel used Steve Roberts' old nickname.

"Shit, you're kidding! Say no more, head in here straight away!" John ordered hanging up. Stationed in New York, Nigel quickly jumped on a plane early that morning, travelling to FBI Headquarters in Washington.

Arriving at Washington Airport, he was greeted by a field agent who quickly drove him to their headquarters. Ushered into John Wilson's office when he arrived, Nigel was surprised to see Ross

Stuart, the head of the CIA, there as well. Getting straight into it, Nigel told them of the phone call and Ali's reaction to the attempt on Steve Roberts.

"He's got a hide threatening our country again!" Stuart said dangerously.

"Did you send someone after them?" John growled at Stuart, who sat there like a stone.

"I shouldn't even bother giving you an answer, using that tone to me!" Stuart shouted back, giving Wilson and Nigel the 'you're beneath me' look.

"Well how about me Mr Stuart," sounded a voice from the door, as Vice President Baker, walked into the room. The three men jumped to their feet.

"Good morning Vice President Baker, good to see you," Ross Stuart said first, a friendly smile on his lips.

"Can the fake smile, I want to know what's going on, right now!" Baker replied, steel in his voice, as he sat down waiting for an explanation. Nigel, again for the Vice President's sake, explained what had happened, before Baker signalled for Stuart to tell what he knew.

"A lot of this information is top secret Sir, I don't know if I'm allowed to reveal it."

"Well you can either tell me now as head of the CIA or fetch the files as a janitor over at the CIA, it's your choice!" Vice President Baker snapped, as beads of sweat appeared on Stuart brow.

"We're all friends here, I'm sure it would be okay to reveal the facts as I know them," Stuart replied, his fake smile not quite getting there. Stuart had upon hearing from John Wilson, checked through Don Brooks' secret files. He found, that not only had Brooks had his own Wet unit looking for Ali's unit, he also had hired several hit men to go after Steve Roberts as well.

"Why did Brooks have it in for Roberts more than the others?" Nigel interrupted, intrigued by what was going on.

"In the late 80s, Brooks tried for the first time, to get rid of the unit. Roberts cut off the heads of two of Brooks' best men. He left the heads in boxes at the American Embassies in Karachi, where Brooks was staying at the time," Stuart explained, not impressed by Nigel questions.

"Yes, I can see how that would upset you," Nigel replied a little shocked.

"They're hard men Agent Chambers, I was hoping they could just retire, now this!" the Vice President added sadly realising, that the whole deal was going downhill.

"Can you call them off?" Wilson asked as Stuart sat there watching the Vice President's reaction.

"Only three were paid in advance, the others have been called off as of this morning," Stuart replied his eyes filled with loathing for Wilson.

"How much were they paid?" Wilson asked.

"Ten million each, a further ten to the one who nails him!" Stuart replied uneasily.

"My God, that's a lot of money!" Nigel stammered out.

"Can we freeze the bonus at least?" Wilson asked angrily, wondering where the money came from.

"No, it's in a Swiss account. We can't touch it," Stuart answered bluntly, having already tried to get the money for his own use.

"I want these assassins stopped or eliminated Stuart! This should have been taken care of when the pardon was given!" the Vice President pointed out.

"That will not be easy Sir. Of the three assassins hired only one works alone, the other two are syndicated, meaning they have numerous hit squads working for them," Stuart answered smugly. Nigel sat dumbfounded, realising how sheltered his life had been when even assassins worked for companies.

"It doesn't matter how many there is Stuart, I want them stopped. How you do it doesn't matter, just stop them," Baker ordered, his voice shaking with rage.

"And what if they can't be stopped?" Stuart replied just as angrily.

"Then, unfortunately, Ali, Roberts and the rest of their unit will have to be taken care of. We can't afford them on the loose, if they think we had betrayed them," Vice President Baker replied, thinking back to his time in the Marines when he had first met these elite soldiers.

"They're only four middle-aged men, Sir," Stuart thinking to finish them was the best option.

"Tell that to the President. He was the one they kidnapped last time from our most heavily protected location, Stuart. I'm sure he'll tell you otherwise!" Vice President Baker answered forcefully, cutting down the rest of Stuart's bravado.

"It will be done as you order Sir," Stuart assured him, before standing and leaving, his mood clear to read.

Once Stuart had left, the Vice President silently paced back and forward for some time, before making a decision.

"Agent Chambers I know there's no love lost between you and these men, but I'm going to ask you to do something for me." Nigel knew he wasn't going to like it.

"Yes, Sir anything you want," Nigel replied formally, as both Wilson and the Vice President look at each other.

"First ring Ali and tell him everything about the hit men, except what happens to his unit, if they're successful. Number two, get your team together, you're going on a fact-finding mission to Australia. In other words, you're going there to protect Roberts and his family," Vice President Baker ordered watching Nigel closely, as Nigel nodded his head in acceptance before leaving.

"You're putting a lot on him, Sir!"

"Ali's unit were good men John, we made them what they became. I promised them a pardon. I aim to see we honour it."

"I think Roberts can look after himself Sir," Wilson pointed out having seen these men in action.

"It's not him I'm worried about John. What if these killers go after Steve's family to flush him out? God it might put him over the edge, and I won't have the country threatened again," Baker confessed, remembering their fear when they found out Ali's team had a Bioweapon.

"They can't threaten us with that again, it was all destroyed.

"When they said it was all destroyed at the time, I believed them and they most probably told the truth, that's why we gave them a pardon. But what if they didn't John, that's what worries me. See they're protected at all costs!" Vice President Baker ordered, before leaving.

Nigel flew straight back to New York, arranging for his team to be waiting at the airport to pick him up and discuss their next assignment. Walking out of the arrivals gate, a black van pulled up and flashed its lights signalling for him to get in. Once inside Nigel was bombarded with questions. After quieting everyone down, he started his explanation of his sudden trip to Washington and their coming mission.

Ian, Allan and Bill sat quietly, as Nigel at the end asked for questions and unlike before, silence prevailed.

"I thought the FBI stayed inside our own borders?" Allan asked, breaking the silence.

"We usually do, but we can be used to protect American personnel or assets if called upon," Nigel answered, knowing the next question.

"But this guy is neither of those and Ali threatened this country, we should let them get Roberts!" Bill made his position clear.

"These orders come from the White House, my friends. They want Roberts protected at all costs, so who's in?"

"We're all in Nigel, you know that. But after meeting Ali last time and knowing Roberts is just as dangerous, I've got to wonder how we're going to help protect an elite soldier. Let's face it he could kill us all easily, even at his age," Ian replied subconsciously touching his leg, where Ali had shot him last time.

"We won't be protecting Roberts; we're going there to protect his family and friends, anyone who might be a target of these killers," Nigel informed them, loathing hired killers more than Ali's unit.

"That's different, they're innocent bystanders, and they should be protected!" Bill replied, thinking the assignment sounded better.

"Do we know where they are?" Ian asked thinking that a trip to Australia, government paid, sounded okay.

"His brother-in-law is a Fed there, we'll start with him," Nigel answered, having already looked at Steve's history.

"Sounding better, when do we go?" Allan asked happily.

"As soon as possible, so pack your bags, we'll leave as soon as the bureau books a flight. Remember this is just a fact-finding mission, no discussion about the assignment," Nigel ordered, as his team headed back to the office, then home to pack their bags.

WASHINGTON

Back in Washington, Ross Stuart sat at his desk fuming over his treatment by Wilson and the Vice President.

"How dare they threaten me, I'm head of the CIA!" He spat out angrily. Brooks had made mistakes in the past but in no way was he responsible. Picking up his phone, he ordered the hitmen stopped or terminated, fulfilling his promise to the Vice President. Sitting there deep in thought, Stuart ran few several ideas on how to fuck up that arrogant Vice President and Wilson. Finally coming up with a plan, he picked up his phone again, deciding to teach these people what happens when you screwed with the Head of the CIA.

THE NEW YORK TIMES
NEW YORK

Patrick scurried down the crowded hallway to his boss' office. Juggling his paperwork, trying not to drop anything, he negotiated the swarm of employees, all running in different directions, trying to get the paper out on time. He'd been at the New York Times for a year now, fresh out of college. He'd come here in the hope of landing one of the elusive and prestigious reporting jobs at the paper.

Unfortunately, he seemed to have spent nearly all his time in the archives doing research, for one reporter or another. He hated the paper pushing, but everyone thought he had a gift for it, so for the moment, he put up with it. For the last few weeks, he had been researching the terrorist seizure of the White House and was now given the job of briefing the editor and the top journalists of the paper on his findings.

Arriving at the editor's office, his suit covered with dust and grime from his basement office, he was herded down the hallway to a large meeting room, by the editor's secretary. Patrick realised nervously that there must be more than the usual four journos to use the conference room, which held up to fifty. Entering, he found the room packed with reporters, including their Europe section. His heart missed a beat as his eyes locked on Natasha, their senior reporter over there.

"God she is beautiful!" Patrick muttered to himself, knowing she was a good fifteen years older than he was. Even so, he had to admit he was a little in love with her, like every other male in the room. Moving through the crowded room, leaving a trail of paper notes behind him, Patrick set up the projector to show some shots he had collected from the siege and from friends in the FBI.

"Is this really necessary chief?" Ron Helyard, the top New York reporter asked, giving the 'you're wasting my time' look to Patrick.

"Let's see what he's got people," Graham replied bluntly.

"It's just we've run the story to death already." Ron added before Graham gave him the 'can it and shut up look,' signalling Patrick to start.

"Ladies and Gentlemen, I think there's more to the story than we have been told!" Patrick said seriously, getting chuckles from Ron and some of the others for his introduction, causing him to hesitate.

"I for one would like to hear his report!" Natasha shouted, silencing the room, as Patrick continued.

"We all know that four men disguised as decorated war veterans entered the White House taking the President hostage for more than twelve hours. Then in a coordinated attack by Special Forces soldiers, the President was freed and the four terrorists killed. On the surface, it looks like a breakdown in security which four men took advantage of and were killed in the attempt. The problem is that in all that time, even though they were holding the President of the United States, they never tried to speak with the media. Also, no one claimed responsibility for the attack, something I find out of the ordinary."

"I think you're guessing Patrick sounds like they just didn't get a chance," Ron replied, unhappy with Natasha for shutting him up.

"You got anything else, Patrick? What you say is strange, but it is not much to go on." Graham put forward, staring at Ron, showing he was annoyed.

"There's one other thing. General Mosley, who was retired, was brought in by the Vice President to handle this situation. We've got a video of him talking on the phone to someone after the siege was over. I had a lip reader look at the video, in it he says. 'I hope the Ghost retires now. Roberts deserves to live out his life in peace'. We believe the general was talking to the Vice President."

"Doesn't sound like much to me, it could mean anything?" Ron replied, this time getting backing from the editor.

"I have to agree with Ron, Patrick. It could be code for all we know."

"Have we got any pictures of these men before the attack?" Natasha asked excitedly, her eyes shining, as Patrick nodded confirming he had.

"Have you got something, Natasha?" Graham asked smiling. He too was a little in love with her.

"I'm not sure Graham, it could be nothing, but it might be the greatest story this paper has ever had!"

"Care to fill the rest of us in," Ron asked giving her his best smile.

"No," Natasha said neutrally, crushing Ron before continuing. "Graham, can I meet with you and Patrick immediately and in private!" as the editor spellbound by this woman, dismissed everyone else.

"Can I look at the photos?" Natasha asked Patrick who passed them over without a second thought. Sitting there, Natasha looked at the many different photos taken by ordinary people. They'd taken them to remember the four brave soldiers, two with the Medal of Honour.

"Oh my God it's them, a lot older and well disguised, but it's them!" She exclaimed as the two men sat there stunned.

"You know them?" Graham said shocked.

"Yes, as incredible as it seems, I do."

"How?" Patrick asked, his instinct telling him she was onto something big.

"One of my first assignments was in Afghanistan. I was reporting on the war, giving the Russian point of view. These men were part of an elite unit, fighting the Taliban at the time."

"You mean Russian Special Forces soldiers attacked the White House?" Graham asked thinking of the explosive story and how many papers he could sell.

"No they weren't Russians; I think they were working for the CIA," Natasha answered merrily. Silence descended on the room, as Graham and Patrick both looked at each other, as they took in what she had said.

"Are you out of your frigging mind Natasha? What a load of bullshit! It doesn't make sense?" Graham said angrily, his love for her evaporating with this nonsense. Natasha stood there looking at him indignantly.

"I've got to admit, it's a bit weird Natasha, back then the Taliban were our friends, why would a CIA unit attack them?" Patrick said softly, not wanting to upset her. Going over to the photos Natasha grabbed several shots, each showing a semi-clear shot of each of the terrorist faces.

"Do you see this guy on the far right; his name is Cody, he's from Scotland, a paratrooper if I remember rightly. This one here his name was Aaron, he's a French commando. The one in the chair is Ali, formerly of the Shah's Iranian Special Forces and their commander.

He was badly hurt in Afghanistan. There was another one, a Japanese Marine named Sukai. I'm not sure why he's not here. Finally, there's Captain Steve Roberts of the Australian SAS, whose nickname is the Ghost and one of the bravest soldiers I've ever met, you smartarse!" Natasha explained angrily, as Graham's face froze.

"Shit that means the phone call from General Mosley to the Vice President was about this Steve Roberts, and he's not dead!" Patrick exclaimed putting the pieces together as the editor stood thinking, of where this could go.

"I don't get it. If they were working for us, why were they fighting the Taliban?" Graham said trying to sort it out.

"From what I heard, while I was held captive by an Afghan tribe, they were there to free a tribal leader loyal to the Americans. The Taliban was holding him captive, Ali's unit was sent to free him. During the attempt, Ali was shot, and the Taliban pinned down his unit in a dead-end canyon. Robert's, who was retired, was sent to find them. He succeeded against all the odds, stealing the helicopter I was on." Natasha smiled, thinking back to that kiss she'd given Roberts teasingly after he had told her he was married. Looking across the room, she saw the astonished looks on the two men's faces.

"Someday you'll have to write down what you did back then Natasha, I think I could sell that story." Graham smiled, back to loving her.

"If this is a giant cover-up, I can't see the President wanting it printed?" Patrick put in, sounding a little nervous.

"That's if we can prove it" Graham replied, thinking of the sales.

"I remember he had a friend named John also in the SAS, who lived on the coast near their base in Western Australia. He adopted an Afghan girl, we could start there," Natasha suggested, giving her editor one of her best smiles.

"You're right, back then there can't have been many adoptions from Afghanistan, they'll be easy to find." Patrick agreed, trying to impress Natasha.

"Okay, you can take Patrick with you." Graham decided, surrendering to her smile.

"I'm not sure I can get away," Patrick answered sensing danger.

"Pack your bags you're going!" Graham ordered, as Natasha smiling, gave Patrick a hug.

"We'll have a great time, and who knows you might end up with a Pulitzer!" Natasha said excitedly, winning him over.

"Okay, as long as it is not posthumously presented," Patrick replied, before leaving apprehensively to pack.

BALLINA LOCKUP

"Remember this is a police station, let me do the questioning," Dave told Steve, as they pulled up opposite the station. It was just after 5am, a bit early to be questioning a prisoner, Dave thought but he wanted it done before his boss, and the other daytime staff arrived. Steve had wanted to be alone with the prisoner, Dave though tempted, knew it was not on; this guy had rights no matter what they thought privately. Walking into the station, Dave was shocked to find the duty officer, not at the front counter.

"Bloody hell, where are you, Constable Simons!" Dave bellowed, angry at this young officer leaving his post. Dave was just about to head back into the lunch area to see if Simons was asleep as he had been in the past when Steve grabbed his arm. Signalling for him to be quiet, Steve pointed to the floor behind the counter. Dave took one look and drew his weapon. There was no doubting the liquid on the floor was blood, as Dave cautiously led the way towards the cells.

Following the blood trail, Dave walked with suppressed rage and shame, knowing poor Simons who moments ago he'd been accusing of being slack was probably dead. Coming to the cell section of the station, Dave's fear was found to be true. Having a quick look around the corner, he found Simons and another officer named Ruddick dead on the floor, both shot in the head. Steve moving past Dave checked both constables before checking the cell finding the assassin dead as well.

Three hours after Dave had first walked into the station, he finally walked out to his car where Steve was waiting for him. They had both decided it would do no good for Steve to be involved, so as Dave called for backup, Steve left the station waiting in his car across the road.

Keeping watch on the surrounding area, Steve had tried to puzzle out what had occurred at the police station. He could understand killing the cops to cover their tracks, what confused him was why the hitman had been killed? Looking towards the police station, Steve watched Dave emerge and cross the road cautiously, before getting in. His face said it all, as he told Steve to drive back to his unit, he sat quietly deep in thought. Once inside his apartment, Dave brought Steve up to speed on what had occurred.

"They're putting it down to the offender grabbing one of their guns while in the cell, killing them before killing himself," Dave sounding tired and upset, as he sat down heavily into one of his lounge chairs.

"You don't believe that bullshit do you?"

"No, Simons might have been lazy, but Ruddick was a good cop. No way he'd let that guy grab his weapon from him, or let Simons near the prisoner alone. There's also the trail of blood from the front counter, how'd it get there?"

"I agree, but why kill him, why not just break him out?" Steve asked.

"That's my fault," Dave confessed, as walking over to the television and picking up a set of keys. "When we took that clown in last night and locked him up, I mistakenly brought the cell door keys home with me. We only got into the cell today because a spare is kept in the safe. Only the boss and I know the combination."

"He'd still have killed them, Dave, remember that," Steve knew Dave blamed himself for his men's death.

"Anyway, I've been given medical leave until this mess is cleaned up. Where do we start looking for these guys?"

"Dave, you've been a good friend to Justine and me, but I don't want any more people killed especially friends."

"They killed two of my men. There's no way I'm not going after them!" Dave growled his voice as hard as a stone.

"Did you get anything on the guy?" Steve asked, giving up, knowing arguing was useless.

"Not much, the guy's a zero. I did find out where he stayed though."

"That's good, it's a start and Dave another thing, I'm going to need a gun." Steve wondered how Dave would take it his request. Reaching into his coat pocket, Dave pulled out a Glock pistol with two magazines.

"It was Officer Simons' weapon; I borrowed it from the lockup. No one will miss it for about a month with luck," Dave replied, handing it to Steve. Expertly checking it, Steve put the safety on, before tucking it in the back of his pants, covering it with his jacket.

"Let's go look at his motel room," Dave suggested, as they left, knowing this time that they were the hunters.

The unit was pretty basic, rented to a tourist who wanted an ocean view, without paying too much for it. It had a lounge area, with a medium size flat screen TV, with cable. To one side of the lounge was a small kitchen; to the other were two plain bedrooms and a small bathroom. Looking through the bedrooms, Steve came up empty. The guy had several changes of clothes, shaving gear, a travel bag and nothing else. Dave, on the other hand, did this for a living; one look and he knew this guy was a professional. He didn't bother looking through the guy's belongings like Steve was doing; he just stood in the middle of the lounge room, slowly walking around, taking in his surroundings.

"How are you going, I can't find anything?" Steve admitted, coming back into the lounge room.

Walking across to the TV, Dave looked behind the unit pulling the DVD player out, noticing it wasn't connected.

"So what, it's a DVD player!" Steve asked wondering what he was getting at.

"The units got cable, and there are no DVDs or a rental guide on where to hire them!" Seeing Steve's uncomprehending look, Dave raised the player above his head, dropping it onto the concrete tiled floor, shattering the back of the player. Reaching into the back, which should have been filled with electronics, Dave pulled a large plastic bag out of its hiding place.

"That was good work, Dave. Mind you, I'm glad there weren't any more explosives in there," Steve smiled, as Dave nervously considered that he could have been blown to pieces. Moving on, he spread the contents on the coffee table.

In the collection was a British passport, ten thousand in Australian dollars, a return ticket to London and a bunch of snapshots and a phone. The photos were what caught Steve's eye; one was of him in his army uniform, another of Justine talking to Dave, only taken a short time ago. The third was a shot of Steve's girls standing with his sister Louise, and the final one was a photo of John, Steve's friend and his Regimental Sergeant Major in the SAS. Dave watched Steve, seeing the pain in his eyes as he stared at the photos.

"They're okay Steve; at least this guy isn't going anywhere," Dave said softly trying to make him feel better. Looking at the clock, seeing it was about three in the afternoon, Steve pulled out his mobile phone, calling the Federal police headquarters in Sydney.

"Federal Police, can we help you?"

"I like to speak to Agent Edward MacCalland thank you," Steve asked pleasantly back. Waiting for several seconds while the phone rang, Steve began to have doubts about getting Edward involved.

"Hello, can I help you?" A voice said all business, but not Edward's.

"You are not MacCalland."

"Edward is on an assignment, can I help you?" The still unidentified voice asked as Steve dropped the phone. Taking a chance, Steve tried his sister's home number getting an answering machine, forcing him to hang up in frustration. Sitting there Steve looked again at the photos making a decision.

"No luck?" Dave asked watching Steve on the phone.

"No, unfortunately. I know people in Europe; they can run down our friend here and find out who his friends are. I'll ring them tonight," Steve decided, as they gathered up the contents of the bag, driving back to Dave's place.

That night Steve called Ali, telling him what had occurred. He then gave him the address of the assassin's home in London from his passport, hoping it was real. Ali then informed Steve of his conversation with Nigel, confirming his fears that there could be a large group looking for him and his family.

"Don't worry Steve. I'll check out the hitman's address on his passport as soon as I can. I'm picking up Aaron, and Cody shouldn't be far behind."

"I'm just worried about my family Ali. I can't find any of them!"

"I've got good news on that front Steve. I talked to Agent Chambers last night. He was on his way to Sydney, with his team to guard your family, on orders from the President. Even with delays, they should be there tomorrow night at the latest!" Ali hoped Steve took it as good news.

"That's something at least. Thanks for your help."

"Forget it, Steve, at least the Americans are sticking to their deal, that's the important thing."

"Still I wonder what their plan is if I get hit, they must be worried about what you'll do?"

"Yes, that thought had occurred to me too. For now, let's be hopeful, they haven't got you yet."

"I'll ring you in a few days, be careful Ali," Steve warned, feeling better as he hung up.

"Good news," Dave asked having listened.

"Yes and no. Seems the Yanks are sending some people, to look after my family, that's the good news. The bad news is there could be a large number of men looking for me."

"Sounds like good news for your family at least!" Dave reassured him, as Steve stood silently, his mind working on a solution.

"Pack light and for a week at least," Steve said coming to life.

"Where to?"

"Sydney first, by then I should know what we're up against," Steve told him, as they made ready to leave.

Loading up the car Steve had hired, Dave jumped behind the wheel, as they left on their nine-hour drive south to Sydney.

"You can take over driving, when we stop for something to eat," Dave suggested, as Steve relaxed in the passenger seat intent on getting some sleep. Turning on the radio, Dave drove south accelerating to just above the speed limit, wanting no unnecessary problems. Subconsciously, both men glanced at rear vision mirrors, watching for a tail, as they drove south, wondering what awaited them.

SYDNEY THE FIRST ENEMY

After driving all night, Steve dead tired pulled up at a motel. It was on the main approach road to Cronulla, and only a couple of kilometres from where Steve's daughters lived with his sister. Booking in for a couple of days, Steve and Dave then drove to his sister's house. Stopping just up the road, afraid to go closer, Steve saw lights on inside, as his family prepared to go to work.

"Are you going in?" Dave asked softly yawning, watching for anything out of the ordinary as the pre-dawn light gave way to an overcast day.

"No. Everything looks okay, I just want to sit here and watch for an hour or two to make sure. If it looks safe, we'll come back tonight, after a good sleep" Steve suggested, as two young women exploded from his sister's house giggling, as they hurried to a small sedan. Steve's heart nearly broke, at being so close to his daughters and not being able to approach them.

"Are they your girls?" Dave asked, getting a nod from his silent companion, as the girl's car past them. "They're beautiful Steve; I guess they look like their mother," Dave continued, trying to lift Steve's spirits.

"Yeah they do," Steve smiled.

Twenty minutes after the girls left, Louise and Edward left the house as well. They both looked a little older to Steve, though Steve could see the spark was still there, as Edward opened Louise's door for her. Hopping into the driver seat, Edward reversed their dark sedan out of the driveway, before driving past Steve's car, talking happily to his wife, as Steve hid his face behind his hand.

"The guy looked like a cop!"

"Yeah Edward's a Fed, works in Williams Street in the city."

"That's who you tried to ring the other night?"

"Yes, I was going to warn him, he's a good guy," Steve replied still watching the house. The two men sat there silently for another ten minutes, before Dave tired, thought they should leave.

"Everything seems to be okay here Steve. Let's head back to the motel?" Dave suggested starting the car, as looking in the rear vision he saw a van edge around the corner behind them. Dave instincts made him kill the engine immediately, as both men for some reason ducked down. The vehicle drove slowly passed, stopping in Louise's driveway. As the van came to a halt, a young Asian looking man climbed out and walked up to the house. Knocking on the bottom level door and receiving no answer, he went around the side and up the second level of the home knocking there as well, before returning to the van.

"Could be just a delivery?" Dave suggested casually to Steve. Both men though continued to watch the van, as Dave's hand involuntarily went to his pistol, as if it sensed trouble. For five minutes the van just sat there, until the side door suddenly flew open and six young men leapt out. Carrying an assortment of baseball bags, the group went upstairs to Steve's sister's house.

"That was bad planning on someone's part. They've only just missed my family, now they'll have to wait all day for their return."

"What do we do now?" Dave asked, knowing he couldn't just run in showing his badge, as the van reversed out of the driveway. It sat there for several minutes, before driving further down the street parking at the end. Pulling off the road, the driver adjusted his side mirror so he could watch back down the road.

"That to was a mistake, no one can watch a mirror all the time, it would have been better to face the car this way," Steve muttered, working a plan of attack out in his head. Looking across at Dave, Steve realised he hadn't answered his question, so focussed was he on planning.

"Sorry, Dave. Look every one of my family members who live here works, so that gives us some time. This road is a dead end and my family who all drive to work, will have to pass us to reach their home. Best bet is we pick a time and hit the house before the others turn up. The hard part is I want one of them alive," his eyes dead as he watched the house.

"Look, Steve, I know you like doing this kind of thing yourself, and your plan sounds good. Can I suggest an alternative, where we don't have to do any dirty work?" Dave put forward, before explaining to Steve what he intended to do.

After waiting for an hour and seeing no movement, Dave put his idea into play. Ringing the local police station, Dave identified himself as a detective on holiday from Ballina. He told the local cops that he'd seen a large group of men carrying weapons enter a house in Cronulla, suggesting that they might be doing a home invasion. After giving the address, Dave hung up, promising to keep watch till they arrived. Steve getting the go signal from Dave reversed the car further up the road, towards the street entrance and waited.

It didn't take long before Steve noticed a squad car nose around the corner before backing out of sight. At this point, Dave got out and walked back showing his badge, before returning.

"SWAT is setting up around the corner. I'll go talk to them. Make the call," Dave suggested, with a slight grin. Steve, picking up his mobile phone, dialled his sister's home number. Getting the answering machine, he left a brief message.

"If you morons in the house can hear this, the cops are closing in!" Several minutes after the call, the young driver in the van got out and started slowly walking up the street towards them. Looking around nervously, his phone in his hand, he continued towards their car. Coming abreast and seeing Steve sitting casually behind the wheel, he approached the driver's side window.

"Are you a fucking cop?" He muttered in broken English, shoving an automatic pistol into the side of Steve's face.

"No, I'm the devil!" Steve answered, grabbing the surprised youth's wrist and smashing it against the windscreen. Removing the youth's pistol, Steve then slammed his door open into the head of his moaning assailant, knocking him to the ground. Climbing out of the car, Steve shoved the unconscious youth into the backseat, binding his hands and covering him with an old blanket. Picking up his phone, Steve recognised someone speaking excitedly in Vietnamese. 'Probably trying to find out what happened to their spotter' He thought, knowing they couldn't see what had occurred. Being a caring person, Steve brought them up to speed, on what was happening.

"The cops have killed your friend, you're next!" Steve spoke into the phone, a slight smile on his face, as a SWAT police officer came around the corner, moving past him.

"Officer, I just saw a guy with a gun at that window!" Steve stammered out, sounding scared. The officer quickly passed on the information to his team members, that he'd been spotted.

"Thanks, now move your car, get away from here," the Officer ordered, giving Steve a well done. Thankful that Steve had warned him, the officer didn't bother to look in Steve's car as he should have, before moving on. Reversing slowly away from his sister's house, a smile appeared on Steve's lips, as all hell broke loose behind him.

It always amazed the police how stupid gang members could be. At this stage, the young men could have surrendered and maybe spent a year in jail for possession of a firearm, plus break and enter. But no, they thought they could beat the police and escape. As the gang members exploded from the house, firing wildly, not knowing where the police snipers were, well-aimed return fire smashed into them. It was over quickly with three down fatally shot and the others screaming for their lives as the police cautiously moved in and handcuffed the survivors.

"God, I'll most probably get a medal for this!" Dave admitted happily, getting into the car, as Steve drove away.

"No problems?"

"No, they took my details, that's normal, but your sister's house is in for a hard time, you'd better warn him." Looking back, Steve saw the police entering his sister's street in force. He knew Dave was right and the cops would give the house a good going over, trying to find out why this particular house had been invaded in the first place.

"There's not much we can do about that, so let's get our friend back to the room first, for a talk. I'll ring my brother-in-law from there," Steve suggested, as they drove away.

Arriving at their unit, Steve again tried Edward's work number, getting the same voice.

"Is Edward there thanks?"

"You're the guy who hung up on me yesterday aren't you?" The voice answered sounding unimpressed.

"Yes, I was. I can only talk to him, it's urgent!"

"Look he was here, he's gone to the airport for some reason. Other than that I can't help," The voice informed him, sounding truthful.

"Actually that's great news, thank you," Steve answered, ending the call.

"Good news?" Dave asked as he tied the young gang member to a kitchen chair.

"Yes I think so, Edward went to the airport. I'm hoping it's to meet the Americans flying in. The time's about right."

"Good, we'll go back to their house tonight. Now, what are we going to do with him?" Dave asked pointing at their guest. To his credit the young man stared at them bravely, saying nothing.

"I'm not sure, he mightn't even speak English, let's cut off a couple of his fingers and see if he yells in English!" Pulling out his knife, Steve advanced on the young man, who clenched his fingers together.

"Well that was easy, he does speak English," Dave smiled, watching the young man's hands, chuckling at the surprised look on his face.

"Look, son, I don't want to hurt you, but you were going to hurt my family. One way or another you're going to tell me what I need to know," Steve told him, his face devoid of emotion. Moving closer Steve slowly traced the youth's face with his knife, cutting him in several places, just to show him how sharp the knife was.

"You can't do this, I want a lawyer I know my rights!" the youth bravely responded, though a tremor of fear could be heard in his voice.

"There are no rights here son, this is family, and I'm not with the police," Steve spat out angrily, as placing the knife against the youth thumb he started to cut. Dave next to him stood silently, his face too showing no emotion, as he shoved a rag into the youth mouth, smiling evilly. Feeling the pain of the cutting, the youth looked into Steve's eyes and saw no pity whatsoever, as the knife cut deeper. Trying to scream he shook violently in the chair nodding his head vigorously.

"I think our friend wants to talk?" Dave smiled. He was secretly glad that the kid had given in, as he was just about to stop Steve from going further.

"From the start son, let's hear it," Steve asked dangerously, as the youth gladly told them all he knew.

At around six in the evening, Steve and Dave drove back towards Louise's home. Their new friend gagged and blindfolded lay silently on the backseat. Pulling up at a park, Dave looked around, making sure there were no witnesses. Opening the rear door, he unceremoniously, dragged the youth out the rear seat, throwing him onto the sidewalk. Quickly cutting the binding on the young man hands, Dave climbed back into the vehicle.

"Next time you won't get off so lucky scumbag!" Dave yelled as they accelerated away, leaving him to find his own way home.

Turning into Louise's street, they drove past the house, spotted a police car sitting in her driveway. The house's doors had been boarded up. Getting out of their car, they walked back to the police car.

"What happened officer?" Dave inquired, showing his badge.

"Some type of home invasion. Didn't go well for the badies," the Officer smiled.

"The owners know?" Dave asked a slight smile on his lips.

"No, we're having trouble contacting them, I'm just waiting here to see if they come home, but so far nothing," the Officer replied, sounding bored. Driving back down the street and around the corner, Steve and Dave parked. Getting out of the car they walked over to a small coffee shop. From there they could watch Louise's street, and at the same time relax.

"Steve it's eight! Surely someone would've come home by now?" Dave pointed out, as the police car they'd seen outside his sister's house earlier, drove past.

"Yeah, whatever happened at the airport with Edward, has made them not return home I'd say," Steve replied sipping his third coffee.

"What now?"

"I'm not sure where they've gone, but our friend told us where the threat is coming from, I thought I'd neutralise that first," Steve replied as if talking about mowing the lawn.

"The scumbag did mention that it's a large gang remember!" Dave was a little worried about confronting a triad.

"They've got to be stopped Dave, and there's no evidence for the police to act on. You can sit this one out if you want to?" Steve suggested, knowing Dave was getting out of his depth.

"You know I'm in Steve. It's just your solutions, though effective; usually involve the loss of blood for a lot of people," Dave pointed out, a slight grin on his face, as they drove back to their motel to plan the next step.

Their young friend had willingly told them a great deal, about their enemy. It appeared the gang leader was the son of a General Tran Vin, formerly of the North Vietnam army. Steve's unit first assignment over thirty years ago was to eliminate this man and his black market weapons business. His son had been visiting relations with his mother at the time and wasn't there during the attack. She had managed after her husband's death to migrate to Australia, hoping to start a new life. Someone had recently, told his son the identity of his father's attackers and of a five million dollar bounty on Steve's head. Their friend wasn't sure if the son really cared about his father, but the money was something else.

"There's one thing I don't understand Dave. Ali said the CIA had cancelled the contracts, where is the five million coming from?" Steve asked bewildered.

"There are the three hit men contracted, who have been paid a shit load; I'd say they've farmed the hit out, to lessen the odds. They'll still get a lot of money anyway."

"I just find it hard to believe the Yanks would tell a bunch of hitmen about an operation. That seems strange to me," Steve replied seeing no sense in it.

"Well there's only one way to find out, let's pay the triad boss a visit," Dave said confidently, wishing he had his bottle of bourbon with him now.

LA AIRPORT

Natasha's flight from New York had been smooth as silk, only interrupted by the stopover in LA to refuel. There they relaxed in the airport's business class lounge, before reboarding their flight to Sydney. Upon arrival, they would board a domestic flight, straight to Perth, where Steve's friend John, had been located. Sitting in the Business Class lounge, Natasha received many sympathetic looks from the other passengers, having seen her on the news. Her face had been splashed across many of the world's newspaper and television channels, after the death of her husband in Bosnia two years ago.

He too had been an investigative reporter. While trying to find an ex-Serbian General in hiding, he'd been ambushed and executed. Seeing the looks, Natasha feeling uncomfortable, ordered drinks from the steward for Patrick and herself. Patrick sitting opposite was reading various, at times vague military reports on Ali's unit, trying to come up to speed on Roberts' history.

"These guys were pretty dangerous soldiers weren't they?" Patrick asked, downing the vodka Natasha order for him without thinking, before coughing violently. Nearly choking, Patrick came to the attention of the attendant, who came over to see what was wrong.

"Are you alright Sir?" the young woman asked, helping Patrick and Natasha, pick up the photos and files he had dropped.

"I'm okay, I thought it was water," Patrick admitted embarrassed, as Natasha and the attendant shared a smile. Picking up a blown up picture of Steve Roberts taken outside White House before the attack, Holly froze. Seeing her hesitate, Natasha looked at the photo then back at the attendant.

"Have you seen this man?"

"Yes, he was sitting in the corner there about a month ago, I think," Holly answered, trying to remember.

"You must have a good memory for faces?" Patrick added nervously, happy to talk to this pretty girl and cover his early embarrassment.

"Well not really, he had quite a bad turn, that's why I remember him," Holly replied, thinking back.

"Was he okay?" Natasha shot back, sounding honestly concerned.

"Yes, he seemed okay when he left" Holly answered, wondering if she should tell them anything.

"Look, Holly isn't it?" Natasha asked, looking at her name tag before continuing. "You most probably recognised me from the news. I'm a reporter for the New York Times. We need to find this man urgently; his life may depend on it. Can you tell me anything?" Natasha had a pleading sound in her voice. Looking at them both and seeing the look in Natasha's eyes, Holly told them the whole story of Steve's collapse, after realising his girlfriend had been murdered while he was overseas. At first, he'd thought it was his fault somehow until she told him about the serial killer who had been caught.

"I seem to remember the story, but I'm not sure where it happened?" Natasha asked, knowing how Steve felt and wondering what happened to his wife.

"It was in Ballina in Northern New South Wales, Australia," Holly said hoping she somehow had helped, as, after thanks from Natasha and Patrick, she went back to work.

"What a stroke of luck!" Patrick said excitedly, as he looked at Natasha, seeing the real concern in her eyes. "Are you okay?"

"Yes, I'm fine Patrick. It's just I once felt deeply for Steve, and I think there's something sinister going on," Natasha replied distantly, before sitting up straight becoming alert. Patrick realised she'd made a decision.

"Find where Ballina is and get us there straight away. Forget Perth for now," Natasha ordered, her eyes unreadable, as their boarding call was announced.

AIRBORNE

Sitting in Business Class, Patrick adjusted his seat for the fifth time. It wasn't because he was uncomfortable, but because in Business Class you could. He'd never flown Business before and was pleased as punch to do so. Beside him, Natasha sat smiling at his boyish antics. Like Patrick, she too was excited about this trip. Since Afghanistan, she longed to meet Steve again, wondering if he remembered her and that kiss.

Looking around the cabin excitedly watching the poor people head through to economy, Patrick was just about to order himself a drink, when four men in suits entered the plane and headed down the aisle to economy. There was something familiar about the men, as looking down at his files, he remembered.

"Holy Shit!" Patrick spat out, causing Natasha and several other passengers close by to look his way, as he hid his face in a magazine.

"What's wrong Patrick?" Natasha asked, not impressed with his language.

"Do you see those four men in suits?"

"Yes, what of it?" Natasha replied looking at the men, as the second man in the group locked eyes on her, before moving on.

"The second one was the lead agent with John Wilson, involved in the White House affair, the others are FBI agents as well, I'm sure of it!" Patrick informed her, scared stiff, knowing it was too much of a coincidence.

"Relax Patrick, it could be nothing, but it's interesting the FBI is travelling overseas."

"Could they know we're after Roberts?"

"I'm not sure. There could be a leak at our office?" Natasha answered, thinking it unlikely, as the plane readied for takeoff.

As the 747 reached cruising altitude and the seatbelt light extinguished, Natasha asked Patrick if he would mind swapping seats with Agent Chandler. She thought rather than wait till Sydney; she could have a talk with him now. Patrick was pretty unimpressed with what she was asking. Reluctantly agreeing, he got up and walked back into economy. Coming up on the four men, Patrick felt the sudden urge to urinate as all their eyes locked on him, sensing somehow he was a danger.

"My boss asked could she have a word with you," Patrick asked shakily, addressing Agent Chandler, who just stared at him.

"Who's your boss?" asked the agent, next to Agent Chandler.

"Natasha Saunders, she works for the New York Times," Patrick stammered out, as the four men sat there silently watching him.

"Okay you sit here until I return," Nigel ordered bluntly, as he went forward allowing Patrick to sit down in his seat, next to Bill. Looking around Patrick realised how cramped it was back here, compared to up front.

"Boy, you're really packed in back here!" Patrick smiled, trying to break the ice with the other agents.

"Open your fucking mouth again, and I'll snap your neck like a chicken!" Bill growled, staring Patrick in the eye.

Petrified, Patrick shrivelled up in his seat, turning to face the other way. In the seat in front of them, Ian and Allan tried not to laugh out loud, chuckling quietly, tears running down their faces as turning around they saw Bill grinning, then wink.

Up in Business Class Nigel sat down casually in the seat next to Natasha. Looking across at her, Nigel felt the sexual attraction this woman projected. She was wearing a tight skirt and blouse. The top two buttons of the top of her blouse were undone showing an impressive cleavage. Looking away, he stared down at her shapely legs, revealed as she seductively crossed them. Trying to concentrate, forgetting her appearance, Nigel waited for the questions.

"Would you like a drink Agent Chandler? My name's Natasha," She asked pleasantly, her eyes watching him.

"No I'm okay and call me Nigel," he replied settling in, he had to admit it was comfortable up here, as his eyes again wandered over Natasha.

"Why is the FBI travelling overseas Nigel, it seems unusual?"

"Just a fact-finding mission, pretty dull really, even though visiting another country is fun," Nigel answered smiling back, knowing she was fishing.

"Maybe I can do an interview with you and your team. Where are you staying?" Natasha asked still holding that alluring smile on her lips.

"I couldn't tell you! Who knows where we've been booked, until we get there, you know the agency?" Nigel replied fencing with her, not falling for the sexual allure she was projecting.

"You were involved in the terrorist attack on the White House?"

"Yes I was on assignment in Washington, it was a terrible incident," Nigel replied, his smile holding. Seeing her charms weren't working, Natasha changed tactics.

"Funny though, my friend Patrick who swapped seats with you, said you were there guarding a terrorist, who was appearing before a Senate Committee!" Natasha pointed out casually, seeing the agent's smile start to disappear, as anger appeared in his eyes.

"That's partly correct; I was pulled off that assignment to assist at the White House. For security reasons, I can't go into it in any more detail."

"The witness was Ali Mustaffer, who was the commander of a CIA run unit wasn't he?"

"He was a suspected terrorist, that's all I know," Nigel replied fear and anger in his eyes this time, his smile long gone.

"I have it from a reliable source."

"Well your source obviously got it wrong," Nigel said flatly, his anger just held in check.

"I'm the source Agent Chandler. I met Ali Mustaffer and his unit in Afghanistan in the eighties when I was a junior reporter," Natasha confessed, watching Nigel's taken aback reaction, as he sat there saying nothing.

"Let's cut the bullshit Nigel, I'm going to Australia to find Captain Roberts, or the Ghost to his army friends; does the name ring a bell?" Natasha told him, having had enough of playing cat and mouse, hitting Nigel right between the eyes.

"Never heard of him!" Nigel replied, his eyes full of anger, as he stood to leave.

"You're looking at twenty years in Leavenworth for your part in this cover-up, so where is he," Natasha barked, losing it, as passengers turned to stare at the two of them.

"Be careful what you say, Natasha, being a hotshot reporter won't protect you!" Nigel replied, starting to head back towards economy, as people sat bewildered listening.

"The truth will come out you bastard! You can't kill people and get away with it!" Natasha yelled after him, bringing him to a halt, as passengers looked on horrified.

"You're in over your head Natasha! Back off while you've still got one!" Nigel spat out. Hearing the intake of breath from the passengers around him, at the apparent threat, Nigel realised he was out of control. He retreated back into economy, as Natasha stood up.

"What's the President sent you out here to do, assassinate Roberts!" Looking around at the surprised and distressed faces in the cabin, Natasha realised she'd gone too far. She was just about to apologise to them for her rudeness when the Captain appeared.

"Please sit back down madam, you're scaring the other passengers," the Captain told her, shocked by what he had heard, as Natasha realising she had gone too far, sat down. After the pilot had finished giving her a dressing down, he headed back to Nigel's seat. Passing Patrick on the way, the Captain forced him to flatten against the aisle wall, as Patrick did his best to hide.

Finding Nigel was an agent; the Captain verbally abused him in front of the other passengers for the trouble he'd caused, warning him to stay out of Business Class. He also informed Nigel, that he'd sent a full report ahead, so when he and Natasha landed in Sydney, they could sort it out with the authorities. Throughout the whole incident, the other agents shaken, looked on quietly, wondering what the hell was going on. Twenty minutes after the plane had returned to normal, Nigel signalled for everyone to meet him at the rear.

"What went wrong Nigel? We heard you yelling from back here!" Bill asked, surprised by Nigel's loss of control.

"She after Roberts my friends; she knows everything! We're in deep shit!"

"How'd she find out?" Bill asked sounding worried.

"She met Ali's unit in Afghanistan in the eighties, she knows the unit was run by the CIA."

"Can she be silenced?" Allan asked softly, causing everyone to look at him. "I didn't mean it that way" Allan admitted nervously, but everyone there thought about it.

"Look she's only got circumstantial evidence. Unless she gets to Roberts before us, she's got nothing," Bill pointed out, giving them hope.

"When we get to Sydney, I'll ring Washington, they can sort it out. The main thing is we get to Roberts and his family and protect them!" Nigel pointed out, as they all returned silently to their seats. In Business Class, Patrick had resumed his seat. Happy to be back, Patrick looked around innocently at the other passengers, who to him appeared somewhat hostile.

"So how'd it go?" Patrick asked softly, as Natasha looked at him astounded, before bursting into laughter.

"God Patrick, I'm glad you came!" Natasha smiled, trying to get over her own stupidity.

Walking towards customs at Sydney Airport, Nigel was glad the flight was over. Grabbing his phone, he tried to ring John Wilson, hoping to sort out this mess, as quickly as possible. Looking down he saw the phone still had no signal, so he decided to wait till they cleared customs. Glancing across through the sea of people, he saw Natasha and the messenger boy she'd sent back, waiting their turn in another queue. From behind the customs barrier, two Australian Federal police approached her, making both Natasha and Patrick follow them into an adjoining room.

"Looks like your girlfriend's in trouble?" Bill said grinning, as two Federal Police stopped in front of Nigel, taking the grin of Bill's face.

"Follow me, Sir!" An Officer instructed, giving Nigel no choice, as his men were also detained. Ushered into a room, Nigel sat there quietly wondering if the situation could get any worse. Ten minutes into his detainment, Nigel was just about to get up and knock on the door, when it flew open. Shocked by the suddenness, Nigel sat there speechless as a plainclothes officer entered the room, pushing Natasha ahead of him.

"Sit over there madam and shut up!" the Officer ordered, clearly irate, as he pushed Natasha into a chair.

"How dare you manhandle me?" Natasha replied angrily, making Nigel smiled.

"Shut the fuck up and sit down!" the Officer ordered, pulling out his automatic from his shoulder holster and placing it on the table in from of him, which made Nigel's smile evaporate.

"Hey take it easy," Nigel said inoffensively, seeing that the agent was overreacting.

"Did I say for you to talk?" the Officer shouted, swiftly picking up his weapon and pointing it at Nigel's face. Both Natasha and Nigel froze; they both knew they were in serious trouble.

"Good, you both can co-operate. It's too bad you couldn't do it on a crowded fucking plane!" the Officer said pulling out a recorder. Nigel sat there angrily, swallowing his pride at being treated this way, as the tape revealed their conversation had been recorded on the plane.

"Under the Federal aviation laws of this country you could both be sent to jail here for up to ten years, have you anything to say in your defence?" the Officer asked, turning the tape to record.

"I want a lawyer. Till then I'm saying nothing," Natasha answered defiantly, but her voice sounded a little shaky.

"I think this is all a misunderstanding Officer," Nigel said thinking his job was over. Putting his gun away, the officer turned off the recorder, before standing and walking to the door. Reaching up, he pulled a wire out of the surveillance camera, which Nigel had only just noticed.

"Is Steve okay?" the Officer asked softly, looking at them both, his eyes showing a mixture of anger and fear. Natasha and Nigel look at each other, both wondering what was going on when Nigel remembered.

"How did you know his first name was Steve, Officer? We didn't mention it?" Nigel replied, a little worried by this man.

"My name's Edward, I'm his brother-in-law, Agent Chandler. We've been worried about Steve since the CIA killed his wife about eighteen years ago," Edward replied, anger back in his voice.

"So that's what happened to his wife, I wondered about her!" Natasha said sadly, thinking of her husband.

"You knew Steve?" Edward asked astonished, Nigel's face showing surprise as well, thinking she had only seen Ali's unit, not knew them personally.

"Yes I met him in Afghanistan on my first assignment," Natasha replied, wiping tears from her eyes.

"What, when he killed the Russian Defence Minister and that General Sokolof?" Edward asked, amazed by Natasha knowing Steve.

Both Natasha and Nigel sat staggered at the enormity of killing the Defence Minister. Nigel had secretly wondered what the CIA used Roberts' unit for. Assassinating government ministers of the USSR, which could've triggered a war, was something beyond what he thought possible.

"No, he kidnapped my film crew and me. He needed our helicopter for his hurt friend," Natasha stammered out, remembering the report of the Defence Minister's plane crash, realising how big this story could get.

"My God! You're the young woman who kissed him?" Edward replied as Natasha nodded her head giving a little smile. Nigel beside her, lost for words, trying to work out what the hell was going on.

"If you're his brother-in-law I need to speak with you urgently!" Nigel pleaded.

"Spit it out Agent Chandler!" Edward said looking at him.

"I can't in front of her, she's a journalist."

"She seems to know more than you my friend, you may as well tell me."

"We've been sent by the President, to protect Captain Roberts' family. We believe the ex-head of the CIA contracted three different hit men to terminate him," Nigel explained, seeing Edward's and Natasha's eyes go wide. For a few seconds, Edward stood thinking. Making a decision, he reached into his pocket and pulled out a mobile phone, dialling a preset number.

"Hello love it's me, we've got trouble, get the girls and head straight to Annette's place. Yes, it's serious hurry. I'll meet you there. Oh, inform the girls we could be gone for a while, so they'll have to tell their bosses they need indefinite leave."

Signalling for them to wait, Edward left the room, returning with Nigel's team and Patrick. Being only three seats, Edward told them all to sit on the floor.

"Why does Steve Roberts need protecting Agent?" Edward asked Nigel, bringing the others up to speed on what was happening. Looking around and knowing the damage had been done, Nigel let it out.

"As I told you, there are three groups of hit men looking for him. They were sent by Don Brooks, ex-head of the CIA," Nigel informed them, as Patrick and Natasha stared at him.

"So you think they'll try for his family, to flush him out. Shit, how much blood does your country want for working for them?" Edward answered heatedly.

"Don't lecture me, he kidnapped our President and threatened our country with a Bioweapon!" Nigel exploded back, as the occupants of the room all gasped in mouthfuls of air and went silent. His own men appeared frightened at the mention of a Bioweapon.

"Well that explains a lot," Edward said sadly before continuing. "Several months ago Steve rang my wife, his sister, who thought at the time that he was dead. He said he had a way to stop running and get the Americans and the Israelis off his back. The attack on the White House must have been it!" Edward replied, realising how desperate Steve had become.

"Look I'm not defending him Edward, but that's not how it happened, Captain Roberts asked for a pardon after wiping out the CIA's Wet squad responsible for killing his wife. The President refused and tried to ambush Steve's unit. It was only after that failure, that they seized the White House, out of desperation," Nigel replied, as Natasha's eyes drilled into him, wondering what else he knew, and what would happen if he failed.

"Why are the Israelis after him?" Natasha asked trying to make sense of what had happened.

"Ali's unit while working for a gun runner out of Singapore, destroyed a Bio lab in Turkey, thinking it was run by a terrorist group. In truth, the Israelis had set it up that way to do research for themselves on Bioweapons. They've been trying to get Ali's group ever since " Nigel explained having read the report.

"Then they did the world a favour." Allan pointed out.

"What about the rest of his team?" Edward asked sounding worried by this new bit of information.

"They're in no danger at the moment. Steve Roberts is the only target."

"Why is he only targeted?" Edward inquired. Nigel looked around the room, wondering if he should tell them. He realised he had no choice.

"Back in the eighties, Don Brooks tried to kill Roberts' whole team off in Afghanistan. He sent them on a suicide mission to rescue a friend from the Taliban. By some miracle they survived, so he sent two of his own killers to do a recon of Roberts' unit. Steve's leader Ali and another member were injured making them easy targets. They were to observe Roberts and wait for backup before eliminating all of them.

"Somehow Roberts found out and killed the two assassins. He chopped off their heads, placing them in two boxes in the American embassy. Brooks was staying there at the time and got the message, cancelling the hit squad. Since then Brooks has always been scared of Roberts, more than the others," Nigel explained, seeing the look of revulsion on the faces in front of him.

"Why didn't he just let them retire?" Ian asked angrily wondering what else Brooks had been up to.

"He was scared it would affect his career!" Nigel answered, having heard it from John Wilson.

"That bastard caused all this mess!" Bill pointed out, seeing Roberts from another angle.

"What happened to Sukai, the fifth member of Ali's unit?" Natasha asked, wondering why he wasn't in the raid on the White House.

"He was killed after the raid on the Bio Lab by the Israelis. Even though Steve said he took down eight Israeli paratroopers in the shootout," Edward answered, having heard it from Steve many years ago.

"He was a good man," Natasha whispered, remembering the happy Japanese marine.

"Look I don't want anything to do with this. Let me go home, I'll say nothing!" Patrick blurted out, trying to stand.

"Walk out that door my friend, and we'll find a kilo of heroin in your luggage, is that understood!" Edward threatened as Patrick collapsed back onto the floor, head in his hands. Bill, a small grin on his face, looked Edward in the eye, seeing him give him a wink in return. Holding back a laugh, Bill realised that except for the accent, this agent could be his twin.

"What happens now?" Bill asked wanting to move on.

"Two things, I'll take up the offer of protection for Steve's family. The second is we've got to find Steve."

"What about the reporters?" Allan asked indicating Natasha and Patrick.

"We're coming with you. Let's face it; you're better off keeping us with you!" Natasha replied her winning smile back.

Patrick in the corner sat comatose, wishing he was back in his little office. 'What have I got myself into' he asked himself not wanting anything to do with this business as the others prepared to move.

"One question before we go anywhere, Edward. How did you just happen to be here?" Nigel asked, knowing nothing about this man.

"One of my friends named Shane got transferred over to the computer centre for awhile. He put a tag in the computer for me, so anyone mentioning Ghost or Captain Roberts sends a copy to me," Edward said secretively watching the door, before continuing. "I'm not the only one looking Shane told me, so remember that when we leave here," Edward warned, herding them out the door.

Edward first went to an office where several police officers were seated. After a brief conversation with them, they waved Nigel and the others group through customs, no questions asked. Walking to a car hire counter, Edward flourished his badge picking up the keys for two vans. He then shepherded the group through the car park to the vehicles.

Loading their bags quickly, Edward signalled Nigel, Natasha and Bill to get in with him, telling Allan to drive the other van, handing him a phone in case he got lost.

THE TAIL

Driving south from the airport, Edward watched the rear vision mirror regularly. For nearly an hour no one said anything, as the radio droned on softly. His three passengers sat there watching him, waiting for him to say something.

"Allan's a good driver Edward, he won't lose you. Even on the wrong side of the road." Bill assured Edward, breaking the silence, a small grin on his face.

"Yeah he's doing okay, I'm not really worried about him my friend. It's the car that's been behind him since the airport, that's what I'm worried about!" Edward replied watching their reaction. Natasha and Nigel instantly turned around, looking to the rear, while Bill looked at Edward waiting. Pulling out his pistol, Edward passed it to Bill, who checked the safety. Winding down his window, he quickly adjusted the mirror so he could see backwards.

"How are we going to do this?" Nigel asked from the rear, as Edward looked at Bill.

"He's okay, just young. I'd take a bullet for him," Bill said seriously to Edward, who nodded his understanding.

"I'm going to try not to do anything! Watch this!" Edward answered a small grin on his face. Picking up a phone, he dialled a number, as they sat listening.

"Hello I'm driving south on the M3, I just passed a car, a white sedan number XYD 8732, the guy had a gun, he pointed it at me," Edward said his voice sounding scared. After giving the police his details, Edward hung up, before explaining. "The phone I'm using, I kinda borrowed from a known drug dealer. The state police will act on this call because I gave them the owner details on his phone. Our friends back there, will soon be spotted by the cameras on this freeway and detained. When the calls found to be a hoax, they'll go after my druggy mate!" Edward explained grinning. Twenty minutes after the call, three police cars came down a side ramp at high speed, cutting off the car behind Allan's van, forcing it to the side of the road.

Edward using the diversion accelerated, turned off at the next exit, before switching to another freeway heading west. Once he was sure the tail had been lost, Edward let Bill drive while he told them what he knew about Steve and his friends.

He first told them about Steve's involvement over the years with his unit giving them a brief rundown of his life, finishing up with what he knew about them now.

For nearly twenty years they had all been on the run, scraping out a living and staying off the radar. Ali, he knew lived in Switzerland somewhere with his wife and two kids, under an assumed name, working in finance. Aaron had a vineyard somewhere in France; Steve said he never slept in the same place in his house two nights in a row, always on guard. Sukai was dead, killed with his girlfriend in Hong Kong by the Israelis, and Cody well, no one knows anything about him.

Finally, Edward got around to Steve, who they believed he had been working on a farm up in Northern New South Wales, somewhere near where they grew up.

"I think he's in a town called Ballina," Natasha told them when Edward was finished.

"How do you know that?" Nigel asked astounded.

"Quite by accident," Natasha replied, telling them about the steward named Holly at the LA Airport.

"I think you could be right Natasha. There was a report the other day of a pub being blown up. The local police have a cover story out that it was a gas leak," Edward replied.

"Ali said someone had tried to kill Steve Roberts with a bomb, it's got to be the place!" Nigel added, his opinion of Ali's unit slowly changing, by what he'd heard.

"One thing Edward. The two vans at the airport were already hired. How'd you know you'd need them?" Bill asked as he drove along.

"Let's put it this way, friend or foes, you people were going to go for a ride!"

"Fair enough," Bill said a slight smile on his face, realising he'd have done the same thing.

"Anyway first we'll check on the girls, and then we'll worry about Steve," Edward decided, as the freeway headed up into the mountains.

THE GUEST HOUSE

Stopping several times to eat or just to check for tails Edward lead the group further into the mountains to the west, away from Sydney. As darkness closed in, the two vehicles arrived at a small village called Mt Victoria. After another scan of the road behind them, Edward, who seemed more relaxed, turned off the highway onto a little side road. This road wandered through the main town, passing turn of the century buildings, mostly filled with antiques and souvenirs. Turning again, Edward followed another side road, passing a small park, finally pulling into a dirt driveway lined with flowerbeds.

Entering a large grass cover area, the two cars stopped, turning off their engines. A chilled silence settled over the group, as they exited the two vans, feeling the cold mountain air. Beside them, through the thick hedge, a large building could be seen, nestled amongst tall pine trees. Walking through an archway, Nigel and the others stared up at the turn of the century two-story building, complete with a bell tower. It was a prime example of the boom times of early Australia and the gold rush that opened up the west. Two verandas, one on each level, encased the structure, designed to take in the bush view, and protect the occupants from the hot summer sun.

"Nice place, who owns it?" Bill asked impressed by the tucked away guesthouse.

"I do, I suppose!" came a pleasant voice out of the dark, as a well shaped, middle-aged woman, came into view, standing at the guest house entrance. "Hello Edward," she smiled, giving Edward a kiss on the cheek and a 'who are these people look'.

"This is Leone, Steve's sister-in-law," Edward said introducing her to his travelling companions.

"I thought you said on the phone your family was staying with someone named Annette?" Nigel asked confused.

"I didn't know you then Nigel."

"Come inside, I'll make you all something to eat," Leone suggested with a welcoming smile.

"God, you can cook too!" Bill smiled, laying on the charm, making the men chuckle.

"You better keep it in your pants my friend, or I'll show you what I can do with a knife," Leone replied with a slight smile on her lips. Bill embarrassed went quiet, causing the others to smirk at his discomfit.

At this time of the year being out of season, the guest house was empty, meaning they all got their own rooms. Once the group was settled, they met in the dining area for a thrown together meal. At one table sat Edward and his wife Louise with Leone and Natasha. On the second table, were Nigel's team and poor Patrick, who was still having trouble mixing with the agents. The meal was eaten quietly, as each person privately considered the present situation, wondering what the future held for each of them. Louise feeling the silence had gone on long enough broke it.

"What's going on Edward?" Louise asked softly, as Edward finished eating.

"Some bad guys are after Steve again," Edward replied, not wanting to go into detail.

"Why are all the Yanks here?" Louise asked sounding a little scared.

"The Americans think there might be a small chance that these guys might try to hurt Steve's family to flush him out," Edward said trying to make light of it. Both women looked at him, seeing the truth.

"Will I go get the girls; they went up the road to the pub for a few drinks!" Leone exclaimed sounding worried.

"Look it's no big deal, I'll send Ian and Allan up there in a minute, they're all about the same age, and they can keep a discreet eye on them," Edward said looking at Nigel.

"No problems Edward," Nigel replied, having heard the whole conversation. Ian and Allan quickly got to their feet, wanting to see what these two women their own age looked like.

"You can go to Patrick," Natasha ordered smiling, as Patrick got up a little more reluctantly than the other two.

"I thought all three of them were Feds?" Louise asked, seeing Patrick take orders from Natasha.

"He's my researcher and a good one. He's the reason why I'm here," Natasha said giving Patrick a winning smile, making him feel a little better, as he followed the two agents out the door. When the three men had gone, Bill and Nigel helped clean the tables off, before they all sat down in a lounge area, Bill taking the chair next to Leone, making her smile.

"Now we're all comfortable, can someone explain why you've brought a reporter along?" Louise asked studying Natasha.

"Remember how Steve told us a story of a young girl kissing him in Afghanistan when he went out of retirement to save Ali and the others?" Edward explained a small smile on his face.

"Yes, I remember. Michelle wasn't happy!" Louise replied laughing, then going quiet, remembering Michelle, looking at Leone.

"So you're the Russian reporter?" Leone asked, touching Louise on the arm reassuringly, before looking hard at Natasha, an amused look in her eyes. Natasha sitting there stared back at Leone, as a small smile played across her lips as well, realising she wasn't the only one who had feelings for Steve.

"It was a long time ago," Natasha replied, as Leone gave her slight nod before smiling, signalling that they shared an interest.

"I don't get it, what was he doing in Afghanistan if he was retired?" Bill asked puzzled.

"From what we've heard, Brooks, who at the time was in charge of the unit, decided to abandon them there. Ali's wife found out and was on her way to Australia to tell Steve. The CIA knew she'd contact him, so they sent him instruction to rescue them hoping to kill him off as well, leaving no links back to them," Edward replied an angry tone in his voice, as Bill and Nigel sat there feeling a bit uncomfortable.

"We know it's not yours or America's fault, it's just been hard especially on the girls," Louise explained, excusing herself to go clean up, as the other two women rose following her.

"So what's the plan?" Nigel asked Edward after the women had gone.

"Simple, a couple of us are going after Steve, the rest stay here and guard the family," Edward answered, watching Nigel.

"I'm worried about that car Edward," Nigel confessed.

"So am I, if they were after us, it won't take them long to come here," Edward replied a little uncertainty in his voice.

"So who's going?" Bill asked.

"I thought Nigel and I should go. I trust you and the others two agents, can keep an eye on my family," Edward replied looking hard at Bill.

"I won't let any harm come to them!"

"You can keep an eye on Leone as well!" Nigel added.

"Stuff you!" Bill growled curbing his swearing, as the women reappeared. The rest of the night was spent just getting to know each other, avoiding any talk about Steve, until looking up at the time; Leone noticed it was getting late.

"Your men are taking their time getting the girls," Leone pointed out a little apprehensive.

"I'll go have a look," Bill suggested, standing to leave, as a bang, signalled the front opening and closing. Down the hallway staggered Ian and Allan, backed up by two beautiful young women, practically carrying Patrick. The room went silent as the two women dumped Patrick in a chair, his face showing several bruises, as did Allan's and Ian's.

"What happened," Nigel angrily asked his men, but his eyes went to the two young women, who stood giggling to each other.

"I'm sorry Agent Chandler, I started the fight!" Patrick confessed, holding his head, as Natasha gasped, choking on her drink. Seeing everyone watching him, Patrick explained.

After Patrick had left with Allan and Ian, they suddenly realised that none of them knew what Steve daughters looked like. Rather than go back and look silly, they went into the public bar, asking the barman if he knew the two nieces of Leone, the Guest House owner.

"Oh you mean Lindsey and Robin," the barman smiling, pointing. "That's them over there dancing with half the locals." Patrick looked upon two of the most beautiful girls he'd ever seen.

"God they're both beautiful!" Patrick murmured, his eyes drawn to the shorter one as she twirled around the floor, grabbing different males from the crowd, who gladly danced with her.

"Don't tell me it's those two?" Allan asked grinning beside him, breaking Patrick's concentration on the girl.

"Yes, that's them alright. After seeing Leone, we should have known they'd be pretty!" Patrick replied, still watching the girls.

"How do we get them to go home, is the question?" Ian asked as he too had become spellbound watching them.

"I'm not sure, but this assignment's looking better by the minute!" Allan grinned, as Patrick and Ian laughed. Looking up still laughing, Patrick saw the shorter young woman watching him. With a glint in her eye, she swung across the room, grabbing Patrick and pulling him out onto the dance floor.

"What's so funny?" the girl asked Patrick as they hurtled around the dance floor, doing a square dance similar to ones he had learnt in Texas when he was young.

"We were trying to work out how to get you two, to come home with us," Patrick answered, before realising his mistake and starting over, much to Robin's amusement.

"I meant to Leone's Guest House." Patrick finally stammered out, as Robin giggled.

"You're Americans! My name's Robin," She told him, her smile bewitching him. Getting over the spell, he was just about to tell her why she had to go home when a huge arm came around his neck throwing him across the room.

"Don't come into our pub and dance with our girls!" the ugly giant growled, looking down on Patrick. "Now you'll dance with me, prickteaser!" The giant commanded Robin, grabbing her by her hair and having a quick feel of her body. Her sister about to intervene found herself held by three of the giant's friends.

"Let the girls go, no one wants any trouble," Ian stated, as he and Allan planted themselves in the middle of the room.

"Back off Yanks, we're just teaching these girls a lesson. They just can't come in here tease us and leave us empty handed!" The giant grinned evilly, waiting for them to try something.

Ian and Allan looked around the room at the other men, seeing if there was any support. No one stepped forward. Knowing they would take a beating, they moved forward regardless. Behind the giant and his friends, Patrick lay on the floor coming out of his daze. Having heard what was said, and after the day he'd had, this put him over the edge. Climbing to his feet, he grabbed a wooden barstool from a corner table. In one fluid motion, he brought it up over his head, then down onto the giant's head, knocking him to the floor. The giant's friends taken aback by the sudden attack, charged at Patrick, intending to finish him quickly. Seeing them coming, Patrick desperately tried to defend himself with the barstool, as an amazed Allan and Ian rushed to help.

It was over quickly, as while the giant's three friends were concentrating on finishing Patrick, Ian and Allan smashed their legs out from under them, taking the fight out of the three. Ian and Allan, knowing trouble could flare again at any moment, grabbed Patrick and the girls hurrying home.

"So he's our hero!" Robin announced giggling, as all present looked at Patrick impressed.

"I told you two about playing up to the local men!" Louise stated heatedly, knowing who was really to blame.

"We were only dancing, we didn't lead anyone on," Lindsey said back defensively. Unfortunately, standing there in tight-fitting jeans and a short blouse didn't help her case much.

"Anyway, what's going on here?" Robin asked changing the subject, as she looked at Patrick, giving him a secret smile.

"Someone's after your father, these men are here to keep us safe," Louise replied neutrally.

"Is Dad okay?" Robin asked her voice childlike as she held back tears.

"We think so kiddo, it's just a precaution," Edward smiled.

"Will we get to see him?" Lindsey asked excitedly.

"In a while Lindsey," Edward replied before continuing. "Agent Chandler and I will be going to find your father, while the others stay here. Unfortunately, there's no more going off on your own, is that understood," Edward said sternly to the girls.

"Which one of them, is going to tuck us into bed?" Lindsey asked innocently, causing the Ian, Patrick and Allan to blush and the others to smile.

"Lindsey! That's enough!" Louise ordered, not impressed as the others hid smiles.

"I'm going after Steve as well!" Natasha stated as Nigel started to say something Natasha continued. "If it weren't for me you wouldn't know where he is. I promise not to print anything until you've looked at it first, is that satisfactory Agent Chandler?" Natasha asked politely, her winning smile in place.

"It sounds acceptable," Nigel replied, thinking it better to have her with them than left here.

"Well it's been a rough day; I think we should all turn in," Edward announced, before taking his wife's hand and walking down the hallway to their room. The rest of the group after introductions were over, followed their lead and retired to get some sleep. Bill walking with Patrick, Ian and Allan smiled at the reaction of these young men, to Roberts' two girls.

"Rough assignment boys?" Bill suggested chuckling, causing the others to grin.

"Just remember who their father is!" Nigel replied, appearing at the end of the hallway, wiping the smiles off their faces, as they all took in what he had said.

TRIAD

Edward had just showered and climbed into bed when his phone rang.

"Edward here, who is it?"

"It's Shane, have you still got that druggies phone?" Shane asked excitedly.

"Yeah, why?"

"Smash it right away!" Shane ordered, sounding anxious. Edward grabbed the phone smashing it with his shoe.

"What gives Shane?"

"There have been two shooting incidents, one on the freeway and one at Cronulla. In the freeway one, the police pulled over a car with four Vietnamese triad gang members in it. There was a shootout, two police were injured, and the gang members were shot dead. Did you have anything to do with it?"

"Yeah they were following me; I thought it was just a tail. I didn't know they'd shoot it out with the cops!"

"Don't worry about the state cops; the newspapers are calling them heroes, for taking down some bad guys. What you should worry about is that the cops were going to try and trace that phone. The druggy reported it stolen two days ago. He didn't know we were the ones who took it during that raid on his house."

"Well, it's gone now, thanks for the warning."

"There's more Edward. The second shooting at Cronulla was at your house, there are another three triad members dead there, plus three arrested. The cops are looking for you!"

"It's lucky we didn't go home then," Edward confessed, a little shaken, wondering what had happened at their house at Cronulla.

"I looked at the police record of the shooting; they got a tip-off from a detective on holiday from Ballina. The same one involved in the bombing up there!" Shane was trying to make sense of it.

"Shit it's got to be connected to Steve!" Edward replied wondering who the cop was, then telling Shane about the bomb.

"Shit that brother-in-law of yours has nine lives. Anyway, stay safe I'd better get off the phone. Ring if you need help, my friend."

Edward sat shaken by what had happened. Looking across, he saw Louise watching him fear on her face, having heard most of the call.

"They're really after us aren't they?" Louise whispered, scared the others would hear her.

"Yes, I'm afraid they are. Get some sleep; I've got to talk to Nigel and Bill," Edward explained, giving his wife a reassuring kiss, before leaving.

Edward had never really worried about his job before. He had to admit, that he enjoyed catching criminals. He watched them, followed them and when the time was right, he arrested them. Sure they made threats, but he never really worried about them, until now. This time some crims were being paid to get him and his family. He had to admit he was a little scared.

Going first to his car, Edward took out a metal box from the rear of the car, where he had hidden it under the seat. Hurrying down the hallway, he banged loudly on Nigel's door, before pounding on Bill's. As Nigel half asleep opened the door, Edward pointed him towards Bill's door. Bill upon opening his door moved aside, as the two of them moved in past him.

"I judge there's a problem?" Bill asked seeing Edward's agitation.

"We're in a little trouble!" Edward explained, trying to sound casual about it, but the two Americans knew some bad news was coming. For the next few minutes, Edward told them what had occurred, from the tail to the attack on his house. Then for the next half hour, they tried to work out a plan. After drawing a blank on what to do, they decided to tell the others in the morning, before making a decision. A tap at the door startled the three of them, only Edward had a gun, and it was out.

"Who is it?" Edward asked gun pointing at the door.

"It's Allan and the rest of us!" answered several different voices, as Edward quickly put his gun away, clearly rattled. Bill opened the door letting the others crowd in. With no seats, they all stood around while Louise did the talking.

"Banging on those two doors woke everyone up Edward, the girls came to me wondering what was going on and we found the others outside the door, when we came here," Louise stated nervously.

"Yes, this sneaking around is putting us all on edge, what's up?" Natasha asked looking a million dollars, something the other women noticed.

"We're just planning the trip," Edward said trying to smile innocently, but a wall of frowns greeted it. Coming clean Edward told them what had transpired, as the room listened silently.

"So it's not just a threat, they're really coming after us?" Lindsey said a little tremble in her voice.

"I'm afraid so, even though I don't know why a triad would be involved in trying to abduct us," Edward answered honestly.

"What's in the box?" Allan asked, having used it as a seat since he'd entered.

"It's hard to explain. Sometimes in my job, we pretend to sell weapons to other crim mates to catch them out. Or we might need one which isn't our own for certain situations," Edward explained sheepishly.

Looking around the room, seeing he was losing everyone, except Bill, he stopped. "Fuck it, just forget it!" Edward spat out, receiving hostile looks from his wife for swearing. Inserting a key, he opened the box, revealing a collection of guns. Handing four automatics of various makes to the four agents, he then gave three revolvers to Natasha, Leone and Patrick.

"They're all empty at the moment, Natasha and Leone will each stay with one of the girls. Patrick, can you shoot?" Edward asked.

"A little, I used to hunt as a kid," Patrick answered, a little scared at the gravity of the situation.

"Is this really necessary?" Leone asked looking at the gun in her hand, as Edward placed some shells in her other hand.

"I'm afraid so, and tomorrow everyone's leaving!" Edward informed them, shocking them all.

"But I've got to go to work!" Lindsey exclaimed sounding scared.

"That will have to wait for a while kiddo," Edward answered hugging her, as she started crying.

"I'm beginning to know how Dad feels," Robin admitted sadly, as Patrick gave her a hug as well, which was closely observed by Louise.

"Look it maybe over the top, but tonight everyone sleeps in two's. Tomorrow we'll work out what to do, but for now get some sleep," Edward suggested, as the group slowly left pairing up as they went.

"I'll take the first shift!" Bill announced, knowing Edward intended to stand guard.

"Thanks, Bill. Nigel and I will do three hours each after you, me first. Allan and Ian can drive the vans tomorrow." Edward suggested, giving Bill a nod of thanks as he took Louise back to their room. After the others had left, Bill checked his pistol carefully making sure the safety was on. It was an old Browning automatic and had seen better days. Bill was confident that it would do the job. Walking towards his bedroom door, Nigel voiced his concerns.

"It's not starting out good is it Bill?' Nigel pointed out, from his bed in Bill's room.

"No it's not Nigel and this triad being involved worries me," Bill replied.

"There's supposed to be only three hitmen. Where's the triad come from?" Nigel whispered.

"I don't know, maybe one of them contracted it out, who knows. I'll say one thing, the sooner we leave, the better!" Bill replied sounding for the first time since Nigel had known him, worried.

"Be careful my friend."

"Always," Bill answered, closing the door.

CONFRONTATION

Walking in near darkness, Bill slowly circled the guesthouse taking in his surroundings, trying to commit the grounds of the property to memory. He'd been in the lounge area sitting in the same chair he'd sat in next to Leone, just awake, thinking about the woman, when a light had stabbed through the darkness. It had illuminated the dining room across from where he sat for a split second, enough to warn him. Rising slowly, he had quietly walked to the back door, opening it carefully, before locking it behind him.

Now gun drawn and held out in front two-handed, Bill continued to circle the building. Fear of the unknown put him on edge, as he approached the front door where the road came in. It could be nothing he told himself. Just a couple of youngsters having a quiet fumble in the back seat for all he knew. Because of this, he hadn't woken the others, not wanting to cause a panic. Now as he circled the guesthouse, not knowing the lay of the land, a sense of being out of his depth made him wish he'd at least woken Nigel.

Seeing nothing out of the ordinary, Bill was just about to continue his circle of the house, when soft click like sound came from the darkness. Barely visible, parked fifty metres up the driveway from their vehicles, sat a black sedan. The type of vehicle was unknown to Bill, as he pivoted around silently, checking behind him, before continuing towards the vehicle. 'Shit this is how a brave fool gets killed' Bill thought to himself, his gun feeling like it weighed a ton, as he held it out in front of him, sweat running down his face. Walking cautiously straight up the driveway towards the car, Bill released the safety on his weapon, as he started to close the distance, preparing to fire.

Darkness vanished in a flash of brilliant light, as the vehicle roar to life. Hurtling straight at Bill, the car screamed as the wheels fought for grip, the driver flattening the accelerator to the floor. Like a startled deer, caught by a spotlight, Bill for a split second was confused by the sudden intense light, as the vehicle raced towards him. Diving into a garden bed beside him, Bill rolled behind a large tree trying to focus. This move saved his life, as the car cannoned passed him sideswiping the tree in an attempt to get him.

Bill, getting over being scared shitless, became angry. Coming to his knees he took aim, firing two shots at the retreating vehicle, which drove through another flower garden, before gaining traction with the road and accelerating away. Breathing heavily and badly shaken, he continued for several seconds to stare after the car, before standing up. Staggering to the front door he collapsed onto the front steps, gasping for breath. Inside the guesthouse, the sound of running feet could be heard rapidly approaching. The noise stopped, as the front door flew open, banging into the outside wall. Nigel cautiously looked out before moving out onto the steps.

"You okay?" Nigel asked stepping past him, his gun travelling from right to left checking the surrounds, as Edward also appeared, gun out taking the same stance.

"Yeah someone tried to run me down when I surprised them, only had time to get two shots off!" Bill replied softly, calming down sounding disappointed.

"That's because you're getting old," Nigel pointed out, stone-faced, still scanning the darkness that surrounded them.

"Fuck you," Bill spat out, before chuckling, as Edward and Nigel joined in as well, relieving the pressure.

"Did you get a look at the vehicle?" Edward asked as the laughter subsided.

"Yeah a dark coloured sedan most probably black, got the first two letters on the plate, LD, that's it, unfortunately," Bill replied, wishing he'd been more observant.

"You did great Bill, do you think you hit it!" Edward asked, impressed with Bill.

"Not sure, I think one tagged the rear of the car," Bill said softly, as hearing the approach of more people from inside, he quickly lowered his gun, the others following suit.

"What happened?" Louise asked as the whole group exploded out onto the front steps. Edward told them the truth about Bill's run-in with the night visitors, before telling them all to get some sleep.

"Wouldn't it be better to leave now?" Allan asked nervously.

"No, it would make it too easy for them. There are only two roads out of this town and at this time of night, we'd be vulnerable. No, its better that you all sleep. Bill, Nigel and I will stay awake till we leave; the rest of you will have to drive, so go to bed," Edward ordered, as the group reluctantly drifted back inside.

"Before I go, can I make you a coffee or tea?" Leone asked sitting down beside Bill and giving him a hug.

"That would be great," Bill replied thankfully, realising his hand was shaking slightly, from the night's excitement.

"Could we have one too?" Edward asked, a slight smile on his face, seeing Leone's full attention was on Bill.

"Of course, I meant all of you," Leone said defensively before standing up and heading for the kitchen leaving Edward and Nigel watching Bill.

"What the fuck are you two looking at? She's just worried about us, that's all!" Bill replied grumpily, before getting up and heading in for a coffee.

For the rest of the night, the three men patrolled the Guest House. Bill, while keeping watch, thought back to Leone's hug. It had been a while since a woman had held him. Sure he'd had plenty of dates and one night stands, but tonight had reminded him, how good it felt to have a woman care for you. He felt fear tonight, mind-numbing fear, it made him realised how old he was getting. Ten years ago he'd have emptied the whole gun into that car, and hit at least a couple of the scumbags, in a fraction of the time. Now he'd been lucky to stay alive.

'Get over it' he smiled to himself, thinking of Leone.

He thought of retiring just before this assignment had come up, knowing he was slowing up. That was before he'd become part of his present team. He'd come to like Nigel and the others, making the decision to stay with the team a while longer, passing on his experience. Now after meeting Leone he felt maybe his life wasn't over, perhaps it was just getting started again. Looking down at his hands he noticed the shaking had long gone and he chuckled, his confidence returning.

"Next time you come near these people, I'll be ready," Bill whispered, feeling better, as he continued around the house.

Two kilometres down the road just outside of the township, the black coloured Ford sedan turned off the highway. Driving up a deserted road into the National Park, the car stopped, and the occupants climbed out. 'The Blade' stood silently, as the three triad men pulled the fourth man from the car. One of Bill's two bullets had hit the rear boot door penetrating the rear seat stopping in the poor bastards back.

"Just bad luck," One of the triad men groaned sadly, the others agreeing, as they tossed the luckless man's body into the undergrowth beside the road. 'The Blade' knew better. The agent back there that had fired those two shots was no amateur and luck had nothing to do with his aim. Whoever the Yanks had sent to help Roberts family, were good and mounting another attack on them could be costly.

'The Blade' knew officially the hit had been cancelled, and the Americans would now protect Roberts and his family. Unofficially someone high up had told them to see it through, something 'The Blade' found amusing. Watching the three remaining triad men and growing tired of their constant tough guy stance, a plan came to mind. Gathering them round, 'The Blade' decided to thin the American escort down by sending these fools in to take them out. Working them up over the death of their colleague, 'The Blade' suggested they attack again at three in the morning when the agents would be either asleep or exhausted from standing watch.

The plan was for the three triad men to approach from the south, at the rear, while 'The Blade' backed them up, attacking from the north near the front door. Excitedly the three men agreed, hoping to end this mission quickly and return to their boss Lenny Tran Vin as heroes.

Two hours after their meeting, at three in the morning, the three triad men, carefully made their way through the thick scrub bordering the rear of the guesthouse. Moving cautiously they approached the house, hoping to avenge their dead comrade.

Nigel, who at the time was on the south side standing half asleep, heard the distant sound of twigs breaking underfoot. The triad men were good standover men but not soldiers, trained to move silently through any terrain. Fear made Nigel come fully awake, as hurrying to the front; he warned Bill and Edward of the noise from the bushland at the rear.

"Bill, you go with Nigel, I'll stay here in case someone comes in from the North," Edward suggested, as Bill and Nigel rushed back to the rear. Taking up positions on the veranda, behind a brick wall, Bill and Nigel silently waited. The triad men unaware they had been detected broke out of the scrub, into the cleared area behind the guesthouse. Fanning out in the near total darkness, they moved confidently towards the house.

"Halt and drop your weapons!" Nigel yelled into the darkness, where waif-like figures could be seen moving. The triad men surprised at the command to halt, open fire, aiming at where the voice originated. Bill, not so fussy about giving a warning had already taken aim, opening fire at the same time, as the three triad men did. The exchanged in the dark, proved one-sided, as while Bill and Nigel were well protected by the brick veranda wall, the triad men were in the open.

Both sides were armed with pistols, which were highly inaccurate over long distances. After they'd all shot off most of their ammo at each other, a strange ceasefire broke out, while they reloaded. It was during this break that the triad men found that one of them had been hit. Both Nigel and Bill thought they'd hit at least two of the attackers each, out of six attackers, but in reality, both had hit the same triad member, once each. The triad men seeing their friend down gave up the attempt at killing the agents.

Gathering up their friend, they retreated back into the undergrowth, disappearing from sight. Nigel and Bill stayed put on the veranda for a further ten minutes, listening to the sound of branches breaking becoming distant, before moving forward. Finding only one blood trail on the ground, they came to the conclusion that they'd both hit the same guy.

Awoken by the shooting, Allan and Ian raced from their room to the back of the guesthouse; opening the back door cautiously they joined Bill and Nigel on the lawn.

"Who were they?" Allan asked looking around as if expecting an army to burst from the darkness.

"Does it matter?" Bill replied bluntly, as looking up, he saw the women arrive on the veranda. "Get them back inside!" Bill ordered angrily, as Allan and Ian surprised by Bill's anger, herded the others back inside. Edward arrived from the front moments later, having sent Allan to keep watch while Ian kept the women indoors.

"Nothing at the front, what happened here?" Edward asked Nigel, seeing the tension in Bill. Nigel quickly brought him up to speed on what had eventuated, as the sound of a departing car sounded in the night.

"Someone sent those poor bastards in here blind!" Bill growled, seeing no sense in the attack.

"Does seem strange, their boss must have known we'd be on guard after the attempt on Bill. On the other hand, if they were set up or not, they intended to do us harm," Edward pointed out, seeing Bill nod, admitting he was right. In the distance, the muffled sound of sirens could be heard, getting rapidly closer.

Two shots earlier in the night might be put down to a car backfiring; multiple shots from an intense shootout must've woken every neighbour for a kilometre. Some of them would've called the police. Bill and Nigel looked to Edward, wondering how he'd handle the police.

"Give me one of your guns, and make yourself scarce. I'll handle the local boys. Just make sure everyone stays out of sight!" Edward ordered, as Bill and Nigel obediently moved inside.

The state police were unconvinced by Edward's explanation of a home invasion. The bullet holes in the rear veranda and a blood trail on the lawn indicated there had been an exchange of fire, with someone though. Confiscating Edward's weapon, the police promised a full inquiry into the shooting. Warning Edward not to leave the guesthouse until their superiors were informed, the police cordoned off the crime scene before leaving. Promising full cooperation and to stay put, Edward walked them out, happily waving goodbye. Hurrying back inside, he told everyone to start packing; they were leaving.

The triad members drove back towards Sydney, pulling up, where they'd dumped their friend's body. 'The Blade' had arranged to meet them here if anything went wrong. The three men sat quietly, fingering their weapons as they pulled up next to their supposed boss, in charge of this operation.

'The Blade' sensing they knew they'd been set up and wanting revenge, walked casually across the road from her car. Leaning on the driver's door her jacket open revealing her impressive breasts, she gave the driver a winning smile. The Blade explained how the FBI agents had opened fire at the same time on the north side, forcing her to retreat. The triad men though angry were confused by her seductive stance, each looking spellbound at her cleavage, as she intended.

When the triad men had first met 'The Blade', they had been stunned to find a beautiful woman. Lenny Tran Vin, their boss, had given them no description of the assassin. But their orders were to do whatever the assassin told them, which they had, not knowing their boss thought 'The Blade' was a man.

"Your friend doesn't look too good. I'd take him straight to a hospital!" The Blade suggested, putting the men at ease, as their thoughts were clouded by the woman's sexual pose.

"Yes, we will take him right away," The driver replied, stammering slightly, as he looked away from the woman's breasts, trying to concentrate. Placing his gun on the seat next to him, he put the car into gear, preparing to drive off.

"Are you sure you didn't hit any of the men shooting at you," The Blade asked seriously as all three men shook their heads indicating no. Hypnotised by her breasts, the triad driver shifted the car into gear, slowly moving forward.

"Wait!" 'The Blade' suddenly yelled making the driver hit the brake, slowing the car. Swiftly drawing a silenced pistol, 'The Blade' opened fire at point-blank range on the surprised driver, before switching to the two men in the rear seats. Shooting at least two rounds into each man, 'The Blade' swiftly moved forward, opening the driver's door of the still moving vehicle, steering it to the side of the road.

Breathing heavily, her breath coming in great gulps, 'The Blade' felt the rush, course through her body, making her moan. 'The thrill of the kill' she told herself giggling insanely, as she wiped sweat from her forehead, recovering from the rapture.

Once the vehicle had hit the gutter and stopped, 'The Blade' lifted the bonnet, cutting the fuel line of the still running engine, before walking to her car. Looking back, watching the fuel spray from the vehicle, 'The Blade', rolled up a newspaper, before climbing into her car. Turning back towards Mount Victoria, she lit the newspaper with a match, tossing it at the triad's vehicle, before accelerating away. Looking in the rearview mirror, seeing the dark sedan burst into flames, 'The Blade' smiled. 'The arrangement with the Triad was now void' she told herself smiling.

TRAN VIN'S HOUSE

At the same time that Bill had dived into the bush to avoid being run down, Dave and Steve arrived at Lenny's home. Unlike the image of triad bosses living in fortified drug houses, in dangerous ghettos, Lenny Tran Vin's house sat on twelve acres, on a riverfront property. His neighbour on one side was a famous actor, while on the other was a state politician, close to the Premier. All the neighbourhood were on friendly terms with Lenny, who through his import company gave generously to charities and political parties. Sitting on the balcony overlooking the water, Lenny sat with five of his lieutenants, and a special guest discussing the day's events.

"Will any of them talk?" Lenny asked dangerously to his men.

"No way boss! They'll do their jail time and say nothing. They know we'll look after their families," Jimmy his headman answered.

"Do we know what happened to the young driver?" Lenny asked wanting all loose ends tied up.

"Nothing yet, he's most probably in hiding, till things settle down," Rick another lieutenant answered softly unsure.

"The police haven't got him. I checked with our sources inside the police department, no one knows anything about him!" Jimmy replied, watching Rick who had been in charge of the two failed missions.

"Do we know how the police got onto our people at Cronulla and on the freeway?" Lenny asked staring at Rick, making him wince.

"Our sources say someone in another car on the freeway, reported seeing our men with guns. The Cronulla mission was a phone in by a cop on holiday from Ballina," Rick replied nervously, feeling his life hung by a thread.

"What was the name of the cop from Ballina?" Lenny's special guest asked suddenly, his French accent giving away his nationality, startling them.

"We're not sure, but he was a detective," Rick answered, hoping he had an ally in this mysterious guest.

"What is wrong?" Lenny asked seeing the look on his guests face.

"It's Roberts; he left Ballina with a detective. Your driver, did he know much about your business?" Lenny's guest asked bluntly, looking around the grounds.

"Yes he's been with us about a year, but I can assure you he wouldn't talk," Lenny replied, a slight smile on his lips.

"Bullshit he won't! Roberts is a professional; he could get a confession out off a fucking rock. I suggest we get out of here immediately!" Lenny's guest suggested, as he stood and walked towards the door.

"You're perfectly safe here my friend!" Lenny assured him smiling; amazed at this famous hitman's lack of courage.

"Your father thought that Lenny, and he was surrounded by an army in a foreign country!" Lenny's guest spat out angrily, hurrying through the balcony door, as the first shot rang out.

Dave sat nervously near the front gate, down the driveway from Lenny's house. His job was twofold; one was to watch for cars in the street. The second was to wait twenty minutes for Steve to get close and then take out the two guards standing watch at the gate. Once he had achieved this task, he was to fire one shot and drive up to the front door, picking Steve up, easy.

When they had first approached the Triad leader's house, Dave had been riddled with doubt. He knew he was a good cop, and he took pride in upholding the law. Sure he'd broken the rules heaps of times, to get the bad guys, like he had with Justine's killer. Delivering rough justice was part of the game when there was no other way to stop evildoers. Tonight was different, and he knew it. Going after a triad to do murder, was down a road he didn't want to go, that's why he was in charge of the gate.

Steve had seen his conflict in coming tonight, so he gave him this task to keep him away from the house. Still, he knew what Steve was planning, which made him just as guilty. Sitting there he remembered Simons and Ruddick's blood-spattered bodies at the station, this took away his doubt, making tonight acceptable.

Crawling towards the gate Dave jumped the first guard, knocking him unconscious. He was in the process of tying him up when the second guard appeared behind him. Pulling his gun he'd told the guy to halt. The bastard instead sliced Dave's arm with a hidden knife, forcing him to shoot the mongrel in the chest, being the widest part. 'Now look what you made me do, you dirtbag! So much for not taking part in the killing,' Dave chastised himself, cranky at having shot the fool. Moving on, Dave swiftly tied a bandaged around his arm with the unconscious man's shirt, before opening the gates.

Standing there feeling dizzy, Dave suddenly realised that he'd fired the warning shot. Racing back to the car he jumped in and started the engine.

"Shit Steve, I hope you're doing better," Dave cursed out loud, as he drove up to Lenny's front door.

After leaving the car, Steve had taken care of all the outside guards, before entering the house through a side window. He had been standing in the shadows, watching the seven men, waiting for Dave's signal. The unknown guest was to have been Steve's first target when he opened fire. To Steve, he seemed the most dangerous as he argued with Lenny. Now his shot was blocked by Lenny's men, as the unknown guest walked swiftly towards the door.

Everyone froze as Dave's shot rang out into the still night, giving Steve his chance. Walking into plain sight, Steve dropped the five lieutenants in a heartbeat, wanting to keep the other two alive. The guest had other ideas, as he dived inside an adjoining room, making good his escape. Lenny impressed, and he had to admit a little scared, raised his arms in surrender.

"My neighbours will have called the police by now!" Lenny informed him, his voice shaking slightly. Standing up, Lenny slowly turned coming face to face with his father's killer. He was quickly frisked before being forced to sit down again, as Roberts stood over him, the barrel of his pistol rammed against the side of Lenny's head.

Across from where they stood, the door the hitman had dived through slowly opened. Voices of children crying hysterically, filtered out to where Steve stood, making him hesitate. His first thought was to eliminate Lenny. The sound of Lenny's family crying caused him to rethink.

"Stay away from my family Lenny, or next time I come for you and them. Do we understand each other?"

"You've have made your point crystal clear Mr Roberts. Though I must warn you, there are other assassins out there, plus the one that just left," Lenny pointed out.

"I'll take care of them, just back off!" Steve commanded, his voice showing no emotion, as he slowly backed away and disappeared into the night. Walking swiftly towards his rendezvous with Dave,

Steve cursed himself for not killing Lenny. His gut told him the guy wasn't going to stop, no matter what threats he made. 'I'll have to watch him' Steve thought to himself as he spotted Dave.

Standing frozen for several minutes, Lenny thought carefully what his options were, before making a decision. Running into his bedroom, Lenny found his wife and children hiding in the corner crippled by fear. Reassuring them, Lenny went to his wife's jewellery boxes emptying it into a pillowcase before going to his safe and emptying it as well. He then took all the valuables to the garage, hiding them in his car, as the sound of sirens started to fill the air.

Dave in the meantime could also hear the sirens, as he sat nervously waiting. Like a ghost, Steve materialised out of the darkness jumping into the car, scaring Dave half to death, as he flattened the accelerator, gunning the car away from the area.

"Go okay?" Dave asked breathing heavily, not really wanting to know.

"Yes I think Lenny got the message, even though I should've killed him," Steve replied spotting the bandage on Dave's arm. "What happened?" He asked, seeing blood seeping through the material.

"The second guard got the jump on me."

"Pull over, I'll check it."

"It's nothing Steve, it can wait," Dave replied stubbornly as they drove on in silence. By the time they'd reached their motel, Dave was sweating badly and running a fever.

"Get in the passenger seat now!" Steve ordered Dave, as he quickly checked Dave's bandage. It was severely swollen and had an ugly dark blue colour; Steve knew he had to get Dave to a hospital straight away or he might lose his arm. Driving to the emergency section of a local hospital, Steve dragged Dave inside, as he called out for help.

"How did this happen?" A young doctor asked, rushing over and examining the wound.

"He cut himself with a knife while we were fishing," Steve replied sounding worried.

"It looks badly infected; the knife must have had some type of bacteria on it. Do you have it with you?" the Doctor asked cleaning the wound with an antiseptic solution, as Dave winced.

"No it went over the side, unfortunately," Dave answered, looking pale and in a lot of pain.

"No matter, but you'll be staying overnight, just in case," the doctor declared, as a nurse connected an IV drip, before giving Dave a shot for the infection.

Three hours after they'd entered the hospital, Dave awoke. Looking around he found he was lying in a single bed ward. Groggily he focused on Steve, who was sitting half asleep beside him on a plastic chair.

"Go home Steve," Dave stammered out, seeing Steve was fighting to stay awake.

"Are you sure?"

"No one knows I'm here and I didn't use my name, so take off. Let's face it, you need sleep badly, I'll see you tomorrow morning," Dave answered groggily. Steve looking around and seeing no one watching, placed Dave's automatic under his blanket beside him.

"Just in case, a nurse tries to rape you."

"Thanks, I really didn't need to think of sex right now," he smiled weakly, pointed at the door. "Go," he said, before going back to sleep.

"Take care, my friend," Steve whispered as he walked quickly out to his car, driving back to his room.

BACK AT LENNY'S PLACE

Police roadblocks covered the entire area for ten square miles, after the shooting at Lenny's house, as the search for the home invasion gang commenced.

"What did they take Sir?" The detective asked, looking at the five dead men.

"They took my wife's jewellery and forced me to open my safe."

"Much in it?'

"Yes, about fifty thousand!" Lenny replied softly, as his wife and children could be heard crying from the adjoining room.

"Well at least they didn't hurt your family, that's something," the detective said trying to reassure Lenny as the coroner started removing the bodies.

"Yes, detective it certainly is!" Lenny answered, looking at the bodies of his former employees.

"I know it's not the right time to ask, but were you insured?" the detective asked a bit embarrassed; unfortunately the question had to be asked.

"Yes, all of my losses will be covered, but my friends cannot be replaced," Lenny replied sadly, happily thinking of the million dollar claim he would be submitting, making nearly as much as going after Roberts. With the assistance of some of his newly appointed lieutenants, he bundled his family into several cars, before driving them to a secret location. As Lenny sat in one of his lieutenant's vehicles following his family's car, his mobile phone began to ring. It was his guest.

"I'm amazed he didn't kill you!"

"He spared my life and my families, in an attempt to get me to back off."

"Are you going to?" the guest asked sarcastically.

"He has made me look a fool in the eyes of my employees. That, I cannot forgive!"

"What will you do?"

"Get my family to safety, and then I'll take care of him, and his family!" Lenny snarled, before hanging up wondering if his men had got Roberts, family, already.

The local police at Lenny's house did a quick sweep of the property before coming to the conclusion that the home invaders were long gone. Detective Mackenzie sat looking at the front gates deep in thought.

"What do you think detective?" One of the local policemen asked him, coming back from searching the river bank.

"Seems Mr Tran Vin has got some enemies."

"I thought it was a home invasion?"

"How many gangs do you know that take on twelve armed men, killing six of them and knocking the others unconscious?"

"You think its drug related?" The officer whispered, knowing Lenny's connection with politicians.

"I'm not sure, but I'll give everything I've got to the Feds, see if they can uncover anything," Mackenzie replied, as the other officers returned from the search.

RUNNING

Scanning the surrounding area, Edward stood watch, as his family and his American friends loaded the two vans, plus Leone's sedan. He knew he needed sleep, but that could wait till they were moving. Nigel after loading his gear walked over to Edward. Making sure no one was listening, he asked Edward what he'd planned to do now.

"We're heading south until we know what's happening," Edward replied still unsure.

"What about Ballina?"

"Look I'm sure he's in Sydney now. He's come south to help us I think, and for some reason, that detective from Ballina is with him."

"Anyway if we can lose the rest of our night visitors today, I'll feel a lot better," Nigel replied even managing a small smile as he pulled out his phone.

"What's with the phone?"

"I've got to ring my boss and tell him roughly what's occurred. Don't worry I won't be mentioning anything about our location," Nigel replied honestly, getting an approving look from Edward, as he checked the area once more.

John Wilson looked down at his phone as he drove home. Seeing the caller was Nigel, he hurriedly pulled over to the side of the freeway, pressing the answer button at the same time.

"God Nigel, where have you been?" John asked angrily, and he had to admit a little worried.

"We're okay, though we've had a few problems," Nigel answered a little concerned how his boss would handle it.

After going through what had happened from the flight to the intruders and finally packing to run this morning, his boss sat quietly taking it all in.

"Considering what you were sent out there to do, you've done well my friend. It was a mistake having that fight on the plane with that journalist Nigel, even though it hasn't been reported," John replied thinking carefully about the implications.

"Natasha is a strange one; she seems more interested in finding Roberts, than the story!"

"Yes, I think her feelings for Roberts are more than just good friends. Anyway, keep safe Nigel and ring when you can," John replied, seeing he been on the phone for twenty minutes.

"Another thing boss, can you ring the Australian Federal Police and get them off Edward's back. The local police are looking for him, and I thought you could scare them off a bit?"

"I'm not some dark demon Nigel, but I'll do my best, and from now on call me John, not boss," John Wilson answered, before hanging up and ringing his office. "Matt, John Wilson here, send a message to the Federal Police in Australia. Warn them they're interfering with one of our anti-terrorist operations, involving one of their agents named Edward MacCalland. Tell them to back off, or there'll be trouble. Let them know, that the Vice President will be ringing the Prime Minister soon to explain everything," John said grinning. Hanging up he then rang the White House, wondering if the Vice President was the devil.

AFP HEADQUARTERS CANBERRA AUSTRALIA

"Excuse me, Sir, there's a message here from the Head of the FBI in America!" George, the Commissioner's assistant said excitedly, as he entered his boss's office.

"Let's have a look?" the Commissioner replied grumpily. Reading quickly through the blunt message, the Commissioner was far from impressed. "They've got a hide running an operation here with one of our men without our consent. Who does this Wilson think he is!" the Commissioner roared, preparing to send a hostile reply back.

"He did mention the Vice President ringing the Prime Minister, Sir," George said worriedly.

"Bullshit he's bluffing. He's trying to get me to roll over and do as I'm told, well he's in for a shock," the Commissioner smiled, as the phone on his desk started ringing. George dutifully picked it up for him.

"Commissioner's office, who is it?" George asked politely, as his face went white.

"Yes Sir, I'll put him right on," George replied softly, pointing to the message and putting his finger under Prime Minister on the message in front of him.

"Commissioner here," he answered politely, as the Prime Minister exploded on his end of the phone. He wanted to know what was going on, after the Vice President of America had thanked him for Australia's cooperation. It was to do with a secret anti-terrorist operation here in Australia, which he knew nothing about.

"We're right on top of it Sir. As a matter of fact, one of our best agents is in the field with them. Even though, I can't go into more details because of the sensitive nature of the operation," the Commissioner replied starting to sweat.

For several seconds the phone line went quiet as the Prime Minister discussed what the Commissioner had said with someone there with him. The Commissioner sat there too scared to breathe, wondering if the Prime Minister had bought the bullshit he was feeding him. Moments later the Prime Minister resumed.

"Good work, Commissioner, I knew you'd be on top of it. Keep me informed, better still, come to the Lodge this Friday, we'll talk about it then," the Prime Minister suggested hanging up. Sitting as if dazed, the Commissioner wiped sweat from his forehead. Looking up, he saw his frozen assistant watching him.

"Give the agent involved and the American agents every assistance George. Find out what's going on. I'll need something to give the Prime Minister on Friday night at his residence. And George, keep this between us." the Commissioner whispered nervously, as George hurriedly left the office, leaving the Commissioner staring at the phone.

AFP SYDNEY OFFICE

Shane Smith sat uncomfortably in the office of the Director of Sydney operations, being grilled as to the whereabouts of Agent MacCalland. The men doing the grilling were the Director's special team of interrogators from internal affairs or dogs as the feds called them. Everyone there knew that the Director had it in for Edward, it went back nearly twenty years, and since then the Director had stopped Edward from getting any advancement or recognition in the Federal Police force.

"Where is MacCalland?" Stevenson, the lead interrogator, asked Shane angrily, as he bumped his shoulder supposedly by accident.

"Haven't the faintest."

"You can kiss your career goodbye, along with your mates if you don't answer soon!" Morris, another interrogator bayed, again bumping Shane's shoulder accidentally, as he passed him.

"Next one of you paper pushers who bumps me, is going to have his jaw wired!" Shane sat staring at Stevenson.

"Are you threatening us?" Stevenson said bravely, as they all moved a little away from Shane, knowing he had a reputation for violence.

"I don't know anything, so unless you got something else I'm leaving," ignoring Stevenson's question and standing up. Stevenson was just about to push Shane back into the seat when the Director charged into the room.

"Stevenson, Morris and the rest of you back off and leave Agent Smith alone!" the Director said patting Shane on the back, as the interrogation team nearly fell over.

"But Sir!" Stevenson replied, clearly amazed at the Director backing Shane against them.

"I said get out!" the Director yelled, leaving Shane astonished, as Stevenson and the others departed. "Sorry about that Shane, I had no idea that Edward was working with the Americans to break a terrorist group here in our country," the Director smiled, waving Shane to a seat near his desk.

"It's pretty secret Sir," Shane replied, not knowing what else to say, before getting an understanding nod from his boss.

"So this triad gang has something to do with these terrorists?" the Director asked, digging for information the Commissioner badly needed. Shane sat there thinking what to answer when an idea came to him. This morning the intelligence department had asked him if there was a link between the triad shootings and the attack on a Vietnamese businessman named Lenny Tran Vin. Shane had done a little digging and had come to the conclusion that Tran Vin was dirty. Sitting in the director's office, Shane knew he had to give the director something, so he decided to give him that.

"Look Sir I can't say much, but Edward and the Yanks thought Tran Vin was involved!" Shane told him nervously, which the director put down to telling him something he shouldn't.

"It's safe with me Shane. Don't worry it won't go beyond this office. By the way, if you hear from Edward, tell him we're right behind him if he needs help," the Director replied dripping sincerity, as Shane headed back to his office.

Shane hadn't been gone for more than five minutes when the Director called Stevenson and his men back in.

"Get a strike force together Stevenson. I want you and Morris to raid Lenny Tran Vin's business and smash his terrorist group!" the Director stated angrily.

"Are you sure he's involved Sir, he's got some powerful friends in high places," Stevenson answered, having heard of Lenny from a friend in Parliament.

"Look, Shane said in confidence that the Yanks are onto him and I'm not going to let that shit MacCalland get all the credit. Get as many men as you need and wipe him out, is that understood!" the Director said menacingly.

"Understood boss, consider it done," Stevenson replied nervously, before hurrying out.

After Stevenson had left, the director sat there thinking of the coming raid and the credit that would come to him.

"Shane you trust too easily," he said to himself smiling, as picking up his phone he rang the Commissioner.

Down the hallway, Shane watched as Stevenson gathered all the field units in for a briefing, excluding him. After it had broken up, Shane rang a friend in an assault group connected to this office.

"Hey, Joe what's going on with Stevenson?" Shane asked secretively.

"I'm not supposed to say anything, but we're raiding Lenny Tran Vin's warehouse this afternoon, the bastard is linked to a terrorist cell!" Joe said excitedly, having had two months of doing nothing.

"Sounds big, be careful Joe."

"Don't worry, we're going in heavy. There'll be no mucking around," Joe answered, his hatred for terrorists evident, as he hung up. Shane sat there for a while wondering what he'd triggered, before bursting into uncontrollable laughter.

EUROPE

After contacting the Americans, Ali called Aaron and Cody. Both calls went to message services, where Ali left an urgent message for them both to ring him on his mobile. Aaron immediately rang back giving his address in Southern France. Ali, after telling him what was happening, asked if he'd been in contact with Cody. Aaron unfortunately hadn't heard from Cody for over a year. Packing for a few days away, Ali told his family about Steve's problem.

Over the years as his children grew into adults, he'd come clean explaining about his past. After America, they'd all thought it was over, now this. To be safe, Julie his wife, and Michelle his daughter would move into hiding at a friend's place in Milano. Peter, his son, wanted to go with him. He had just turned twenty and was now one of the youngest officers in the Swiss elite paratroopers. Blue-eyed like his mother and dark skin like his father, he stood just over six feet tall with an athletic build.

"Father let me help. I can bring my unit with me no questions asked."

"Thanks, son but I need you here in case they come for our family," Ali replied moved by his son's love.

"You're not getting any younger Dad, remember that," his son put in smiling, though his eyes showed misgiving.

"It's just a recon son. Don't worry and I've got Aaron and Cody with me."

"Remember that skiing holiday Dad. I was only young, but I remember it," Peter reminded him, as both men went quiet.

"Look I've got your number; if things get dodgy, I'll ring you," Ali conceded getting a nod from Peter, as Ali departed.

Four hours later Ali arrived at Aaron's vineyard. It was a beautiful spot overlooking Lyon, with the Swiss mountains in the distance. Aaron had been apparently waiting, and as Ali's BMW pulled into his driveway, he pointed for him to enter a garage where the door was opening. Driving inside Aaron greeted him, as behind him the door closed.

"Privacy is always important," Aaron smiled as he opened a rear door in the wall of the garage revealing an armoury.

"You've been busy," Ali frowned looking at the extensive collection of weaponry.

"I'm a careful man Ali. They won't again catch me off guard like last time," Aaron declared, Ali agreeing.

"Funny you should mention that. My son also brought it up just before I left."

"It was a bad time for him. Mind you, they wouldn't try it now the way he's grown."

"It wasn't as bad for him as you think Aaron," Ali smiled, having never told Aaron all that occurred.

"Let's have some lunch, and then we'll pack what we need," Aaron suggested, confused by Ali's answer, as they moved upstairs to the kitchen. The two men briefly went over their plan of action over lunch, both concerned for Steve and Cody. Aaron, who'd been a close friend of Cody's admitted over the last few years how he'd become distant as if he was hiding something.

"He could be just keeping his distance for safety sake," Ali concluded, admitting since the skiing trip he'd been reluctant to call Aaron.

"I can't blame you, Ali, it was close, very close. On our own we can blend in, together we're easy to spot," Aaron put forward, as the men lapsed into silence.

Moving on, they quickly returned to the car, breaking down several weapons hiding the parts all over Ali's BMW. Aaron throwing a bag with his own gear in the back seat signalled they were ready, as Ali opened the garage door. Standing in the driveway was a pretty woman with long black hair, aged about 35. She was typically French with an hourglass figure and a pretty smiling face. Coming forward she grabbed hold of Aaron pulling him to her kissing him not letting go. In the end, Aaron pushed her away hurrying to the car as she stood there forlornly watching them leave.

"Who was that?" Ali asked surprised, even though she looked familiar.

"She works for me here as a storeman, used to be a cop," Aaron admitted smiling.

"She seems to like her job," Ali smiling as he suddenly remembered where he'd seen her. "Was that Petra?" Ali asked shocked, as Aaron nodded. Saying nothing more, they drove down the driveway, heading for London.

Aaron looked through his binoculars at the house for a third time, in as many minutes, still seeing no movement. It was a typical cold miserable morning in London, as the fog swirled around aimlessly, slowly flowing west, with the prevailing wind. The row of two-story semi-detached brick homes was a common sight in the western suburbs of London. The only difference from this one they were watching, to the thirty other ones in this block, was a now dead assassin had lived in this one.

"I wish Cody or Steve were here Ali! With only two of us, it's going to make this a lot harder," Aaron whispered, his growing unease being felt by Ali.

"You're right I don't like it either. I know Steve said he copped it in Australia, but there's something not quite right here," Ali replied as he too watched the house.

They had arrived the night before, setting up across the road from the suspect's house in a derelict pub. Their drive across France to the channel tunnel had been routine. Ali had waited for Aaron to mention the woman at his vineyard, but so far he'd said nothing. Ali sensed Aaron wasn't completely convinced the Yanks would leave them alone by the sizable armoury he kept at his house and his reference to their skiing trip. This was maybe the reason why he kept his private life secret Ali presumed, understanding. Driving to England through the channel tunnel proved easier than Ali had hoped, having spent a great deal of time worrying about a customs check.

Aaron explained that to the English police, they were just two pathetic old guys driving around Europe. Ali had his doubts though; Aaron seemed to be right as they passed through customs with barely a look. Ali had been secretly worried about being Arabic in appearance. This made no difference, as he was too old to fit the profile of the men the police were looking for.

Now they both sat in the derelict pub, feeling their age, hesitating. Both knew that in their prime, they would have acted without a second thought, now even something as simple as checking out a dead man's house required planning.

"So do you think it's a trap?" Aaron whispered.

"There's only one way to find out!" Ali chuckled, as giving Aaron a grin he checked his weapon, taking the safety off and placing it in his coat pocket. Going out the back of the pub, away from the house, Ali walked casually around the block, strolling as if looking for an address. Going past the house, Ali continued up the street before turning and walking back. Seeing no imminent threat, he walked up the three small steps to the assassin's front door. In the meantime, Aaron climbed up the rickety stairs to the first floor. Training his sniper rifle across the road, he checked each of the windows of the houses opposite, making sure there were no surprises.

"So far, so good," Aaron said into his transmitter, as Ali made a clicking noise, showing he had heard him, as he approached the door. A feeling of impending disaster gripped Aaron, making his guts grumble, as he went back to the binoculars, for a more comprehensive look at the area. Still seeing nothing out of the ordinary, Aaron watched Ali approached the door.

Knocking, Ali stood looking relaxed, on the inside his nerves jumped at being so exposed. Putting his hand on the door handle, Ali turned it to find the door give. Slowly closing it again, he stood there knocking again pretending to wait.

"The doors unlocked my friend, it's too easy!" Ali whispered into his microphone. Swiftly turning, Ali sprinted across the road towards the safety of a bus shelter. As he raced across the road, two automatic weapons opened up from the neighbouring house. Luckily for Ali, his erratic behaviour at the door had caught the two shooters of guard. Feeling the aim of the shooters close on him, Ali dived in desperation. He just made it, as bullets belted rhythmically into the concrete bus shelter.

Laying gasping for air, Ali thanked his creator for making it, cursing his own stupidity. He knew he was safe here behind the concrete bus stop, the problem was he was also trapped. Lying there unable to move, he realised he was entirely in Aaron's hands.

When Ali had turned to sprint, Aaron had dropped the binoculars, snatching up his rifle. A split second later, the two windows on the house to the right of their target house, burst out onto the street, as the enemies weapons came to life. Not having time to aim, Aaron sent several shots through both windows causing both shooters to stop and take cover. Looking through the scope this time, Aaron waited for movement.

A blurred shape was all he needed, as he fired one round at the window on the far right. His reward was seeing the figure spin backwards and then drop. The sense of achievement was short-lived, as the second window erupted, spewing hot metal from the shooter's weapon. Round after round impacted on Aaron's window forcing him to take cover. Pinned down by the shooter, Aaron knew he had to do something quick, as in the distance sirens could be heard, approaching.

"Sometimes, it's no fun being right," Aaron, said out loud, thinking of Ali running shit scared to that bus stop, after his warning not to go. Crawling to another window, he was just about to return fire, when the sound of a timber floorboard downstairs creaking, told him that someone was behind him. Without hesitation, Aaron pulled a grenade from his pocket, pulled the pin and tossed it underarm out through the doorway onto the stairs. He heard it bounce several times, before a voice screamed out in horror, a split second before the grenade exploded.

Up until this stage, the condemned building's frail structure had held itself together by sheer will. As the shock wave from the exploding grenade roared through it's failing walls, the building gave up its fight to stay erect, imploding into itself. As a cloud of debris and sound mushroomed out into the street, the shooter opposite blinded by the dust, stop shooting, waiting for it to clear.

It was the break Ali needed. Coming to his feet he took aim at the shooter's window, sending a full clip into the shooter's position. Reloading Ali stood silently waiting for a response. As the second's tick by, he lowered his weapon and ran to the pub. Kicking down the front door, Ali quickly entered the dust filled wreckage.

"Aaron, where are you?" Ali screamed as the siren grew louder, only moments away.

"Over here!" Aaron groaned as Ali climbed over the debris, finding Aaron in the corner. The force of the explosion had made the upper levels floor collapse, sending Aaron down landing heavily on his left leg. Quickly examining him, Ali dragged him out what was left of the rear door, causing Aaron to moan in agony, his left leg hanging at an unnatural angle.

Shoving the near-delirious man in their car, Ali swiftly jumped behind the wheel. Gunning the car down a side road, Ali tried to get as much distance as he could between them and the ambush site.

Driving for a good two hours, Ali, seeing hospital signs pointing to the right, followed them. Pulling up at the emergency entrance, Ali called out to a nurse for assistance.

"What happened to him?" a doctor asked, as Aaron was dragged into the emergency department and place on a bed in front of him.

"We were doing renovations on my house, when he fell through the floor," Ali answered showing genuine concern at the mishap.

"Well next time hire professional tradesmen to help, you two aren't getting any younger," the doctor answered, examining Aaron's leg.

"Yes, we were certainly taken by surprise!" Ali replied getting a small grin from Aaron as the painkillers took effect.

"Looks like a straightforward break, but he'll be in plaster for several weeks at his age. And next time be more careful!" the doctor informed them sternly as if talking to children before he hurried off to another patient.

"If he says old one more time, I'm going to cut his throat!" Aaron groaned trying to smile, as Ali sat there solemnly thinking about the ambush.

"They knew we were coming my friend, how did they know?" Ali asked softly, as they both waited for Aaron's leg to be set in plaster, trying to work out what was going on.

Against the doctor's advice, who told them they were two silly old men, Ali piled Aaron into his car, rather than stay exposed at the hospital. Travelling back to London, they booked into a freeway hotel, on the outskirts of the city, where they could plan their next move.

"I'm going back to the hitman's house!" Ali stated coming to a decision.

"It's too dangerous Ali. Give me a couple of days, or better still, wait for Cody," Aaron was concerned for his friend.

"The last thing they'd expect is a visit to the house from us, while the cops are still there."

"What about weapons? I lost the rifle when the roof came down, and they're hard to get in England," Aaron told him, knowing smuggling more weapons in from France in the back of their car would be pushing their luck.

"I've still got the pistol, which will have to do for now. So stay here and hope Cody rings while I'm gone. I shouldn't be more than three hours," Ali assured him, before departing as dawn started to break.

Driving past the street, where the shootout had taken place, Ali found road barriers in place. Police forensic units could be seen in the pub and the shooters house, luckily not in the hitman's home next door. 'They don't know the house is connected with the shooting' Ali thought to himself, as he continued into the next block of houses, parking.

Walking casually past the barrier, Ali saw the ordinary police were in attendance as well, watching the barrier and keeping the public back. Going completely around the block, Ali noticed that the dead end alley behind the block of houses was cordoned off but deserted. Quickly looking around, he slowly walked down the alley counting houses. Coming to the rear of the hitman's house, Ali opened the gate, walking casually up to the door, finding it locked and barred. Retracing his steps, he came to the garage, noting it was a remote control type door.

Borrowing a steel bar from the yard, Ali cautiously jimmied the door at the bottom corner. It lifted just enough for him to crawl under, before pulling the door closed behind him. Dusting his clothes off, Ali went up a small staircase, finding another door locked. This door wasn't barred, and with the help of his steel bar, it folded quickly under pressure. Waiting for several seconds, to see if his door breaking had been heard, Ali then checked the ground floor, making sure he was alone.

The ground floor area consisted of a small kitchen, a lounge area, and a dining room. The place was spotless; the only thing out of place was the trip wire across the front door. The thin black wire, waited patiently for some unfortunate fool to open the door and stretch it. He realised then, why the ambush had come undone from his last visit. The two gunmen had expected him to open the door and be blown away.

"Luckily they hadn't locked the door, or I would have forced it!" Ali said to himself angrily, slightly shaken, by how close he had come to death. Walking cautiously forward, he carefully disconnected the trip wire, which led to a bucket full of explosives, surrounded by nails.

Opening the door slightly he peeked outside, checking the area seeing the police were still there, he closed the door, locking it.

Moving upstairs, Ali thought how lucky it was, that the local cops hadn't tried that door when they'd cleared the area. The second level consisted of two bedrooms and a bathroom. Like below, the rooms were clean, to the point of boring. 'Whoever lives here doesn't like mess that's for sure' Ali thought grimly, as he began to strip the rooms looking for a clue. Two hours later, Ali sat exhausted on what was left of the main bed, after destroying the whole top floor.

"What a waste of fucking time!" Ali spat out angrily, as he walked back downstairs, repeating the process downstairs, looking for something to give him a lead. 'Another hour and still nothing' Ali fumed, as he made ready to leave, totally dispirited. Exiting through the kitchen, Ali stopped getting himself a glass of water. It tasted so disgusting that he threw the glass angrily on the floor smashing it. Leaning against the sink, Ali took a few deep breaths calming him, knowing coming here had been for nothing.

Looking down at the mess he'd made, knowing he was getting stressed out, he saw the water drained through a large crack in the floor.

"Thank you God" Ali whispered, smiling at his luck, as he quickly pulled back the floor rug, tracing the crack in the floor. It revealed a cleverly hidden trap door leading to a basement. Slowly lifting the door, Ali looked for any sign of bobby traps, before descending down the improvised staircase, to the wooden floor below. Finding a hanging piece of cord in the semi-darkness, Ali pulled it, turning on the lighting system.

This illuminated the whole area allowing him to carefully check the area. Like upstairs the room was spotlessly organised, divided between a store room and an office section. The first thing that attracted Ali's attention was a shot of Steve, taken at Fort Bragg. There they had all received their training from the Americans, in the early 80s. Besides, it was more recent pictures of Steve's family, and the other unit members, including Ali and his family.

'How'd did they get these?' Ali asked himself angrily, worried by this group's knowledge of the unit's locations, all over the world. Looking around at the treasure trove of information, Ali became wary, knowing no one would leave this unguarded. Walking back to the staircase, Ali carefully searched the ground and the surrounding walls, till he found what he was afraid of. In the wall was a miniature LED light and opposite was another glass tube obviously the receiver.

The beam operation was simple, anything getting in the way of the LED light and the receiver, set off an alarm; the question was what happens now? If it were meant to go bang, it would've by now Ali surmised, so that meant someone must be coming. Hurrying up the stairs, Ali rushed to the front door, carefully peeking outside, checking the street. The police still had the street blocked off, so that side was safe. Going to the kitchen window, which faced the back entrance, Ali cautiously took a look. Ali at first saw nothing out of the ordinary, but as he looked towards the entrance to the alley, he saw a white van blocking his escape route.

Reaching into his pocket, Ali drew his pistol, remembering Aaron's words about coming back here too soon and with only a pistol.

"I hate when Aaron's right!" he chuckled, before going back down into the basement. The storeroom section contained many boxes, and it didn't take an expert to know by their shape, that they were weapons. Opening several Ali found what he was looking for, in the shape of an M16 assault rifle. Going through a series of small boxes he then located some ammo for the rifle, plus of all things, a silenced pistol. Smiling, Ali grabbed both the rifle and the pistol, before moving upstairs to the bedrooms for a better look at the van. Four men now stood behind it, all were watching the house and visible in their hands, was an assortment of weapons.

What was more worrying was the way they professionally checked their weapons before moving forward in a two by two formation, showing they had military training.

"Not good!" Ali whispered to himself as he prepared to open up. Taking aim, he was just about to fire when a figure appeared from a garage doorway behind the four men. Staying behind a brick wall, the shadow fired a silenced pistol at point-blank range into the surprised group of men. When all four men were on the ground, the figure slowly advanced, reshooting each man in the head. Finished, the figure casually walked to the back door, where he knocked before speaking.

"Ali, its Cody, are you there?" a voice asked in a normal voice, looking around casually. Tapping on the glass from upstairs, Ali saw

Cody look up, as Ali signalled him to wait. Rushing downstairs, Ali unbarred the back door forcing it opened so Cody could enter.

"So how are you enjoying London?" Cody asked neutrally, going to the fridge and grabbing out the only beer and passing Ali a coke.

"About the usual!" Ali replied just as casually before they both came forward giving each other a bear hug.

"Might be best if we hurry up, those dead guys out there are going to be noticed soon," Cody pointed out, as Ali grabbed what Intel he could, including a laptop computer from the basement. Cody in the meantime, grabbed a selection of weapons from the storeroom, throwing them into a large baseball bag, they then swiftly departed.

The trip back to the hotel where Ali had left Aaron, was mostly filled in by Cody bring Ali up to date on where he'd been. When Cody had first been contacted, he'd been fishing off the Irish coast, helping out a friend who owned a trawler. It had taken a few days to reach port, and after contacting Aaron, he'd found out Ali was on the way to the hit man's house. Not wanting to surprise Ali, he decided to wait near the alley's entrance. While watching the house, he'd seen the van slowly come to a stop at the alley. This forced him to duck into the shadows of a neighbouring driveway. Knowing Ali was trapped inside he decided to intervene, as the men's attention was on the house.

"I went through their pockets and bagged it. We can go through it later. There's one thing they have in common though, they're all your brothers!" Cody informed him, as Ali stood trying to work out what he was saying. "They're all Muslims," Cody smiled. Ali for one minute thought he was joking, seeing he wasn't, lapsed into silence.

"Somehow that makes this whole business far worse," Ali admitted. "Anyway, I've got the assassin's laptop. When we get back to the room, we'll see what Aaron can find out. Like how they knew we were coming," Ali suggested, as they drove the rest of the way in silence.

When they arrived at the motel, Aaron was overjoyed with both Cody's appearance and Ali's survival. He was unimpressed by how lucky Ali had been.

"Getting yourself killed isn't going to help Steve or our families when these killers decide to come after the rest of us," Aaron chastised him; his anger and fear plain to see.

"It's okay my friend, it worked out okay," Ali answered trying to sound confident.

"You were lucky! In the old days, you would've been the first to reject the operation you just did," Aaron spat out, silencing Ali.

"What's done is done, let's move on people. At least we have a lead on who we're up against," Cody added settling everyone down.

"Your right Cody and so is Aaron. I was rash, and I apologise. From now on we'll plan like we did in the past, as a unit.

Ali prayed that night before going to bed, thinking how lucky he had been. Cody turning up had saved him, from either death or arrest. Even if he'd managed to kill the four men, the chances were at least one of them would have got a few shots off. Their weapons weren't silenced so the police would've been alerted. He knew he couldn't shoot a cop, meaning he'd have been arrested. He owed Cody his life, the only thing nagging him, was how quickly Cody had gunned down those men.

Cody hadn't missed a beat, he'd shot them and walked forward finishing them, something Ali would've had trouble with. 'Am I the only one who has trouble with killing' he thought, as he lay there missing his family. It was then that Ali remembered the skiing trip, there he had no problems killing he reminded himself.

THE SKIING TRIP

When Peter was 16 years old, Aaron, who had been visiting, asked if he could take him cross-country skiing in the Ardennes near Bastogne. At the time, Julie, Ali's wife was taking their daughter Michelle secretly to Australia to visit with Julie's mother, who was unwell. Peter, who was on holidays from school, seemed overly excited about skiing.

Ali found this unusual since he'd just returned from a ski trip with his friends. Aaron too seemed keyed up, which made Ali suspicious knowing Aaron hated getting cold.

"Why Bastogne?" Ali asked the pair, as they sat in Ali's study, sipping hot chocolate.

"It's historic Dad. It's where the Allies turned back the Germans during the war," Peter piped in, showing he'd done his homework.

"Bullshit! Now I know you're both lying," Ali replied heatedly, knowing Peter's hatred of studying history. Sheepish looks passed between Aaron and Peter. Aaron, in the end, came clean.

"Well, I thought since we were cross-country skiing there, we could try for a couple of deer. There's supposed to be quite a few in the hills to the east of the town," Aaron answered, as silence settled over the room.

"You've only just turned sixteen Peter," Ali said before stopping unable to continue.

"Dad, I'll be careful and in our situation knowing how to use a rifle could come in handy," Peter replied, looking into his father's eyes. Ali had told his children from a young age about his background and why they should always be on guard against strangers. Looking at his son, Ali realised he was no longer a child.

"Where are you getting the rifles from?" Ali asked.

"I've got a good hunting rifle. I can borrow another for Peter," Aaron replied smiling knowing Ali was letting them go.

Getting up Ali pressed a button beside his desk, as behind him the wall cracked open. He walked to the concealed room entrance, indicating for Aaron and Peter to follow. Several weapons lined the wall, Ali reached up and grabbed a Swiss sniper rifle, passing it to Peter. The last time Ali had prepared to use this weapon, was when drug cartels men had come for him. Luckily it wasn't needed. Watching his son work the bolt, making sure it was empty, Ali saw

Peter's surprise, when he found a round in the chamber and the magazine loaded.

"Always watch for that son. In this family, a weapon is always ready to be used."

Two days later at six in the morning, an excited Aaron and Peter waved goodbye to Ali and drove off. They would first stop in Lyon, where Aaron lived, to pick up his gear. From there, they'd drive to Bastogne, where Aaron had hired a hunting cabin in the mountains to the east. Altogether they would be gone for ten days. Ali had been tempted to go with them. Work like usual had stopped him, as he drove towards Zurich, to attend a finance seminar hosted by his bank's investment arm.

He had secretly bought into a Swiss bank; using the money he'd built up working for the Americans to become a silent partner. This gave him employment and a career without anyone being able to check on him. Julie would be away with Michelle for at least another three weeks, so Ali thought he'd use this time to watch how his team ran the seminar. He felt guilty he hadn't told Julie of Peter's real reason for going skiing with Aaron. Ali decided to tell her after they'd returned, rather than have her worry.

The first day of the seminar ran smoothly, Ali was impressed with the staff, telling them so. That night he opted to stay in Zurich rather than drive home. Settling down at a local hotel for the night, he watched the news, before ringing his wife at two in the morning which was lunchtime in Sydney. They were having a good time, and Julie's mother was feeling a lot better. He promised to keep in touch, before turning in.

Seven the next morning, Ali dressed readying himself for another day. Turning on the news, he listened to it in the background, while he enjoyed his hot breakfast. He was just about to take his plates to the sink and walk out the door when he heard Lyon mentioned on the news. A house in a leafy, affluent suburb could be seen ablaze. The caption underneath gave the street address indicating two people had been murdered.

"Saint Vincent Boulevard," Ali whispered, a sense of foreboding gripping him. Ripping open his briefcase, he pulled out the address and phone number of Aaron's home.

"No!" He cried out loud, seeing the same address as he pulled out his mobile, dialling. An engaged signal came in reply, so he tried again. Over the next ten minutes her tried at least twenty times, always greeted by the same engaged signal. Making a decision, he called his bank telling them he had to go overseas immediately. He then gathered his belongings, before leaving the hotel driving towards Lyon.

Ali had never felt such fear, as he felt now. When in Afghanistan, where he'd been shot while rescuing a tribal chief from the Taliban, he'd faced death like a soldier. Sure he'd been scared, but that was a soldier's lot. When the drug cartel had come for him and his family, he'd at least been ready for them. Steve had rung and warned him, allowing him to get his family out of harm's way. This time, his son and Aaron could already be dead, and there was nothing he could do about it.

Fear was an emotion Ali had always been taught to control, now as he sped towards Aaron's home he felt completely at a loss which scared him.

LYON

Arriving at Aaron's home, Ali was greeted by smouldering ruins, surrounded by police tape. Getting out of the car his heart labouring in his chest, Ali walked towards what could be the spot where his son and a good friend had been executed.

Detective Petra Marroe, looked towards the barrier as the BMW screamed to a stop, the driver looking clearly upset, got out. 'What's your story,' Petra asked herself, as the man stood looking at the crime scene. Being new to the town having just transferred from Paris, she had been handed this mess to see if she could cope. So far the crime scene and what had happened was unbelievable, to say the least. They had two dead people, believed to be renting the ground floor of this two-story house, from the owner who lived on the top floor.

Both had been murdered after being tortured before the building was set alight. The only reason they knew that had occurred was a passing police car had seen the fire before it took hold. Pulling up, the police officers had kicked in the front door, dragging the two unfortunate people outside. It was only then that the police got a look at the bodies they'd rescued.

To complicate the situation, the owner's name was found to be false, further hampering the investigation. Walking towards the man, the Inspector noticed he appeared Arabic in appearance and about fifty. He was well dressed in an expensive suit and from the female point of view, not bad looking.

"Can I be of any help Sir?" Petra asked approaching the man.

"What happened here?" He asked his voice full of emotion.

"Are you related to anyone who lives here?" She asked.

"The owner was a friend," Ali replied neutrally. Both the Detective and Ali stood there silently, sizing each other up, waiting for the other to talk. In the end tired of waiting for a reply, Petra started.

"The two people dead were renting here. They were tortured and murdered before the house was set alight. We can't locate the owner, can you help us?" Watching him, she saw a look of relief cross his face. She also noticed he didn't seem to be surprised that the victims had been tortured.

"Thank you, Detective, you've been a great help," the man replied, starting to move towards his car.

"Wait, where do you think you are going?" Inspector Petra spat out, signalling to two uniformed officers to move in.

"I've done nothing wrong Inspector, you can't detain me. I'm a Swiss citizen," the man answered his eyes bluntly studying the two officers closing on him. Something in his eyes warned Petra that he wouldn't go quietly, as she told the two officers to wait.

"That might be so, but you know the owner, who was using a fake identity to live here. Look you can either talk to me here or at the station. Something tells me you don't want the law involved," Petra smiled watching him. The man eyes seem to drill into to her, as he nodded his acceptance, pointing to a small coffee shop across the road. Dismissing her men, Petra accompanied him into the shop, sitting at a table inside the door. Petra noticed he grabbed the chair facing the outside street.

Ali too had been studying Petra. She was a pretty woman with a good figure, but there was something more. She walked with cat-like grace as if she was ready to attack. She was also well muscled, Ali guessed she been in the army or done some serious training. Sitting down he ordered them both coffee as Petra waited.

"Were you in the Army?" Ali asked.

"Yes for a couple of years. Took a hit in Algiers, put me in the hospital for six months," she answered truthfully.

"Aaron the owner of that house and I were in a unit too," Ali replied leaving it there.

"Is that why he's using a fake name?" Petra asked guessing by the way he brought the army bit up, that it was connected.

"Yes. Who we were working for wasn't happy with us retiring."

"You've got to give me more than that!"

"They'll kill you for just sitting here with me," Ali answered watching outside. The way he said it made Petra look outside too, as if sensing they were being watched.

"Don't try to scare me, my friend. Anyone who did this is long gone."

"Maybe they're gone, though if it were me, I'd have left someone here to see if any of his friends turned up," he suggested, watching a van edge out of a parking space at the end of the block, moving down to park opposite his BMW.

"You could be a terrorist for all I know and your friend was a sleeper here."

"Would you like to get the men responsible?" Ali asked, liking the Inspector.

"Of course I would, where are they?"

"Do you see that van opposite my car?" Ali asked as she nodded seeing it. "Tell your men to cover that van, but warn them to be careful," Ali added, deadly serious as Petra used her radio, then standing.

"And what will we be doing?"

"We're the bait. Let's walk towards my car." Ali suggested, offering his hand.

"What's your name, since we're holding hands?" she asked, as crossing the road she noticed the van start its engine.

"Ali. Just Ali," he answered, tackling her to the ground, as the first shot rang out.

Inside the van, Jake and Robby had watched Ali with greedy grins on their faces. After a tipoff from a CIA cell in France, they'd come with four other men to get Aaron. He been located through a fake passport he was using. The forger who'd been caught had rolled over on Aaron, in exchange for a lighter sentence. After arriving at the address, they'd found him gone. The couple staying downstairs didn't really know him, but they knew he was taking a young kid skiing near Bastogne.

Even so, they'd tortured them just in case they knew something else, before slicing both their throats. Robby and Jake had been the lookouts at the time, and the others had left them here, just in case Aaron returned.

When Ali had arrived, Robby had nearly jumped from the car to terminate him. Jake had stopped him as the police presence was too strong. Now having moved their van opposite his car, they could take him out and accelerate away. Brooks, their boss had been excited just to get Aaron. How would he react if they got Ali, the unit's leader? Excitedly they'd rung the others telling them of Ali's appearance. To their surprise, their leader told them to back off and tail him.

"They're just worried we'll get all the glory," Jake snarled, watching as Ali walked towards them with the female cop.

"Well, I'm not waiting!" Robby laughed, raising his assault rifle and taking aim, before firing. It was this movement that Ali had seen, as he shoved Petra down onto the ground, behind a parked car. Robby thinking he'd hit Ali shouted wildly.

"Got him! The bastards down!" he screamed, as he jumped from the car and ran towards where Ali had hit the ground.

"Wait Robby, get back in the car!" Jake yelled seeing the cops reacting. Robby wasn't worried by the local cops. They were only armed with pistols, no match for assault rifles he and Robby carried. Spraying the surrounding area, he made the police dive for cover as he continued across the road looking for Ali. Jake in the van had no choice but to jump from the van and lay down cover fire.

Petra on the ground, getting past being knocked over, looked under the car seeing the feet of the man heading towards them.

"Any ideas?" She asked Ali.

"Yeah, don't get shot," he smiled as the surrounding police opened up.

Jake was the hit first. He hadn't seen the police move in behind him before the shooting started. Shot twice in the back, he crumpled to the ground, shouting out a warning to Robby. Nearly to the car, Robby heard Jake scream his warning. Turning he saw him slide down the van to the ground, realising he was now exposed. 'I can still get Ali' he thought as turning back around he saw the female cop take aim and fire.

When Jake had screamed out, Ali told Petra to take the shot. Standing swiftly, she took aim and fired, as the man with the rifle turned back towards her, preparing to fire. At first, she thought she missed as the man continued to stand there. His gun dropping from his hands and the spreading stain on his chest told her otherwise, as he stumbled, falling face first onto the road. Shaken by the shootout the local police slowly rose from their positions walking towards the two gunmen, kicking their weapons away.

Ali, climbing to his feet rushed from the first gunman to the next, checking if they were still alive. Robby was gone, Jake was still breathing. Getting down on his hands and knees Ali tried to stem the bleeding as Jake cried out in pain.

"You'll be okay my friend, just hold on," Ali assured him.

"Save it arsehole, I know I'm finished! By now our team has got that fucking French paratrooper mate of yours and his kid," Jake spat out, spitting blood at Ali.

"You're right, you're a dead man. Shit, whoever trained you anyway, they didn't do much of a job?" Ali laughed, trying to rattle him.

"We mightn't have been a part of an elite unit like yours killing for the CIA. But we're good enough to get your friend, while he's skiing near Bastogne," Jake laughed, showing Ali he knew where they were, as coughing up blood, he suddenly froze, his eyes staring into space. Getting up, Ali wiped his hands on his handkerchief, tossing it beside Jake.

"Rot in hell!" Ali growled, as Petra and the other cops stood watching him.

"Handcuff him," Petra ordered, as two of her men moved behind Ali, securing his hands.

"You're making a mistake Inspector. You've got your men," Ali pointed out, as she led him towards her car.

"Spit out your story Ali, or you're going to jail," Petra ordered. Ali, anger in his eyes sat there watching her. "Have it your own way," She continued starting the car.

"Wait Inspector!" Ali stammered out, his eyes for the first time showing fear. "I got to go to Bastogne. The boy's my son," Ali confessed.

"He said you worked in an elite unit for the CIA is that true?"

"Yes, they tried to retire us permanently. We have been on the run ever since."

"Where are they staying in Bastogne?" Petra asked.

"I don't know? Aaron was taking my son cross-country skiing and hunting, somewhere in the mountains?" Ali explained wondering how he'd find them.

"Then having a cop along will help won't it?" Petra smiled driving off. It took three hours to reach Bastogne, only then did Petra take the cuffs off.

"Look Officer!"

"Stop! Don't try to talk me out of it Ali. I want the men who tortured those two poor souls back in Lyon to close this case, so shut up," she ordered, before walking into the local tourist centre. Showing her badge, she asked the manager to check all the rental lodges in the area, checking for a man and boy. There were several fathers and sons staying in different lodges, as it was a popular spot to teach sons to ski and shoot. Ali, in the end, furnished several aliases which Aaron used, one, they got a hit on.

The lodge was twenty miles to the east, deep in the forest, meaning they'd need a 4WD vehicle. The manager arranged it for them, supplying them with a map as well.

"Thanks for your help," Petra said to the manager as they walked out to the vehicle.

"No problems. Still, if you'd got here earlier, you could've travelled with those Interpol cops."

"When was that exactly?" Ali asked neutrally.

"About seven this morning, they're looking for the same people I'd guess. They didn't know his name though, just took a list of the five different father and son groups," the manager replied, as Petra put the vehicle into gear driving off.

"Ring the lodge where your friends staying, warn him," Petra suggested, putting her foot down racing out of Bastogne. Ali tried the lodge several times the phone failing to be answered.

"The whole lodge could be out skiing or shooting. Don't read too much into it," Petra put forward, seeing Ali's eyes staring out the window. Petra driving onto a side road covered with snow engaged the 4WD.

"These men we're after will show no mercy Detective, be ready," Ali answered his mind far away, as he continued to stare out the window. "Stop the car!" he yelled, as Petra shocked, slammed on the brakes.

Jumping from the car Ali ran back down the road, gazing at the line of wires running next to the road. Petra running back, gun out, wondered what he was looking at when she saw the wires. On one of the poles all the wires had been cut, it was clearly deliberate.

AARON AND PETER

Waving goodbye at dawn to a crestfallen Ali, Aaron and Peter had excitedly started off, heading for Lyon's. Aaron had planned to stay at his home overnight, and then drive the next day to the shooting lodge. However, Peter's enthusiasm had been contagious. Arriving at Aaron's home, Peter had breathlessly told the people living downstairs about Aaron taking him deer hunting. Aaron watching had caught his enthusiasm, deciding to drive straight through to Bastogne. There he suggested they have a late lunch, and take in the war museum, before driving to the lodge.

Peter had of course agreed, so Aaron had quickly thrown his gear into the car and driven on, inadvertently saving both their lives.

Leaving Bastogne after visiting the museum, Aaron pulled over to check his map. Sure he was going the right way, they continued on, making good time on the surfaced roads. Reaching the halfway point, Aaron turned onto a dirt road for the second half of the trip. This proved far more daunting, as the snow had started falling heavily. Aaron worried about the road condition, thought maybe he should wait till the next day. Peter beside him was overjoyed, talking excitedly, encouraging Aaron to keep going, enjoying the adventure.

When after blindly travelling for two hours and only being able to see the road in front of the vehicle, Aaron concerned, decided to turn back. Clearing a ridge, looking for an area wide enough to turn around, Aaron looked down onto the lodge in the valley below.

"My God! It's incredible!" Peter exclaimed spotting it too. Staring down at the complex, Aaron punched Peter's arm playfully.

"I told you we'd make it," Aaron smiled confidently, all doubts were forgotten, as they drove down to the parking area.

After booking in, they carried their gear to their hut, unpacking. It was simple in design, just two bedrooms off a lounge room, with a small bathroom. It gave them a feeling of privacy, while at the same time; you could eat and drink in the main building. Dining that night in the restaurant, the owner welcomed them, giving them advice on where to hunt. As the night continued, the talking moved to the bar area, where the stories grew in size. The hunters gathered there, secretly smiled, knowing the owner was having Peter on.

Peter knew they were joking, but didn't care, this trip meant everything to him. Listening to the men talk, feeling the comradeship, he could only just contain the excitement, at going hunting the next day. Aaron too was enjoying the night. He had no family and sitting there watching Peter, he realised why Ali had been torn in not coming with them. This was as close to being a father as he'd ever get he realised, as downing another glass of scotch, he laughed merrily at the owner's antics.

Looking up, laughing at himself, for being taken in by the owner yet again, Peter noticed a pretty girl his age, appeared at the door. Walking forward she gave the owner a big hug and kiss on the cheek.

"This is Marlies, my daughter," he proudly told them, watching Peter's reaction. "What are you looking at young man?" he growled, causing Peter to go crimson, as the room again exploded with laughter. Giggling, Marlies looked over at Peter winking, indicating her father had done this before. Seeing Peter watching the girl, Aaron suggested he go watch the TV in the adjoining room, while the older men told tall stories and drank.

Seeing Aaron was having a good time talking to the other hunters, Peter took his advice, wandering to the next room. Closing the adjoining door, cutting down the noise, he'd switched on the TV looking for something to watch. Finding an action movie, he sat down, as Marlies came in and sat down beside him.

"Sorry if my father embarrassed you. He likes doing that, it secretly warns off the young men," She smiled.

"That's okay," Peter replied feeling out of depth with this young woman, as they sat watching the movie. Peter sat quietly trying to concentrate on the movie, while stealing glances of Marlies. When he'd first seen her, he'd thought she was pretty. Close up, she was beautiful and Peter for the first time, felt a stirring of arousal. He'd had this problem before, while fantasising about the opposite sex on his own at home, but never in their presence. In time he managed to relax, though looking sideways, he saw her smiling. He wondered quietly if she was aware of his problem.

"Have you hunted before?" she asked him softly, watching him.

"No it's my first time," he replied hesitatingly as if he was admitting to something else.

"The first time they say, you'll remember always," She whispered, moving closer. "How old are you?"

"Nearly eighteen," he croaked out, smelling her perfume as arousal started again.

"So am I. If it's okay with you, I might ask my father if I can come with you tomorrow. Would you like that?" She asked.

"That would be fantastic," He smiled back, as standing, she moved towards the door.

"I'll see you tomorrow then," Marlies promised, disappearing down the hallway, leaving Peter frozen. In the other doorway, Aaron watched the exchange.

"If we don't get to bed Peter, we won't be able to get up early," Aaron told him, watching Marlies disappear.

"Marlies wanted to know if she could go hunting with us tomorrow," Peter told him, his voice sounding dry.

"I suppose its okay if her father gives her permission," Aaron smiled, thinking of when he'd been a young man. Peter, feeling Aaron was onto him, quickly stood up grabbing his jacket, as they trotted through the fresh snow back to their hut.

"She a beautiful young woman, that Marlies, isn't she?" Aaron asked from his bed, later in the night, breaking the silence.

"Yeah she's okay," Peter replied thinking about her, from his bunk in the next room, as Aaron started laughing.

"What's so funny?"

"Nothing Peter, I was just thinking how much you're like your old man. Now let's get some sleep," Aaron answered smiling to himself, before falling to sleep.

It was a cold morning, the type of cold that hurt your throat when you took a deep breath of air. Despite his excitement, Aaron was happy to stay in bed, keeping his old bones warm. A banging on the door made him bolt upright as looking at his watch he saw it was just on six. Being cautious he grabbed a pistol from under his pillow stowing it in his jacket pocket that he'd just thrown on. Opening the door and looking out through a crack, Aaron saw Marlies standing there.

"You two are going shooting today?" She asked grinning, as Peter hearing her voice jumped from his bed dressing in record time.

"You know these young men; they are hard to get out of bed," Aaron smiled, as he swiftly threw on his gear. While doing this, Marlies sat quietly waiting. She was dressed in a tight-fitting pure white ski suit, which accentuated her figure. In stark contrast Aaron's and Peter's suits, which were old army, cold weather uniforms. Inside out they were camouflaged, brown and green, while the other way around as they were now, was white with dark splinter patterns like branches. Aaron, even at his age, seemed at home in his suit, making him look every inch a soldier.

Peter's suit seemed two sizes too big making him look younger, something he wanted to avoid. As if guessing his thoughts Marlies smiled knowingly, before moving to the door.

"We'd better hurry if we're going to have breakfast." she declared, leading the two men across to the lodge. Leaving their weapons and skis in a rack near entry foyer of the restaurant, Peter saw several hunters look at his rifle.

"That's quite a weapon son. Is it yours?" One asked, looking at it closely, impressed.

"It's my father's," Peter answered proudly, as several men nodded approvingly.

"It's a beautiful weapon. What's your father hunt, men?" another man asked, as the hunters all laughed. Seeing Peter's uncomprehending look, Marlies' father answered.

"That rifle is what we call a sniper rifle. They're mostly used by the army or police, too expensive for hunting," the owner smiled. "Your father must own a bank."

"He does!" Peter replied, as all present burst into laughter.

"I don't get it, why are they laughing?" He asked Aaron and Marlies, who had tears in their eyes.

"They meant he must have money," Aaron smiled, as finishing their breakfast they headed out to hunt.

Cross-country skiing was a slow and energy draining way of travelling through a snow-covered mountainside. It's also the only way Aaron thought, as breathing heavily, he stopped just short of the ridgeline spying over into the next valley. Trying to keep his silhouette hidden from the elusive deer, Peter looked down seeing movement in the shadows of the forest below. They'd been hunting for over two hours, and this was the first movement he'd seen. Pulling out his binoculars, Peter saw the shape of three does magnify, leaping closer.

They were grazing on small tufts of grass amongst the snow, unaware of their presence. 'Where is the stag?' He asked himself, knowing this small herd of females must have a male close by. Movement behind him indicated Aaron and Marlies had arrived. Backing down from his observation spot, Peter filled them in on what he'd seen.

"He can't be far," Aaron pointed out, sounding short of breath as Marlies stood there silently not even breathing heavily. 'This is a walk in the park for her' Peter thought as pulling out his water bottle, he suggested they rest before moving closer to the herd. Aaron gratefully nodded his acceptance removing his ski and sitting down making himself comfortable. He'd overdone it, trying to keep up with these two teenagers, who were in their prime. Still, he wouldn't swap it for anything, glad to be here with Peter. He was so much like his Dad; Aaron smiled, enjoying every minute, watching, as Peter became a man.

Becoming a man had nothing to do with trying to kill a deer. It was observing him becoming the leader of this hunting party, giving instructions, as he had now, in taking a break. Most boys would have been too excited at spotting those deer to stop. Peter had weighed up the situation first, resting his group, taking in Aaron's tiredness. Marlies too watched Peter.

Last night and at breakfast, she'd enjoyed teasing him, now she saw him in a new light. With his tanned coloured skin and deep blue eyes, he was good looking all right, as were many boys she'd met. What excited her was the way he had taken command, his army uniform now suited him as if somehow he'd grown into it.

Taking his skis off, Peter again moved up to his observation spot. Lying down and using his binoculars again he felt Marlies move up and lay beside him. The three does were still there and standing amongst the trees to their right was a large stag. He was magnificent, towering over the females with an impressive set of antlers. Passing the binoculars to Marlies, he pointed to the stag, letting her look.

"He's impressive. Will you take the shot from here?" She whispered her face close to his. Peter looking at her, the deer forgotten, put his hand under her chin, kissing her lightly on the lips. She returned the kiss enjoying it, before pulling back studying him. She was just about to say something when the sound of snow crunching behind them, warned them of Aaron's approach. Moving apart their eyes remained locked on each other, as Aaron lay down beside Marlies. This brought the moment to an end, as Marlies pointed out to Aaron where the stag was.

Aaron took the glasses, cursing his bad timing for interrupting Peter. Looking down he saw the stag, he was just about to suggest a course of action, when three men came into view further down the valley. Watching them, he saw them spot the stag. They stood there looking at it for several seconds, before walking straight towards it, startling the stag and the three does making them stampede up the valley.

"What's going on?" Peter whispered, seeing the movement, knowing the deer had been spooked. Aaron signalled for them both to be quiet as he watched the three men. Only one had a hunting rifle, the other two men had assault rifles. This in itself wasn't worrying, the fact no one had shot at that stag when they had the chance disturbed Aaron.

"Peter, you and Marlies stay here and cover me. I'm going to move closer to see what they're up to," Aaron informed them.

"They're just hunters aren't they?" Marlies smiled seeing the two men exchange glances.

"Then why didn't they shoot that stag," Aaron replied, moving slowly along the ridge towards the men, who had stopped to look at a map.

"What's going on Peter?" Marlies asked softly seeing Peter preparing his rifle unfolding its bipod legs.

"My father and Aaron have enemies. He's just cautious," Peter volunteered watching the men, as Marlies beside him moved closer to him sheltering in his warmth. Aaron moved another hundred metres along the ridge. Stopping beside a large tree trunk, he lay down.

"You in the valley, stay where you are and lower your weapons!" Aaron yelled, as the men below froze. Looking up they located Aaron, as the three men moved away from each other.

"You know why we're here! Give yourself up, and we won't kill the boy!" One of the three shouted back as Aaron raised his rifle.

"I'll give you five minutes to head back down the valley, after that I start shooting," Aaron yelled back, pointing his rifle at the man who'd shouted. The three men softly spoke amongst themselves, before complying with his request and turning, skiing back down the valley. Aaron not waiting pushed through the snow, warning Marlies and Peter to keep their heads down as they hurried down to their skis, putting them on.

"Have they gone?" Marlies asked sounding a little scared.

"For now, but unfortunately they'll be back," Aaron informed them, as a tree beside them shattered as a shot rang out. "Go quickly back down our trail!' Aaron screamed as the three raced away from the ridge. The men had only retreated enough to find cover before deploying up the ridge.

The one with the hunting rifle had taken a shot at extreme range, hoping to get lucky. He'd only just missed, unable to allow for wind across the valley.

"Did you hit them?" Broderick, the leader of the group, asked, as the men crested the ridge, seeing three sets of tracks.

"No, but in this snow, they won't get far. There are three of them, looks like one adult and two young men or maybe a girl and a boy," the shooter informed them.

"Spread out either side of me, I'll follow their trail," Broderick suggested, picking up his two-way radio; he called the fourth member of their group, as the men skied off in pursuit.

Aaron had to admit he was a bit scared. Not for himself but for Peter and Marlies. These men were a lot fitter than he was and they only had to stop one of them to get them all. He was familiar with the countryside having been here before, knowing that if they continued this way, they'd hit a road leading back to the lodge. The chances were that they'd left someone there he assumed, as he thought about their next move.

It was about lunchtime when they reached the road back to the lodge. Snow was again falling heavily, as they stopped to get their breath. Aaron anxious, looked back up the trail they'd just come down. Although he saw no sign of their pursuers, he knew it wouldn't be long till they appeared.

"Marlies, do you know what's along this road," Aaron asked, pointing the opposite way from the way to the lodge.

"Yes, the road breaks up into six different trails, they all dead end in the mountains, except one. That one, leads back to the lodge, although it takes a lot longer, compared to this road. There are also several cabins up there, but at this time of the year, they're not in use," Marlies informed him.

"Okay you two go that way, I'll head for the lodge and get help."

"Wouldn't it be better to stay together?" Peter suggested.

"No best we part company, I'm too slow. If they gain on me, I'll just turn off and hide. In this snow it would be easy to lose them," Aaron assured them.

"How long do we wait?" Peter asked.

"At least till tomorrow morning, then head back to the lodge, but not on this road," Aaron warned them.

Cutting off any more talk, Aaron turned and skied towards the lodge, as Marlies leading the way, skied in the opposite direction, followed by Peter. Looking back, seeing them heading away from him, Aaron breathed a sigh of relief. He was the target, as long as he kept away from the others, they should be safe. Using his remaining energy, he propelled himself forward towards the lodge, hoping he'd make it.

Petra drove as if she was part of a rally. Flying into the corners, she used every bit of the road to turn, as the four-wheel drive fought to grip the snow-covered road. Twice she'd ended up off the road, forcing them to back up. The further they went the more dangerous the road became as beside her Ali sat quietly, his mind churning over what to do when they reached the lodge.

Cresting the same ridge where Aaron had thought to turn around, Petra's luck finally ran out. Taking the bend way too fast, they'd skidded off into a ditch, burying the vehicle in a deep snowdrift.

Climbing out through the rear door they'd both stood looking at the 4WD, wondering what they'd do when Ali sighted the lodge. Leading the way, Ali carefully walked down the slippery ice-covered road, followed closely by Petra. At first, he was relieved at making the lodge. As they moved closer, his optimism died, as he spotted two figures lying in the snow.

Signalling Petra to stay close, he left the road, coming through the trees behind the main building. Glancing in a window, which Ali took for the bar area, he saw about fourteen people sitting on the floor their hands and feet secured by ropes. To one side having a drink, sat a man holding an assault rifle, pointing it threateningly at the group of people. Whispering to Petra what he'd seen, he asked for her pistol. At first, she seemed about to say no. Staring at him, considering the situation she reluctantly handed over the gun.

Walking to the rear door of the building, which was the kitchen, Ali ghosted inside. Moving carefully through the building, he looked for any more gunmen. Sure the armed man was alone, he positioned himself just outside the bar area.

"Stay on the floor and don't try anything or you'll end up like your brave friends outside," The gunmen snarled, downing his drink watching the group. He'd been babysitting this bunch of so-called hunters for more than four hours, having arrived at the lodge at eight that morning. Their target had just left, so his three friends had gone after them, leaving him to hold the fort.

Since then all had been quiet except when two hunters who'd slept in had seen him holding their friends hostage. They'd tried to rush him, only to be cut down. 'Some hunters' he thought, it was different when what you were after, could shoot back he smiled. Now it was coming up to lunchtime, and he was hungry.

"Hey who owns this shithole? Get out to the kitchen and get us all something to eat!" The armed man, named Phil demanded, as the owner reluctantly got up, holding out his hands for the shooter to untie. "And don't try anything or I'll shoot a couple of your friends," he chuckled, cutting the ropes. Watching the owner leave, Phil saw hate in his eyes. 'I should kill them all now' he thought seeing the unbridled anger they all had for him.

Broderick, their team leader, had said no. He believed in keeping them alive to the last minute, in case they needed leverage. They'd kill them all just before they left; when they were no longer needed Broderick had assured him. After half an hour and no food, Phil began to worry, wondering if the owner, to save his skin, had taken off. Walking to the entry door, Phil saw the owner moving towards him carrying a large tray of sandwiches.

"It's about time arsehole. Bring them to me first!" He demanded as he turned to check on the others. Hearing a crash, he turned swiftly, nearly shooting the owner, who'd fallen over, dropping his tray full of sandwiches.

"You fucking clumsy oath!" Phil screamed, running forward and kicking the owner in the stomach several times. "I should kill you now!" he roared, as out of nowhere, a pistol came rapidly towards him. It struck him across the bridge of his nose, knocking him to the floor. Semi-conscious, Phil felt his gun ripped from his hands, as the same pistol came to rest on the side of his head.

"Don't even breathe," A voice threatened besides his ear, as looking sideways he saw a woman untying his hostages. Once released, the mob rushed towards Phil kicking and punching him, until the woman who'd released them, fired a shot in the air, making them back off.

"Settle down! I know what he's done, and he'll face justice, so move back," Petra ordered showing a badge, as the badly beaten gunman blacked out. After securing him in a lockable room with no windows, she asked the owner what had happened.

He described how four men had arrived taking them all by surprise. Three of the men, after finding out where Aaron had gone, had taken a four-wheel drive and skis before heading into the mountains over four hours ago. The one left behind had been watching them when two hunters, who had seen the rest of them captured, had rushed the building, only to be gunned down. The owner then explained how after going for the sandwiches, Ali had told him to drop them, while he surprised the shooter.

"You didn't mention he'd kick the shit out of me," the owner smiled.

"Yeah I'm sorry about that, I didn't think he'd lose it that much," Ali apologised.

"Forget it. The problem is what are we going to do about the other three, my daughter is out there?" the owner informed him sounding scared, as the others in the room indicated they wanted to go after them.

"Look these men are professional killers, best if we leave you all here to protect this lodge and the prisoner, while the detective and I find them. Let's face it, if they get past us they'll come here," Ali put forward. No one was happy about staying, but the thought of the men coming back and freeing their friend made them all agreed to stay put. Grabbing a rifle each and some ski gear, plus another 4WD vehicle, Petra and Ali drove up the road into the mountains.

Aaron couldn't run any further. Twice they'd shot at him, always getting closer. He'd made a good distance before the first shot had sent him into a ditch, avoiding a second shot. They'd cleared the ridge behind him and were about five hundred metres away when they'd taken the shot. He'd been forced to crawl around a corner, while they kept skiing, moving closer. The second time they'd halved the gap.

This shot tugged at the arm of his jacket as he frantically dived for cover. Looking around Aaron saw the track bend to the right up further, where the road went through a cutting.

Scrambling to his feet he pushed himself, skiing to the end of the cutting, deciding to make his stand there.

"Don't tell me you missed him again?" Broderick exploded, seeing Aaron disappear into the cutting.

"If you think you can do better, you take the fucking rifle," Brad replied heatedly, as the third man Stevenson kept watch.

"Where the other two go?" Stevenson asked noting only one set of tracks in the snow ahead of them.

"Who gives a shit, Aaron's the one we want!" Broderick snarled.

"I'm just saying, that we could've held the kids until he showed, save chasing him," Stevenson replied.

"Forget it! We'll take care of Aaron and get out of here," Broderick told them, moving forward.

"What about Phil, why haven't we been able to contact him?" Brad cut in, stopping Broderick.

"Who knows? It could be the radios don't work in this valley, or he's had trouble. Either way, we've got to get back there, so let's get moving," he ordered moving off.

Approaching the cutting Broderick stop skiing. Looking carefully around the corner he saw nothing out of the ordinary, as Brad beside him skied past.

"Wait!" Broderick shouted as a shot rang out. Hit, Brad was slammed backwards off his skis. Using his ski pole, Broderick pulled Brad back around the corner, as Stevenson laid down covering fire.

Brad had taken a hit in his left shoulder. The round luckily had passed straight through, hitting nothing vital. Bandaging the wound, Broderick handed back his rifle.

"I think I hit him!" Stevenson shouted, seeing Aaron drop after his last shot.

"Good! Now Brad you keep him pinned down, while Stevenson and I flank him," Broderick smiled as he and Stevenson climb up into the forest above them. By the time they'd travelled through the forest coming out on the other side of the cutting, Aaron was gone.

"That little shit!' Broderick cursed, signalling Brad that it was safe. Getting no response, he sent Stevenson to get him, while he kept watch.

Resting, Broderick downed half his water from his canteen, before pulling out his binoculars. Looking down the track trying to spot any sign of Aaron, he saw a 4WD vehicle sitting around a bend, only its nose sticking out. At first, he thought it was the vehicle they'd driven up the track. Realising theirs was hidden up a side road out of sight he became alert.

A feeling of impending doom touched him, as reaching for his weapon he dived to the ground. The shot came from across the road not ten metres from him, hitting him in the forehead killing him instantly. Stevenson meanwhile had reached Brad, finding him dead. He was just about to warn Broderick, when the shot that killed him mushroomed out of the cutting, bouncing off the surrounding hills. Knowing they'd been outsmarted, Stevenson put on his skis, swiftly moving back up the track away from the lodge.

Beside the now dead Broderick, Petra and Ali stood looking back up the trail. Checking Broderick, taking his weapons, Ali signalled Petra to move back down to the 4WD, where they'd left Aaron.

Leaving the lodge, they had been travelling up the track for over an hour, when Ali had asked Petra to stop, while he checked the map. Studying it, Ali being cautious, showed Petra where the cutting was, fearing an ambush as a shot rang out. Ali guessing the shot had come from there, told Petra to roll the 4WD back around the corner. Jumping out, keeping low, they moved up the road as more shots echoed around the valley. Reaching the cutting, they found Aaron shot in the arm. He was trying to put his skis on as someone at the other end of the cutting, spasmodically fired shots at him, trying to keep him pinned down.

At first, Aaron was taken by surprise at Ali's appearance behind him, thinking the men shooting at him had called for backup. Getting over it, he told them what was going on. Ali loading his rifle, climbed up the opposite side of the cutting, as Aaron fired off a round. This showed the shooter he was still in the same position. Brad at the other end fired back, seeing Aaron hadn't moved, he edged forward hoping for a killing shot. Ali, spotting him moving, waited. As Brad rose from the ground trying to spot where Aaron was, he saw Ali on the other side of the cutting taking aim at him. Reacting to the new threat, he swiftly lined up Ali. It was already too late.

Petra meantime had bandaged Aaron's arm and was moving him back to the vehicle when the shot exploded above them. Moments later, Ali reappeared, telling them he'd taken care of the shooter. Knowing the other men were coming, Petra took Aaron back to the car, while Ali lay in wait.

Soon after, two men had dropped onto the road together, right opposite Ali. Knowing he'd be too close to them, for a rifle, Ali swapped using Petra's pistol. Even with surprise on his side, a pistol was no match for two assault rifles, so he remained hidden.

Once the men had split up, Ali waited until the one moving up the cutting had nearly reached his comrade, before shooting Broderick. Seizing Broderick's rifle, Ali then waited for the other man to return; instead he fled up the track. Petra meantime had reached the vehicle, putting Aaron in the back seat she drove up to Ali.

"Where's the other one?" She asked.

"He went back up the trail, I thought he'd come back to help his friend," Ali confessed.

"Peter and Marlies went that way, though they've a good lead and we've got a vehicle," Aaron informed them, as Ali climbed in, Petra driving.

"By the way, who is this?" Aaron asked Ali, watching Petra.

"She's the detective in charge of the shooting at your home. Detective Petra Marroe, this is Aaron," Ali said, introducing them.

"What shooting?" Aaron asked as Petra told him of the murder of the people renting from him.

"They weren't renting. I took them in when their winery went under. We planned together to get it going again," Aaron sadly told them.

"We'll talk about it later. At the moment I want this last murderer to face justice," Petra replied, as she drove swiftly through the snow.

Stevenson felt a moment of panic when he skied away from the cutting. He didn't regret for a second leaving Broderick. He considered the man a complete fool, who got what he deserved. Now after travelling for twenty minutes, he'd had time to think. His only chance now was to find those two kids before his pursuers caught up. Hearing the sound of a vehicle coming fast, Stevenson stopped.

Opening his pack, he withdrew a small lump of C4, planting it on a large tree overhanging the road. Inserting a detonator he ran a trip wire across the road, tying it off on a branch. Smiling at his handy work, he resumed skiing, confident he just bought some time.

Petra drove as quickly as possible through the heavy snow. Beside her, Ali tapped his fingers on his assault rifle anxiously. Petra was a fine detective and had been a good soldier, but she had no experience in chasing trained killers. As time went by and they gained on the last man, she should have slowed down. Instead, she continued driving hard.

"Might be best if we slow down a little," Ali suggested, knowing this man wasn't going to just let them catch him.

"I know what I'm doing!" she shot back, wanting the last man.

"Ali's right Detective. He could be anywhere waiting for us. At this speed, he might surprise us," Aaron put forward. Petra thinking it over admitted they were right, easing off she let the 4WD slowdown. Ali looking ahead saw the reflection of light of a wire across the road where the snow had settled.

"Get out! Jump for it!" Ali screamed, as opening his door he jumped. Aaron behind him did the same, landing heavily on his wounded arm. Petra too saw the wire but didn't jump. Thinking she could stop in time, she slammed on the brakes. Realising the vehicle was skidding on the ice and wouldn't stop in time; she opened her door at the last minute and jumped. Landing safely she looked up to see the vehicle hit the wire, only metres in front of her.

The explosion wasn't massive, but it was enough to bring the tree down onto the vehicle. As the tree hit, it shattered, sending branches crashing down all around the vehicle. One landed on Petra's legs, crushing them. Ali, getting up, checked on Aaron finding him hurt, but alive. He then moved to the other side of the vehicle to look for Petra. At first, he thought she was just lying next to a branch, moving closer, he saw her legs were pinned under it.

"How is she?" Aaron yelled from the other side.

"Not good," Ali yelled back, as he examined Petra's legs. A scream of pain answered his touch, as Petra after passing out came to. Moving slowly to the 4WD, Aaron grabbed the first aid kit. Painkiller tablets were the only relief he could give her, as Ali lifted the branch off her legs. Luckily there was no bleeding, so using one of the rifles, they splinted her legs together.

"Next time someone tells you to jump, do it!" Aaron told her angrily, as he and Ali dragged her further up the road.

"I get the point. I'm the fucking one with the broken legs!" She shouted back, before smiling and moaning at the same time.

"Forget it both of you, we've got other problems!" Ali pointed out looking at the 4WD. The vehicle's cabin was a write-off, but the vehicle itself seemed intact. Ali standing beside the driver's door turned the engine on. On the second try it started, so using his hands on the clutch and accelerator, he manipulated the pedals reversing the vehicle from under the fallen tree. Several times he stalled it and one occasion he nearly slipped under the front wheel.

In the end, the vehicle broke free leaving Ali with a difficult decision. Petra needed immediate medical treatment, as did Aaron, so what should he do? He knew he had to find his son, though he couldn't leave his friends.

"I can drive Ali, it won't be easy, but I'll make it," Aaron assured him, reading his mind.

"Are you sure?"

"Yes, we'll be alright, though it's going to be cold," Aaron smiled looking at the 4WD. After breaking off the doors and what was left of the roof, Ali with some help from Aaron dragged Petra into the rear of the vehicle. Turning the vehicle around, Ali got out leaving it running before helping Aaron behind the wheel. Grabbing a spare sleeping bag, Ali wrapped it around Aaron before throwing what other clothing he could find over Petra.

"If you take it easy, you should be at the lodge before dark. Tell them to stay put till I return," Ali told him, as he picked up his rifle and pack.

"They'll be okay Ali. Peter's a fine young man, he can look after himself and Marlies, the girl with him, knows the country. They said if I hadn't arrived by tomorrow they'd head back to the lodge from a different direction," Aaron told him, as throwing the vehicle into gear Aaron, one-handed, drove away.

Peter and Marlies heard the distant sound of the explosion. They'd travelled at least ten miles up into the mountains making good time. Marlies had suggested that they keep going east, as she knew the old track in that direction, that they could use to circle back to the lodge. It was snowing heavily, so hiding their tracks was no problem as they came upon the first cabin. Finding the door unlocked, they went to the phone, finding it disconnected.

"We could stay here?" Marlies suggested.

"No, the cabins are the first place they'd look. Better we gather some blankets and food if there is any and then find a spot of the track where we can hole up overnight. Tomorrow we can get up early and take the other track back to the lodge," Marlies agreeing helped him search.

The cabin proved a treasure trove of supplies, meaning whoever owned it, came here regularly. Loading the gear onto a sled they'd also found, they followed Marlies' map, starting along the trail back to the lodge. Travelling till it started getting dark, Marlies pointed to a valley off to the right. Moving a good hundred metres into the valley, they quickly put their tent up, before covering their tracks, as the heavy snow falling did the rest. Deciding on no fire, they ate what food they'd found settling down for the night.

Laying two blankets under their sleeping bags, they zipped both bags together for warmth. They then covered themselves with their remaining blankets. Lying silently for several minutes, Peter heard Marlies moving beside him.

"What's wrong?"

"Nothing, I'm removing my clothing. It allows your body heat to warm you, so when you get up in the morning, you will feel better when you have to get out in the cold and get dressed again. I've still got my underwear on," she informed him. Following her advice, he did the same, as complete darkness settled on the area.

"Do you feel warmer?" Marlies asked softly, her face only an outline, next to his.

"Yes, you're right I do feel better, though I wish I could use a light."

"Why would you need a light?" she giggled.

"So I can see your beautiful face," Peter answered softly into the darkness, smiling. Silence followed his remark for several seconds before she spoke.

"I still feel cold Peter. Maybe you should hold me?" Marlies whispered. Pulling her to him, Peter felt her body radiating heat, as one of her legs crossed over his. Finding her lips, he kissed her, as his hands explored her body.

Pulling off her underwear, Peter entered her as she screamed, making him hesitate, worried about the noise.

"What wrong?" Marlies asked breathing heavily.

"Just the noise someone might hear us," Peter admitted.

"We're miles from anywhere Peter, and I don't want to stop," she moaned, wrapping her legs around him, as he gave up worrying.

While Peter and Marlies were setting up their tent, Stevenson had reached the hut, where they'd gotten their supplies. Seeing someone had been there and left, Stevenson pondered what action he should take. He knew at least two of Ali's unit members were after him by the ambush at the cutting. His bobby trap he believed would've stopped the vehicle and may have even injured them. He doubted that with one of their kids up here, it would stop them. He knew of their past, and even with age they were still formable soldiers, the cutting had proved that.

Getting killed wasn't part of the deal, he decided to toss in the search for Aaron's kid and get out of here. Looking at the map, he saw if he continued northeast, he'd hit the main road between France to Germany. Kissing his career of working for the CIA goodbye, he decided to keep going, glad to be alive. Writing out a note he left it on the door, before skiing away, making the decision like Peter, to camp away from the road.

It was pitch dark when Ali arrived at the cabin. Doing a quick search of the area, Ali cautiously entered. After checking the cabin he returned to the door, picking up the note that dropped when he entered. Reading it, he smiled to himself, knowing he would've liked working with the man who left it. He showed good tactical sense. The note said he'd had nothing to do with the torture of the couple in Lyon. It also told whoever found the note, that he was abandoning the mission, heading away from the area. It warned not to try and follow him.

Knowing it was now too dark to travel; Ali found a comfortable bed and settled down for the night. There was still a chance that the last man was out there and Peter and the girl could be in danger. The note convinced him somehow that the danger, for now, had gone. Having no choice, he went to sleep early, setting his alarm to wake him at daybreak.

"Wherever you are son, I hope you're keeping safe and warm," Ali whispered, pulling his sleeping bag tight feeling the cold.

Peter lay covered with sweat; he'd never felt so alive and exhausted at the same time. Marlies beside him, moan softly in her sleep, her body hotter than a radiator. His guilt at making so much noise had long since vanished, knowing he didn't care. Making love was worth dying for. Still, he worried about Aaron, wondering about the explosion they'd heard. Tomorrow they'd head back, and then he'd know what had taken place. For now, he'd keep Marlies safe, something he enjoyed.

Ali woke the next day, his back aching. He missed his hard mattress at home. Smiling he realised what an old whinger he was becoming. Eating a hot breakfast, warming his insides, he looked outside to see the snow had stopped falling. Getting out his map he saw there was another trail from here to the lodge. Guessing this was the way they went, he put on his skis starting out.

Peter awoke to find Marlies' watching him. Moving closer to her he kissed her.

"Good morning," he smiled stretching.

"That was quite a night," she giggled as she moved on top of him.

"We will have to head back soon?" Peter suggested feeling his body react to contact with her heated body.

We've got all day," she purred, biting his ear playfully, as he tickled her, making her squeal with laughter.

"I suppose it won't hurt to wait for a while," Peter smiled pushing her off him and pinning her beneath him, kissing her again.

Ali had been travelling for just over an hour. It was still pre-dawn as the light started to break through the trees above him. Stopping he check his map, the only noise being his laboured breathing, as a scream shattered the silence. Swiftly preparing his weapon, Ali tried to work out where the scream had originated. Standing trying to slow his breathing, Ali listened as a faint sound of laughter resounded through the trees.

'What the hell's going on?' Ali asked himself. Moving forward silently, he came opposite the entrance to a valley. Stopping he heard moans and laughter erupting from inside the valley. Smiling Ali knew what was going on. Some young couple were making love and had picked an area where he was looking for his son and his female companion. His smile disappeared as he thought over what he'd said.

"My God, it's Peter," he whispered to himself. At first, he was angry, wondering what his son was doing having sex, while someone was chasing him. He remembered Aaron saying how Peter had become a man on this trip, made his anger dissipate. Who was he to judge, he smiled, recalling his own escapades when he was Peter's age. 'I haven't even given him my father, son talk,' Ali confessed knowing it was a bit late. Moving along the trail towards the lodge, Ali decided to wait, further along, letting them enjoy the morning.

When Peter and Marlies finally packed up and skied back to the trail, they found ski tracks on it. Not sure if it was friend or foe, they moved cautiously following the trail towards the lodge. It wasn't till lunchtime that they caught up to Ali.

He was sitting beside a tree resting, when after seeing him through his binoculars; Peter with Marlies hurried to meet him. Overjoyed to see his Dad, Peter excitedly introduced Marlies. Ali, in turn, explained what had happened since he heard the news on the radio. He was amazed how he'd missed them on the trail. Peter explained how they were afraid to stay at the cabin and had camped of the track instead.

"Wise move son, though it must have been cold."

"We shared body heat," Peter admitted without thinking, as both he and Marlies went red.

"Maybe we should say I met you at the cabin where we all stayed. It might save Marlies' father worrying," Ali suggested, getting agreement from both of them.

Arriving back at the lodge, Ali found several police and a medical helicopter waiting. They were told that Aaron and Petra had been flown to a hospital at Bastogne. The police had already taken the live gunman and the two dead ones back to Lyon, they had returned to look for the fourth gunman. Ali gave them the general direction he would've gone, as they flew off to look for him. Marlies' father was overjoyed with his daughter's safe return, hugging Peter thanking him, much to his embarrassment.

After a couple of hours of questioning by the police, Ali and Peter were allowed to leave. Digging his hired 4WD out of the snow drift Ali said his goodbyes, wanting to be gone. Peter, gathering his and Aaron's gear quickly loaded the car, as a tearful Marlies, kissed Peter passionately, telling him to ring. Her father stood in the background, quietly pondering what had gone on that night, as Ali waving, drove away.

Arriving at the hospital, they found Aaron with Petra. She was in plaster unable to move, so Aaron was looking after her. He seemed upset that his passport blunder had caused the death of the people in Lyon and nearly his and Peter's. Ali told him to forget it; the three of them should be going. Aaron surprised him, by wanting to stay and look after Petra. Ali started to argue, pointing out it that it would be dangerous staying. Looking down, he saw Petra hold Aaron's hand.

"Very well my friend but be careful. Our enemies could still come looking," Ali warned him, saying goodbye.

"We'll do it again someday Peter. Next time you'll have a better time," Aaron assured him.

"That's hard to believe," Ali laughed, as Peter went red, leaving Aaron and Petra completely in the dark.

Aaron disappeared for several years after that, only keeping in contact by phone. Ali knew he'd bought a vineyard but not where. It wasn't till this present mission when he'd picked him up that he knew where it was. He'd kept to himself out of fear of endangering Ali's family again, though Peter especially missed him.

THE WAREHOUSE

Steve woke up feeling better for having slept. It was still early, so he quickly showered and dressed, driving straight to the hospital. Parking on the street, he casually wandered into the hospital watching his surroundings, looking for anything out of the ordinary. Sure he wasn't being watched, he walked to Dave's room hoping his condition had improved. Entering the room, Steve found Dave fast asleep, though he looked a lot better. Grabbing a chair near the entry door, Steve sat down next to Dave's bed, waiting for him to wake. As if Dave sensed he was being watched, he slowly opened his eyes, adjusting to the room's lighting.

"Been here long?" Dave said groggily, his stomach cramping, as pain came to the surface making him wince.

"Not too long. You've looked better my friend."

"Yeah, I don't know what shit was on that blade, but it has really stuffed me up," Dave admitted, his pain making him summoned a nurse.

"What's your problem darling?" A nurse asked. She was about the same age as Dave and had a cheeky smile on her face.

"Just a little pain that's all, can I have something for it," Dave asked wincing again with the pain. Seeing his face, the nurse disappeared returning with a small needle, which she connected into his drip. Dave felt the pain immediately lessen, bringing a smile to his face.

"Thank you, you're an angel."

"Get to know me better Detective, and you'll learn I'm really a devil," She replied, wiggling her eyebrows, as Steve chuckled. Dave, on the other hand, appeared shocked, stopping Steve's laughter.

"How did you know I was a Detective?" Dave asked the nurse seriously. Seeing his intense look, the nurse after looking towards the door answered.

"When you were knocked out last night, the doctor was suspicious of your knife wound, so we checked your pockets and found your police badge. He realised then that you must be working undercover, that's why you had used a fake name," She whispered.

"Look your doctor did the right thing. The problem is that some bad people are looking for Dave, hence the false name," Steve said walking to the door and checking the hallway.

"I'm sorry, but there's another problem. He entered your real name on the computer, the doctors kind of anal on that type of thing," She said apologetically. The room went silent as Steve and Dave digested this information, wondering how much danger there was in staying.

"Get dressed Dave, we'd better leave," Steve decided it was best to keep moving.

"He can't be moved, it's too soon!" The nurse replied with a mixture of fear and anger in her voice.

"Look I know you want to help, but you and the rest of the staff could be in danger if the people who are after me come here," Dave admitted, taking the nurse's hand to reassure her.

"Look there might be another way," She suggested a little embarrassed before continuing. "You could stay in my room in the nurse's quarters out the back, at least that way I can keep an eye on you,"

"You're taking a big chance," Steve said seriously.

"Look, I don't want to be any trouble and isn't that against the rules Susan?" Dave asked getting her name from her security pass.

"Of course it's against the rules stupid, but my brother's a cop, and I want to help. It's still early if we move you now no one will be the wiser." Unsure, Steve looked to Dave seeing him nod his acceptance.

"Okay let's go," Steve replied, making a decision, as Susan quickly disconnect Dave's monitor, before pushing his bed into the hallway. Luckily the nurse's quarters were joined by a covered walkway making the transfer easier. Susan hurried ahead opening her door, as Steve guided the bed inside.

"Are you sure you're okay with this?" Steve said to Dave, as they transferred him onto Susan's double bed.

"Yeah I'll be right Steve, but you'd better get moving, your family is out there somewhere."

"Thanks for your help Dave; I wouldn't have got this far without you."

"You're not going mushy on me are you?" Dave asked smiling, but he too felt a bond with his new friend. "Anyway I've got a private room and a pretty nurse, what more could I ask for?"

"Don't get any big ideas fellow," Susan smiled. "Oh and by the way what's this?" She asked sternly, pointing to Dave's gun, which was still under his pillow in his hospital bed.

"It's my comforter, I can't sleep without it," Dave answered smiling sheepishly, as Susan giving him a stern look, stowed it in the bedside drawer next to him.

"Anyway I'll leave you two to say your goodbyes; I got to go back to work and return this bed," Susan declared, before leaving, wondering what she had gotten herself into.

"She's nice," Steve said smiling after Susan had left.

"Hey, she's just helping me out!"

"Of course she is," Steve replied chuckling, as taking down Susan's phone number, he left to check on Lenny Tran Vin.

LENNY'S WAREHOUSE

Lenny sat in his office staring out the window, as his French business partner conferred with 'The Blade'. Watching the man, Lenny for the second time, wondered what all the fuss was about. The Frenchman was supposed to be one of the best assassins in the business, yet he and his men had stuffed up their attempt on Roberts. As good as they were, an old man in his fifties had escaped the hit, and one of 'The Blade's' men had been captured, forcing his termination. True Roberts was good, he'd seen it himself at his home, but these men were supposedly pros.

"How many men can you supply?" the Frenchman asked suddenly, staring at Lenny as if he read Lenny's mind.

"I have gathered forty of my most skilled men here today. You can take half, but the rest stay here, in case you fail."

"I hope they're better than the ones guarding your home," the Frenchman shot back angrily, wanting to put this upstart in his place. Lenny sat there silently watching his so-called partner. He had prepared a good retort, but realised that arguing amongst themselves, was pointless.

"I suggest you pick them yourself, that way there will be no problems. Remember they're just muscle, not soldiers."

"Thank you, that's a good idea, and my name is Claude," the Frenchman said smiling, as he put out his hand, in a sign of mutual respect. Lenny took his hand shaking it, sealing the deal.

Lenny knew deep down that Claude couldn't be trusted and he'd tried to take Roberts himself, cutting out paying Lenny. Even so, he knew he needed his expertise to get Roberts, so, for now, he'd play ball.

"Do they have weapons?" Claude asked politely, putting the ill will behind them, planning to settle with Lenny when Roberts was dead.

"Yes, I have brought in a large collection of weapons from overseas; you can point out how to use them effectively, while you're here," Lenny suggested as they left the office.

Walking to the rear of the warehouse, Claude saw Lenny's men unpacking a large assortment of weapons. They were mostly older models, but they were in good condition. Claude was impressed by the variety, quickly giving all the men some basic training, on each type. Picking out the twenty of the most competent men, Claude looked around at the containers, realising the huge amount of weapons Lenny had.

"Are you going to war with someone?"

"No, but several groups in this country have shown interest in them, so I thought I'd expand from drugs into weapons."

"I have had dealings with some of these religious groups my friend and I can tell you, they're dangerous!" Claude replied seriously.

"I'd thought the same thing. So after they purchase the weapons, I discreetly inform the authorities of their whereabouts, after the money, of course, is in my possession," Lenny smiled.

"As long, as they don't find out," Claude replied neutrally, knowing how dangerous these groups could be. "There is one other problem. Four of my men who went with The Blade have failed to check in this morning. Do you trust The Blade?" Lenny asked neutrally watching Claude's reaction.

"As you know, we just talked, and I find it strange that there was no mention of any problem or your men."

"If you find out The Blade has terminated my four men, I expect you to take care of it."

"Consider it done! If they're dead 'The Blade' betrayed both of us," Claude answered angrily, as both men deep in thought, watched the men train with their new weapons.

Claude, thinking over what Lenny had said, excused himself, making a phone call. When Claude had come to Australia, the cartel of assassins he belonged to had sent four more men secretively to back him up, if trouble arose. He'd kept this a secret from Lenny and 'The Blade', just in case things didn't work out. Giving them the information on how to find Roberts, family, he gave them the go signal, having no faith in Lenny's men.

Walking back to Lenny, he gave his twenty men a quick rundown on his plan of intercepting Roberts' family; he then gave them instructions on where to meet, once they'd left here to get their personal gear. He'd decided to continue with Lenny Tran Vin for the moment, using his men, hoping to weaken the team protecting Roberts' family with them. Afterward, it would make dealing with Lenny that much easier.

A shout from the front office made both Lenny and Claude turn around. One of Lenny's new lieutenants ran towards Lenny, handing him a message.

"Good news. One of my contacts has located one of the men involved in the attack on my house last night. He is injured and in a hospital, in the south of the city. I'll take some of my men and detain him," Lenny smiled.

"Lenny, after the raid on your house, it would be better if your men stayed out of this. I have some friends here in Australia. Let them take care of him. The police are not stupid they might connect you to his disappearance," Claude put forward, secretly wanting a learn Roberts location. Thinking carefully about it, Lenny agreed.

"Okay, you take care of it, but I want him alive!" Lenny ordered, handing him the address, wondering where these friends had sprung from.

Claude immediately rang his men, telling them to forget Roberts' family. He gave them the address of the hospital, making it clear that he wanted Roberts' friend alive. Telling Lenny his friends were on their way, he turned back to the men, seeing how their weapon training was going. Satisfied that no one would shoot themselves, Claude turned to leave, when a small object smashed through a skylight window above them, landing at his men's feet.

"Shit no!" Claude screamed in French, as he dived for the ground.

Steve casually parked his car in a parking station across the road from Lenny's warehouse. This gave him a good view of his objective. The warehouse was in Botany, adjacent to the docks, giving Lenny's company good access to their overseas shipments. It was a large structure which had probably been designed as a hangar for planes. Now it had been adapted, as a container storage shed. Taking out his small pair of binoculars, Steve scanned the area, seeing nothing out of the ordinary, he decided to go to the rear of the building and scale the fence. Walking quickly through the car park, he was just about to cross the road, when he saw several dark vans nose around the corner, pulling up opposite the main entrance gate and the office front door. Acting like he'd forgotten something, Steve quickly retraced his steps arriving back near his vehicle.

"Keep your hands where we can see them!" A blunt voice ordered behind Steve, as two armed men came into view.

"I've got two hundred dollars in my wallet!" Steve spat out sounding scared, knowing full well the men were cops.

"We don't want your money friend! What are you doing here?" one of the men asked as the other tried not to laugh.

"I imported some furniture from Indonesia. The shipments short, I just thought I'd look around see if they are hiding it here somewhere," Steve said nervously while he prepared himself to act.

"Well, your shit out of luck my friend. We're police, and Lenny Tran Vin is about to be arrested. We're just setting up now to take him in!" the same officer informed him, before putting his gun away. "Stay in your car, we'll talk again when this is over," the officer ordered, before moving to the corner of the car park, as his radio began to squawk.

Stevenson had watched the exchange in the garage with interest, wondering if they'd been made, as the units moved into position. Grabbing his radio, he called his two men stationed there to find out what was going on. The officer there gave him a brief report on his conversation with Steve, telling Stevenson he'd made the guy wait in his car.

"Go back and tell him to piss off, he can come back tomorrow. We don't want any witnesses running to the media about this operation. Do it now!" Stevenson exploded over the airways, getting his message across loud and clear. Steve watched the officer talking on his radio, as appearing angry, he started to walk towards his car. Steve thought he'd had it, as he slowly drew his weapon, pointing it at his driver's door, as the officer leaned on it.

"Look there could be trouble here Sir. My boss has said for you to leave immediately. You can come back tomorrow or better still go to the local police about your furniture," He informed him sounding sincere.

"Thank you, officer, I appreciate it," Steve replied sounding grateful, which he was, as he quickly started his vehicle and drove away.

Driving several blocks, Steve stopped at a multi-story office building. Racing inside, he pressed the lift button to the top floor. Luckily it had a foyer, with a fire door leading off to the side of the lift, sparing Steve the problem of talking to someone. Arriving at the roof door Steve quickly forced it, hurrying across the roof to a spot where he could see Tran Vin's warehouse. It was at least a kilometre away, but with his binoculars, he could roughly make out what was going on.

The Federal Police were all over the building. Some were cautiously climbing along its roof structure, preparing to cover the men entering below. Even at this distance and with the background street noise, the sound of gunfire and explosions started to echo around the building as the police disappeared inside.

When Claude saw the percussion grenade hit the ground, he swore. He then covered his ears and closed his eyes dropping to the floor, having seen them used before. Lenny and his men had not and unluckily took the full force of the stun grenade. Disorientated and confused, the men furthest from the explosion hearing the police closing in, opened up, bringing their new weapons to bare.

Shocked at first by the large number of weapons firing at them, the police retreated taking cover. Returning fire, the police sprayed Lenny's men with well-aimed shots, as they stood in the open firing wildly. Coming to his senses, Lenny shouted for his men to cease fire, as Claude lying on the floor, saw his chance to escape.

Taking careful aim, Claude shot Lenny twice in the back, watching him drop to the floor. He then yelled to Lenny's men, to make a run for the containers towards the front of the warehouse. As one, the large group of men surged forward, forcing the police back by the weight of numbers. Claude seeing his chance, slipped behind a container at the side, heading towards the rear of the factory. Reaching the rear without being noticed, Claude hid himself in a pile of carpet and waited patiently, for the inevitable.

Lenny's men, despite their lack of training, managed to push the police out of the warehouse wounding several in the process. However, unlike the police who were all wearing bulletproof vests, which kept causalities to a minimum, Lenny's men had no protection at all. As their numbers dwindled with each passing minute, most of Lenny's men who were still firing, sought cover. The clever ones, seeing they were losing, dropped their weapons and lay down on the ground, waiting for the end of the shooting.

Police reinforcements now entered from the rear, coming up behind Lenny's men, catching them in a deadly crossfire. With nowhere to go, the ten remaining men dropped their weapons. Filled with rage, the police rushed forward to secure the prisoners, dealing out rough justice to anyone who gave them trouble. Sirens then filled the air, as ambulances swamped the streets racing to the warehouse.

Buildings along the way emptied out, as people raced into the street to see what was going on. On the rooftop Steve found that it was soon standing room only, as people joined him, looking as he was, towards the warehouse. Knowing it was time to go, Steve quietly left, surrendering his spot to another person, who gladly gave his personal view, as to what was happening to the growing crowd.

Shane sat in his office glued to his radio, which screamed out details of the raid on Lenny Tran Vin's warehouse. At first, he felt a little guilt, when the first officers were hit, knowing he'd made up the whole story. As reports of the number of men captured and the huge amounts of weapons came to light, Shane realised what a huge blow the Federal Police had delivered. Walking down to his boss' office, Shane was intercepted by one of Stevenson's goons. He informed him of the raid, reassuring him that the credit would go partially to him and Edward.

It was also suggested he go to the crime scene to help with the cleanup and search for evidence. In other words, the boss wanted him gone when the cameras got here Shane figured, as he left for the warehouse.

When Steve had first arrived at Lenny's factory, it had been ten in the morning. Now as he sat a block from the warehouse, he realised it was close to seven at night. The warehouse was finally quiet, and except for an officer at the gate and one patrolling, the only other person was a plainclothes officer who had arrived earlier. Steve judged by the detective's expression that he wasn't too happy about being there, as he slowly worked his way through Lenny's office paperwork. Steve knew he had to get in there and find some link to the assassins who were after him, hopefully before the police removed everything.

As darkness descended, he silently approached the rear of the warehouse, quickly scaling the fence, before making his way into the warehouse. Gliding forward, Steve came to an open area covered with chalk outlines of dead people. This he surmised was the main battle area. Moving towards the front area, he came upon a body. It was the patrolling guard Steve had seen earlier, but who'd killed him?

Cautiously, weapon out, Steve approached the front office area. A quick look inside revealed an interrogation was going on. Handcuffed in a chair was the plainclothes officer he'd seen earlier. At his feet was the policeman from the front gate, obviously dead.

For more than twelve hours, Claude lay hidden in the back area of the factory waiting for the police to leave. As things grew quiet, he slowly rose to his feet stretching, before fitting a silencer to his pistol. Standing in the darkness, Claude thought about his next move before moving cautiously towards the front office. He had decided to search Lenny's office before leaving, worried at what information had been left there. Rounding a corner, he'd come face to face with the patrolling policeman, shooting him at point-blank range in the chest.

The officer still managed to grunt out a warning into his radio, in an effort to warn his partner. Hurrying forward, Claude had just reached the office section, when the officer from out front, raced inside warning the plainclothes officer, who drew his pistol. Claude, firing twice, dropped the policeman, ordering the plainclothes officer to stay still. Shane taken entirely by surprise, angrily stared down at the dead policeman, as he dropped his gun. Forced to kneel on the floor, he had his hands handcuffed behind his back.

"Have you found anything?" Claude asked.

"About what?" Shane asked sarcastically, knowing he'd seen the bastard's face, and he'd shoot him anyway. A pistol slapped across the back of his neck, caused him to fall forward onto the floor, groaning in pain.

"About Roberts!" Claude yelled smiling, enjoying inflicting pain.

"So you're one of the hitmen!" Shane answered chuckling, "How's that going so far?"

Claude, his smile gone lowered his weapon, placing it against Shane's knee, before squeezing the trigger. The pain was overwhelming as Shane screamed in agony. Close to blacking out, he fell forward onto the ground.

"Tell me what you know, or the other knee goes!" Claude screamed angrily, kicking Shane at the same time, as he pressed the weapon against Shane's other knee. Through a wall of pain, Shane taking several breaths answered.

"Go fuck yourself!" He screamed, knowing it was over and not wanting to die begging to this shit.

"Well said!" a voice sounded behind Claude, making him frantically turn towards the voice. Steve, with the speed of a cobra, smashed Claude's hand, in which he held his weapon. Dazed, Claude looked down at his ruined hand minus his pistol, as a hand chopped him across the throat, knocking him to the floor unconscious.

Shane, coming to terms with still being alive, tried to clear his vision to see his rescuer, as pain racked his body. Looking to his side, he saw a man of about fifty years old quickly open the office first aid kit, before hurrying to his side, working on his leg.

"Thanks!" was all Shane got out as he felt the cuff leave his hands.

"You're welcome!" Steve replied, amused at the situation, as Shame got his first look at his rescuer.

"You're not a cop?"

"No. But my brother-in-law is if it makes you feel any better."

"Shit! You're Steve Roberts!" Shane exclaimed truly amazed.

"How could you possibly know that?"

"I work with Edward; we've been secretly looking for you for ages," Shane admitted, before filling Steve in. He told Steve about everything that had happened, from his family running to the mountains, to the raid here, while Steve tied up the unconscious Claude.

"Well, whoever was after them up at Leone's place in the mountains, it wasn't him. He was at Lenny's place last night," Steve informed him, remembering him jumping through the porch door.

"I wondered who called in on Lenny's house, should've known," Shane replied quietly, knowing how dangerous Steve could be.

"Do you know where Edward was heading?"

"Somewhere south I'd say, and I've got his cell number," Shane added trying to help before he stopped. "There's someone on their tail Steve. One of Lenny's men told us that the arsehole here was gathering men to go with them. He somehow knew they were headed south."

"Let's get that bleeding stopped first, and then I'll ring them," Steve answered worried at the loss of blood, as he swiftly bandaged Shane's leg, making him a little more comfortable.

"Can I have the number now?" Steve asked, as Shane without hesitation, read out the numbers, as Steve dialled.

HEADING SOUTH

Edward drove steadily, keeping to the speed limit, and continuously watching the rearview mirror. He was driving Leone's car followed by the two minivans he'd hired at Sydney airport. The day had been quiet, as the group silently motored along each wondering what tomorrow or tonight would bring.

Louise sat beside him taking in the scenery, which at any other time would be considered breathtaking. In the back seat, Bill and Leone sat fast asleep. Leone slept across the seat, her head resting face down in Bill's lap. Edward smiled thinking of both their reactions when she woke up. Nudging his wife, Louise turned to see what Edward was getting at, giggling softly, breaking her sombre mood.

"Wish I'd bought a camera!" Louise whispered, thinking what a strange pair they made, like beauty and the beast.

"I think they're cute," Edward replied laughing lightly, as Bill stirred.

"What's so funny?" Bill asked, as looking down he saw Leone's head resting in his lap. 'God she must be dead tired to sleep with her face in my crotch' Bill thought smiling, as he gently stroked her hair. Unfortunately, the heat of her breath on his pants started to cause Bill a problem. Reaching back into the back area, Bill, quickly grabbed a pillow. Lifting her head carefully, he placed it between her and his pants, relieving his discomfort. Slightly red in the face, Bill sat quietly, as Edward smiled having guessed what had happened.

"Comfy back there, Bill?" Edward asked neutrally, getting an angry look in response, as his phone began to ring. Pulling the car to the side of the road, Edward quickly pulled out his phone. He knew Shane was the only one who had this number and would only ring in an emergency. Edward apprehensively pressed the answer button. Behind him the two vans seeing him stop, both pulled over, waiting.

"That you Shane?" Edward asked cautiously, not recognising the number of the sender.

"It's Steve, how are you, Edward?" Steve asked, wondering how Edward would react.

"Thank God Steve, where are you?" Edward asked relieved, as the whole car came to life.

"In Sydney, I'm here with your friend Shane."

"How'd you run into him?" Edward inquired, as Louise indicated she wanted to talk with him as well. Steve quickly filled Edward in on what had happened at the warehouse, as their prisoner awake now listened with interest and a little fear.

"Those poor local cops, what are you going to do with him?"

"He's coming to at the moment. Soon we're going to have a long talk," Steve replied his eyes dead, as he stared at Claude.

"He's got it coming!" Edward agreed, knowing they had to know what he knew. "Oh your sister's here; she wants to talk to you," Edward reluctantly handed the phone to Louise.

"Are you okay Steve?" She asked close to tears.

"I'm fine sis, I'm sorry for all this trouble I've caused," Steve told her what was going on.

"It's not your fault Steve, we all know that, but your daughters need their father, so be careful," Louise pleaded, tears on her cheeks as she handed the phone back to Edward.

"I'd better get off the phone Steve, just in case. Can you meet us in Melbourne?" Edward asked watching the time, knowing his phone might be being monitored.

"Yes, sounds good. Remember what I said, they know where you are, so be careful," Steve urged him, before hanging up.

Not liking sitting out in the open Edward signalled the others to follow him. Driving further south, looking for somewhere to stop, they crossed the border into Victoria. Seeing a sign indicating a fuel stop and refreshments, Edward pulled in, the other two vehicles following.

Topping up the tanks, Edward suggested everyone get something to eat and then meet across the road. There in a small park, the group sat at some picnic tables, discussing their situation in private. Edward filled them in on his talk with Steve and the fact they were still being followed asking if anyone had seen anything.

"Look I've been watching behind us most of the time. I haven't seen anyone following us constantly unless they've got several cars," Allan put in, gulping down the rest of his coffee.

"Yeah I'm with Allan, I haven't noticed anything suspicious behind us," Nigel added, noticing how Lindsey again opted to sit next to him, something that put him off balance.

"Steve said Shane was sure they knew where we were," Edward pointed out, wondering what he'd missed.

"They wouldn't be tracking us somehow, would they?" Patrick asked neutrally, his eyes always going to Robin, whose eyes sparkled brightly back at him. Silence followed Patrick's remark as all the agents looked at each other wondering why they hadn't thought of it. Natasha seeing the agents surprised expressions, burst into laughter, causing the others to join in.

"No kidding Patrick. Have you ever thought of being a cop?" Edward asked shocked that he hadn't thought of it yet. Seeing if Patrick was right, Nigel and Bill hurried back across the road, with the other agents behind them. Bill seeing nothing obvious grabbed two torches out of the vehicles.

On the other side of the road, Robin praised Patrick.

"Our hero again!" Robin exclaimed, reaching across the table and kissing Patrick on the lips, causing the other women to giggle.

"I just read it somewhere!" Patrick replied stuttering, as the women broke into laughter.

"What the hell's so funny?" Bill asked bumping his head on the bumper bar in the dark as he crawled underneath, turning on his torch.

"Who knows, but I've got to admit Patrick's proving very handy on this assignment," Nigel admitted looking back across the road, as darkness settled over the countryside.

"Well don't get too excited, we haven't found anything yet!" Edward said, watching back down the highway where two lights, indicated a vehicle had stopped.

"Allan, go get the others, tell them to prepare to leave," Edward ordered, his voice distant, as Allan hurried across.

"Could be just someone stopping for the night?" Nigel put forward, as everyone spotting what Edward was looking at, watched as well.

"Got something," Bill mumbled, banging his head again and swearing, before crawling out from under their van. As Bill shone his torch, the others gathered around looking at the object.

"Yeah, it's a tracking device all right. The problem is, is it the only one?" Nigel asked, cranky he didn't think of it himself.

"Well let's find out!" Edward smiled, as he watched a truck pull up for fuel.

When the truck left, so did their three vehicles continuing to head south, as before. The truck was a large semi loaded with cars going to Melbourne. Edward, while the truck was stopped had placed the bug on the truck's trailer, hoping their mysterious shadow would follow the truck and not them. The truck was sitting just over the speed limit, as Edward got in Leone's car again leading the other two vehicles tailing the truck.

"Is anything behind us Allan?" Bill asked speaking into his phone beside Edward.

"No not now, there was before, but they've dropped back," Allan answered from the last vehicle, as Nigel drove.

"Okay, the turns coming up. When you see me turn, kill your lights," Edward ordered, as Bill passed it on to Allan, and then to Ian in the middle car. Sighting the turnoff ramp, Edward turned onto it, killing his lights as he did, allowing the car to come to a stop without using his brakes. The other two vehicles did the same, as they all sat in the darkness waiting, out of sight from the highway.

They'd been sitting there for about five minutes before the sound of another vehicle passed them, continuing along the highway, followed by several other vehicles. Edward waited for another ten minutes before returning to the highway.

"There could still be another bug!" Bill whispered next to Edward as they drove along in the pitch dark, with only their lights to show the way.

"Yeah, I've thought about that. We'll hole up somewhere for tonight and tomorrow, we'll get rid of these cars," Edward decided, an idea coming to mind as they continued on towards Melbourne.

"Then what?" Bill asked softly.

"The best idea is to make sure that once we get rid of the vehicles, they can't follow us. The only way we can do that is to hop on a plane, where we can see if someone's after us. If we time it right, we should be able to leave by booking a ticket at the last minute. That should leave our friends tailing us, no time to board the flight," Edward suggested.

"Sounds good, have you thought where we'll go after we lose them?" Bill asked.

"To where it all began," Edward smiled, turning onto another side road.

Shane listened to Steve's conversation with growing unease. He knew what Steve intended to do to the bastard, lying across from him. Killing two cops and shooting him, put the assassin in line for a bullet, but torture was something else. Listening to the conversation, Claude also knew what was coming, and he had to admit he felt a little afraid. Though he'd tortured his fair share of people in the pursuit of his career, he wasn't looking forward to the role reversal. Shane was just about to try and stop Steve when Claude jumped in.

"I will tell you everything in exchange for my freedom," Claude exploded nervously, making both Steve and Shane turn in his direction.

"You're in no position to demand anything," Steve smiled, pulling an evil looking flick knife from his pocket.

"I at least demand to be turned over to the police!" Claude shouted his fear plan to see.

"Maybe later!" Steve laughed, as he came closer to Claude, his knife tracing a line across Claude's face.

"Steve let's hear what he's got to say," Shane asked softly.

"Talk my friend, if you tell me everything, I promise to turn you over," Steve whispered, as Claude gladly told his life story.

His syndicate was based in Amsterdam. His group plus two others had been hired by the CIA to take care of Steve for ten million dollars apiece. The bonus was a further ten million to the one who got him. He'd arranged to meet with the other two groups over an Internet connection, as each wanted to keep their identity hidden. One of the groups was from England, calling themselves the British Freedom Brigade, their leader here, was nicknamed 'The Blade'. The other group turned out to be a lone assassin, who called himself, 'The Thistle'. He'd told them point blank to keep away from him, preferring to work alone.

Despite this blunt warning, he for some unknown reason had furnished each group with a complete history of their target, plus photos, which proved invaluable. After giving it a lot of thought and having never been to Australia, Claude had thrown in with 'The Blade', as they too, had no links here.

With one of 'The Blade's men, Claude had gone to Ballina to stake out Steve's girlfriends unit. Upon arrival they found she'd been murdered, forcing them to rethink their plan. Leaving The Blade's man in Ballina, Claude knowing they'd needed more manpower, had contacted Lenny Tran Vin. He knew from the Thistle that he would help him, because of his father's murder by the unit and the money.

The Blade's man who had stayed behind in Ballina had after several weeks, decided to leave. By chance, while waiting for a flight out of Brisbane airport, he had spotted Robert's hiring a car. Tailing him south in a van he'd stolen, he had been foolishly spotted.

Abandoning the pursuit, but informing Claude, he continued looking. After checking all the motels in the area, he tracked him down to a small hotel in the centre of Ballina. Throwing caution to the wind, he had tried to finish him with a bomb, rather than wait for Claude's return. Not only did he fail, but he was captured, leaving Claude only one option, to silence him.

'The Blade' in the meantime, with eight of Lenny's men, in two cars, followed Steve's brother-in-law, to the airport. Tailing Roberts family and the FBI agents from the airport, one carload of Lenny's men had been intercepted by the police. The Blade's group, seeing what had occurred pulled back, contacting Claude. He told them of the guesthouse owned by Roberts' sister in law.

'The Blade' had then driven to the mountains and was to have waited for Claude, while the triad men bugged their cars. 'The Blade', Claude assumed had gone back on the deal and was now following them, trying for the extra cash bonus, cutting his group out. That was why Claude had come here for reinforcements, before resuming the chase, not mentioning his four syndicate men.

"This Blade character, how many men does he have with him?" Steve asked softly.

"I'm not sure? Maybe there were three of them, including The Blade. Remember I only met one of them and he's dead."

"And you killed those two cops at the Ballina police station as well!" Shane asked, his face showing pain from his injury.

"It was necessary, unfortunately," Claude answered showing no emotion, as Steve's eyes grew dark.

"We have a deal, Roberts! I want to be handed over to the police, I have information they will find invaluable!" Claude demanded watching Roberts closely. Steve was just about to answer, when Shane fired two rounds, into the surprised Claude's chest. Steve bending down on the floor beside Claude checked his pulse. Finding none, Steve undid the restraints securing Claude, before going through his pockets. After he finished searching, he placed Claude's pistol back in his hand.

"Why?" Steve asked Shane, as he worked his way through Claude's possessions

"He was the type that would do a deal. Those policemen deserve justice!" Shane answered angrily, willing to live with it.

"You'd better call it in my friend, you need medical attention," Steve suggested, patting Shane on the shoulder, showing he understood.

"Anything?" Shane asked seeing Steve hesitate.

Steve stared at the piece of paper, showing Dave's name and the hospital address. Dread filled him as he grabbed his phone, dialling the nurse's quarters where Dave was staying. Shane sat watching him, wondering what was going on. The phone rang for several seconds before being picked up.

"Hello, is someone there?" Steve asked pleasantly, as he waited for a reply. The only sound he could hear was muffled breathing before the line went dead. Standing, Steve tried to think what to do.

"What's wrong?" Shane asked seeing Steve's confusion.

"This address is the hospital where a friend of mine is staying at the moment. He was hurt in the raid on Lenny's house."

"Then you'd better go!" Shane suggested, getting a nod from Steve in return, "And for the record, you were never here," Shane smiled, nodding his thanks again, as Steve hurried to his car.

THE TRADE

Lying half asleep in Susan's bed, Dave was feeling much better. The antibiotics had done their trick, clearing the infection from his system. Susan had been watching over him most of the day, making sure he stayed in bed and out of sight. Looking outside, he guessed it was close to five in the afternoon. Susan, he knew worked till six giving him another hour of lying there, bored. Restless he decided to go for a stroll to the canteen and grab a coffee.

Putting on his clothes from the night before, he went for the door then hesitated, reaching into the side draw, he pulled out his automatic. 'Better safe than sorry,' he told himself with a smile, as he tucked it into his belt at the back of his pants.

Walking groggily at first, then more confidently he proceeded up the ramp towards where his room had been in the hospital. Hoping to spot Susan, he looked into each room as he passed knowing it was her ward.

Coming to his old room, he heard the unmistakable noise of someone moaning. A sense of danger swept over him, as reaching back he rested his right hand on his weapon. Stealing a quick glance around the corner, he saw a 'doctor' standing over his doctor and Susan.

"Where's the Detective?" he asked Susan slapping her across the face, as he grabbed Dave's doctor, shoving a gun in his face. "Answer or he dies!" he snarled at Susan.

'There's got to be a lookout' Dave's mind screamed, as turning around he saw another doctor emerge from the room behind him, one hand behind his back. He smiled at Dave as he moved towards him. At first, Dave thought he might be overreacting until he looked into those dead eyes. Having no time to draw his weapon, Dave surged forward, head-butting the surprised doctor, knocking him to the floor.

Caught off guard, the doctor put his hand back to brace his fall, causing him to drop the knife hidden in his hand. Recovering from the attack, his cover blown the imposter yelled a warning to his friend. With no time to think, Dave drew his pistol, putting two rounds into the big mouth's chest, before turning swiftly and charging into his old room.

The other supposed doctor was in the process of coming out of the door, pistol drawn when Dave cannoned into him. Both fired their weapons at the same time, Dave was luckier, fatally hitting the assailant, while he took one in the upper arm.

As the hospital's alarm system screamed to life, a stabbing pain erupted along the length of Dave's arm. Close to fainting and feeling nauseous, Dave felt something grip his arm, stopping the flow of blood and easing the pain. Looking up he saw Susan above him applying a tourniquet to his arm, before wrapping a large bandage over the wound. Her face was badly bruised, but to Dave, she looked beautiful, as she continued treating his bullet wound. Once his arm had been taken care of, she turned her attention to her colleague, working on the doctor's head wound.

"Is he okay?" Dave asked Susan having trouble focusing, as his wound throbbed.

"Yes, thanks to you, they really worked him over," Susan answered sounding scared, before continuing. "They wanted to know where you were. Doctor Wain knew nothing, but they didn't believe him."

"You did great Susan, now we've got to get out of here!" Dave pleaded, knowing others could be coming.

As he slowly climbed to his feet, Susan checked the doctor, making sure he would be okay. She then raced to medical cabinet, grabbing a packet of tablets. Coming back, she put two in the doctor's mouth, then handed two to Dave. "Take these, they'll kill the pain," she ordered, as grabbing his hand, she led him out of the room.

Running sometimes staggering, they both made their way back to Susan's room. The journey took twice as long as usual, as several fire doors had closed automatically when the security alarm activated. Each had to be pried open before they could move on to the next.

Practically falling into her room breathing heavily, Dave relieved, heard the sound of sirens.

"Thank God, the cops are here! Lock the door until they arrive!" Dave moaned, close to blacking out. He didn't see a shadow sweep in from his left side, thumping him on the back of his head, knocking him to the floor. The last sound he heard was the muffled sound of Susan's voice screaming, as his world went dark.

It was near midnight when Steve arrived at the hospital. The police had the whole block to the hospital locked down, allowing no entry or exit. Turning up a side street running parallel to the hospital, Steve parked his car. Deciding to sneak in, he left his car walking to the rear of the hospital. Here a broken down fence gave easy access as he prepared to climb through. His phone ringing made him stop. Grabbing his phone, Steve looked down to see it was Claude's phone ringing not his own. Pressing the receive button, he waited.

"We got the detective and a nurse who was helping him. Where are you?" The voice asked. Steve looked at the phone, trying to think of a way out for Dave, before answering.

"It's Roberts here, not Claude. How about we meet somewhere, and I'll swap you your boss, for my friends?" He answered. Silence followed, punctuated by the distant sound of voices having a whispered conversation, on the other end of the phone.

"Okay. West of this hospital, is a bridge near the town called Sutherland, across the Woronora River? Do you know it?" The same voice asked.

"Not really, but I'll find it."

"Meet us in the middle of the bridge on the northern walkway in two hours. There's an observation platform located there. Don't bring anyone or your two friends will have their throats cut before we throw them from the bridge," The voice chuckled, before hanging up.

Pocketing the phone, Steve sprinted back to his car. Starting up, he flattened the accelerator to the floor, speeding away from the hospital as fast as he could. He knew where the bridge was, having crossed it many times, to travel to his sister's house, when he was stationed at Holsworthy army base. Driving as fast as possible, Steve hoped to arrive there first, knowing it was his only chance of saving Dave and Susan.

Parking his car in a breakdown lane on the eastern side of the bridge, Steve hopped over the safety wall, walking down the concrete walkway. The path passed under the bridge to the northern side, where a suspended metal walkway ran under the bridge across the river. It was just before three in the morning as Steve looked towards the middle of the bridge, where a viewing platform stuck out over the river. He could just make out two hazy shapes, lying there.

Silently he prayed it was Susan and Dave. Looking around, seeing nothing, Steve hesitantly started out, walking onto the bridge walkway.

Twenty metres from the platform, Steve could see his friends bound and gagged, their heads turning towards him, hearing his footsteps on the metal grating. Standing over them was a tall, thin man dressed in a black suit, making him hard to see against a background of steel beams.

"Keep coming Mr Roberts and keep your hands where I can see them!" The man shouted, as Steve silently obeyed. Stopping twenty paces from the man, Steve waited.

"Where is Claude?"

"He is in my car. I'll go and get him, now I know my friends are okay," Steve answered his eyes studying the man.

"I thought you were more professional than this!" he chuckled "I can't believe you were stupid enough to come out here in the open!"

Shawn and Michael, the two remaining men of Claude's team of four, had never intended to exchange prisoners. Claude's life meant nothing to them, compared to the contract on Roberts. When Claude's support team had arrived at the hospital, Shawn and Michael, being the two juniors of the group, had been told to wait in the car. When the other two posing as doctors, found a nurse was involved, they'd sent Shawn and Michael to check her unit.

Hearing the alarm go off in the hospital, they came to the same conclusion that the others had run into trouble. Deciding to wait until things settled down, they had opted to wait in Susan's unit and leave later. Luck had been with them when Dave and Susan had staggered into the unit and been subdued. Transporting them first to their safe house, they had then moved them to the bridge as bait.

They'd planned this, as the final hit on Robert's and it had worked all too easy. Shawn and the two prisoners waited on the bridge, while Michael on the hill above the bridge was the executioner. At this moment, he was lying on the cliff above them with a snipers rifle, waiting for Shawn's signal. Putting a cigarette in his mouth lighting it, thus giving the signal, Shawn waited smiling. As seconds passed by and nothing occurred, Shawn lost his smile.

Swiftly drawing his weapon, preparing to fire, Shawn cursed Michael's incompetence, as he saw Roberts already had his weapon out, taking aim.

"Too late!" Steve informed him, firing before Shawn could get a shot off. Hit in the upper body, Shawn was catapulted back against the rail. Dazed Shawn looked down at the water below him, wondered what had gone wrong, as Steve grabbed his feet, shoving him over the rail. "Say hello to Claude for me," Steve snarled, as Shawn wide-eyed, hurdled down towards the water far below, screaming all the way. Pulling his knife out, Steve cut loose Susan, then Dave, who both continued to sit silently comatose, having thought they would both die tonight.

"How'd you do it?" Dave asked savouring life, hugging Sue, both of them crying.

"I got here first and saw his friend heading up to the cliff."

"So he's dead too?" Dave asked; Steve nodded.

"I'm glad!" Susan snarled, before getting to her feet on unsteady legs. "Thank you. I don't know who you are, but thank you," Susan smiled hugging Steve, before helping Dave up.

The drive back to their motel room was made in silence, as each person tried to come to grips with what had happened.

"What are your plans now?" Dave asked Steve after Susan had gone to have a shower.

"I'm going to meet my family, I've found out where they are."

"I can't go, Steve, I had enough!" Dave confessed.

"That's okay my friend. I wouldn't be here without you," Steve admitted. Shaking Dave's hand saying nothing more, he walked out the door into the morning light. Watching him leave, Dave stood silently riddled with guilt for letting him go alone.

Susan having finished her shower, walked out into the lounge area to find Dave standing mutely, staring at the door. Walking up beside him, seeing his eyes, she gripped his hand.

"He's gone, hasn't he?"

"Yes, he's trying to save his family, from more of those swine's!" Dave answered close to tears, as he closed the door.

"I wouldn't want to be the guys chasing his family Dave. I've got a feeling he'll keep them safe."

"I just couldn't go with him after last night, it's rattled me."

"I thought we were going to die on that bridge," Susan whispered, remembering how Dave had begged them to let her go, getting beaten for his trouble.

"I'll never be able to repay you, for what you did for me, Susan!" Dave blurted out, hugging her to him, crying like a baby, releasing the pressure.

"Let's go to bed, we'll talk about it later," Susan smiled, leading Dave towards the bedroom.

"God its close till eight, I don't know if I can sleep and there's also sorting out the trouble at the hospital," Dave admitted, his mind working out a story they would tell.

"Who said anything about sleeping?" Susan giggled, as Dave at first surprised, laughed as well.

Returning his car to the airport rental station, Steve hurried to a Qantas departure lounge to purchase a ticket to Melbourne. Unfortunately, all economy seats were booked out for the next two days business class was another story. Paying the extra, Steve managed to book a seat in two hours time. Having a quick breakfast, he then boarded the flight, wondering what the reception would be like from his family. He hadn't seen them for over ten years, and with all the trouble he'd caused, he realised they might not be too happy to see him.

Landing in Melbourne about midday, Steve went straight to a small hotel, down the road from the airport. Getting a room, he tried to calm down and get some much-needed sleep. Showering first, he lay down, thinking about what had occurred. He'd come close to losing another friend he realised. Dave was at least safe and out of this mess, though he missed having him with him. Lying there, feeling sleep settling over him, Steve remembered another good friend, who he hadn't been able to save.

OWEN

After the failed attempt by the Israelis, Steve had decided never to stay in any place for more than one year. Three years on he found himself in South Australia, working on a vineyard in the Barossa Valley. Doing general farm duties under an assumed identity, he stayed off the grid, burying himself in the local community. Picking grapes might not have been the most exciting job in the world, but Steve enjoyed it, plus there was the extra bonus of being paid in untraceable cash.

He'd been there for nearly a year and was just about to move on when reading a local paper; he found a small story on the death of Owen Elliot. Owen had been the senior partner in a stock broking firm, that Steve had once been part of. More importantly, they'd been good friends. Needing more finance to expand, they had taken on Steve as a silent partner.

After his army career had ended, Steve, with Owens help, had started working for the firm. He'd trained with him first in Sydney, before setting up a branch in Perth. Although he'd enjoy working with Owen in Sydney, the building the Perth office to a size were it rivalled their Sydney office, had been exhilarating. The murder of his wife several years later had made Steve leave though he hoped to someday return.

The article informed their clients, that Warren, Owens partner and his daughter Mary, who had married Warren would take over the running of the company. Silently Steve remembered a good man, who'd help him through some tough spots in his life. Owen had given him a chance to make something of himself, outside of the Army.

Driving his old rust bucket of a 4WD he'd bought for getting around town, Steve went to the local post office. Stopping around the corner, he casually walked back having a good look around. Entering the phone box located out front, he dialled Owen's private number.

"Good morning, how can I help you?"

"Is that you Mary? It's Steve Roberts," Steve answered softly. At first, the only sound was an intake of breath, followed by silence, as Mary came to grips with Steve being alive.

"Is it really you Steve?" the voice asked sounding wary.

"The first time we met, you were wearing an extremely small skirt and a tank top, I still remember it."

"My God Steve, it's been years. We thought the worst I'm afraid," Mary whispered, sounding guilty.

"Well I'm still alive, though my former friends are still looking for me," Steve admitted. "Anyway, I saw the article in the paper. How'd it happened?"

"We're not sure, the police are still looking into it, but it appears he disturbed someone breaking into his home. In the scuffle it's believed Dad fell and hit his head," Mary tried not to cry.

"He was a great man and a true friend, I'm sorry he had to go this way."

"If he hadn't been attacked, he'd have died anyway Steve, he had cancer of the lungs. In a way, the thief saved him a horrible death, though I want him to rot in jail anyway,"

"I'm sure the cops will get him, Mary. When and where is the funeral to be held?" he asked, cutting the call short.

"Four days time, at the Auburn Cemetery, at two in the afternoon. Our family has a plot there."

"I'll see you there, and then if you and Warren aren't too busy, we'll catch up," Steve answered, saying goodbye before hanging up.

'Get away from the phone box!' his mind screamed, as looking around at his surroundings, Steve nervously walked back to his car. Once inside, he grabbed a sawn-off shotgun from under the seat, loading it. Driving cautiously back to his rented farmhouse, Steve regularly checked the rearview mirror, expecting at any minute to see a car following him.

For over an hour he waited in his farmhouse on edge expecting the worst. Finally, after another thorough look around, he relaxed, knowing his location hadn't been known before that call. They might now know where the call came from, but unless they had assets here, he was safe. Owen had been murdered, Steve was sure of it, the problem was, what did he do now?

If he just disappeared, they'd just keep killing other friends until he showed up. 'They may even go for my family' Steve thought nervously. If he attended the funeral, he knew they'd be waiting, though he couldn't see an alternative. Knowing it was a trap helped, the problem was how to turn it his way? Packing his bags, Steve looked around the farmhouse sadly, knowing he wouldn't be coming back and his anger grew.

"Unlike the last time my friends, you won't be getting off lightly this time," Steve promised, as grabbing his bags he drove to the airport.

SYDNEY

As Steve's plane touched down, his stomach turned over. It was not from fear of the plane landing, but the realisation that an assassin could be waiting at the airport. Letting the other passengers push and shove their way off the plane, Steve patiently waited. Standing up, he walked casually off the plane and up one of the new walkways just installed at the airport.

There were only four flights a day from Adelaide to Sydney. They knew he had to come on one of these flights, so would either try for him here or wait till he'd left? Looking neither right nor left, Steve walked straight down the concourse, heading for the baggage pickup area. Once there, he waited for his bags to wander around the automatic baggage conveyor, before picking them up.

Now came the scary part he realised, bracing himself as he walked out to the taxi rank. Outside the airport, building was the first place where a weapon could be used without being detected. He'd already spotted two men near the boarding area. By using the windows on the sides of the concourse, he'd watched them follow him through the terminal; were they here to follow him or point him out to a waiting shooter.

It was a cold day in Sydney, though you wouldn't know it by the sweat that ran down Steve's back. Across the road sat a multi-level car park; the perfect place for a sniper Steve thought, as he tried to blend in with the crowd. Glancing to his right Steve was relieved to see a large contingent of police arrived, rushing into the terminal. Someone had called in a bomb threat, from a mobile phone inside the terminal. Steve smiling casually tossed a spare mobile phone he was carrying, into a garbage bin walking towards the taxi queue.

Stealing a quick glance behind him, he saw the men tailing him talking on their phone, as Steve unhurt climbed into a taxi. 'Thank God that's over," he said to himself, giving the driver instructions on getting to his hotel in the centre of Sydney's business district.

Glancing casually in the taxi's rear view mirror, Steve watched a blue car take station behind the cab. Ten minutes on, the blue car disappeared, replaced by a white van. Another ten minutes and the van disappeared, replaced again by the blue car. The changing of the vehicles happened like clockwork, occurring several times on the way to the hotel, making Steve smile. It was a good technique changing cars, but in this case only using two made the whole exercise pointless. It told Steve one thing though, whoever was after him, didn't have unlimited resources.

Arriving at his hotel, Steve went straight to the front desk, picking up his key. Exiting the lift on the twelfth floor, Steve raced to his room. Throwing his bags inside, he turned on the TV, before rushing back outside locking his door. Moving swiftly down the hallway he entered the fire escape. Safely inside the stairwell, he watched his room through a crack in the door. Moments later, two men exited the lift approaching his room. They stood listening for several minutes before walking back to the lift, leaving.

Time was now critical, as he recklessly rushed down the fire escape, cursing that he hadn't asked for a room on a lower level. Opening the exit door at the bottom of the building Steve found himself in a back alley behind the hotel. Walking warily around the block, he crossed the road, watching for tails. The white van and the blue car were sitting opposite the hotel. Buying a paper, he watched the two men from the twelfth floor, walk out of the hotel. Crossing the road to the cars they were met by two other men.

Steve recognised these two from the airport. After the men had a brief conversation, one man walked back to the hotel. The other three entered the two cars, one in the van. This was Steve's chance to find out where they were staying, as hurrying across the road, he flagged down a cab.

"Where to?" the Cabby asked sounding bored.

"Do you see that white van up ahead about to take off, follow it."

"Are you kidding me, man?"

"There's two hundred dollars in it for you if you don't lose them."

"Okay you're on, but why are you after the guy?" The Cabby asked worried something bad could be going down.

"I think he's screwing my wife. I just want proof it's going on. He's my best friend," Steve told him, wiping his eyes.

"That's a bitch man. Happen to a friend of mine. Don't worry I won't lose him." The cabby promised him, feeling the man's pain. The cabby was worth every cent, as he wove through the traffic staying behind the unsuspecting van driver. In the end, the van drove into a unit complex parking area, forcing the cab to drive down the block. Handing over the two hundred, Steve was surprised to find the cabby wanted to come with him to help handle the situation.

Steve assured him he'd be all right, though the driver insisted he take his card in case he needed help. Waving his thanks, Steve walked back towards the unit; the happy taxi driver leaving. Reaching the front door, Steve encountered his first problem; the entry was by swipe card only. The problem was solved, when a young couple came up behind him.

"Forget your key?" The young girl asked, hugging her boyfriend.

"No, I'm meeting some of my mates here. They're renting one of the apartments here for a few months," Steve replied.

"You mean the Yanks. They're the only ones here renting. How do you know them?" The young man suspiciously, noticing Steve hadn't mentioned they weren't Aussies.

"I was in the army and served in America for awhile. We were part of the same unit there."

"Yeah, I figured they were ex-military. They're staying on the second floor, apartment 22," He informed Steve, before grabbing a handful of his girlfriend's backside and steering her along the ground floor hallway, into an apartment. Making sure they'd gone, Steve walked down a staircase into the garage, deciding to check the car park first. Locating both the blue car and the van, Steve looked through the car windows, seeing nothing out of the ordinary. Moving to the van he repeated the process finding a large shape hidden under a blanket in the rear section.

No time to be neat, Steve grabbed a fire extinguisher smashing the rear window. Ripping open the door he carefully removed the blanket seeing a tripwire connected to it. Removing the clip holding the wire, Steve pulled the large box out of the van. The box was locked, but the extinguisher again proved useful, breaking the lock completely off in one hit. Inside Steve found a sniper rifle and an assortment of pistols, plus ammo.

"Put your hands where I can see them!" A voice ordered behind Steve, making him do as he was told. "Now turn around slowly," it commanded, as Steve slowly turned. "Fuck it's you, Roberts, I can't believe it was this easy," He laughed, as Steve watched him take up the slack on the silenced pistol's trigger.

"What's going on?" A voice challenged, from the car park entry door.

The gunmen surprised, instantly turned his weapon towards the new threat, firing twice, before turning back towards Steve. It was the chance Steve desperately needed, as rushing forward; he struck the shooter across the neck, crushing his throat. Staggering backwards, the shooter tried to reacquire Steve and finish him, when the extinguisher crashed into his forehead killing him.

His breath coming in great gulps Steve looked towards his saviour, seeing the taxi driver lying in the entrance. Running to the downed man, he felt for a pulse. Unfortunately, the shooter was an excellent marksman; he'd hit the poor cabby twice in the chest.

"Why the fuck did you come back?" Steve whispered sadly, knowing the guy had saved his life and died for it. Getting up knowing there was nothing he could do, Steve returned to the shooter going through his pockets. Gathering everything he had, Steve gathered up the box of weapons placing them back in the van. Two of the many items in the shooters pockets were his car keys and swipe card.

Closing the cars back door, Steve drove the van out of the garage and further down the street, in case he'd needed to get away fast. Knowing time was rushing by; Steve went back to the garage moving both bodies behind the blue car out of sight. He then walked up to the second floor, hoping no one would spot the bodies before he left.

Locating number 22, Steve quickly checked the hallway, before returning to the door. It was a solid wooden door with a steel frame; he knew kicking it in was out of the question. Pulling out a silenced pistol taken from the killer in the garage, Steve placed it on the ground beside him, as he bent down to examine the lock. Inserting a small piece of wire into the key section, he was just feeling for the tumblers, when the door swung open.

"I'll see what's keeping Roger!" a bald-headed man shouted back into the unit, as he opened the door and saw Steve bent over working on the lock. He reacted instantly, screaming out a warning, as he went for his weapon. If he had kicked out at Steve instead of going for his weapon, the result would have been different. Instead the time it took to draw his gun, allowed Steve to recover and grab his own weapon of the floor and fire.

Two shots to the body, catapulted the man back inside the apartment, as weapons inside fired out into the hallway. Backing away, knowing surprise was gone; Steve beat a hasty retreat downstairs and out of the building.

"Shit, what a stuff up!" He cursed loudly, as jumping into the van, he drove away.

Dumping the van two blocks away in a back alley, Steve torched it, taking only some ammo for the pistol. Walking to the nearest railway station, Steve watched as several fire trucks raced past him, heading towards the plume of smoke rising in the distance.

Getting off in the city, Steve decided to take a chance and return to his hotel, knowing the man there watching would've been tipped off by now. Commonsense told him to abandon his gear and move on. The reason why he couldn't, was the only photos he had of his kids and his wife, were there.

Watching the hotel for several minutes, Steve, in the end, walked straight through the front door. The man left to watch him, was standing near the front counter. As Steve walked to the lift, the man smiling walked over, hopping into the lift with him.

"My boss said to tell ya, that today's going to cost you, two friends," He chuckled confidently.

"You tell your boss that if he goes near anyone I know, I'll take out your Ambassador here in Australia and let the media known why it happened."

"Bullshit, you're bluffing! I've seen your file, my friend, you're what we call a true blue hero. Your type wouldn't hurt an innocent man."

"Your boss back in America didn't tell you about his two other men in Pakistan, did he?" Steve smiled. For the first time since Steve had met this creep, he saw a slight crack in his confidence.

"Well, why don't you tell me then Roberts?"

"He sent two men just as confident as you. They were to watch me until more men arrived. I cut their heads off and sent them back to Don Brooks. Surely they told you what you were up against?" Steve smiled.

"Sounds like more bullshit!" He smiled, as he swiftly drew his gun. Steve expecting the move didn't try to draw his own weapon. Kicking out, he smashed the man's kneecap, causing him to collapse onto the floor screaming. Ripping the man's gun from his hand, he kicked him in the guts taking out any fight left him. Pressing the button for the floor below his own, Steve waited for the door to open, before throwing the man out.

Knocking him unconscious, Steve emptied his pockets, before hopping back into the lift. Getting out swiftly, gun drawn, Steve moved to his room, hoping he didn't run into any more of the man's friends. Grabbing his bags, he again started the long walk down to the rear alley exit. Why they hadn't tried for him at the hotel, Steve had no idea. Commonsense would have told them he wouldn't return. Steve figured this guy had been left here just in case.

It amazed him that the guy had expected him to just come quietly, after threatening to kill more of his friends. Killing the Ambassador and going public was indeed a bluff, for he knew in custody he'd be easy meat. The problem for the yanks was, it would open a can of worms for Brook's the head of the CIA at the time. Steve was banking on Brook's fear of discovery to stop more killings. Realising he was back to square one, Steve hailed a cab, looking for another hotel.

Waking from a troubled sleep, Steve had his breakfast delivered to his room along with a paper. Splashed across the front page was the killing of the cabby and his unknown friend. The reporter covering the story had the murder down to being 'in the wrong place at the wrong time'. He believed the cabby was taking his passenger to pick up his car from the garage. On the way, they must have come across a drug deal going down or some other underworld activity. The imagination of the reporter was truly inspiring, as Steve visualised how many copies this story would sell.

More worrying, was a description of a person of interest that the police wanted to talk to it fitted Steve. The report said that a young couple had given him entry to the complex earlier. There was no mention of the Americans or the shootout at their unit, meaning they'd left soon after he had. Steve's problem was how to locate them before they found him.

Clearing his breakfast from the small dining table, he spread the two men's belongings onto it. There was the usual mixture of odds and ends, including their wallets. Something he found strange was that neither of the men had passports. Except for a couple of hundred Australian dollars, there was nothing else in each wallet, even licenses and credit cards were missing.

Both men, however, had a small key with a tag indicating a safety deposit box at a bank in the city. Obviously, all their valuables would be kept there. Unfortunately, the other members of this hit squad, including the one Steve hadn't killed, would know Steve had the two keys. By now, they would have emptied their friend's lockers, but it did give Steve an idea.

Fronting up to the bank, Steve introduced himself as Edward McClelland of the AFP. Showing a fake badge he'd had made, which was an exact copy of his brother-in-law's badge. He asked to see footage of the safety deposit box area, supposedly looking for money launderers. Watched by one of the bank's security men and a bank clerk, Steve quickly looked through the morning's footage. Spotting the two men from the airport, Steve asked for a copy to be made.

"Are you sure it's those two men?" The clerk asked sounding suspicious.

"Look I can't tell you too much, but we think these two and some other men might be planning a major drug import into Australia," Steve whispered looking around as if making sure no else heard.

"You could be right officer. This morning they came in here and tried to clear out two lockers supposedly because their friend's keys were taken. The manager told them to come back in the afternoon, after he checked their story," The security guard volunteered, excited about helping apprehend some bad guys, instead of picking up coins that customers dropped.

"So they're coming back?" Steve asked surprised, not believing his luck.

"Yeah, the manager wanted time to see if the keys turned up, before handing over the contents. He's okayed it now, so I suppose they'll be back in soon," The guard informed him.

"Do you think we should stop them from having the contents?" The clerk asked softly.

"No let them have the contents, I'll ring for backup and have them followed. Thanks for your help; you two may have saved someone's life today," Steve smiled shaking their hands, knowing it was his life they'd saved.

Looking outside seeing no sign of the yanks, Steve quickly walked across the road to an adjacent car park. After walking along several rows of cars, he found what he was looking for, an old white Toyota Landcruiser. A quick search revealed a window slightly down on the passenger side. With the help of an aerial from the car parked nearby, Steve had the door open.

Quickly hot-wiring the ignition; Steve then drove to a spot in the car park where he could watch the bank. Speed was not something he needed to follow the men, what he needed was something big enough to come out on top, if push came to shove.

Two hours of watching and Steve started getting worried. If the men didn't show soon, he'd run the risk of having the owner of the Toyota turn up. He was just thinking of abandoning the car when across the road opposite the bank, appeared the blue car. Driving to the car park entrance, Steve produced the car-parking docket, paying the fee. Once the boom gate opened, he drove slowly out onto the street, coming to a stop five cars behind the blue car.

Twenty minutes more of sitting there exposed passed, before Steve's adversaries walked out of the bank and hopped straight into their car. While getting in, one of the men appeared to stop and look straight at him. Steve froze as the man looked away hopping in as the blue car moved off. Tailing someone was new to Steve, as he tried to keep his distance. He'd watched his fair share of cop shows and had watched the cabby tail these guys the other day. Doing it yourself, however, was something else.

He couldn't get too close, or they'd spot him. Then again he couldn't leave too big a gap, or he'd lose them. Even being careful not to fall too far behind, he still lost them three times. The first two were just a matter of catching up; on the third time he'd thought he'd stuffed it. The car in front of him braked for a red light while their car, two cars ahead kept going. Panicking he accelerated, overtaking several cars as he hurdled through heavy traffic running the red light.

Losing sight of them, he looked down every side street trying to spot them. In the end, he saw them just as they were turning left, forcing him to turn suddenly, causing several cars to brake and honk their horns. Slowing down, Steve again tried to relax as the blue car continued on driving out into the suburbs. At last the blue vehicle turned onto a side road, driving to the end and turning into a private driveway.

'Why so far out of the city?' Steve asked himself nervously. Following them cautiously, Steve realised it wasn't a private driveway, but a park entrance.

The road ran through several areas of playing fields winding into a lightly forested area, where Steve saw a sign indicating a jogging track; deserted at this time of day. The vehicle ahead had now disappeared, and Steve's guts started to knot up. Rounding a corner the road started to slope downhill, Steve opened the door and dived out, letting the car continue. The Toyota continued on, slowing as it reached the bottom of the slope. Thinking he'd given away his main advantage at being mobile, Steve was just about to walk down and hop back in, when shots rang out from the surrounding tree line, peppering the vehicle.

Being just over the rise and out of sight, Steve sprinted into the trees making his way down the slope. It had become deadly quiet, as he silently moved down opposite the trees where the shots had come from. Hidden behind the trees opposite, Steve could just make out the outline of the blue car, with another vehicle parked beside it. They'd either spotted him at the bank, or his tailing them, had given him away. At this point though, it really didn't matter. He was in big trouble.

Looking out towards his Swiss cheese car, Steve saw two men moving cautiously up to its side, looking in. They'd soon all know he was still alive, so taking a chance; he lined up the two vehicles, shooting out a tyre on each. Even with a silencer, the two men near his car scattered, as voices in the distance called to each other, trying to find out where the shots had come from. 'Now we're all stuck out here,' Steve smiled, starting to hunt.

Crawling through the undergrowth, Steve cursed at not wearing his old clothes, which made him smiled. Clothing was the last of his problems he figured, as he stopped and listened for movement. To his right, the muffled sound of feet creeping through the scrub brought Steve's pistol up, as he froze and waited. As if sensing Steve lying there, the man stopped and whispered.

"Can you see the bastard?"

"Yes, I can!" Steve answered in a soft voice, firing two rounds. The man screamed and fell with a muffled thump, as Steve moved forward to his body. Going through his pockets and finding nothing, he moved further into the trees. It wasn't any of the men Steve had seen so far, so there were more than just four.

"Adrian, where are you?" came a voice to Steve's left, meaning someone had heard the scream. When no answer came, Steve heard him summoning the others. More people approached, a least five men were now combing the brush, looking for Steve. Each man was carrying a light machine gun or rifle, and by the way, they swept the scrub always turning right to left, Steve could tell they'd had some training. This meant he couldn't open fire, knowing no matter how good he was he couldn't take out five well-trained men at once.

The group came towards Steve's position in an extended line, each man covering the area in front of him; backed up by the man on either side. Lying motionless in a thick stand of bramble, Steve held his breath as the line moved passed him.

'What to do?' Was the burning question, as Steve slowly got to his feet, watching the line of men disappear over the next ridge. Moving in the opposite direction, Steve slowly walked towards where the American's had left their two vehicles. Not everyone was searching he realised, as a shadow moved in one of the vehicles, bringing him to a sudden halt. Still, in the tree line, Steve silently retraced his steps coming around behind the rear of the parked cars.

'He's been left here to keep watch' Steve thought, creeping forward until he was nearly right beside the man's window. The idiot was asleep, enjoying the afternoon sun, a fatal mistake, as Steve drove the man's own knife between his ribcage. Opening the door of the car, he quickly tossed the body out onto the ground searching it. He then went through the rest of the car finding nothing. Pulling the boot release, he searched the rear coming up blank. The other car was a station wagon which he also searched, coming up empty. 'Surely the guy had a weapon other than a knife," Steve surmised.

Disappointed he was just about to leave when he spotted a black box under the rear of the car. Reaching underneath he pulled out a long case that held a sniper rifle and its ammo. Moving back up the hill where he'd jumped from the car, Steve found a spot where he couldn't be flanked. Lying down in a depression in the ground, he built a small support rampart in front of himself. The sniper rifle had folding legs, which Steve extended, setting the rifle up facing down towards the trees. That was where the two cars were hidden and the most likely place where they'd launch their attack. Now he waited knowing his enemies would soon return to the vehicles thinking Steve had fled, to find their dead comrade instead.

After lying motionless for over an hour, the sound of a vehicle starting came to him. The blue car noised out of the trees then stopped. 'Shit, they know I took the rifle and are baiting me into firing!' Steve realised as shapes could be seen moving towards him through the trees. The car was just a diversion he concluded. Training his sniper rifles sights on the closest moving shape, he pulled the trigger. The shape exploded away from him, as moving to the next shape, which had dived to the ground, he fired again.

The second shot missed, as two automatic weapons immediately opened up, spraying the bushes around him. Ducking down behind his hastily built rock wall, Steve kept his head down praying the rocks were thick enough. Over the sound of gunfire, Steve heard the car accelerating. Glancing down the hill, he saw the blue car rushing towards his position. Pinned down by the men shooting Steve taking a chance, rolled sideways. He'd barely cleared his hiding spot as the wheels of the car ploughed into the depression, shattering his rock wall.

Slamming on the brakes, the driver used the vehicle as cover, jumping out. He immediately went on the offensive, pumping round after round into the scrub around Steve. His friends down the hill, blinded by the car, stop firing afraid of hitting the driver. His rifle gone, Steve whipped out his pistol, pumping a full magazine into the direction the driver was shooting from, making him move behind the car. Both had missed their targets, emptying their weapons, causing both to reload.

Reloading a pistol is a lot faster than a rifle, especially when you'd left the spare magazine to the rifle in the car. As the driver reached into the car to reload, Steve came to his feet racing around the side of the vehicle. Firing at point-blank range, the driver's head exploded as his body smashed backwards against the side of the car. Seeing him go down, the driver's two friends immediately opened fired as they sprinted up the hill. Closing the gap swiftly, Steve in desperation grabbed the driver's weapon firing blindly into the two men from under the car. Seeing both men go down in a hail of bullets, he stopped firing.

A deadly silence settled over the area, as Steve getting over the rush of adrenaline; listen for any movement, as his lungs gulped down oxygen. A moan from one of the men, made Steve drop the rifle and advance towards the two men's bodies, pistol held out in front. One was dead, the other had been hit twice; once in the shoulder, the other through his lung.

"How bad is it?" he asked, groaning again.

"You're not going to make it."

"Put one in me and finish it!" he begged, the pain overwhelming him.

"Why should I?"

"I'm not like the others. I don't enjoy killing for the fun of it. I was in jail for a robbery I did while in the army. They promised me freedom in exchange for coming here with this lot. I had no part in the killing of your friend!" he replied honestly.

"Is this all of them?"

"No, the boss isn't here, but you've met him. He was the clerk at the bank!" The man croaked out.

"Okay, close your eyes," Steve said sadly, placing the muzzle against his head.

"Thanks," was all he got out, as Steve pulled the trigger. Walking to the car, Steve found the engine had received a few rounds finishing it. Having no choice, he walked back down the hill finding the other car's tyre had been changed. Climbing in, he took a few deep breaths, before starting the engine.

"You little shit!" Steve said out loud, thinking how helpful the clerk had been, as he gunned the engine, driving back into the city.

Getting back to the bank, just before closing time, Steve waited near the car park, like he had before. Watching the bank, Steve felt quite a fool, for being taken in so easily. He should've inquired about how long both the clerk and the security guard had been there for, before taking them into his confidence. Angry at himself, Steve looked up to see the clerk exit the front door of the bank. Following him, walking along towards the railway station, Steve noticed how fit the man was and the way he practically marched along. This in itself should have warned him.

Entering the railway station, Steve followed the clerk down onto the platform. It was packed, as the crowd stood five deep, waiting for the train to pull in. Steve watched as the clerk positioned himself at the front of the crowd, trying to be first on to claim a seat. Inching his way through the crowd, Steve came to stand behind the clerk, his face practically touching the man's back. As the train entered the station, Steve ready himself to push the clerk onto the tracks, when looking out the corner of his eye, Steve saw two police officers standing several spaces away.

So intent was he on getting the clerk, he'd failed to take in his surroundings and the people standing there. Cursing his mistake, Steve wondered what to do, when the train came to a halt in front of him. The clerk making ready to enter, glancing into the glass doors seeing Steve's face reflecting back behind him. Reacting, the clerk reached for his weapon, as Steve retreated into the crowd. Getting a brief sighting of Roberts the clerk opened fire as mayhem erupted. Two people in the crowd, a young man and an old woman, were hit in the clerk's attempt to get Steve. The rest of the crowd stampeded away from the gunman, all except the two police officers.

Caught off guard at first, they fell back on their training, dropping to one knee on the ground drawing their weapons. Both officers took aim, calling on the clerk to drop his weapon. The clerk reacted instantly, turning and firing at the police officers, hitting them both. The officers surprised by his swift response still managed to get off several shots off at the gunman, before dropping to the ground both hurt. Lying on the platform, the officers thought they'd both missed when the gunman suddenly toppled backwards into the train unmoving.

By this stage, more police who'd been alerted by the shots poured onto the platform. Racing through the crowd, they dragged the shooter of the train, disarming him. It was obvious he was dead, by the two holes dead centre in his chest. Still, the police dutifully went through the motions of checking for a pulse finding none. The area was then cordoned off, while the two police, the young man and woman were stabilised. Moved to a hospital, all four people were treated, only the woman proved to be serious. As with all shootings, a detective was sent to the hospital to get both Officers' statements.

"Nice shooting!" Detective Watts said to the two officers, having been called to investigate the shooting.

"Yeah, even though we're not sure which one of us hit him?" One of the officers confessed.

"Where were you two standing?" Watts asked, getting a feel for what had happened. After going over the police officers stories, the detective again checked the offender's wounds and photos from the crime scene. Looking at the photos, he again checked the positions of the offender and the two policemen.

"Are you sure you two were standing there, and the offender was facing you here?" Watts asked scratching his head.

'We're positive, why?" the second officer answered.

"He was hit from this direction," Watts informed them, pointing towards the exit stairs on the station.

"That means there was another shooter?" The second officer suggested.

"Who cares, he saved our lives. Most probably had an illegal firearm?" The first officer pointed out.

"Anyway, it makes the bookwork easier for you two. The blame for this whole mess can now be loaded on this nut and the other shooter," Watts informed them smiling.

"Have you identified the shooter?" The first officer asked.

"No. He had no ID on him," He answered, thinking back to the cabby shooting where again the guy with him was a nobody.

"Just as a matter of interest, this guy wasn't in the crowd was he?" Watts asked showing a picture of the man wanted in connection with the cabby murder.

"I can't be certain, but there was a guy behind him in the crowd, who looked a lot like this picture," The first officer replied.

"Shit I wonder if the bullets will match?" Watts said more to himself than the others, as he hurried back to his office.

By the next day, the shooting at the park had been discovered, and an investigation got underway. Several men had been identified as being shot by the same weapon as at the cabby shooting.

Two days after the shooting at the railway station, Detective Watts and the detectives assigned to the cabby shooting and the park shooting sat down together for a briefing. Watts found that he'd been right, that his shooting was tied to the other two.

At the briefing, the lead Detective explained how the cabby, was believed now to have been shot by the unidentified man at the scene, not by the man in the photo. The person in the sketch was then believed to have shot the unidentified man after he'd killed the cabby.

Also, it was revealed that a group of Americans staying at a unit where the cabby was killed were the victims at the park shootings. Detective Watts then got up and told them of the shooting at the station.

There, yet another American with no ID had been shot by the mysterious man in the sketch. He told them how he believed the shooter had tried to kill the man in the sketch, wounding the other four people including the two police officers. Instead of making good his escape, the man in the sketch, had open fired on the shooter killing him, undoubtedly saving the two cops lives.

"What the hell's going on?" A detective asked from the rear.

"There's another problem gentlemen! The American Embassy wants the unknown men's bodies returned to them immediately, and they're not answering any questions on their identities," The lead Detective admitted, looking none too happy.

"So what do we do about the case?" Watts asked angrily.

"We drop it, men. The only thing we're to do is look for the man in the sketch."

"That's bullshit. He looks like he was doing our job, these yanks are dirty you can smell it!" Watts put forward, getting nods from the others.

"Look I'm not happy about it either, but there it is. And remember, it's up to us how hard we look." The lead Detective smiled, before closing the meeting. Watts left the meeting feeling like the police were being used. The bright side was now he could attend the funeral for Owen, which he'd thought he'd miss today. Jumping into his car angry, he put on the blue light to get through the traffic, smiling happily at breaking the law.

THE FUNERAL

That morning, Steve got out of bed feeling terrible; he was sure he'd got rid of the threat to himself, but at what cost? The cabby and those poor people at the station had paid for keeping him alive. Looking at the paper, he was a little relieved to see no one at the station had died except the clerk. All three separate shootings were linked somehow to the man in the sketch the paper screamed but gave no details of why. Again his photo, though rough, appeared on the front page.

Luckily getting around that was easy; most people were looking for a low life, not someone wealthy. After the shooting at the railway station, Steve had gone shopping. He ordered a handmade suit to be delivered to his hotel by 11am that morning as well as a collection of other clothing. It was an expensive way of getting a suit, but necessary for his cover. Finished with clothing, he returned to his hotel, ordering a limo to take him to the funeral the next day. The suit arrived just in time, as after dressing, he was informed his car was waiting for him.

Walking through the foyer, Steve noticed many admiring looks from some of the women there, at his suit and limo. Several even held papers with his profile flashed across the front, proving his disguise was working. Jumping into the limo, he instructed the driver where to go before sitting back and relaxing.

The funeral was a sad affair. Owen had been immensely popular with his friends and clientele. Several family and friends including Warren and Mary had got up giving small testimonials to a great man. Mary even approached Steve, who after being introduced as a silent partner, gave a tearful salute to a man who had been like a big brother to him. When the service had finished the group of friends and clients went back to Warren and Mary's house for refreshments.

Many people there knew Owen and Warren had a mysterious partner, but no one had ever met him. This caused quite a stir, as Steve was introduced to a great many people. Towards the end of the wake, Steve was introduced to a detective named Jim Watts. Owen had at one stage helped the detective break a share fraud scam being run out of Sydney. Afterwards, he and Owen had become good friends, having a passion for golf in common. Shaking the detective's hand, Steve saw more than just a friendly hello he saw recognition.

"You Mr Roberts look a lot like a man I'm looking for," Watts said with a smile on his face.

"I hope he doesn't owe you money because I'm not paying," Steve laughed, as inside his heart skipped a beat.

"No, it's nothing like that, just a case I'm working on at the moment," Watts explained still smiling, before moving off to get a drink. Steve watched the man move off, his survival instincts telling him to get away from here as quickly as possible. 'No he'll know something was wrong if I left, better to stay put' Steve decided, as Mary took his arm introducing him to someone else.

Across the room, Watts felt like he'd confronted a lion. Even though Roberts hadn't moved an inch over his deduction's something warned him the guy was a killer. Seeing Warren refreshing his drink, he asked him about Steve.

"I can't believe he's here Jim! He must've really loved the old guy to risk coming back," Warren whispered secretively. Watts figured he'd had quite a bit to drink.

"Why would he be in danger?" At first, Warren hesitated about answering. Unfortunately, alcohol has a gift for making a man talk when he shouldn't.

"Steve was once a soldier in the SAS. Owen told me he also worked for the CIA as well. Some drug cartel in Columbia put a hit out on him for killing members of their cartel, while working for the CIA. When they came for him, they killed his wife instead. Unarmed he still managed to kill all the attackers, though Owen said it had affected him mentally. After that, he and his army mates went after the cartel and wiped them out completely. No one's seen him for years, and Owen found out through a friend in the government, that the CIA has a kill order out on him," Warren blurted out, before suddenly sobering, realising what he was saying. "I shouldn't have told you that Jim, can we keep it to ourselves," He asked looking a little scared.

"It's safe with me Warren, forget about it," Jim assured him, as Warren hurried off, obviously embarrassed at saying too much. Jim stood there working through what he knew. Owen had once told him of Steve Roberts, saying he was one of the most honest men he ever met. Jim had always wondered about Owen's murder, he didn't buy the robbery angle especially when the thieves took nothing.

Could the yanks have killed Owen to draw Roberts out? Knowing how much Steve had cared for him, they'd know he'd surface for the funeral, giving them a chance to finish him. It certainly fitted, and it could explain why Roberts' description matched who they were looking for. He decided to wait until everyone had gone before confronting Roberts. He had to know what was going on, friendship with Owen or not.

It was very late when Steve decided to call it a night. Everyone had gone including Steve's limo driver meaning he'd have to call a taxi. Mary and Warren had wanted him to stay, but the run-in with the detective had worried him. It was time to disappear again, even though he had one more thing to do before leaving. Steve seeing the taxi pull up outside, said a quick farewell to Warren and Mary, before walking down the driveway to the street entrance.

Walking out through the front gates he approached the taxi, seeing the driver lying on the kerbside.

"Are you okay?" Steve asked rushing to his side.

"Put your hands on the roof of the cab!" a familiar voice ordered him from behind, as a figure stepped out of the shadows beside the gate. Moving to the cab, following the man's instructions, Steve felt a whack across the back of his head. Grabbing his head as he collapsed onto the ground, Steve saw the man move in closer. "Remember me from the hotel? I missed the meeting with you at the park because of the beating you gave me arsehole!" He screamed as he laid the boot into Steve's stomach. Dizzy from the beating, Steve focused on the man, recognising him.

"Then I saved your life' you know what happened to your friends," He smiled, as another kick to the stomach made him wince.

"You're a real comedian aren't you?" The man replied angrily, his gun staying trained on Steve.

"Yeah, though I can see why you don't get the joke," Steve groaned."You didn't kill the driver of this taxi did you?" Steve continued, trying to distract the scumbag.

"Nah just knocked him out, I'll kill him later, after I finish with your friends inside, like I did their old man," He laughed.

"You're gonna die badly for that arsehole," Steve snarled, making ready to attack.

"Well, you won't be there to see it," He smiled, pointing his gun at Steve's head.

"He's right, you are going to die!" A voice spat out behind the gunmen, making him turn. Two pistol shots echoed around the neighbourhood, as the 'would be' assassin's body fell across Steve's crushing him to the ground. Pulling himself slowly out from under him, Steve groggy, tried to stand, as a hand reached down pulling him to his feet.

"Move back a bit!" Detective Watts ordered Steve, as he fired a shot directly into the assassin's face. Shocked, Steve looked down at the mess wondering what was going on. "Get the taxi driver into the house. I'll fill you in after I ring this in." Watts explained, as Steve doing what he was told, picked up the driver shaking him awake.

"Hey before you go, I'll have that gun you've been shooting everybody with?" Watts demanded as Steve reached into his coat pocket, passing over the pistol and the silencer. Not sure what was going on, Steve staggered up the driveway with the cabby. Halfway to the house, he was intercepted by Warren and Mary, who had come out to see what was going on? Taking the driver from Steve, who at this time was coming around enough to walk on his own, he told them to go inside while he checked on Detective Watts. By the time Steve reached the detective, he found his gun with silencer-fitted in the assassin's hand.

"It's neat this way," Watts told him. Seeing his confused look, he explained. "I was going to take you in for questioning when I heard this guy confess. With his face a mess I can say he fitted the description we've got of you. They're all looking for a random killer, so I'll say he was attacking the cabby and just about to kill him when I came along."

"Thank you, detective," Steve said softly.

"I didn't do it for you, I did it for Owen. I want you gone as soon as possible, understand!" Watts told him angrily.

"Thanks anyway. Give me another day, and I'll disappear," Steve replied, walking up the driveway to Mary's house.

This shooting closed the case as far as the cops were concerned. A bad guy was in the right place at the right time as far as they were concerned. Steve stayed the rest of the night at Mary and Warren's house, saying a sad farewell the next morning before disappearing into another taxi. Returning to his hotel, he hired a car for the afternoon to be returned to the airport in the morning. He then booked a flight to Tasmania for the following day, having one last thing to take care of. Changing into dark clothing, Steve prepared for his three-hour drive south to Canberra.

At one in the morning, the United States Ambassador, Brad Anderson, showered and changed into his pyjamas. It had been a tough day after leaning on the Australian Government to hand over some bodies belonging to his country. Usually, he didn't get his hands dirty with this type of problem; this time he'd made an exception. The order had come from the CIA of all places, which had intrigued him. He knew in the future he could use this to barter a better position within the government.

Another reward for his hard work was waiting for him in his bedroom upstairs. His wife having divorced him a few weeks earlier had finally left, returning to the States. His secretary, who he figured wanted to advance her career, was staying over for the night. Wondering if he was up to it, the ambassador entered his bedroom to find his secretary lying naked on the bed. His tiredness vanished in seconds as he stood there marvelling at her young firm body. Moving beside the bed, he ran his hand along her thigh getting an answering moan of pleasure. If it was faked or not he didn't care, as he swiftly stripped, preparing to thoroughly enjoy her career advancement.

After an hour of mind-blowing sex, the ambassador staggered to the bathroom urinating loudly, not caring if it offended her or not. Coming back out wondering what he'd try next, he found his playmate hiding under the blankets.

"I know where you are!" He laughed, racing to the bed and throwing back the covers. His laughter stopped abruptly, as he saw his secretary's arms and feet were taped as well as her mouth. "What's going on?" he asked not understanding, wondering if this was another game. The butt of a pistol hitting the side of his head ended his questioning. Waking up confused, Anderson found his hands and feet secured like his secretary's.

"What's going on?" He stammered out, clearly frightened.

"She's a beautiful woman Ambassador, you're a lucky man!" A voice said to his right, making him turn that way.

"How dare you assault me! Do you know who I am?" the Ambassador asked angrily. A gun being shoved under his chin stopped him from saying more.

"I know who you are. You're the man who's helping Don Brooks try to kill me!" Steve replied, his voice sounding like death.

"I've got nothing to do with the CIA! I'm just cleaning up a mess for him that's all," Anderson answered, his voice quivering with fear, as the silence stretched out as each person waited for someone to talk.

"You tell Brooks if he comes after my friends again, I'll start killing Ambassadors, starting with you. I'll then work my way up through your government leaving a message on each one, telling the world that Brooks is responsible," Steve warned him, before walking to the door and vanishing.

Anderson and his secretary lay there for at least twenty minutes, before trying to free themselves. Once free, both sat there silently as Anderson thought about what to do. Making a decision, he decided to pass the message onto Brooks, telling no one else. His secretary recovering climbed out of bed swiftly dressing, preparing to leave.

"Where are you going, Linda?"

"I figured it was time to go," She mumbled.

"Come back into bed!"

"You can't still want to make love after that?"

"No not really, but then after what happened I'd rather you stay with me. I'd rather not be alone," he admitted sheepishly. Dropping her clothing back onto the floor, she quickly climbed back into his bed, snuggling up next to him.

"That was pretty scary. Does your head hurt?" She asked softly.

"Yes, it does a bit, though it's fading."

"Your secret's safe with me, you can always trust me, Brad," His secretary replied softly. Jumping out of bed again she ran to his bar fridge getting out some ice. Wrapping it in a small towel, she returned to the bed putting it on Brad's head.

"That feels great thank you, Linda," Brad answered feeling the throbbing slowly ease. "He didn't hurt you when he first arrived did he?" Brad asked sincerely

"No, he was quite a gentleman, he even apologised for having to do it," She said, snuggling up next to him.

"Yes, he's seemed quite a professional didn't he?" Brad admitted wondering why Brooks was after him. "Linda, about your promotion, we never discussed what you wanted?" Brad asked hoping she wasn't offended, thinking he was buying her silence.

"I'm happy working here with you," She admitted softly, kissing him on the side of his face. Surprised Brad looked closely at Linda seeing her blush slightly. 'My God, she isn't faking it, she really likes me!' Brad realised as the heat of her body warmed him.

"You know, now it's over, and he's gone, I've got to admit, I'm a bit horny," Linda giggled, her body rubbing up against Brad's thigh.

"So am I now," Brad chuckled, knowing the night had changed his life, in more ways than one.

That was the last time Steve had been cornered. Since Owens's death, no one till now had made a move on Steve's friends. The ambassador had scared Brooks enough to make him back off, which at least kept his friends out of harm's way.

Waking from the dream, as if coming out of a coma, Steve bolted upright. Looking at the clock, he saw that he'd slept right through the day and into the next night.

"Shit!" He groaned, realising that he'd missed a chance to catch up with his family. Through his confused state of mind, he heard his phone ringing.

"Who is it?"

"It's Ali, how are you, Steve? This is the third attempt I've made at ringing you tonight. Are you okay?"

"Better now, I'm on the way to meet my family. The reason why I didn't answer is I haven't slept for some time, today I caught up," Steve replied, before filling Ali in on what had happened. Ali, in turn, told Steve of their problems and how Aaron had been hurt.

"Will he be okay?" Steve asked concerned.

"Yes, though the doctor was lucky not to get his throat cut when he told Aaron at his age it would take a while."

"So there are three different groups of assassins. One based in Amsterdam, one in England and this Thistle character, who is a loner. Where do you think we should start?" Steve asked, knowing Ali had been through a fair bit already.

"Since we're in London, I'll see what I can learn about the British group, but there's only Cody and me, Aaron's out for now," Ali replied neutrally, knowing nothing of this group's size or location.

"This Thistle character, do you think he's CIA, he seems to know a great deal about us?" Steve asked puzzled by this assassin.

"Yes, the fact they were waiting for us, shows someone either tipped them off from your end," Ali answered, worried by the third assassin.

"Anyway keep safe my friend, and come out here when you get a chance, I could use your help!" Steve admitted, knowing he was a little afraid of this unknown adversary.

"We'll see what we can learn here, and then we'll come. In the meantime be careful!" Ali replied, before cutting the connection. Steve sat thinking about Owen, and other innocents that had paid for his freedom. How many more he asked himself, would continue to pay for his sins.

THE BLAME GAME

The death of two state police officers at the warehouse had turned a successful counter-terrorist raid into a nightmare. The blame game for not securing the warehouse properly went back and forth between the Feds and the local cops. Shane, his leg heavily bandaged, had been moved from the hospital to their headquarters that morning, to try and find out what had happened. He was surprised to find the Commissioner himself there, looking none too happy. Entering the conference room, Shane shuffled to a spare seat, wondering who would wear the blame for this one.

Looking around the room, he saw Stevenson and Morris sitting with the Director, while Jeff and the rest of the special weapons group sat to the side, clearly wanting nothing to do with Stevenson or the Director.

"What the hell happened? I want to know why the warehouse wasn't secured," the Commissioner shouted, as he looked around the room.

"Yes Jeff, you headed up the special weapons group, why didn't you search it?" the Director spat out, trying to put the knife into someone, other than himself.

"Several of my men were hit, we did a quick sweep, but the wounded men were my main responsibility," Jeff answered his eyes boring into the director.

"Stevenson, you were in charge, why didn't you call the state police to help?" the Commissioner asked angrily. Stevenson looked to the director for support and saw none coming, so he decided to save himself, and tell the truth.

"The Director wanted all the credit, he ordered me not to get the local police involved," Stevenson answered, sweating badly.

"That's a lie, I gave no such order!" the Director replied smugly, dropping Stevenson in it.

"Stevenson, can you prove Director Ray gave that order?" the Commissioner asked, as the room grew deadly silent.

"No Sir, but Agent Smith was the one responsible for the raid in the first place, he's responsible for this whole mess!" Stevenson yelled, desperately trying to pass the blame.

"Is that true Agent Smith? Is this mess your fault?" the Commissioner bellowed, as the room looked at Shane.

"No Sir! I told Director Ray of the link, between Lenny Tran Vin and a terrorist group, but it was in confidence, Sir. The Americans wanted it kept secret, as part of an ongoing operation they have going at the moment!" Shane replied angrily, as all eyes went to the Director.

"That's bullshit" the Director got out before the Commissioner stopped him.

"Director Ray, I briefed you on the American group here didn't I!" the Commissioner asked.

"I thought it would be good for the Federal Police," the Director stammered out, as the Commissioner asked the others to leave, while he talked privately with the Director.

"He's fucked!" Jeff said smiling, as he entered the lunchroom, along with the members of the weapons group, who burst into laughter.

"I'd be careful if I were you," Stevenson threatened from across the room, at Jeff.

"Your boss is in big trouble Stevenson and so are you I'd say!" Jeff replied angrily, staring at Stevenson for trying to dump it on Shane and himself.

"There'll be a new boss here soon, remember that!" Stevenson smiled back, indicating it could be him. Shane was just about to jump in and tell Stevenson where to go when another agent burst into the room.

"Shane! We checked the prints of the guy you shot, with Interpol. He's in their top ten most wanted lists! They're ecstatic that someone got him, they're sending you a medal!" he laughed, as Jeff and the other agents in the room came forward, shaking Shane's hand. For several seconds, Stevenson and Morris stood in the background silently watching, before admitting defeat and leaving.

The killing of Claude Dopar or 'The Guillotine' as he was known had made Shane an instant hero. Wanted all over the world, accolades from other countries law enforcement agencies started pouring in congratulating him. They also stated how sorry they were for the loss of the two police officers, who had also been given credit for his demise. In Director Ray's office, the Commissioner sat with the director trying to figure out this mess, when the news was given to them.

"Well this changes everything!" the Commissioner smiled. "Trapping a wanted high profile criminal like the Guillotine clears up the warehouse mess. Unfortunately, the agents all heard Shane say he gave the information to you in confidence, so we've got a problem."

"I was just trying to help!" Director Ray blurted out.

"Don't worry John, you're my brother-in-law, and I promised that you'd replace me when I retire, so hold it together!" Bill, the Commissioner, replied patting his brother- in- law on the shoulder, while he thought about the situation.

"We'll move our plan forward, and you can take over the office in Canberra, as my deputy. Because of his bravery and silence, I'll elevate Shane to the head job here. That way our family maintains control at the top," Bill smiled, knowing how both John and his family members and friends, had taken up senior positions in the AFP, to protect their hold on power.

"I just hate giving this position to that little shit!" John spat out angrily.

"Don't worry; he's a 'do-gooder' who likes seeing action from his men. Sooner or later he'll stuff up, and we'll be rid of him. For now, we'll let him enjoy his success, which we'll share," the Commissioner said smiling before they both departed for Canberra.

After getting over the shock of promotion, Shane called Jeff in giving him the number two position in the Sydney office.

"I thought you'd give this position to Edward?" Jeff admitted honestly.

"This business with the Americans rules that out, and if I know the Commissioner, my stay here won't be for long."

"Well, while your boss here we might as well enjoy it!" Jeff smiled, amused by the situation.

"Talking of Edward, get everyone together, and try and find them. He was last reported heading south towards Melbourne, with the Americans and his family!"

"What's going on?" Jeff whispered secretively.

"Better you don't know," Shane replied, leaving it there.

"No problem. What do you want done with Stevenson and Morris?" Jeff asked an evil smile on his lips.

"Send them over to records department. They'll like it over there," Shane smiled, as Jeff happily left, to reorganise the staff and arrange the search for Edward.

Sitting in the director's office, Shane thought long and hard about his new job. He knew it was a setup, but he wanted deep down to give it a go.

"Well here goes nothing!" Shane laughed as he forgot his misgivings, and got down to work.

MELBOURNE AIRPORT

While Steve down the road was sleeping soundly, his family was arriving at Melbourne airport. Leaving the others in the vehicles on the second level of the car park, Edward got out looking around. Telling them to stay put, he casually walked across the overpass joining the car park to the terminal. Walking up to the ticket counter Edward asked if there were any spare seats on the flight to Adelaide. The counter girl quickly looked through the flight information, finding twenty seats still not booked.

"I'll take nine tickets thank you," Edward smiled at the surprised attendant, took down details of each passenger. Tickets booked, Edward rang Bill's phone, giving him the signal to leave the car park with the others. In groups of two and three, the group enter the terminal, going straight to the flight check-in counter. Here their bags were processed leaving them free to board.

The tricky part of travelling by plane was they couldn't carry weapons on board. Bill and Edward had decided to strip the weapons, smashing the firing pins, before discarding them. Once they were in pieces, Bill dropped them into several different garbage bins throughout the car park. To cover the others, Ian kept his, staying behind waiting till the others made it to the terminal. Seeing they'd all made it, he dropped the pistol into a mailbox near the entrance, before joining them.

Walking through the internal airport security barrier, Bill at least felt a bit safer, as no one else could enter here with a weapon either.

"Any sign of a tail?" Edward asked softly, as he walked beside Nigel.

"No nothing, I think we got away clean," Nigel whispered, as they both glanced back the way they'd come, not spotting anything out of the ordinary.

"Where are we going to Adelaide?" Louise asked, coming up beside Nigel and Edward.

"Nowhere love, we're changing flights there to Perth as soon as we land. I'm only doing this, to make sure there isn't a tail," Edward smiled, as he gave his wife a reassuring hug. Gathering the others, they quickly boarded their flight.

Back in the car park, 'The Blade' watched the group enter the domestic terminal. She'd been tailing them since they'd left Leone's guesthouse, waiting for the right time to strike. Unfortunately, they'd discovered the bug on one of the two vehicles they'd targeted, distracting her for half the night, while she'd followed the decoy. Finding she'd been tricked, she'd angrily turned around, tracking them down to a motel on the outskirts of Melbourne. Here she tried to get close, but the agents were always alert, forcing her to back off. Now she was at the airport, and if she didn't do something quickly, they would get away.

Grabbing a small carry-on bag, 'The Blade' quickly disposed of her weapon leaving them in her stolen car. Walking briskly, dressed in a short mini skirt, low cut blouse and a tight-fitting leather jacket with black boots, she appeared seductive, to say the least. Upon entering the terminal, she felt the appraisal of many men's eyes, confirming her disguise was working, as she searched for her prey. Spotting them through the crowded terminal, The Blade watched Edward's group proceed to a boarding gate showing a flight to Adelaide.

Quickly walking to the ticket counter, she tearfully told a sob story about a death in her family and needing to get to Adelaide urgently. Touched by 'The Blades' grief; the assistant arranged for her to be rushed onto the flight. Only just making it before the door closed, she thanked the flight attendant for her trouble, inwardly fuming, that her seat was located near the toilets.

"It will do," she told herself smiling, watching Robert's family and their security get comfortable, as the plane taxied out onto the runway. Sitting watching the targets, 'The Blade' felt her passions rising, at the thought of killing so many men and women. As the plane accelerated into the dark sky, The Blade tried to control the waves of exhilaration that swamped her as the thought of the kill flooded her senses. Settling down, calming herself she closed her eyes, breathing deeply. In control, she smiled to herself. 'God this is going to be good!' she said to herself giggling insanely.

Natasha sat quietly next to Patrick as the plane glided through the night skies, taking them west towards Adelaide. She knew they were heading to Perth to meet Steve, at his original home he'd shared with his wife, Michelle. Edward had explained how Steve had rebuilt his home years ago after it had been gutted in an attempt on his life. He'd always hoped to return here someday, but events overseas had ruled that out. His army buddy John had since then maintained the house in the hope his friend would return. She smiled in anticipation of meeting John again and the girl Mary, he'd adopted in Afghanistan.

She remembered how they constantly argued over anything, wondering if they had calmed down. Steve though was the main reason why she'd come and story or not, she wanted to see him again. He'd turned her world upside down, when he'd commandeered her helicopter, in Afghanistan back in the eighties. He needed it to rescue his friends, who had been injured in that hostile, dangerous land, so many years ago.

Natasha and her fellow journalist had spent several tense weeks, as uninvited guests of an Afghan tribe waiting for Steve Roberts to arrive. After he'd captured their helicopter, he and two Afghanis stayed behind as the chopper was overloaded. Against all the odds he'd made it, or her stay there could have been far different, as his promise of her crew's safety kept the Afghans from finishing them off. As a captive Natasha had seen the Afghans side of the conflict, far different than the story the Russians had peddled to her before she'd arrived there.

She still remembered the day Steve had come hobbling into the tribe's camp, dirty and blood covered, to a hero's welcome. His unit's exploits had spread throughout the countryside, but his last escapade to rescue his friends and Abdul the tribe's leader, from the Taliban, had become a legend. While in the camp, Natasha had heard much discussion of Steve's unit, sensing an undercurrent of fear that the west had such fearsome soldiers. Omar, the chief's son, smoothed these fears by pointing out that Steve's unit was the elite of the elite. Not all western soldiers would survive in this country so easily he told them.

At the celebrations for his safe return, Natasha had sat down next to him and found herself drawn to this strange man. Losing her usual control, she had openly flirted with him, sitting so close that her body heat had radiated into him. So blatant were her intentions, that he had suddenly blurted out that he was married, making her burst into laughter, mostly to cover her own embarrassment. That night, she had gone to his tent and waited for him, wanting to be with him.

Part of her had been shocked by her need for him, but as he walked towards his tent like a hunting lion, she lost control completely. Rushing into his arms, she had kissed him hungrily, thrusting her body against his, her blood boiling. She was just about to beg for this one night together; when she looked up to see his friends emerge from the darkness. Covering her mistake, she said she was just showing him what he was missing, before she walked off into the darkness, leaving him standing, bewildered with his friends.

She had never forgotten Steve and had buried the story of his unit out of love for him, moving on with her life. Now she sat in this plane as giddy as a schoolgirl thinking of finally meeting Steve again, wondering if he would remember that night as she did.

"Are you okay Natasha?" Patrick asked from beside her, bringing her back to the present.

"Of course I am why do you ask?"

"You had a strange look on your face, and you've gone red as a beetroot," Patrick explained sounding worried.

"It's nothing, must be all this travelling that's all," Natasha snapped back, sounding out of breath, as she wiped her face with a wet cloth.

"Okay, I was just worried, that's all," Patrick replied defensively.

"Thanks for your concern Patrick, but I'm really alright," Natasha smiled, as Patrick returned to his book. 'God Steve really excites me,' Natasha told herself, feeling out of control, which worried her. She was a professional reporter and had a duty to find out the truth no matter what. On the other hand, she wasn't going to lose Steve again, and this story could see him dead or behind bars.

"I'll think about it" she whispered smiling, knowing she'd already made up her mind.

Across the aisle, Leone sitting next to Bill listened to Patrick and Natasha's conversation, guessing what Natasha was thinking about, before smiling. She had felt the same way about Steve for a long time until this lump beside her had come along. Bill was no Brad Pitt, but since the night when the intruder had tried to kill him, while he was protecting them, something had happened to her. For some unknown reason, she liked having him close to her. Leone, like Natasha, had been married once, but it hadn't lasted. She'd had countless dates and boyfriends since then, but no one for a long time had made her feel safe like Bill did.

Despite his bluntness and his hardened bachelor traits, Leone could sense his loneliness and longing for female companionship. It was easy playing the tough, rugged cop all the time, with his male fellow cops, but a woman could get under those defences. Leone could see the real man, hiding behind the tough outer exterior that Bill projected.

She smiled to herself at Bill's problem, when her head had been in his lap in the car, forcing him to quickly grab a pillow from the rear. When Edward had been forced to pull over, she'd woken up and realised the problem, pretending of course that she hadn't, to stop his embarrassment. Now he dozed beside her dead tired, his head resting uncomfortably against the window. Putting her hand behind his shoulders, she pulled him towards her, letting his head rest against hers, keeping him safe for a change.

At first, he had grumbled in his sleep about being moved until his head came to rest on her soft shoulder. Sensing the security he had snuggled up to her, before entering his bone-weary sleep again.

"God you big lump, you'd better be worth it," Leone whispered wondering where this would lead.

Leone's and Bill's seats were in front of Louise and Edward. They watched silently, seeing how Leone had pulled Bill to her, giving each other a knowing smile. This was the first time they'd seen Leone take an interest in a man for a long time, and they were both glad that it was a man like Bill. Yeah, he was gruff, but he was a good cop, and they both trusted him.

"This will be interesting," Edward said softly to Louise, as they both tried not to laugh.

Across the aisle, behind Natasha and Patrick seats, sat Robin and Lindsey. They were excitedly talking about meeting their father, while Nigel, on his own, sat behind the two girls. Looking over the group of people his government had made him responsible for, Nigel admitted he'd changed his opinion of Ali's unit. He'd formed his first opinion about Ali and his team in America, and it wasn't good. He wanted them behind bars, seeing them as a rogue group of assassins, who'd killed on American soil. That to the FBI and to him was unforgivable.

His opinion had changed over time, as he watched over the Roberts' family, becoming accepted, sharing their fears. The hell they'd all been through for nearly twenty years was chiselled into their personalities. It had hardened Edward, Louise and Leone, while making Lindsey and Robin vulnerable, always seeking their father's attention from a distance. Lindsey had feelings for him, a blind man could see it, but Nigel pretended indifference. He knew he couldn't do his job correctly while at the same time dating Lindsey.

Unfortunately, it had backfired as the more he ignored her, the more she found him a challenge. As if sensing his thoughts, Lindsey turned around in her seat giving him one of her winning smiles, before turning back to her sister.

"God, you're beautiful!' Nigel said out loud, without realising it, as both Robin and Lindsey spun around, looking at him suspiciously.

"Did you say something?" Lindsey asked softly, her eyes sparkling with excitement.

"No, just talking to myself," Nigel stammered out, going slightly red as the two sisters watched his face closely, before turning around. Nigel sat there guiltily, breathing a sigh of relief that his blunder hadn't been heard clearly, as, in the seat in front, Robin gave her sister a raised eyebrow. This was confirmation that Lindsey's plan was working, which caused them both to started giggling. Edward looked back towards his two nieces and saw them both giggling, as behind them Nigel's face went crimson.

"Poor bastard doesn't have a chance!' Edward whispered to his wife smiling, as Louise turned, seeing what was going on, smiled as well.

Allan who also had heard the exchange between Nigel and Lindsey smiled, wishing his boss good luck. He had also prayed that one of the girls would be drawn to him, but that hadn't happened he told himself with a smile. He'd been sitting with Ian opposite Nigel for most of the flight. Ian's snoring had made him move back to an empty row of seats behind them. A hand touching Allan's shoulder interrupted his thoughts. Looking up he saw a stunning woman of about thirty, standing beside him.

"Do you mind if I sit here, my seats a little too close to the toilets?" The woman asked merrily, her eyes sparkling watching him.

"No, not at all," Allan replied happily, thanking God that Ian had snored, forcing him to move. Squeezing past Allan to sit in the window seat, Allan stared at her athletic firm body.

"My name's Morgan," the woman smiled as she made herself comfortable, removing her jacket, showing an impressive pair of breasts, just held in check by one straining button.

"My name is Allan," he stammered out, trying not to stare at her breasts, as she smiled back seductively as if she knew what he was thinking.

"What brings an American to Adelaide?" Morgan asked pleasantly, her beautiful elfin features watching him, her eyes tempting him.

"Business trip, I'm here with some of my law firm's partners, and our Australian representative's family," Allan replied swiftly, as this was the cover story Nigel had suggested.

"Well, I'm glad you came. You can keep me company on this flight," Morgan suggested seductively as she made herself comfortable.

Landing at Adelaide, the group quickly booked another flight for Perth. This left in an hour time, giving them only enough time for a quick bite to eat before they boarded their second flight. 'The Blade' or Morgan, stood near the entrance to the boarding area, talking to Allan. A hand signal from Nigel to rejoin the group, made Allan say his goodbyes, after first getting her phone number. Morgan leaning forward kissed Allan seductively on the lips, biting him softly, before smiling and waving goodbye. Inwardly she cursed angrily.

There was no way of getting on the second flight without being spotted, so after seeing the group purchase the tickets to Perth, Morgan decided on taking a later flight. There was only one place the group could be headed for Morgan mused, and that was to meet Roberts, at his home.

That's where 'The Blade' would finally terminate him, along with as many of his family members as possible.

After Steve got off the phone with Ali, he quickly dialled Edward's number.

"Is that you Steve?" Edward asked groggily, sounding as if he just woken up.

"Yes it's me, I'm in Melbourne, where are you?"

"We're on our way to your home on the coast, via Adelaide," Edward replied yawning before continuing. "We found a bug on one of the vehicles. We dumped them at the airport, before taking a last minute flight to Adelaide, where we changed for Perth.

"Are you sure that's a good idea?"

"We checked for tails Steve, no one is following," Edward reassured him. The problem Steve realised was Edward didn't know about the manuals photo's from Ballina. Explaining the photo's indicating the hitman knew John's identity, and he was a target, brought Edward fully awake.

"Shit Steve I didn't know!" Edward whispered seeing Louise stir beside him.

"It's not your fault Edward. Anyway, this might work in our favour. Don't go there, go south maybe to Margaret River, do some wine tasting. I'll meet you at my house in seven days time. For now, keep out of sight. I'll contact you in a few days."

"Okay Steve, but the girls are going to go crazy!' Edward replied before saying goodbye and hanging up.

Steve, after the call, sat thinking about what to do. There was a good chance these killers knew his family might go to Steve's house in Western Australia. 'They might even have the place under surveillance' he thought, as he came to a decision. Picking up his phone again, he dialled a number he hadn't rung in nearly twenty years, wishing he didn't have to.

"Hello who is it?" asked a friendly young female voice.

"Is John there thanks, it's Steve?"

"My father is not here at the moment, can I help you?" the voice said pleasantly not recognising the name.

"My God, is that you Mary?" Steve heard an intake of breath.

"Ghost! You're still alive!" Mary screamed, into the phone.

"Yes I am Mary, but someone's still after me. Where's John?" Steve asked, close to breaking at hearing one of his friend's voices.

Mary explained that John and his wife Joan were overseas on a cruise in Canada. She was here minding their home while they were gone. Steve at this stage cut her off, telling her what was happening and that the assassins could be heading there or worst, were there already.

"I'll have my husband look around Steve, but I haven't noticed anything," Mary replied her voice sounding slightly alarmed, as Steve suddenly took in what she said.

"You've married Mary that's fantastic, but these guys are dangerous Mary. Can your husband look after himself?"

"He's seen some action Steve, and he controls me, that should tell you something," Mary giggled making Steve smile.

"I'll be there tomorrow night Mary. I'll come in from the beach in the dark, Okay."

"We'll be waiting for you," Mary replied happily.

Sitting there Steve wondered what type of guy Mary would marry. She'd been a tough Mujahidin fighter in Afghanistan, battling the Russians. Then in Australia, she and her father had gunned down several men trying to kill him. On top of all that she was a devoted Muslim. It made whoever she'd married a brave son of a bitch, he thought. With a smile on his lips, Steve booked a flight the next morning for Perth, trying to get some more sleep, before leaving for his home.

THE STAKEOUT

Arriving in Perth, 'The Blade,' seeing no sign of Roberts' group, hired a car and made a phone call. Two men had come to Australia with her from their group in England. One was dead in Ballina by his own stupidity, the other was here in Western Australia, watching Roberts' house. Dialling his cell number 'The Blade,' waited for six rings before the phone was answered.

"Hussein, it is me, is anything happening?" The Blade asked bluntly keeping the call as short as possible.

"All is quiet at the address, even next door only the daughter and her husband are home."

"I am two hours away, a group should be arriving soon, be watchful!"

"I know my job Blade, remember that!" Hussein replied angrily before hanging up, causing the Blade to smile. 'Men are so touchy about taking orders from a woman, especially Islamic men' she thought, chuckling to herself.

It had been her one major drawback in her successful career, having to remain subservient to her male leaders. Right from her first day of training in Libya she learnt the hard way how contemptuous her male trainers were, at being forced to train a woman. Arriving at the camp, she'd been asked to parade in front of the Camp Drill Instructor along with forty other recruits. The Drill Instructor had flown into a rage taking her admission to his camp as an insult to himself personally.

Walking up and down the line of recruits he spat at her feet, calling her a slut, explaining that her only use here was to be the camp whore. He openly told the others that anyone finishing behind her in any class would be considered less than a man, before storming off. All eyes had turned on her, their anger at her presence plain to see, their silent voices urging her to leave. Through all this, she stood there unfazed yawning as if bored by the Drill Instructors speech.

"Have you no respect for our Drill Instructor?" an Officer barked from the far end of the parade ground, making the Instructor stop and turn to face her.

"Oh is he the Drill Instructor here? I thought you hired a clown," Morgan replied, smiling. The parade ground grew instantly quiet as the Instructor fought for control, his men watching his reaction to the woman's insult.

"You need a lesson in manners whore?" drawing a small riding whip from his belt, the Drill instructor advanced on a silent Morgan. Ripping her shirt from her back, he struck her across her shoulder blades, making her cry out in pain.

"Please don't hurt me?" Morgan screamed sobbing loudly, as she fell to her knees, crawling to the Instructors feet. Looking down, the Drill instructor stared at her naked breast, liking what he saw, as she climbed to her feet crying hysterically. Most of the men watching were either smiling or openly laughing at Morgan's humiliation, as the Drill instructor grabbed her by the hair turning her around in a circle showing her off. Looking at the men's reaction the instructor smiled raising his free hand in the air at his victory, his prisoner forgotten.

It was what Morgan had planned, as while he was distracted, she sprang backwards crashing the back of her head into the instructor's face. Concussed by her headbutt, the instructor dazed, let go of her hair, staggering backwards. Morgan now her arms free thrust her knife deep into the surprised Instructor's left eye, killing him instantly.

"I told you that you're a clown," Morgan giggled. As the recruits and trainers looked on in absolute horror, Morgan moaned in ecstasy, pulling her knife from his eye letting his body fall.

"What have you done?" One of the instructors shouted. Drawing his pistol, he pointed it at Morgan.

"Lower your gun Sergeant!" the same Officer ordered, walking across to stand in front of Morgan. "Well done recruit. Now cover yourself," He smiled turning to the others.

"Remember this day well men, burn it into your minds, once you leave here, everyone is a possible enemy! From a battle-hardened soldier fighting beside you to a pretty half-naked girl, it could be anyone. Our enemies will do anything to stop us nothing is beneath them. This man in his arrogance forgot that; don't let it happen to you," he shouted before leaving, giving Morgan a well-done nod.

After that day no one doubted Morgan's commitment or ability again. Finishing first in the group she went back to England, her reputation preceding her as a cold-blooded killer.

Appling her makeup carefully before driving off, she drove sedately away from the airport, heading for the Roberts home. Arriving at their stakeout location, the Blade walked to their unit tapping three times, before Hussein opened the door.

"Anything?"

"No nothing!" Hussein answered angrily, still smarting from her talking down to him.

"I need some sleep, wake me in the morning. I'll relieve you then, so you can rest," the Blade said pleasantly before retiring to the second bedroom. Morgan smiled as she closed the door on Hussein. She had once been asked by Hussein to marry him but had turned him down. He was a devout Muslim and would have treated her well, but her past made marrying any man much too dangerous.

When she was only ten years old, her mother left her husband taking Morgan with her. Her father was a Pakistani doctor working in England, and her mother had been his receptionist. They'd married after dating for a short time, her husband insisting, she convert to Islam. She had readily agreed, but after the birth of Morgan, she grew tired of strict Muslim customs.

Leaving him, she soon started dating a long line of men friends, drinking heavily. With her looks failing, her male friends soon turned their attention to the beautiful young daughter living with her. At the age of thirteen, she was awoken one night, by a hand being placed over her mouth. The drunken boyfriend stripped and raped her, while her mother lay passed out down the hallway. It continued on and off, for the next five years, as a long line of boyfriends abused her, while her mother pretended to know nothing. On her eighteenth birthday, after a visit by her mother's latest boyfriend, she'd had enough.

Hopping on top of her naked visitor, she'd driven him crazy, pretending to enjoy his lovemaking. Reaching under her mattress, she swiftly pulled out an old hunting knife, before ramming it into his right eye, killing him instantly. Excitedly she looked down at the now dead man, feeling more alive than she'd thought possible. She had her first orgasm, screaming with exquisite pleasure. Dressing she packed her bags, hiding them in the alley behind their home. Going back into the house, she went to mother's room and killed her the same way. She didn't this time feel the rush she'd got by killing the boyfriend, but it still felt good.

Smiling, feeling free, Morgan rushed to the kitchen, turning on the gas oven jets to full. Taking several deep breaths to calm herself down, she walked to the front door. Lighting a small candle, she placed it inside, before closing the door.

Checking the street, seeing no one around, Morgan casually walked down to the corner pub. There she sat quietly, watching a football match with a group of locals. Twenty minutes passed when an explosion rattled the pub, followed by the sound of glass smashing. In a panic the pub's patrons ran outside to see what had occurred. Standing there frozen by what she saw, Morgan gave the impression of a distraught daughter in shock, watching her mother's house burn. The fire took four hours to extinguish, leaving nothing except the outer brick walls.

The police having heard from the locals, that Morgan lived with her mother in the house, took her back to the station. There they tried to find a relation to take care of her. It was an open and shut investigation put down to being drunk and leaving the gas on. As Morgan was seen at the pub before the fire, no one even bothered to question her.

Worried for her safety the police tracked down her father, who rushed over picking her up. Once they'd left the station, Morgan had her father stop while she picked up her belongings, before heading to his home in London. Not once did he ask about the clothing, or how it managed to be outside before the fire. He had his suspicions about Morgan's treatment for some time, but not any supporting evidence for the authorities to investigate. That he believed she might have killed her mother didn't worry him at all, as long as she was with him.

Emil, Morgan's father, belonged to a local Mosque in London, where his moderate political stance had made many close friends. Taking Morgan along the week after he'd picked her up, he asked could his daughter be counselled. The female members of the mosque had taken her under their wing; delving into her past, they had discovered her mistreatment.

Emil had wept when he found out what his daughter had been through, even though she had not told them of her revenge. In the safety of the mosque, where woman were protected, and modesty of unmarried women was paramount, Morgan finally found sanctuary. Here she could hide from her deep depression at being violated, while her mother had done nothing. After talking to her father, explaining all that had happened; she converted to Islam, with her father's blessing. Covering her face, hiding behind the rigid law of her new religion, Morgan felt at peace, even though her dreams reminded her of the pleasure of killing. The rush she'd had felt was all consuming, and like an addict, she knew she needed another hit.

When the split between the mainstream Mosque and the British Freedom Brigade happened, Morgan decided to go with the more radical group, hoping for a way to release the frustration she felt. It would be one year before their leader discovered a purpose for Morgan, making her 'The Blade'. It occurred when Ahmed, the leader of their split away movement, became aware that his group had a spy in their mists. After several members had been arrested, when trying to smuggle explosives into England, Brennan, Ahmed's second in command, smelled a rat.

One night at a small gathering of Ahmed's most trusted men, at which Morgan was serving refreshments, the matter was discussed. Brennan knew of only one man outside this group, who had knowledge of the explosives. Alit had converted to Islam after being in England for four years. He had proven resourceful, and being a medical student at a London hospital, could arrange for drugs and medical treatment for Ahmed men when it was necessary. At first, Ahmed was unconvinced that the mole was Alit, but Brennan was certain.

"Can you prove it?" Ahmed asked softly, knowing Brennan wouldn't have accused him without having some proof.

"When he left the meeting last night, I followed him. On his way home I noticed he talked to himself a lot. My first thought was that he was praying, but as he passed a trash bin, he tossed something in. I was about to check the bin when a car pulled up, and two men got out. They retrieved something from the bin then left. I believe it was some sort of cassette!" Brennan growled his loathing clear to see. Morgan looked around the room seeing anger and fear written on all the men's faces, as they realised the danger they were in.

"You are right my brother, but next time tell me what you are doing," Ahmed suggested, not happy with Brennan following Alit, on his own.

"How do we handle this situation, without bringing his handlers down on us?" One of Ahmed's men asked not wanting more trouble with the police.

Many ideas were suggested, all agreeing it should look an accident, but how could they get close when he knew them all?

"He doesn't know what I look like!" Morgan put forward, causing all the men to turn, some angrily towards the woman who had spoken out of place.

"You are not here to speak," Several of Ahmed's men answered angrily.

"Wait!" Brennan shouted stopping any further argument. "Let's hear what she has to say," he continued getting a nod of support from Ahmed.

"It's just he's never seen me without a veil on and dressed as a westerner I could get close, even lure him into an alley where I could make it look like a robbery," Morgan's eyes were shining with excitement.

"It is not becoming for a woman to do this," Ahmed said sounding confused.

"Why not, I want England to be a Muslim state like everyone here. Surely women must martyr themselves as well." The room lapsed into silence, as the men there considered her statement. Excusing the others, Ahmed asked Brennan and Morgan to remain.

"Killing is not to be taken lightly, Morgan. Do you think you can kill?" Brennan asked softly. At this point, Morgan told them of her life with her mother and in the end what she had to do to escape. Both Ahmed and Brennan were appalled at her treatment and a little shocked at her way of ending it, but all doubts of her ability to carry out the job ended there.

"Okay Morgan you can go ahead with the assignment, and if you're successful we may find other uses for your talents," Ahmed said his voice still sounding unsure.

"I will not fail," Morgan replied leaving the two men to plan the operation.

"What do you think Brennan?"

"I know it is against many of our teachings Ahmed, but on the other hand, would you suspect a woman of being an Islamic warrior," Brennan smiled.

"No, she'd be the last one I'd suspect. Maybe we're onto something here my brother," Ahmed replied thinking of his grand vision.

"One thing worries me though," Brennan confessed before continuing "She seems somehow unbalanced?"

"Yes my brother, I think she could be damaged by her childhood nightmares. Let's see how she carries out this assignment before we make a final decision on using her again," Ahmed answered softly, secretly not caring, knowing there would be many martyrs for the cause ahead.

Alit proved all too easy Morgan thought smiling. She had waited near the tube station where Alit boarded for his trip home from the hospital. As Alit entered a train carriage, Morgan followed him sitting opposite. Almost immediately Alit's eyes were drawn to her long legs, which were extenuated by a short dress half way up her thigh. Catching him looking Morgan had given him a seductive smile, her eyes shining drawing him closer.

Getting up, Alit moved across to her seat, engaging her in friendly conversation. Impressing her by talking about his career, and his bright future, Alit laid on all his charm, as Morgan sat smiling, appearing to hang off his every word.

Bending over to adjust her skirt that had ridden up showing her black underwear, Alit's heart nearly missed a beat, as her breast surged forward, as she knowingly smiled. Resting her hand on his thigh to support her as she stood, she asked if he would walk her home to her apartment, as it was quite late. Looking up and seeing it was his station anyway, he gladly accepted.

The station was nearly deserted when they left the train. Walking beside her Alit could hardly keep his excitement under control, as he watched her hips sway from side to side occasionally brushing his causing his excitement to mount. Stopping opposite the entrance to an alley, Alit turned her towards him kissing her hungrily on the lips. At first, she tried to protest saying no not here. But as their passions grew she suggested moving into the alley entrance.

Ripping at her clothes he pulled her blouse open rubbing his face in her breasts overwhelmed with passion. Looking up to see her reaction, he saw a silver flash of light race towards his right eye, ending his life. Blood covered her arms and the front of her dress, as

Morgan moaning with pleasure, looked down at her fresh kill. Opening her bag, she quickly changed her clothes putting the blood covered ones in the same bag. Adjusting her new clothes, she made sure all the blood was removed, before stripping Alit of his watch and wallet. Making sure he had no other valuables, she continued down the alley, coming out in an adjoining street where she'd left her car. Driving away her body covered with sweat, Morgan smiled, knowing she'd found her perfect career.

Assassination became her speciality, and they had trained her well. No one could get as close to a target as a woman could, her instructors had told her. Through experience, she found men were easily deceived by a pretty face or a good body, something she luckily possessed. With the hard-line Islamist wanting women kept at home, Morgan's looks and way of dressing, made her invisible to her enemies. Western countries who were on constant watch for terrorists took hardly any notice of a young woman travelling.

The main thing was, she got the job done, and that had earned her the nickname of 'The Blade'. As the English Freedom Brigade grew in size, 'The Blade' was freelanced to different agencies, like the CIA, earning much-needed money for the group and their vision. This assignment to get Roberts had proved her toughest by far.

Working outside of Europe was one thing. Trying to track down people, who didn't want to be found, was driving her crazy. Near impossible or not, she knew her group needed the ten million, plus the bonus for something big and Allah willing, it would soon be theirs. Changing out of her clothes, she glanced at an up to date photo of Roberts, taken at Ballina by some reporter there. She saw a man in his fifties still good looking and fit.

Other than that, he meant nothing to her, just another stepping-stone, to achieve their group's goal. Still, terminating an adversary as professional as Roberts, gave her a high, as she lay down for a much needed night's sleep.

"Your time has come my friend," the Blade whispered confidently as she closed her eyes, thinking of the coming kill.

After hiring a small car, Steve drove cautiously towards his home. He hadn't been back here since his wife had died, not even to see the home he'd had rebuilt, nearly twenty years ago. His street was still the same; his house was at the point overlooking the beach, while John's was up the road about two hundred metres. He'd bought the other blocks in the street secretly, to keep it the same. On the other side of John's home, houses and units stretch for kilometres taking in the ocean views.

'They could be anywhere' Steve thought watching the surrounding homes as darkness settled slowly over the coast. Driving down to his house, he quickly looked over his once happy home remembering the good times he had there. Driving back down the road for a couple of kilometres, he parked his car, in the car park of a block of sandstone coloured units.

Swiftly changing into dark clothing, he left the rest of his belongings in the vehicle.

Walking down onto the beach, Steve silently jogged towards his home. After a quick recon of his own house, Steve carefully approached his neighbour's house from the beach side. Ghosting through the small growth of scrub growing on the dunes, Steve came at last to his John's back door. Here he hesitated, wondering how to warn Mary's husband he was here, without scaring him. The touch of the cold metal barrel of a pistol to the back of his head told him that it wouldn't be necessary.

"There was a time Captain Roberts when doing this would have been impossible?" a familiar voice whispered in his ear, pushing him towards the door, which swung open. Turning slowly around, Steve tried to work out where he'd heard that voice before when two arms enfolded him hugging him in the semi-dark.

"Steve, it's really you!" Mary laughed excitedly, as her mystery husband closed the door, turning the light on.

"My God, it's you, Omar!" Steve replied shocked, that the son of a tribal leader in Afghanistan could be here, let alone married to Mary.

"It's a long story Captain Roberts, I mean Steve," Omar replied smiling, before hugging Steve as well.

"I'm not going anywhere at the moment," Steve replied, as Mary turned on a small light in the kitchen. Closing the curtains, to cut down on light, the three of them sat down for good talk.

Mary had returned to Afghanistan three years ago to find out what had happened to her tribe. After years of fighting the Russians and then the Taliban, Abdul, Omar's father and leader of the tribe had joined with a much larger tribe to survive the continuous attacks. Abdul's death five years ago had hit the tribe hard and Omar seeing unity was needed, handed over leadership to a larger tribe that was supporting them. He then took over the defence of the area against the Taliban.

Upon her arrival, Mary found Omar badly wounded and demoralised, after a life of constant fighting. Nursing him back to health, the two found mutual support in each other, leading over time to love. A year later, Mary's adopted father John and his wife Joan turned up looking for Mary, as she'd been gone for a longer than expected. John had received a hero's welcome for his part in rescuing Omar's father so many years before; it was still well known amongst the Afghan tribesmen.

Knowing she couldn't stay Mary broached the subject of Omar returning to Australia with her. Omar, who at first rejected the idea of leaving his people, became conflicted, wanting to both be with Mary and stay with his people. Discussing it with his men on patrol one night, Omar found his men wanted him to go. 'You need to find peace' they told him forcefully, knowing no man could fight all his adult lifetime. Surprised by their reaction, Omar had gone to John, Mary's father and asked him, why they wanted him gone.

"If you can find peace Omar, then one day so can they too. They want you to be happy my friend. Look in the mirror my friend, and see what they see," John suggested softly, patting Omar on the shoulder, leaving him to think. Going to a nearby stream, Omar stared at his reflection, seeing a face far removed from the laughing young man he once had been. His face had hardened from years of combat, capped off with the scar running down the side of his cheek, where he stupidly had got too close to an exploding Russian gunship.

"No wonder they are worried!" Omar said to himself smiling. Looking again at his reflection, he saw his face soften with a smile, and he knew at that moment what was missing. Going straight to Mary he had asked her to marry him, before going to her parents to ask their approval. He was ten years older than Mary, but he loved her, and that was enough for John and Joan.

The whole tribe gathered for their wedding, the chieftain of the tribe wishing them eternal happiness, assuring them they were always welcome. Omar still remembered the time of his leaving. The tribe lined the road as John drove, Omar, hanging out the window tears in his eyes waving madly like a child. It was only on the road further south after his village had disappeared over a rugged mountain peak that Omar felt a weight lift from his chest, knowing the burden of responsibility for others had gone. Breathing deeply he gulped in mouthfuls of air, hugging Mary and for the first time in a long time he laughed.

Arriving in Australia to Omar was like walking on the moon. People walked around talking freely, not fearing snipers or artillery. Everything was green; the houses looked fresh with no signs of battle damage. At John's house where they stayed at first, no one had to stand guard while they all slept peacefully, without the fear of attack. It took him months to get used to this, while Mary brought him up to speed with his English, both in speaking and writing.

Finding a job for a chieftain's son, whose occupation was guerrilla warfare wasn't easy. He, in the end, got a job as a linguist, translating for the governments in the foreign affairs department. There he helped new immigrants like himself settle into Australian culture, something he found immensely satisfying.

For a while, he and Mary had lived in Steve's house needing their space from John and Joan. Now they lived in their own townhouse halfway between here and Perth. So when John and Joan travelled overseas, they agreed to babysit their home, till they returned.

"That's quite a story. I'm glad for you both," Steve said softly seeing the love these two shared, making him slightly envious.

"What is your story, Steve?" Omar asked neutrally, though Steve saw in his eyes the unasked question. 'Are you a danger to my family?'

Steve left nothing out, owing these people the truth. An hour later, when he had finished, he wasn't the only one with tears in his eyes.

"And you think they will try for you here?" Omar asked softly, not knowing if he could live without Mary if someone killed her.

"I would!" Steve answered coldly, as the three of them sat in silence.

"Then we have to give them something to go after, don't we?" Omar suggested smiling, as the sun outside started to rise from the sea.

Hussein was tired and frustrated, as he watched the house. Nothing had happened for over two months, it had become totally boring. The frustrating part came with Morgan being so close. She was his superior now, but he still found her desirable, and he wanted her.

"Who am I kidding!" he whispered to himself, going back to his assignment of watching Roberts' house. Quickly looking through his binoculars, he ran his eyes swiftly over the entire property, even noticing flaws in the paintwork, where a slight difference in colours could be seen in the paint near the front veranda. 'Must have run out of paint, just before they finished?' Hussein said to himself, as moving on, he saw the slightly opened front door. His heart nearly missed a beat, when looking closer he saw an outline of a person moving freely about the house.

"Morgan, come quickly he's here!" Hussein excitedly yelled, banging twice on her door, before returning to his binoculars to keep watch. Running into the lounge room beside him, Morgan grabbed the binoculars from him, focusing on the house and recognising Roberts from her photo.

"We got him, Hussein!" Morgan laughed excitedly, turning to see Hussein staring hungrily at her. In her hurry to see Roberts, she had come from her room naked, as she slept. Both assassins looked silently at each other, drinking in the moment.

"No Hussein, I forbid it!" Morgan ordered, trying to stop him.

"You come naked before me to tease me, now you will satisfy me," Hussein demanded reaching forward. Pulling her to him and kissing her savagely on the lips, she tried half-heartedly to push him away. The excitement of the morning's events and the thought of the coming kill had sexual charged Morgan. She gave up fighting, raking him with her fingernails, as they both crashed onto lounge room floor. Pinning her there, Hussein brutally entered her, screaming with unbridled lust as he took what he needed, enjoying every moment of his conquest.

For her part, Morgan let him enjoy the moment of domination, knowing what would follow. When Hussein had fully satisfied his lust, he fell asleep snoring loudly. Careful not to wake him, Morgan lifted Hussein's leg, sliding out from underneath him, as she again checked Roberts' house. She saw no sign of Roberts, but the windows were now open, and the front veranda door stood ajar. Looking back at Hussein, Morgan, 'The Blade,' felt a touch of guilt over making love to Hussein. She had enjoyed it to a certain degree, but it was not the high she was looking for.

Crossing the room going into Hussein's bedroom, she returned with his pistol. Fitting the silencer, she approached her sleeping lover. Placing the pistol just out of reach of Hussein she went to the kitchen returning with a carving knife. Shivering with excitement, she thrust the knife into his right eye, as she screamed and moan, as multiple orgasms ripped through her. Weak at the knees, she slowly stood throwing a rug over his body. Thinking of the next kill, Hussein forgotten, she went into her room showering, before changing into a brief two-piece bikini.

Emptying the contents of her bag, she placed the pistol and knife inside, covering them with a towel. Looking at herself in the mirror she examined her body making sure she looked desirable. Finished, she walked out the door, trying to control the rising hunger, as she thought of the coming kill.

THE SETUP

Steve sat in his bedroom deep in thought, remembering the happy days he spent here with Michelle and his two daughters. The place had been completely rebuilt, a perfect copy of the original house. A sudden beeping from his phone disturbed his thoughts, as he pressed the call button hearing Mary's voice.

"No sign of any threats yet Steve," Mary informed him, as both she and Omar watched the surrounding area hidden from view inside John's house.

"They might not even be here, but we'll give them today and tonight to see if they try anything," Steve answered; feeling exposed sitting in his own home. Omar's plan was simple, use Steve as bait, while Mary and Omar neutralised any threat.

After spending the whole morning wandering around his house, Steve decided to go for a jog. Ringing Mary and telling her his plan, Steve changed into a pair of shorts and t-shirt, and moved out onto the front veranda, to have a look around. Being cautious, he picked up a pair of binoculars and quickly scanned the beach. It was deserted except for a young woman lying topless on her back, getting a tan. She was very attractive with an athletic build Steve noticed, as he adjusted the glasses bringing her into focus.

"I'll definitely jog by her later!" Steve said to himself smiling, as he started off, signalling to Mary his intentions.

Across at John's house, Omar too was studying the young woman on the beach. She was impressive he thought, but rather white to be out in the full sun.

"Enjoying the view?" Mary asked from behind Omar, making him look at anything else, but the girl.

"Don't be jealous," Omar replied smiling, as he turned back to the beach. Steve, in the meantime, angled away from his house heading north away from his and John's homes, also bypassing the girl who was opposite John's place. Mary and Omar had both picked up binoculars, and both followed his progress, as his silhouette grew smaller. On the beach, the young girl also followed his progress, as she rose from the sand and started walking in the same direction. Omar was fascinated by this woman, who boldly stood up walking along the beach topless, before casually putting on her bikini top.

"That's strange?" Omar said out loud.

"What's strange?" Mary asked looking for trouble and seeing nothing.

"The girl on the beach, she has left her towel, but has taken her bag," Omar replied his eyes following the hypnotic flow of the girl's body as she walked north. Mary was just about to give Omar a serve for concentrating too much on the woman when she took in what Omar had said. Watching the girl closely Mary notice now the woman held her bag over her shoulder, but her right hand was in the bag. Looking north Mary saw Steve turn to start back, realising now he would pass right by the girl.

Grabbing John's hunting rifle from the kitchen bench, Mary opened the bipod legs steadying the weapon on the bench, facing out the window, as she looked again at the woman this time through the powerful scope on the rifle.

"What are you doing Mary?" Omar asked, as his wife followed the woman's progress.

"She's got her hand on something in that bag."

"It could be anything love," Omar replied fearfully, an edge to his voice, thinking of the consequences if she shot the wrong person.

"Let's find out shall we!" Mary answered distantly as she held her breath releasing it slowly before she pulled the trigger. It was a spoiling shot, aimed to miss, landing just in front of the woman, raising a pillar of sand into the air. An ordinary person would have been startled or frightened to be shot at. This girl, on the other hand, somersaulted, doing a commando roll, coming up with a pistol in her hand.

Steve still one hundred metres further up the beach dived to the ground as well, upon hearing the shot. Looking up he saw the young woman holding a weapon, trying to locate the shooter, before turning her attention to Steve. 'The Blade' dropping to one knee, took up a shooting stance, before opening up on Steve. Diving again to the ground, Steve rolled several times before getting up and zigzagging up the beach towards the dunes. He was just entering a grassed area when a sickening slap to his left leg sent him sprawling onto his back.

"Shit, now I'm in trouble!" Steve groaned, as he slowly turned over, and crawled further into the dune scrub.

Morgan too had her problems. As she raced after Steve, she felt the whip of two more bullets pass by her, as the unknown sniper tried to finish her off. The first shot had taken her by surprise, making her react as she had been trained to, giving away her profession. Not being able to locate the shooter, she quickly changed focus going back to Roberts. He had gone to ground with the rifle shot, giving her a chance to line him up, as he came to his feet and started running. Unfortunately, the distance was too great for a pistol, and she'd only managed to tag him with the sixth shot. Now it was her turn to run and dodge, as Roberts' friend fired at her.

As the woman disappeared into the dunes, Mary chastised herself for missing. When she had discovered the woman's true purpose for being on the beach, she had reloaded for a second shot only to have the mechanism jam. Clearing it, she had reloaded firing twice more, and missing, as the woman ran for cover.

"Can you see her?" Mary screamed in frustration, as Omar tried with his binoculars to spot her.

"No, she's gone, my love. It's up to Steve now," Omar conceded, as they both watched the sand dunes.

"I hope he's okay Omar. Do you think we should go look for them?" Mary murmured sounding unsure.

"It's too dangerous. Either of them could target us in the scrub. Better to wait here, sooner or later one of them will come for us," Omar admitted picking up Mary's assault rifle, wondering who it would be.

In pain Steve ripped his shirt into strips, applying a tight bandage over the wound. Luckily it had gone straight through without hitting something vital, or loss of blood would have killed him long before the assassin found him.

"A beautiful half-naked young woman, shit I can't believe it!" Steve muttered to himself, as he noiselessly crawled deeper into the thick undergrowth, stopping every now and then to listen. Coming to a halt in a thick patch of scrub, he buried himself in the loose sand, leaving only his torso showing. He still retained the ability to spring forward, while cutting down on his silhouette. It was a good spot Steve surmised, visibility was near zero, only a couple of metres at the most, but without a weapon, it was the only way he could get close.

Whoever she was, she was good Steve thought as he weighed up the situation. To hit a moving target at that distance with a pistol was impressive. The big test was how she'd react now when she had to get in close for a kill. Lying motionless sensing movement behind him, another thought came to him, 'Can I kill a young woman'. Steve was no stranger to killing, though he'd always drawn the line at hurting innocent bystanders, especially woman and children. Steve knew this young woman was no saint, but she was still a woman, and Steve knew he couldn't do it.

"But she doesn't know that, does she!" he smiled, as branches to his right moved.

Morgan, on the other hand, had no problem with killing Steve, or for that matter whoever was shooting at her. Walking with her gun held two-handed straight out in front; she slowly worked her way north, checking each section of undergrowth. She knew he was hit, how bad was the question. Either way, he wasn't going anywhere and more importantly he didn't have a gun. The thought of him hiding waiting for her, thrilled her as she stopped, feeling her arousal growing with the coming kill. Calming down, controlling herself she moved forward.

Just inside the dunes, she found what she was looking for, a crawl mark, dotted with blood. It ended in a pool of blood, where Roberts had obviously patched up his wound. Getting down on her belly, she slowly crawled forward, following Steve's drag marks, closing in on her prey's position, licking her lips excitedly.

Twenty minutes of creeping forward brought Morgan, 'The Blade' to an opening in the scrub where a track ran through it, from the beach to a car park. The drag mark left by Steve crawling went straight across, disappearing into a thick patch of scrub on the opposite side. Morgan froze, studying the track, as a small smile appeared on her lips. 'He's waiting across there somewhere, hoping to ambush me,' Morgan smiled, as adrenalin surged through her body preparing her.

This was the reason why she had taken up her career as an assassin. She loved the kill, it drove her wild to have the power of life and death in her hands, and like a druggie hooked on heroin, she needed it a hit now. Pointing her weapon across the clearing, she fired a full clip, into the scrub opposite, spreading the shots out roughly an arm's length between each shot.

Rising slowly from the ground, her breathing coming in short excited breaths she slowly moved forward, loading a fresh magazine, into her weapon. As she cleared her side of the track, two hands rose from under the sand tripping her forward, making her let go of her pistol to stop her fall. Not stopping to think how stupid she was for being fooled, Morgan kicked out backwards, catching Steve in the face spinning him backwards. Scrambling for her pistol, Morgan turned to fire when a dust storm of sand hit her in the eyes, blinding her.

Steve had been shocked by her reaction to the trip, expecting her to try for her gun first. Dazed after her kick, he had seen her moving forward grabbing for the pistol. Having no weapon except sand, Steve had used it, throwing it forward straight into her eyes, as she turned to fire. Amazingly she still opened up, firing wildly in Steve's general direction.

"Good trick, I underestimated you!" Morgan spat out trying desperately to clear her vision. Morgan knew she was in trouble and that was why she had spoken, hoping he'd give some return abuse. This would give his position away allowing her to fire, at the sound. There was no voice or noise of any type, as she stood there waiting for the minutest sound to give Roberts position away.

Morgan yelped as her right arm holding her pistol was hit by a well-aimed chop. Standing there for the first time in her life feeling afraid, Morgan had her legs knocked from under her, as Roberts came forward picking up her weapon. Knowing her life might at any time be over, she casually wiped the sand from her eyes, to see her executioner. She was surprised to see her target sitting opposite her, checking his wound, appearing unconcerned with her. Readying herself to spring forward, in one final attempt to kill him, she saw her gun suddenly snap forward in his hand, pointing right at her.

"Don't be stupid my dear! I have been doing this for a long time!" Steve told her, his eyes unblinking, staring at her.

"Congratulations, I thought you'd be waiting on the other side of the track. What are you going to do with your prize now?" Morgan answered softly, watching him, stretching her arm making her breast strain against her small bikini top.

"I bet you're a handful my dear, but I'll pass. Now get up and head down to the beach!" Steve ordered, keeping his eyes on her constantly.

"Can I fix my hand first?" she asked softly, smiling seductively.

"Go ahead," Steve replied his eyes cold as stone. To Steve's surprise, she pulled off her bikini top supporting her arm with it around her neck.

"I'm ready now," she purred seeing his eyes drawn to her breasts.

"Would you like to touch them, or maybe tie me up and have some fun?" She giggled, her free hand tracing her body.

"Start walking now!" Steve growled pointing to the beach.

"Maybe when we get back to your place, you'll change your mind?" She laughed doing as she was told.

Walking in front of him up the beach towards his house, Steve's eyes kept straying to her hips, as she slowly walked towards his home. She had an incredible body, and against all logic, Steve thought about what she would be like in bed. Morgan knew she had to try something soon or her chance would be gone. She knew he was watching her body and like all men, it was only a matter of time before he thought he could have her. Of course, she would let him if he wanted to; knowing men were at their weakest when making love.

As she approached his house, she hopes were dashed, when she saw a woman of about her own age, covering her with a rifle.

"I guess this is your mysterious guardian angel?" Morgan smiled, turning towards Steve, her breasts tantalising him.

"Yes and she's a Muslim, just like you," Steve replied, her spell over him broken by Mary's presence, wiping the smile from Morgan's face.

"I see you found a pretty one, Steve!" Mary smiled sounding relieved, as Steve and Morgan came up onto Steve's veranda.

"How can you follow the prophet, and be a friend of an Infidel," Morgan spat out, startling Mary with her hatred.

"How dare you judge me? Look at you, where is your shame?"

"I do God's work," Morgan shot back defensively, but standing there topless in a small bikini and having just tried to kill a man, her argument, sounded lame.

"Let's all settle down ladies. I'll get somethingg to cover her with after I call the Feds," Steve told them walking inside. This surprised both women, who both thought Steve would terminate Morgan, after questioning her. Morgan seeing Mary's confusion made ready to attack when a man carrying an assault rifle appeared on the veranda.

"Don't even think about it!" Omar warned, throwing Morgan his shirt, covering her with his weapon while Mary helped put it on her.

FAMILY

At Margaret River, Edward and Louise sat happily at a small vineyard enjoying a quiet moment, when his phone rang startling them both.

"Is that you Steve?" Edward asked guardedly.

"Yeah, I got the hitman named 'The Blade', it's a woman!" Steve told him, as on the other end Steve could here Edward's intake of air.

"You're kidding. I thought the group were Islamic or something."

"Yeah, a woman was the last person I would have suspected. Luckily Mary, John's daughter spotted her," Steve explained sounding proud of Mary.

"What are you going to do with her?"

"I thought you might know some Feds over here, who wanted a big fish," Steve replied happily.

"I'll make a call, where are you?" Edward asked surprised that Steve was handing her over.

After telling Edward that he was at his own house, he warned him to all wait another two days before coming here. Steve then returned to the two women, with a shirt, to find Omar had already covered her. Omar seemed surprised that Steve was handing the assassin over in one piece.

"Won't her group just send more men?"

"Ali is taking care of that problem," Steve replied neutrally, watching the assassin's eyes go wide.

"We know all about your unit friends, they're most probably dead by now!" Morgan spat out angrily.

"Oh, you mean your men who were waiting at the assassin's house in London? I'm afraid those men are dead my dear, sprung the trap a bit late," Steve smiled, seeing it hit home, that he knew about the ambush, that she'd planned.

"They will not have died in vain. With God's help, our group will free all our Muslim brothers in England!" Morgan replied defiantly, knowing even with the loss of the men at the ambush, their vision would be fulfilled.

"And how are they going to do that?" Omar asked condescendingly.

"You will see God's wrath is coming!"

"You're full of shit! You're just another thug for hire," Steve smiled, trying to bait her into saying more, but Morgan remained silent.

"You're like all the others out there filled with hate. You talk freedom only when its suits you, what you really want is the thrill you get from killing," Mary spat out, hitting home, as she walked away.

"When fire rains over London and our brothers are free, followers like you will be taken care of," Morgan screamed, as reaching forward, she tried to grab Mary from behind. Omar, ready, swung his rifle knocking her to the floor.

"If you try to strike my wife again I will kill you!" Omar growled, tying Morgan's hands and feet together, before dragging her inside.

"Thank you husband," Mary smiled as Steve sat down on the veranda, resting.

Edward upon getting off the phone with Steve rang Shane. Getting put through to the Director's office was the last thing he expected.

"Director Smith speaking, who is it?" Shane answered, sounding very happy with himself.

"Have you all gone crazy there? How the hell did you become Director?"

"It's a long story. God, I'm glad to hear from you Edward, where are you?" Shane asked excitedly, having only so far, traced Edward to Perth.

"I'm in the Margaret River area, tasting wine."

"Bullshit, where are you really?" Shane replied, sounding a little cranky.

"I'm not joking! Steve told us to stay here, while he took care of the other hit man, who turned out to be a woman."

"I suppose she's dead?" Shane said bluntly, having met Steve.

"Amazingly, he's holding her for you. Can you get someone to pick her up at his house in Western Australia, where the shootout was back in the nineties?

"No worries, she's most probably on the most wanted list like the guy in Sydney. The Perth office will fall over themselves to get her. What story do we tell them?"

"Go with the yank undercover story, we'll get Steve to say he's Nigel Chamberlain. That way there's no need for him to talk too much," Edward explained smiling, thinking of Nigel's reaction. After working out the details, Edward rang Steve explaining the plan before informing the others.

By the time the Western Australian Feds had been sent to pick up the Blade, her assistant, Hussein's body had been discovered, tying up loose ends, as Interpol was sent a copy of her prints. It didn't take them long to connect her to several hits in Europe, previously thought done by a male assassin. Luckily for her, murdering someone in Australia took precedence over the overseas hits; Australia didn't have the death penalty like most European countries.

Nigel, at first wasn't impressed with being given credit for the arrest, but the other agents thought at least it was something to report positively, on this so-called, fact-finding trip to Down Under. At least the pressure of the assassin's was gone; the only one still out there was the Thistle. Edward hoped, he'd been warned off by the CIA. Bill was still apprehensive.

"He's still out there, and he's the best informed! I say we be cautious, until someone gives us confirmation, that he's not coming after anyone," Bill suggested, seeing the others looking forward to meeting Steve, not of the danger. It was Steve in the end that backed Bill's suspicions, warning the others off for another week. This would give Ali a chance to sort out the London connection before they met at Steve's house.

LONDON MOSQUE

Aaron, Cody and Ali sat silently sipping a freshly brewed pot of tea, watching as the first rays of sunshine as a new day broke through the fog onto the docks opposite their apartment's location. The day was going to be clear, if not a little cold, perfect for tourists Ali thought, as he studied the building opposite them. It had been a warehouse in this once busy dock area, but that was before the developers had moved in turning the area into a tourist haven. Close to the Tower Bridge and Parliament House made it the perfect location, for the sprawling hotel complexes that had sprung up in the converted warehouses, along the Thames.

The warehouse Ali was interested in wasn't a hotel. It was a safe house for the British Freedom Brigade. When Ali had first found out an Islamic group was involved, he'd gone to a local Mosque. He, being on the losing side in the Iranian Revolution hadn't made him too many friends, though it was in the past and Iran had changed. From hunting down members of the Shah's old military elite, Iran policy now was one of letting old wounds heal. In other words, if you kept away you were safe. Still, his name had been tied to the CIA for many years, and that alone made him an outcast to many former Muslim friends.

Coming to this Mosque unarmed was taking a chance. Cody assured him that he'd have his back, as long as he stayed near the front door of the complex. Keeping this in mind Ali had at first entered and prayed, before asking one of the many followers, if he could speak with the head Cleric out front. The man had at first been sceptical if his Cleric would meet him, but after Ali gave his full name, the man said he would inform his leader.

Waiting patiently for twenty minutes, Ali thought at first that his name might no longer carry any significance. When a group of ten men took up station around him, he knew it still did.

"Your name is not welcome here my brother!" an old man in a white flowing robe told him, as he moved to stand in front of Ali.

"I come in peace my brothers I seek no trouble!" Ali replied truthfully, his palms held up showing he wasn't armed.

"You take a great chance coming here American lackey!" a young man snarled, moving close behind Ali, with two other men.

"It would be unwise to come nearer!" Ali warned, dropping a white handkerchief onto the ground beside him. At first, the group wondered what he was doing when a whipping noise like an angry wasp whipped by the group and a hole appeared in the handkerchief. The group, which moments before had been out for blood, stood frozen. The significance of the bullet hole paralysed them, as fear flowed through their minds. This lasted for several seconds until the old man in the white robes burst into laughter.

"It appears your reputation is well earned!" the Mullah smiled, as his men continued to stand motionless, with both fear and shame.

"I said I came in peace, I didn't say I came unprepared," Ali smiled, as the old man dismissed his followers. Sitting down on the front steps, the old man introduced himself as the local Mosque spiritual leader, asking why Ali had come. Ali explained how a group of Muslims were hunting his friend, going by the name of British Freedom Brigade.

At first, the old man seemed to weigh up whether he should tell Ali anything, but his eyes showed something that worried Ali more than his follower's threats, and that was fear.

The British Freedom Brigade had once attended this Mosque. Unfortunately their radical views had made them feared, leading to their expulsion. Giving their address to Ali, the Mullah warned him to be careful approaching this group. He told him that some of the more rebellious members of his Mosque had been warned that something big was coming. Something they said that would free all their Muslim brothers in England.

"Any idea, what they might be planning?"

"No, my brother; God has already given us the freedom to pray and live within our teachings. These troublemakers will only bring death!"

"Thank you for your help," Ali said standing as the Mullah stood as well.

"You could be a great help to our cause in many countries my brother," the old man said looking Ali in the eye.

"I've too much blood on my hands already, I seek only peace."

"Then I hope you find it." the Cleric said smiling, before walking back inside the mosque. Ali stood slowly, picking up his damage handkerchief, which signalled Cody to leave. Strolling away from the

Mosque, a sense of foreboding touched Ali, as he wondered if peace for a man with his history would ever be possible.

THE HIDEOUT

Ali stood at the window, watching the warehouse suspiciously, his mind trying to work out what the group was up to. At any time the warehouse had at least ten members of the group stationed inside. Aaron, while being laid up, had over the last few days, made a rough description of each member, numbering eighty all up. From their position across the street Aaron, Cody and Ali had worked out a plan to hit the warehouse, taking the entire group of men hostage, if possible. They hoped to find out what was going on, but feelings of dread touch them all, as they stood watching.

"We'll go at three in the morning! They'll be at their weakest then. It should give Cody and me an advantage, while you cover us," Ali explained to Aaron, getting a nod from Cody.

"There's something going on here Ali! They're waiting for something, I don't like it!" Aaron warned, his eyes glued to the warehouse as Ali to turned and stared at it.

"What choice do we have?" Ali replied, knowing they were running out of options.

"Vehicle slowing down, it's already gone past once already!" Cody whispered. Looking down, they saw a black Mercedes nose into the curve opposite them, making the three of them move back from the window. Four men in full-length coats slowly got out of the car, as five members of the British Freedom Brigade appeared at the door, sloppily hiding a collection of weapons.

"They're taking a chance that no one calls the police," Aaron mumbled to himself mostly, as the two groups after briefly talking, moved inside.

"What the hell's going on? None of those guys looks like an Arab, or Englishmen for that matter." Cody pointed out.

"Aaron, grab your camera, I've got an idea," Ali smiled, as after twenty minutes the four men emerge, and Aaron snapped away.

John Wilson sat at his desk silently reading over reports as his mind wandered to what was going on in Australia. His career and that of many others hung in the balance, dependent on what happened there. A feeling of helplessness settled on him, hoping Nigel could pull it together.   The rumble of his personal phone startled him, as he quickly wiped sweat from his face, and picked it up.

"Nigel is that you?" John asked excitedly knowing only a few people knew his number, and Nigel was one of them.

"No Mr Wilson, it's Ali Mustaffer. I need your help," Ali answered neutrally. At first, John Wilson looked at the phone as if it had turned into a snake. Calming down, he explained.

"What do you want Mustaffer, and how'd you get this number."

"I need your help identifying four men, mixed up with one of the groups after Steve Roberts. The second part of your question is Nigel gave me your number, in case of an emergency," Ali informed him in the same neutral voice.

"Send the pictures to this phone number, I'll check them out. I'll ring you back on the number you're on now if I find anything," John told him hanging up.

"Shit now I'm doing work for him!" Wilson said out loud, before bursting into laughter.

It took nearly four hours to pass the photos to the crime lab where they ran them against FBI and CIA records. They were sent back immediately marked 'urgent' to the director's office. Picking up the ID matches John Wilson read the Intel of the men, before swearing out loud, as beads of sweat ran down his face. Picking up his phone he rang records to verify.

"Are you sure you've got it right?" John asked Brian the senior man there and a friend.

"Yes, we ran it twice John, it's definitely them," Brian answered.

"My God Brian how'd the Russians get it so wrong," John replied sadly.

"Remember WMD's in Iraq. It's easy to make mistakes my friend when you're sure your right.

"Thanks for the history lesson Brian. Keep this quiet, if something goes wrong I don't want this pointing at us," John answered, before hanging up.

Gaining his composure, John called Stuart at the CIA.

"What is it, Wilson!" Stuart asked flatly sounding bored.

"One of those groups of hit men, your former boss hired, used their ten million to buy a fucking Nuke!" Wilson roared angrily. At first, Stuart remained quiet, unable to reply.

"Are you still there Stuart?"

"This could be a blessing in disguise, John. No one knows it was our money and if they use it, we can put the whole mess on Iran," Stuart suggested happily.

"Are you completely crazy? What about the loss of life?"

"Sacrifices have to be made for the greater good," Stuart informed him. "And anyway, England hasn't been that great an ally to us lately," Stuart continued, as John hung up. Staring at the phone, wondering if the whole world had gone crazy, John grabbed the recording of the conversation and raced out the door.

THE WHITEHOUSE

A meeting between the Vice President and the President was underway when a Secret Service agent burst into the room. Both men look up surprised, as John Wilson rushed in, knowing it must be something big to interrupt them.

"It's okay James you can wait outside," the Vice President told his secret service escort.

"Might be best if all the Secret Service left Sir," John suggested. The President's face showed he was unhappy with Wilson, for telling him what to do. Reluctantly he signalled for his two guards to go as well.

"What is it John?" the President barked.

"I had a problem, so I rang Ross Stuart at the CIA. I taped the conversation without him knowing, so it's inadmissible in a court of law. I'll let you listen then we can discuss the problem," John informed them, before turning on the recording.

For the next five minutes, all three men sat quietly while the tape played. In the end, both men continued to sit deep in thought.

"Stuart's crazy. Even if we got away with it, God the loss of life would be horrendous," the President exploded, much to John's relief.

"What did you think we'd say that he was right?" Vice president asked, looking hard at Wilson.

"I wasn't sure to tell you the truth. Politically it could be a big win," John replied sheepishly.

"At what cost John? I've done some shady things before as President, but I've always been able to look in the mirror without shame," he pointed out, backed up by Vice President Baker.

"Anyway, now you're aware of what's happening, I'll explain how I think we should handle the problem," John put forward, wondering how they would handle it. After digesting Wilson's plan, the President sat silently, an unreadable expression on his face.

"It's the only possible way we can help and still have deniability," John added as the President stood up signalling for him to be quiet.

"I don't like it one bit! I hate that Ali and his cutthroat unit friends," he exploded. "On the other hand, they're just the type of people we need, unfortunately. Go ahead John, but remember if this goes south, losing office will be the least of our worries,"

"What do you think Mr Vice President?" John asked.

"You're right, it's the only way John. One thing though, what will you do, if they say no?" Baker replied.

"Let's hope they don't!" John answered, turning to leave.

"Before you go, John, what would you have done if we sided with Stuart?" The President asked.

"I'd have resigned and gone to the media," John answered bravely.

"You know we mightn't be friends John, but you've got guts," the President smiled waving him away. "Now let's call Stuart in for a little talk," he suggested angrily.

LONDON

It was eight in the evening when Ali's phone started ringing. Having not heard from Wilson, Ali had decided to hit the warehouse that morning. Looking at the caller ID Ali answered, hoping Wilson would play ball.

"Mr Wilson, how did you go?' Ali asked happily.

"Ali, can I call you Ali?" John Wilson replied, his words running into each other nervously.

"Ali's okay. I judge you found something?" Ali asked softly, his sense of humour rapidly fading.

"We have, and it's not good," John replied, before explaining. The four men were Ukrainian, part of a splinter group of rebels fighting the Russians in Chesney. It was believed that these four men had, with the help a large group of their followers, attacked a nuclear storage facility in southern Russia, making off with two small bombs.

The Russians had thought the weapons and men were destroyed when a fuel ignited bomb had been dropped on their base in the mountains. It obliterated the entire area for several kilometres vaporising the base. The photos of the men were only made available in the hope they could track down the conspirators involved with the theft.

"Looks like they got that wrong?" Ali replied.

"Any ideas where the bombs might be?"

"One's most probably in downtown London in the docks area, across from where we're staying, right now!" Ali replied as Aaron and Cody looked on wondering what Ali was talking about.

"What do you need?" John asked seriously, wondering if Ali and his friends would want to help at all. The silence on the other end of the phone lasted only a few seconds; to Wilson, it felt like hours.

"We'll need some way of finding exactly where the bomb is and some more men, about eight, who'll do what they're told," Ali replied, with an underlying edge of uncertainty, wondering if this was a setup.

"Thanks, Ali, I couldn't blame you if you walked. I can assure you, that I'm being honest with you."

"Trust to men like us is an unknown luxury, John. Can you give me an idea of the time frame, on the men and the equipment?" Ali asked neutrally, moving on.

"The CIA has contacted British Intelligence giving them a brief rundown on the situation," John answered before continuing. "Needless to say they're a bit worried and have put their armed forces on full alert. You can have eight of their best and a locating device, in four hours time. Of course, you will have to tell me where you are."

Taking a big chance, Ali gave their address, not their room number, suggesting they meet at the rear entrance of the hotel in five hours. He then told Cody and Aaron what was going down, giving them the option to leave. Neither was too impressed with having eight unknown SAS soldiers at their back, but neither did they want to walk away from this mess.

"Can we trust them?" Cody asked.

"For the moment, yes, but after the bomb is secure, we'll have to be careful," Ali replied honestly, hoping he was doing the right thing.

John Wilson hung up the phone to find his hands trembling slightly. He had just put the fate of an entire city, maybe a country, in the hands of a small group of men who they'd tried to kill several times. The President himself had warned Stuart, pushing him hard. He ordered him to go to England personally, to make sure the President's instructions were carried out to the letter. Even so, John was scared, so many things could go wrong, and the death toll if things went wrong, could be staggering.

America being itself engaged in two unpopular wars in Afghanistan and Iraq couldn't handle another scandal. The people were losing faith in their government and their place as the protector of the free world. Too many enemies were springing up all over the world, waiting for their chance to strike.

"If this bomb goes off, it could make the world descend into anarchy!" John Wilson said out loud, as he walked to the window and stood silently looking out over Washington.

THE RAID

Roughly five hours after Ali's talk with Wilson, a Ford van pulled up in the alley behind their hotel. Eight everyday clothed civilians piled out, each carrying a duffel bag. Checking their surroundings, they walked swiftly towards the rear entry. When Ali walked out of the shadows opposite the door, he scared the shit out of all of them.

"Where'd da fuck you come from?" stammered one of the young men, with a thick cockney accent.

"Settle down corporal!" a tall young man behind the corporal ordered, before addressing Ali.

"I judge you're our contact? I'm Captain Johnson, and these men are my team," the tall man said with a smile, looking Ali over trying to gauge him.

"My name's Ali, Captain, please follow me."

Walking into the room, Johnson's eyes went to the collection of equipment and weapons positioned strategically around the room, while the curtains on the window were closed securely. Putting his gear down, he looked into the adjoining bedroom, seeing a man with a broken leg sitting in the dark peering out through a cut in the curtains.

"Do you want to fill me in on what's going on!" the Captain asked wondering who these three men were.

"What have you been told?" Ali asked flatly.

"Only that we're to obey your orders and give you this," Johnson replied smiling at the situation. Handing Ali a sealed box he quickly opened it revealing an advanced type of Geiger counter. Ali quickly looked over the device, before walking into the adjoining room, handing it to Aaron.

Aaron nodded his understanding of the device, turned it on. Going over to the window Aaron pointed it across the street slowly pointing it at each window scanning each floor. Captain Johnson and his men were no fools; their faces' betraying the fact that they knew what Aaron was looking for across the street.

"Yes, you're right Captain; it's a bomb, the bad type," Cody smiled, watching these highly trained soldiers sweat.

"Much resistance?" Johnson asked nervously.

"Ten armed men and they're fanatics, so there's no room for mistakes!" Ali pointed out, as the group sat down, going over his plan. After an hour of instruction, Ali decided to hit the warehouse in the early hours around three like he worked out before.

"You want to go in tonight?" Captain Johnson asked surprised.

"What's the point in waiting Captain? One more day will only help them; it's a straightforward mission, in and out."

Ali had decided that Aaron and two members of the SAS team would give them covering fire from their apartment, while the others assaulted the warehouse. The assault group would break into two units, three SAS with Cody from the rear, while Ali with the three remaining SAS including Captain Johnson, took the front. Aaron, unfortunately, had some bad news.

"It's not there Ali. I've done a complete sweep of the building, and there's no signature of a bomb," Aaron said softly as if he thought the men across the street could hear them.

"No way you've missed it?" Cody asked smiling, as Aaron gave him the finger. Ali sat there for several minutes wondering what to do, thinking they could just walk away. No matter how you look it, this was a terrorist attack that would do untold horror. Thousands, maybe millions of innocent people would die needlessly. Ali knew if he could stop it happening, it was his duty to try.

"We go in as planned, we have to know what's going on, so that means we'll need prisoners."

"I wish Steve was here!' Aaron said softly.

"Me to my friend! I thought about it, but it would take too long for him to get here," Ali admitted, knowing in this type of operation, the timing was everything.

Three in the morning, the prime time to catch your enemy at his weakest Ali thought, as Johnson and his men prepared to go. Johnson at first had not been too happy playing second fiddle to Ali, but as he and his men watched these three middle-age men prepare for the mission, a sense of being in the presence of experts settled on them.

"You've done this before I judge?" Johnson asked as Ali expertly checked his weapon, fitting a silencer before walking to the window having a last look.

"Yeah we've done this once or twice," Ali answered, giving nothing away, as Cody and Aaron chuckled behind him.

"They're not going to want to be taken alive!" Johnson admitted watching Ali.

"Don't worry Captain, surprise is the key, remember that!" Ali replied sternly taking the measure of the man in front of him.

"We'll do our best Sir," Johnson answered formally as he and his men dressed in black overalls moved towards the door.

"I hope so Captain, we're only getting one shot at this."

THE BREACH

Approaching the front door, Ali swiftly looked through the crack in the door seeing if it was wired before pulling a knife and skilfully opening the door. Two clicks on his headset told Cody at the rear that he was in, as he silently moved inside. Ali was just about to try an internal door when the door suddenly opened. Silhouetted by the light behind him, the man holding a rifle, casually by its barrel, took in the dark shape in front of him. Striking rapidly with the butt of his pistol, Ali smashed the surprised man across the head, before he had time to react. As Ali lowered the unconscious man to the ground, Johnson quickly grabbed the man's rifle, before it dropped to the floor.

Nodding his thanks to Johnson, Ali moved forward, as the SAS soldiers look at each other, amazed at Ali's reflexes. Inside the room from where the man had emerged, Ali found two men sleeping blissfully on the floor. Pointing to them, the two SAS soldiers getting Ali's meaning, moved forward, drawing their knives, killing the two men as they slept. Leaving the two SAS men to secure the first man and keep watch, Ali and Johnson moved further into the warehouse, slowly securing each room, before moving on. Coming to a set of descending stairs, Ali softly told Cody, that his group was heading down into the basement, telling Cody to head up and secure the first floor.

Looking down into the darkness, Ali was just about to take the first step, when a voice yelled out a challenge asking who was there. Reaching into his pocket, Ali grabbed a stun grenade, throwing it down the stairs into the darkness. As the grenade bounced down the stairs the sound of a weapon being cocked made him turn and dive backwards, dragging Johnson with him. Bullets ripped into the timber stairs around them, as the stun grenade exploded with a brilliant flash.

Jumping to their feet, both Johnson and Ali launched themselves down the stairs, firing blindly at the shapes that moved in the pitch dark. The grenade's effect had disorientated the men downstairs, slowing their reflexes, making them easy targets. Finding a light switch, Ali turned it on swiftly moving forward, checking the three bodies on the floor. Johnson covering him moved forward, securing the area.

Hearing shooting above, Ali asked Cody for a situation report. Getting a static-filled response Cody informed him that the floor was secure, but one of the SAS soldiers had been hit. By this time the two SAS soldiers, who had been left to secure the prisoner, had caught up, the four of them then moved forward searching the basement. Realising that the plan now was shot to shit by the firefight, Ali called Cody.

"How many enemy dead?" Ali asked Cody flatly, his mind racing, as he nosed around a large stack of boxes, his weapon held out in front of him.

"Two dead, one's still alive. Aaron got another one at the front window, so that's four!" Cody replied his breath labouring.

"That's all of them!" Ali stated sounding relieved, working out with the three at the front, plus three down here and Cody's bunch added up to ten. Still cautious though, Ali continued forward, not relaxing till the entire warehouse had been secured. Johnson, seeing Ali signals that the building was safe, used his radio to check on his downed man. Luckily he'd taken a hit to the arm, the bullet just grazing him. A quick bandage stopped the bleeding enough to make transporting him to a hospital easy.

"What a complete stuff up!" Ali cursed angrily.

"What's wrong? We achieved the objective, and we've got two prisoners!" Johnson replied, not understanding Ali's anger.

"If they'd had a bomb, someone would have triggered it! We're better than this!" Ali replied still angry at his carelessness, leaving Johnson and his men staggered, as Cody joined him.

"This wouldn't have happened if Steve had been here!" Cody added, having heard Ali's outburst, as he came down to see what had happened.

"You're right; I stuffed up at the stairs. They heard me approaching," Ali admitted still angry with himself.

"Well it's done! Let's move on," Cody suggested seeing Ali nod his acceptance of the situation, as they planned their next move. Johnson and his men looked at each other, wondering who the hell this Steve person was, thinking that even in their prime as they were now, they'd have had trouble getting a better solution out of an attack as this one had.

"Captain, get your men to bring the living members of the British Freedom Brigade, down here to the basement. Then tell your men to search this entire area, there's got to be something here to tell us what's going on!" Ali ordered as Johnson's men broke into groups and started searching. Cody's interrogation of the survivors proved fruitless. Being only soldiers, the two men captured had little knowledge of what was going on. They knew of the plan to detonate the bomb, but not where the weapon was or who was going to detonate it.

Unlike Ali, Cody hadn't seemed to have lost his killer edge, ruthlessly torturing the prisoners repeatedly trying to get anything of value out of them. In the end, Ali stopped him, telling him they knew nothing or they would've talked by now, saying nothing of Cody's methods. Johnson too was sickened by the torture. Under orders to obey these men, he said nothing, but it disgusted him. In the end, the torturing proved unnecessary, as Johnson's men got lucky, finding a small laptop hidden behind a false wall. Johnson immediately went to work on the laptop. After an hour he had the answers.

"The reason why the bomb isn't here, is only half the payment for the two weapons have been made. They've paid ten million, but the Ukrainians wanted twenty!" Johnson informed them, after checking the computer.

"Looks like they were dependant on killing Steve for the rest?" Cody replied solemnly to Ali, as Johnson silently took in this new piece of information.

"No, they must have a backup plan in case their hit squad failed, dig deeper!" Ali ordered Johnson, his nervousness making him appear angry.

For the next two hours, Johnson poured over the laptop's contents finding nothing. He was just about to toss it in, when checking the email, he found a strange message. It mentioned doing some flight training at an aero club airfield to the west of London in four weeks time. The strange part was the booking was for 8pm on a Sunday night. Checking the aero club's site, Johnson found it was closed on Sundays, along with the airfield, except for emergency landings. Johnson told Ali about this information as the others gathered around.

"Sounds like where the exchange might be going to take place?" Cody suggested softly, deep in thought.

"Then we've got a problem!" Ali pointed out. He knew that a sizeable part of this terrorist group was still at large and would soon know their warehouse had been hit. They would automatically change the rendezvous, knowing the Intelligence services might have found the laptop.

"Maybe not!" Cody said smiling evilly.

"How can we hide this mess?" Johnson asked, as Ali too looked confused by Cody's statement.

"We don't hide it. We arrange the police to have a shootout with some men seen with guns. In the end, the building is burnt to the ground by the terrorist, no prisoners. The other group members will think their buddies fought to the last man, and remember these men know nothing," Cody informed them smiling.

"What about the prisoners! They have to be turned over to the authorities," Johnson pointed out angrily, knowing there'd be questions about their treatment.

"What do you thinks going to happen to them Captain!" Cody snarled back, as Johnson stood up, followed by his men.

"Settle down all of you!" Ali ordered them all, bringing silence to the room. Looking hard at Cody, Ali was worried by what he saw there, but he had to concede that it was a good plan.

"Can someone think of a better idea?" Ali asked softly, feeling his guts start to knot knowing at the airport there would be another firefight. Getting no answers, Cody's plan was adopted. Johnson sat quietly as Ali quickly laid down a plan, for the shootout with the police. Gathering up the dead terrorists, Johnson's men positioned them near doors and windows, leaving their weapons positioned at each window. While this was being done, Cody disappeared downstairs taking care of the survivors, before moving them to the ground floor.

When Johnson had first met these men, he'd been in awe of their military training and their natural ability. He now saw them as men who'd gone over to the dark side, men who thought that any action, justified a positive outcome. Ali seeing Johnson studying him pulled him aside.

"Can I depend on you Captain?"

"Yes Sir, I have my orders!" Johnson barked back, his eyes black with anger.

"Well, you remember that Captain! Millions of lives may depend on it!" Ali growled back, walking away from him, and getting out his phone.

The emergency service operator sat at her station counting the minutes that were left on her shift. It had been a boring Wednesday night with only one fire and a few false alarms from several well-known banks. There was also a call about some shooting in the docks area, but nothing had been heard since then. It was now approaching six in the morning when most workers were just starting to get up when the phone began to ring.

"What is your emergency?" the operator asked with a clear, if not bored voice.

"There are several men with guns across from our hotel in the docks area!" a voice screeched into the phone, making the operator jump.

"I'll switch you through to the police," she replied, looking at the time and thinking she'd stay at work a little longer, as she had to travel through that area.

The police at first were sceptical, having already been to check on the earlier report of shooting finding nothing. In the end, a two-man patrol car was dispatched to check it out. As the patrol car slowly came around the corner and drove down past the warehouse, the driver was just about to radio a false alarm, when all hell broke loose. Cody on the first floor carefully lined up the front bonnet of the vehicle, sending a full clip into the metal work, blowing the engine, and sending the two police running down the street, followed by another spray of bullets.

"That will get a reaction!" Cody chuckled into his radio, as Aaron and Ali, looked on from their hotel room across the street.

"Just be careful Cody, we don't want any friendly causalities!" Ali replied, a little worried by Cody's attitude.

"Don't worry it's a piece of cake," Cody answered, watching the street, as three of Captain Johnson's men took up positions beside him.

"Cody worries me, Aaron. There's something about him." Ali whispered to his friend.

"I haven't seen him for awhile either Ali, but you're right, I too sense something different about him," Aaron replied softly, feeling he was betraying his friend in even talking about it.

"When this is all over we'll talk about it," Ali suggested, getting agreement from Aaron, as they went back to watching the street.

The plan was to start a firefight, then torch the building. To give the impression of a larger force, each time they fired they moved to a different location. Cody's shooting spree didn't take long to get a reaction. Black-clad police swat units arrived on the scene in less than ten minutes, blocking off both ends of the street.

After they manage to calm down the two police officers from the car, they got out of them that only one weapon had opened up on them. Inspector Ney, the officer in charge, decided to play it safe, sending two swat teams down each side of the road to gauge what they were up against. When at least four weapons opened up from different locations in the warehouse, showering the street with rounds, he ordered the swat teams to retreat.

"Looks like somebody in there fired at that police car by mistake I'd say, and now we've got the whole bunch trapped in there! Anyone got another opinion?" Inspector Ney asked with a slight smile on his lips.

"Makes sense Sir. Why else would he have fired?" one officer replied.

"This could be a lucky break for us Sir. Who knows what would have happened if this group got into the city?' another officer said voicing his opinion, as more units arrived.

"Okay you know your jobs, evacuate the neighbouring buildings and pick off the shooters," Ney ordered as his men raced to their positions.

When the knock came at Aaron and Ali's room, to evacuate Ali and Aaron obediently cooperated with the police, leaving the building. Aaron informed the police that he was the one who had called in the sighting, telling them there were at least ten men in the warehouse. After receiving a well done from the police, they waited with the other hotel patrons at the back of the hotel. The police getting this information called in backup, from the SAS.

Five minutes later Captain Johnson arrived with the three remaining members of his team. Inspector Ney was surprised by the SAS's quick response, but Captain Johnson informed him that they'd been training in the area when the call had gone out.

As to him only having three, he assured them the other team members would join them shortly. Viewing the warehouse with the swat commanders, Captain Johnson suggested his men work their way around the back entering there, while the police units tied down the shooters. The police readily agreed, as no one wanted to take on such a large group of dug in terrorists. After setting up a time for the initial breach, Captain Johnson and his men headed for the rear of the building keeping out of sight.

"He's a cocky young officer," one of Inspector Ney's swat team officers remarked, watching the SAS men disappear down an alley.

"Why do you say that?" Ney asked, watching the SAS as well.

"He didn't ask for a layout of the warehouse, or the enemy strength. It was as if he already knew," the officer remarked softly.

"Well they might've have been on to these gentlemen already, and dropped the ball and we got here first," Ney smiled, knowing the police would get full credit.

"You could be right Sir. Anyway, they're going in, not us, makes up for any cock up someone's made," The officer replied before joining up with his men. Relieving the police officers stationed at the alley entrance, Johnson's men hurried forward reaching the back door, which was opened, by one of Johnson's men inside. Taking up positions around the warehouse, the SAS along with Cody waited for the breach time to arrive.

Picking up the British Freedom Brigade weapons the SAS soldiers moved the bodies of the dead terrorists to the windows giving the men in the street something to shoot at once the firefight started. As the swat teams moved forward to cover the SAS breach at the rear, the warehouse erupted with flashes of weapon fire, as the swat teams dived for cover.

The police at first were startled by the sudden outbreak of automatic weapon fire. Getting over it, the snipers across the road in the hotel, and on the adjoining roofs opened fired at dark silhouettes, outlined by muzzle flashes.

After several minutes of firing the police outside noticed the firing at them slowly recede, as shooting continued inside. It was apparent to the police outside that the SAS were heavily engaged inside as the shooting grew in volume, the weapon fire moving downstairs to the ground floor. The swat teams worried for the SAS, wanting to enter the building to assist. Inspector Ney told them to hold position as he knew the SAS would fire on anything moving.

It was one of these waiting swat team members, who first spotted the smoke, which quickly spread throughout the building as explosions echoed throughout the structure. The noise mushroomed out into the surrounding area. Inspector Ney immediately called the fire brigades getting them rolling. Captain Johnson's voice suddenly squawked out of the Inspector's radio, informing him that the terrorists had set off some kind of suicide device in the basement and he and his men had safely exited out the back door into the alley.

"Any survivors?" Ney asked, watching as the fire brigade, heavily protected by the police, set up hosing the building, trying to contain the fire.

"No, they fought to the last man, but it was your snipers who did most of the damage!" Captain Johnson informed him, making the police around the radio smile with pride, as they passed it on to the men in the field.

"Well done everybody, even though the terrorists all lost their lives, which were unavoidable, we have most probably saved hundreds of lives today!" Inspector Ney informed his men as everyone moved forward to help secure the warehouse.

Walking forward and looking back at the barricaded ends of the street, Inspector Ney saw several news media groups had set up, along with a large group of spectators. Ney was glad they'd secured the area early, stopping the media from getting too close. In this type of operation, the Inspector knew that keeping a low profile on shootouts was an important part of calming the population's fear of terrorism.

"Well at least they didn't get much footage for the news tonight," he smiled. Above him, in Aaron and Ali's abandoned room, the CNN news crew clapped each other on the back, knowing that thanks to that middle-aged Frenchman; they had scooped the other media outlets.

THE AFTERMATH

Ahmed Garn watched the TV screen with simmering hatred. His plans for detonating the bomb at their base in downtown London had evaporated. Picking up his chair, he smashed it into the TV screen, causing the device to explode into hundreds of pieces.

"Be at peace my brother!" one of his lieutenants shouted frightened by their leader's violence. Calming down, Ahmed quietly paced around the room, while five of his most trusted men sat quietly watching their leader warily.

"Have we heard from 'The Blade' or Hussein?" Ahmed asked suddenly, looking around the room dangerously.

"No, nothing today and they had strict orders to call," Brennan Huda, Ahmed's second in command answered, knowing this information wouldn't help.

"That means we won't be able to pay the Ukrainians the rest of their money," Ahmed snarled looking around the room seeking someone to blame.

"Then we take what we need brother, it is our duty to carry out Gods mission," Brennan replied softly, getting nods from the others.

"And what if the authorities know about our meeting?" Ahmed spat out, looking closely at Brennan for any deception, seeing only his most loyal follower. Brennan had been the first to follow Ahmed after Ahmed had told him of his vision, that God wanted London destroyed utterly. Also, it was Brennan who had first suggested using 'The Blade', which at first Ahmed had been uncomfortable with, being a woman. Brennan convinced him to give her a try, and up till now, it had been incredibly lucky.

"We have all seen the CNN secret filming of the firefight. No one got out alive, and there's no way any evidence survived that inferno, thanks to our brave brother's sacrifice," Brennan answered sadly, his eyes misting up at the loss of their men.

"Forgive me, brothers, you are right. Their lives will not be in vain!" Ahmed shouted, coming forward and hugging Brennan, before repeating the gesture with all his men present.

"Then how do we get the weapons, without paying?" another brother asked softly.

"We take them! Allah wants us to have them!" Ahmed smiled as the others shouted their support. When the other men left Brennan hung back waiting so he could talk to Ahmed alone.

"Are you sure we can't just use one bomb? These Ukrainians are our brothers too!"

"No, one mightn't be enough. The second is insurance to be able to threaten them with!" Ahmed laughed.

"But God showed in your vision that we would be victorious."

"The vision may not have been fully understood by me. This way we can make sure," Ahmed answered softly, patting Brennan on the back, as he walked him to the front door, bidding him goodnight. Outside in the cold night air, Brennan shuffled along lost in thought. He had believed in Ahmed's vision, leaving his passive beliefs to follow a path paved with blood. Now he stood in the dark wondering if Ahmed had misled him. Falling to his knees, he prayed for a sign that would tell him what path to take.

For two hours he lay prostrate on the ground, the cold penetrating his body making him shake uncontrollably. He was just about to give up and stand, when a blanket fell over his body, warming him.

"Are you okay my friend?" asked a croaky old voice, as Brennan looked up and saw an old man looking down at him.

"Yes, I'm sorry to worry you. I had the urge to pray," Brennan answered sounding embarrassed.

"There's nothing wrong with that laddie. If more people prayed they wouldn't fight would they?" the old man replied giving a small chuckle. Standing slowly Brennan wiped his eyes bending to pick up the blanket the old man had given him.

"Thank you!" he said out loud, only to find himself standing there alone, the old man gone. Shocked at not seeing the old man anywhere, Brennan wandered home mystified, not knowing what to make of what had just happened.

THE UNIT RESURFACES

When Steve's phone rang early that morning, and he saw it was Ali's number. Steve thought it had to be good news. Instead, Ali filled Steve in on what had been happening in London.

"We could walk away from it Ali. This bomb business has nothing to do with us!" Steve answered angrily, knowing they wouldn't.

"You know we can't Steve."

"I know Ali, but I'm tired of it," Steve answered his voice betraying how sick he was of killing.

"We all are Steve, but we need your help."

"And here I was thinking you were coming out here to help me!" Steve replied, forcing a laugh.

"Get here as quick as you can Steve, and bring the yanks if you can, I think we'll need them. I took the liberty of ringing their boss, asking for their help," Ali admitted before hanging up. Staring at the phone knowing he had no choice, Steve packed his bags. Next, he booked enough tickets for Nigel's men and himself, on the next available flight, before ringing Shane at the AFP office in Sydney, asking him for a favour.

Ringing Edward next, he told him to bring everyone to the International Airport in Perth that afternoon, saying he'd explain there what was happening. He hadn't meant to sound angry to Edward, but he was. Not with Edward, but with the situation that he again found himself in.

'This is how we all get killed!' Steve thought to himself sadly, as he gunned his car towards the airport.

Robin and Lindsey were beside themselves at meeting their father. It didn't matter what Edward said about meeting at the airport, all they cared about was seeing him. They weren't the only ones, Louise was near tears all the time, and Natasha had a mischievous smile on her face, always adjusting her hair or makeup. The Americans had many different reasons, from just wanting to meet Roberts. Two of them were asking could they take out his daughters, Patrick was one of them. He sat nervously holding Robin's hand, wondering how her father would react.

"You'll be fine!" Robin reassured him, as they crammed into their two mini vans for the trip to the airport. "It's not like he's going to kill you or anything!" Robin continued, as Bill and Allan being in hearing range, burst into laughter.

"What's so funny?" Leone asked, a beautiful smile on her lips, as she came up beside the two agents. Allen explained as Bill became tongue-tied, at Leone's close proximity.

"Of course he won't kill him! Maybe just rough him up a bit, that's all," Leone answered neutrally, watching Patrick start to sweat, before she too laughed, followed by the others.

"How about everyone take a few deep breaths and let's get moving," Edward suggested, as everyone loaded into the vans, saying no more.

Arriving at the airport, the whole group was ushered by Federal Police to a side room, usually used for private functions. Edward was informed that Director Shane Smith had asked that security be tight, plus when they left there, a security detail would protect them at Mr Roberts' home on the coast. As the group entered, they saw a middle-aged man dressed in a smart well-fitting business suit, standing beside a window, watching a plane landing. Before Edward could say anything, Robin and Lindsey broke away from the group running to their father, followed closely by Louise.

The Americans seeing that this was a family affair held back, while Edward joined his family. Nigel was watching Roberts' family with his men when his phone started to ring. Getting some space from the others, he answered the call.

"Is that you Nigel?" John Wilson's voice boomed through the phone, causing Nigel to move the phone from his ear.

"Yes John, what's up?" Nigel replied softly, watching the interchange between Roberts and his family.

"Are you at the airport with Roberts?"

"Yes we just arrived, why?" Nigel asked suspiciously.

"Roberts is on his way to England, you and your men are going with him!"

"I suppose we have no choice?"

"I can't go into details, Roberts will do that. But it's by order of the White House, a presidential decree that you obey Roberts' orders!" John informed him, his voice shaky.

"No problem, don't worry we'll do what needs doing. Is everything okay with you John?" Nigel replied worried by the way his boss sounded.

"You'll understand why I sound like I do when Roberts briefs you. But thanks for your concern and watch your back, my friend, this could get bloody real quick!" John warned hanging up.

Looking across at Roberts, Nigel saw him watching him, so he gave him a nod, letting him know, that he knew what was going on. Turning to his men, he saw their surprise, as a steward handed them each a ticket. Natasha, to the side, looked on, her eyes watching him. Walking across to his men, he broke the news.

"It's not a joke, we're going to England with Roberts!" Nigel confessed.

"Why?" Bill asked, having wanted to stay here with Leone a little longer.

"Orders from the White House, Bill. So that's that. If it makes you feel any better, I'm not too happy about it either." Nigel admitted, ending any further discussion.

"What about me?" Natasha asked angrily.

"You'll have to stay here," Nigel told her, sensing trouble.

"Bullshit I will!" Natasha replied loudly, staring hard at Nigel, as the others turned in their direction.

"Look we're only following orders," Nigel admitted, hoping to calm her down.

"I follow no one's orders unless I choose to!" Natasha countered, standing her ground. As the argument started between Nigel and Natasha, Edward who was happily spending time with his family, started to feel the mood shifting.

"What's going on over there?" Edward asked Steve, as the family group grew quiet.

"Nigel has been told he and his men are coming with me to England," Steve announced softly, as all hell broke loose. Robin and Lindsey broke first, realising they were losing their father again, followed closely by his sister. After a dozen whys went unanswered by their father, the girls quietly sobbed knowing they could do nothing. Steve his eyes misting up, asked for their forgiveness, before walking over to Nigel's group.

"I'm sorry to see you again Agent Chamberlain," Steve said neutrally sizing up Nigel's men.

"Seems we don't have a choice?"

"No you don't, but neither do I. Are there any problems?" Steve asked bluntly, looking at the beautiful woman beside Nigel, wondering where he'd seen her before.

"Natasha wants to come with us, I told her no," Nigel replied, waiting for Steve's reaction.

"Who is she?" was all Steve got out when recognition hit him like a hammer. "My God it's you!" he stammered out, and for the first time in many years, Steve found himself lost for words.

"It's taken me a long time to find you, Captain Roberts. I'm not letting you get away again!" Natasha practically purred; coming forward and kissing Steve on both cheeks, making him go crimson.

"It's too dangerous, you can't go!" Steve finally got out, remembering vividly that night in Afghanistan.

"England's a big country, Steve."

"Nowhere there is safe Natasha!" Steve blurted out without thinking, as Nigel and the others who were smiling at Steve's dilemma, suddenly took a serious interest.

"I'm still going Steve, that's my job. If not with you then I'll follow, asking questions," Natasha shot back, knowing she had the upper hand. Steve stood there for several seconds, trying to think of a way out. In the end, he surrendered to the inevitable.

"I found it better to have them along, than following," Nigel whispered to Steve, getting a nod in return.

"When do we leave?" Natasha asked her eyes sparkling.

"In one hour. I've booked five seats, I'll book another," Steve answered, bending to her will for the moment.

"Can you make it two; I can't go without Patrick, my assistant," Natasha smiled, as Patrick who happily thought he'd missed out on going, groaned loudly.

It took all of the hour for Steve to say goodbye to his family, Robin and Lindsey holding him, right up until he passed into the customs area. As Steve waved to his family, he was surprised to see kisses being laid on Patrick by Robin, Nigel from Lindsey and then Bill from Leone, leaving him stunned. Edward, who because of his job was allowed into the departure section, smiled at Steve's surprise.

"A lot has happened since the yanks have been here!" Edward laughed, seeing Patrick and Nigel look sheepishly at Steve.

"Yes it has, I'll threaten them later. What goes with Leone and the older agent?" Steve asked, seeing Leone wiping her eyes, as Bill went through customs.

"That took us all by surprise, like why you're going to England?"

"The terrorists that tried to kill me have bought a couple of atom bombs with the money. The yanks want it kept quiet, so since we know already, they're letting us handle it," Steve whispered cautiously to Edward.

"No offence, but aren't you guys a bit old?"

"There's also a bunch of SAS soldiers, smartarse!" Steve replied, knowing their ruthlessness was what the yanks needed.

"Good luck Steve, make sure you come home again my friend," Edward said gripping his hand, before turning quickly to hide his misgivings, as he walked out to join his family.

When Nigel and the other agents entered the plane, they were surprised to find that they were in first class.

"Shit this must have cost a few bucks!" Bill exclaimed as everyone made themselves comfortable. Except for their group, first class was empty, which suited Steve just fine. The rushed bookings he'd made were only possible by flying first class, but it did guarantee privacy. After taking off and everyone having eaten lunch, Steve asked for the stewardess to give them time to talk privately. Sitting everyone down in the bar area in the first class lounge, he quickly briefed them on what was happening in England. The main purpose of the agents being there was to secure the bombs once the terrorists had been caught so Steve and the others could depart without being involved.

"A lot could go wrong on this operation!" Nigel said fear in his voice after Steve had finished.

"We know, but surprise is with us, plus the SAS are good soldiers, they should make the difference," Steve answered confidently.

"You could have walked away?" Bill suggested looking at Steve.

"Could you?" Steve asked, seeing Bill acknowledge that they all had no choice.

"Are you even sure they'll turn up? They could know you're on to them," Patrick suggested, as Steve studied him closely, before answering.

"Good point, but for everyone's sake, I hope they fell for the deception or we've failed," Steve admitted, thinking he could like

Patrick; he had a way of grasping the facts, and sorting them out. After going over what he knew several times, Steve called it a night, settling down for dinner.

"Mind if I join you?" Natasha asked sitting down before he could say anything, making him laugh.

"What's so funny?"

"Do you always get your way?" Steve smiled, studying her, which made her blush.

"Not always. But what's the fun unless you try?"

"You know it's never too late to pull out," Steve suggested trying to keep her away from danger.

"Don't even try Steve. This story will be big enough to bury your story, and at the moment I'd rather keep the whole American incident quiet," Natasha replied, fencing with him again.

"You know I still remember that kiss," Steve smiled, finding Natasha's weak spot, as she went quiet looking confused.

"It was a long time ago," Natasha answered, her voice betraying her with a slight tremble, as they both ate their dinner in silence.

Bill sat half asleep, missing Leone. So far they'd only kissed, and if it hadn't been for this trip, it could have gone further, or so Bill hoped. Ali's plan was straightforward and well thought out. Bill thought it had more than a good chance of succeeding. The problem was he knew their full history, along with top CIA and FBI officers. Doing this raid was something these men and their code of honour couldn't avoid and that made them vulnerable.

Once the bombs were secured, their usefulness was at an end, and that's what worried Bill. Though he wasn't impressed with Steve's history, he made a decision to protect him, knowing he couldn't face Leone again if he didn't.

Patrick also saw the weakness in Ali's plan. Steve he knew was ruthless when cornered, but as this mission showed, he was at his weakest, when innocent people's lives were at stake. Seeing Natasha disappear down the corridor to the bathroom, he quickly got up and walked to Steve's seat, sitting down next to him.

"Mr Roberts, have you considered this plan leaves you vulnerable?" Patrick whispered quietly, not wanting the others to hear.

"How serious are you and Robin?" Steve shot back, watching Patrick as he had before, causing him to go blank.

"Spit it out, Patrick," Steve growled as Patrick tried to gather his thoughts.

"I love her, and she loves me! That should be enough!" Patrick answered loudly, daring Steve to say something.

"That's all I wanted to know. And about the other thing, why do you think we've got the FBI involved Patrick? Think about it," Steve smiled knowing he could trust Patrick and that Robin had picked well.

Natasha stood in the powder room, looking at her reflection in the mirror. She still looked good, but for how long? Steve, reminding her of the kiss had excited her, making her weak at the knees, something that hadn't happened in a long time. But how did she compare to his other women? She knew Steve's girlfriend had been a lot younger than herself, so would he still want a woman a bit older.

"Stop worrying you fool, he's a passionate man, he'll want you," Natasha convinced herself, as she walked slowly and sensually back to her seat, giving him her best smile.

HEATHROW AIRPORT

Arriving at Heathrow, Steve's group quickly passed through customs, heading out to the taxi rank. They hadn't been there for no more than a minute, when a black, twelve seater bus screeched to a halt beside him.

"Inside everyone, let's get moving," a Frenchmen, by his accent ordered, from the side door. As they all piled in, Steve and Natasha entered last.

"Who the fuck's the girl?' a Scottish voice yelled from the front, as Steve after hugging the Frenchmen, introduced the others.

"A journalist! Shit, are you crazy Steve?" Aaron roared, nearly choking after Steve introduced Natasha.

"I remember you both from Afghanistan. You two had foul mouths back then as well!" Natasha answered back angrily, silencing Cody and Aaron.

"The girl who kissed me," Steve replied, answering the question both his friends were looking for, making them both look around at her.

"Oh my God, he's right!" Aaron admitted, switching to French in his excitement. "What is she doing here?" Aaron continued after getting over the shock.

"It's a long story, I'll tell you about it later," Steve replied smiling

"Bloody hell, Ali's going to shit bricks," Cody laughed as Aaron joined in.

THE UNIT

Driving casually past the airfield clubhouse, Cody waved to the group of old and middle-aged men and women. They were sitting having tea while watching aircraft land and take off.

"We managed to hire an old hangar on the third runway. The runway is not used anymore, and we're supposedly doing flight training," Cody answered watching his rear vision mirror, just in case. Driving into the hangar, Steve's eyes were drawn to the group of young, fit men, casually watching their approach. As the van pulled up, Ali came outside to meet them. Pulling Steve aside and hugging him, he suddenly caught sight of Natasha.

"It's a long story, my friend, let's sit down," Steve suggested as the group moved inside into the office area. After hearing Steve's story, Ali admitted Steve's only option was to bring them along, and in some ways, it might help. Gathering everyone around, Ali went over his plan, which was a classic 'let the others do the dirty work' scenario. The plan was for the British Freedom Brigade to get possession of the two weapons.

They would do this by either paying the full amount or taking the weapons by force. Either way, it would lower the force facing them, which they would then engage. Because of the large enemy force, Captain Johnson had suggested getting more men to help maintain the perimeter. This would prevent anyone escaping, once the enemy was engaged. Ali had reluctantly agreed.

Their biggest problem was the size of the airfield. They knew it was where the weapons deal would go down, but not the exact location. Johnson had brought in two more teams plus his own, which made twenty-four. Ali thought that this number, plus themselves should be adequate.

Steve, Cody and Aaron weren't too happy about the increase, though if things went bad, the numbers might help. Ali pointed out that even with the SAS, the first minute would be critical. He also needed someone to get in close and try to gain control of the weapons arming devices.

"That's where you come in Steve; do you think you're up to it?" Ali asked seriously.

"I'm not getting any younger, but yes with a bit of darkness I should be able to," Steve replied, though his guts churned with the thought of more bloodshed.

"What about the FBI and the reporters!" Johnson asked not happy with their presence here.

"They'll stay here. They can cover this position till the mission is completed," Ali answered, still unsure of Johnson.

"There is no room for mistakes on this one gentleman. All enemy combatants must be taken out! Do you all understand?" Ali asked as the room went dead quiet.

"What if they are wounded?" Johnson asked angrily watching Ali's reaction.

"There's to be no prisoners Captain! Anyone of them could detonate those bombs. Shoot to kill, do your job. Remember even though this airport is thirty-five miles from London, the blast would kill thousands, and contaminate this area for a hundred lifetimes," Ali warned, hoping Johnson got the point.

Surprisingly, Johnson's men all nodded their support leaving him isolated. As the group got down to the small points of the operation, Natasha got up and walked out into the aircraft storage area of the hangar. Two SAS soldiers watched from just inside the hangar, and they saw no reason not to let her walk outside and along the old runway.

Steve scared Natasha and excited her at the same time. She could see it in his eyes that killing was no longer easy for him, somehow it appeared to hurt him mentally she surmised. In two weeks, with luck, it would all be over, or would it? She could tell Ali and Steve feared something. Maybe betrayal by these SAS units, although except for the officer, Natasha saw respect for Steve's unit in the SAS soldier's eyes.

"Good morning!" a voice said happily ahead of her, startling her, as she came back to earth. Focusing she saw two men standing near the end of the runway. Remaining calm, Natasha waved and walked over to them.

"Hello, how are you? I'm not trespassing, or anything am I?" Natasha asked, wondering if she had walked onto someone else's land.

"No, my friend and I are bird watchers. We come here every now and then to check on the local bird population. We make sure the planes aren't affecting them too much," a young man said happily, but his friend remained silent.

"You picked a beautiful day for it," Natasha replied her journalist instinct aroused for some reason, by these two men.

"What are you doing here?" The quiet young man asked, with a forced smile on his face.

"I'm using the flight simulator in the hangar over there, to try for my license again. Had a bit of trouble landing on my solo flight, so my instructor sent me here," Natasha replied giving her best smile.

"We were wondering what was going on there, it's not used much," the young man said looking relieved.

"I think they hired it for another three weeks, seems there's a lot of us failed pilots being retested, even though I think so far I've passed, with luck," Natasha giggled as the two men laughed as well, for different reasons.

"Anyway, good luck with the bird watching, I'd better get back," Natasha said smiling, as she walked casually back towards the hangar, stopping several times to look around, before entering. Watching her walk away Brennan and Ahmed stood quietly using their binoculars to study the area and the hangar where Natasha was heading.

"They could be a problem if they're still there in two weeks!" Ahmed admitted watching the roll of Natasha's backside, liking what he saw.

"I don't think so Ahmed, they're too far away to interfere, and if they're all like her, they'll run for the hills at the first shot," Brennan laughed.

"Yes, your right brother and at least we know now who's in there, saves going closer," Ahmed replied.

"That woman somehow looks familiar," Brennan said staring after her, trying to remember where he'd seen her.

"You may have dreamt about her, she looks appetising," Ahmed laughed thinking about her too, as Brennan laughed as well.

"Yes she was very attractive," Brennan admitted smiling. Forgetting the woman they crossed to the boundary fence, swiftly getting into their vehicle before departing.

"We're all set my brother! In just under two weeks we'll be able to free all our brothers from the oppressors in this country," Ahmed screamed, startling Brennan as they drove back to their men.

Natasha in the meantime walked without a care in the world, finally reached the hangar. The two SAS soldiers were nowhere to be seen, as Steve walked over all smiles.

"Follow me inside, keep smiling," Steve told her smiling, as they both entered the office area. It was like entering the tribal camp in Afghanistan, as half-dressed soldiers grabbed weapons and silently took up position around the building.

"Who were your friends?" Steve asked softly, a touch of fear in his eyes for her, showing he cared for her.

"I'd say they were the enemy," Natasha replied calmly, although her voice quivered.

"I should have thought of this! I thought they would carry out their recon a few days before the night, not two weeks before," Ali fumed, knowing they'd been lucky again.

"They're most probably just checking early, because of the raid on their headquarters," Aaron suggested, the others agreeing. Natasha then gave them a rundown on her chance meeting, and how she stuck to the cover story, getting respectful nods in return.

"Well done Natasha. They now think we're no threat, and we also have the position where the exchange will take place," Ali beamed, knowing that the deception at the warehouse had worked.

Nigel, who with his men had remained quiet letting the soldiers organise the raid, signalled to Steve he wanted to talk, so with Natasha in tow, the three of them walked outside.

"This new development puts the enemy troops close to this hangar. It might be prudent if my men and I had weapons," Nigel asked softly as they stood in the sun outside the hangar.

"Okay Nigel, you'll find in the rear office a cache of weapons, a couple nights before the raid, you can arm yourselves, but for now no one carries," Steve replied, knowing another group with unknown loyalties, would be armed on the night.

"Don't worry Steve; we'll protect your back!" Nigel said softly as if he had sensed what Steve was thinking.

"Where do you stand with my eldest daughter?" Steve suddenly asked as Nigel made to move away, stopping as if he'd hit a wall.

"She drives me crazy Steve, I don't know where I stand?" Nigel admitted before moving away.

"Your daughter has him so confused he doesn't know which ways up."

"Beautiful women have always had that effect on men," Steve answered his eyes bright as his memory flooded with Lindsey's mother's image. Grabbing Natasha's hand, Steve walked to the end of the runway as Natasha had before. Coming to the fence line, where the two men had crossed, they both stood silently, as Steve studied the surrounding area.

"I like you Natasha; you're a breath of fresh air. But I'm poison, get away from me while you can," Steve whispered his eyes clouding over, as he stared out over the fence line, into the past. Natasha turned swiftly and slapped him.

"Pull yourself together Steve, I've had losses too. My husband was killed by an ex-General, who didn't want his face on TV. It haunts me every day. Let's get through this than worry about tomorrow. People depend on you here for their lives, so wake up!" Natasha replied angrily, as Steve's surprised face broke into a smile.

"Someone slapped me many years ago, over the same thing," Steve answered wiping his eyes, getting rid of his depression.

"She did the right thing then," Natasha answered smiling, reaching forward and holding his hand reassuringly.

"It was Ali actually. He too couldn't stand my complaining," Steve explained, as they walked back towards the hangar.

Ali watched Natasha slap Steve from the hanger, 'Good for you' he thought smiling thinking Steve had met his match with Natasha. Once they'd returned, Ali gathered everyone inside for a meeting. He decided to send most of the SAS away leaving just three men and the FBI agents here. Johnson was far from impressed.

"We're better to stay here and train for the night."

"We now know where the exchange will happen. Furthermore, the enemy could return for another look, with this many person here; they're liable to get suspicious. Better you find accommodation close by and three nights before the attack, reassemble here," Ali put forward, getting a grudging acknowledgement from Johnson. "Cody and Aaron will be the only ones to camp here. The FBI and the three SAS soldiers must leave every night, returning in the daytime, as not to attract attention.   Is that understood?" Ali asked, getting acknowledgement from the group.

"What will you and Mr Roberts be doing?" Johnson asked suspiciously.

"We have other problems outside of this mission, which could affect the outcome here. We'll be travelling outside of the country for the next week to take care of them. Other than that, it's none of your concern," Ali pointed out, dismissing the meeting.

"Wherever you're going, I'm coming," Natasha informed Steve.

"Natasha you can't" was all Steve got out before Ali stopped him.

"She can come to Steve, but Patrick stays. He's not military or FBI, so here he'll help us blend in," Ali pointed out, as the groups prepared to leave.

"One other thing gentlemen, no one contacts anyone at all, even family, is that understood!" Ali ordered, getting acknowledgement from all present before they all departed.

Ali planned to hit the house and the office at the same time, demonstrating the units revolve, giving them a warning to back off. It took another three days to set the breach up, Steve being the one to penetrate the manager's home, decided to do a recon, by hiring a canal boat. Taking Natasha with him, they pretended to sail along the canal. Of course, they didn't actually sail, as being a motor yacht; they'd used the engines to glide past the impressive home.

Once there, they'd tied the boat up beside the wall, having a romantic picnic. Steve taking the camera, snapped off several pictures of Natasha with the fort behind her, the perfect cover. All the time, the guards watched, intrigued and impressed by the passion Steve and Natasha achieved on such a small blanket.

"God there's no way they'll think we faked that!" Natasha laughed, as Steve got the boat going.

"Yeah it's the most thorough recon I've ever done," Steve smiled, as they sat together on the stern of the boat, taking turns steering.

Arriving back in Amsterdam, they walked like two young lovers through the streets, arriving back at their hotel as it started getting dark. Bursting into their room kissing passionately, they were just about to rush to the bed, when Steve saw Ali waiting in the lounge room. Pulling apart, short of breath, Natasha walked into the bedroom stating she was having a shower, leaving Steve and Ali alone.

"How'd the recon go?" Ali asked a red-faced Steve.

"Good, got a good look at it," Steve replied.

"What about the house?" Ali asked, before bursting into laughter. "I'm happy for you Steve, but seriously, did you get a good look around?"

"Yes, it won't be easy, they're no fools, but then again, neither are we," Steve replied smiling.

"Okay, we'll hit both places tomorrow night. Try to get some rest!" Ali smiled before leaving.

'I can rest some other time!' Steve said to himself, heading to the shower.

Ali walked back to his hotel smiling at Steve's situation. Natasha had him spellbound, something he needed. He too had been busy, having spent the day cleaning his way through the syndicates building. He'd arrived early, entering from the rear alley. An Arab greeted him, from of all places, Iran. Gerard, as his name was now, had arrived from Iran ten years ago, changing his nationality and name. He'd been waiting for a replacement cleaner to arrive, from the employment agency.

"So you're the guy, what's your name?" Gerard asked bluntly.

"It's Steve!" Ali answered smiling.

"Yeah, I bet!" Gerard answered chuckling. "Let's get to work," he continued the interview over. Handing Ali a mop, a swipe card and a pair of overalls, he led him to the top floor. Here Ali began mopping the entire floor area, while Gerard vacuumed. Once finished they walked down to the next floor starting over, repeating the process. By the time lunch came around, Ali, sweat running down his back, had a detailed plan of each floor. At one stage Gerard's phone had rung, and an angry exchanged took place, his eyes darting to Ali, as he talked.

"That was the agency. They said you wouldn't be here until tomorrow," Gerard laughed. "Shit no wondered the country's falling apart!" he continued, thinking they'd stuffed it up.

"Well I'm here, so let's get going," Ali smiled, killing any further discussion. By the time knock off came, Ali was stuffed, though he had what he needed.

"You're not bad my friend. Are you coming back tomorrow?" Gerard asked, happy with him.

"That's up to the agency, they might send another. You know what they're like," Ali smiled, covering his tracks, as he departed. Now he sat in his room, thinking of what Steve and he had discussed about getting away from killing.

"Is it really possible?" he asked himself sadly.

THE WARNING

"Shit I'm getting old!" Steve moaned to himself climbing the wall above the canal. It was the worst wall to climb, devoid of handholds, forcing him to use his fingers to grip the rough stone. He'd picked this wall because it was the toughest and the only one unguarded. Now he wondered if he'd make it. Pulling a couple of climbing spikes from his pockets, he inserted one in a small crack, screwing it in, before attaching a small piece of rope.

"Thank God for these pins," Steve thought as he inched higher. While wandering around town with Natasha, he'd spotted a climbing shop, by accident. It was closing down, as climbing in a country with no mountains or hills would make selling mountain climbing gear hard. Germany, next door had heaps of mountains and unfortunately lots of climbing shops. The salesman, who was a fanatic climber, seemed suspicious of what Steve wanted the pins and rope for but the appearance of cash quickly dispelled all his doubts.

Placing another pin further up the wall, Steve tested it before moving up, as his fingers felt the battlements. An hour after he'd started, Steve found himself at the top, where he sat down catching his breath. A gun barrel pressing against his left ear interrupted his rest. A young man about thirtyish said something in Dutch watching him.

"I'm sorry do you speak English?" Steve asked trying to cover his surprise.

"I said that was quite a climb!" the young man replied in rough English, smiling. The way he stood, his physique and his short-cropped hair, told Steve he'd had a few years in the military for sure.

"Yeah, I did it for a bet!" Steve smiled; trying to get to his feet, as the gunman's other hand stopped him.

"Just stay there old man, you're trespassing, and my boss has no sense of humour," the gunman informed him, his voice sounding far from friendly. Fishing in his pocket, the young man pulled out a mobile phone. It was the distraction Steve was waiting for. Reaching upwards, grabbing the surprised gunman's hands, Steve smashed his face into the battlement. Jumping to his feet, Steve looked around for the man's backup. When no one came, Steve realising he'd been overconfident and hadn't reported his presence.

"Not bad for a fucking old guy!" Steve whispered angrily in the semi-unconscious guard's ear, before gagging and tying him up. Moving towards the house, with the utmost care, Steve hoped Ali was doing better.

At the same time, Ali was entering the syndicate's building from the rear, as he'd done the day before. Grabbing a pair of overalls and a mop, he quickly changed, before walked towards the lifts. He'd kept the swipe card from the other day, hoping they hadn't erased it from the system. Swiping the lift, the door opened, saving Ali using the stairs, which was his backup. 'Shit I most probably wouldn't have made it!' Ali smiled, pressing the eighth floor.

From his day here cleaning, Ali learned that this was where the surveillance room that monitored all the floors cameras was located. Exiting the lift, Ali slowly worked his way along the corridor, emptying bins, coming at last to the security room. Knocking on the door, he waved at the camera opposite. Seconds later the door flew open. There were two men on duty, one sat at the controls while the other, gun in one hand and garbage bin in the other, stood in the doorway.

"Empty the bin and hurry up!" the security guard demanded.

"Yes Sir," Ali answered smiling before turning to his cart and emptying the bin.

"You're new aren't you?" the other security man asked.

"Yes my cousin got me a job here, it is very good," Ali answered happily.

"Shit that's all we need, another bloody Arab," the Security guard laughed to his friend, as a fist slammed into his throat. Falling to the floor grasping his throat, Ali relieved him of his pistol, pointing it at the other frozen security man.

"Stay where you are and don't move," Ali ordered, as he advanced into the room.

After handcuffing both men and taping their mouths, Ali quickly turned off the security systems pulling out their DVDs for the past week, smashing them. Locking the door, he then proceeded to the seventh floor that housed the vault. Here two of the remaining four guards stood watch. Both were armed with pistols; however, with video surveillance, the two guards took their job less than serious. They were both asleep at a desk beside the main door to the vault, making Ali's job easy.

Walking silently up to the first guard, Ali belted him across the head with his pistol, knocking him out. The other guard bolted upright, to find Ali gun touching his forehead.

"Would you mind opening the door for me?" Ali asked politely.

"I haven't got access to the vault," the guard replied nervously.

"Look I know there's no money kept in there, only records. So open it up now!" Ali demanded. He came by this bit of information yesterday when Gerard had been asked to clean the vault and took Ali with him.

"The only reason the records are kept in the vault is for fire and security, they're not worth anything," Gerard had told him smiling. The guard in the end not wanting to be shot for paper records, dutifully obeyed, punching a hidden button in the wall behind the desk.

"Thanks for that," Ali said politely, as he belted the guard over the head, knocking him out as well.

Walking into the vault, Ali looked at the massive amount of records, indicating contracts and successful operations the syndicate had run. These were interesting, but what Ali wanted, was the small pile of back up disks sitting neatly in the corner. These could do this syndicate severe damage, revealing not only hits but also clients and victims relations. These two groups would make short work of this Syndicate if they came to light.

Piling the twenty disks into his pockets, Ali turned to leave. Coming out the door, he heard one of the downed guard's radios squawking, as the two remaining guards, failing to contact the other four set off the alarm. The claxon screamed a high pitch wail, as the two remaining guards thundered into the vault room. Racing to the downed guards, they both looked at the open vault doors, fear on their faces.

"Check what's missing," one ordered, as he tried to revive the guards. Ali's gun sticking in his back made him stop his first aid, as he was pushed towards the vault and then shoved inside. Slamming the door on the surprised remaining guard, Ali then caught the lift down to the ground floor, leaving by the rear alley. 'Piece of cake,' Ali smiled, as walking down the street he was passed by several police cars.

Meanwhile, Steve did a loop of the house taking out the security. There were four men, including the first one who got the drop on him, making Steve more cautious. After all four had been secured, Steve moved inside making sure there were no more surprises. He'd been told the guy only had three guards with him, so the fourth he figured must be permanently at the house. It was an impressive house too. No expense had been spared, showing the contract business was doing well.

Arriving at the main bedroom, Steve found the accountant entertaining. The two girls were way too young for the accountant, who was Steve's age, but then again he seemed happy, up until when he saw Steve. Looking towards a set of drawers next to his bed, the accountant then looked at Steve, seeing him nodding no. Walking to the drawers, his eyes never leaving the accountant's face, Steve reached in and withdrew an old German luger.

"That's impressive!" Steve said looking at the gun, as the two girls became aware of Steve.

"Who's he?" the girls asked, clearly not too worried by a man with a gun.

"A problem I'd say. You two stay here, I'll be right back," the accountant assured them. Walking out into the adjoining room, which Steve guessed, was his home office, the accountant poured two drinks.

"I judge your Captain Roberts?" he said sitting down, after giving Steve a drink.

"Thank you, and yes I am," Steve replied, sitting down as well.

"When the partners took that contract, I knew there'd be trouble. My name's Peter by the way."

"Yes, it didn't go well for your men Peter."

"Claude was getting too confident with his contracts. The others were trying to prove themselves, always a problem," Peter answered.

"Not anymore I'm afraid. You seem rather unconcerned by me, why?" Steve asked smiling.

"I read your file. I'd be dead by now if you meant to kill me, so I guess this is a warning."

"You're right, it is a warning my friend, and you only get one. By the way, we're also visiting your office tonight, keeping some insurance for the future," Steve informed him.

"Thank you for the warning, you're professionalism is well known. I judge you've taken the backup files?"

"Yes, and they'll stay buried as long as we live."

"You didn't kill any of my men, did you? They may be not the best, but I like them," Peter asked this time showing genuine concern.

"No, they're okay. One nearly got me though, a young man about thirty with short cropped hair," Steve said impressed.

"That's my nephew, he served in Afghanistan, took a hit, so now he and three of his army buddies work for me," Peter answered happily, glad his nephew was okay.

"Well he won't be happy when he comes to, remind him that just because someone's old, doesn't mean they're harmless," said Steve seeing his business was finished prepared to leave.

"Before you go, can I have my Luger back, it was my father's," Peter asked hopefully, as Steve unloaded it and passed it to him.

"Have a good night Peter. Don't make me come back!" Steve said seriously this time, leaving.

"Don't worry I got the message!" Peter answered watching him leave. Once Steve had left, Peter took several deep breaths. He realised how lucky he was to still be alive, knowing Roberts' reputation for violence. Running out, he untied his men, they all then searched for his nephew, finding him on the canal wall.

"I'm sorry uncle; he got the drop on me. The guy was old; I didn't think anyone could be that quick at his age." Roger, his nephew, confessed.

"Remember you told me about the tribe in Afghanistan, who talked about the legendary western soldiers, the trained killers who saved their chief, back in the eighties?"

"Yes, we thought it was just a story," Roger replied.

"Well, you just met one of them son, be glad he's changed," Peter smiled, helping his nephew inside, as his phone started ringing.

"That'll be the office," Peter smiled answering.

The next morning Peter met with his partners of the Syndicate. After Peter explained what happened at his home, the partners decided that from then on, no one was to take a contract on ex-soldiers, especially Special Forces. Needless to say, the contract on Roberts and his team was dropped; they'd just keep the ten million front money.

Ali sat with Steve and Natasha on the flight, talking about past times and what the future held. Steve admitted this whole operation with the English SAS worried him, so much could go wrong.

"It's the end of it, Steve. After this we can all relax," Ali pointed out, knowing the yanks owed them big time after this.

"I hope your right, Ali. I've had it. I can't keep running any longer," Steve confessed, as Natasha squeezed his hand.

"I know everything Steve. When this is finished so will others, they won't do anything, I can assure you," Natasha smiled confidently, as their flight took them back to England. Ali and Steve both smiled at Natasha reassuringly. Looking at each other they lost their smiles, knowing more about the people involved than Natasha.

THE AIRFIELD

Three days to go and everyone was present at the airfield. The SAS supervised by Ali, went through their paces getting the plan and the location down pat. Steve practised in his own way, running attacks on the SAS soldiers during the night. They were good men, though Steve still managed to get them all. So impressed were they that several asked for instructions from him on night target approach, all happy to learn from a pro. He passed on what he'd learned, as he had when training his battle group in the SAS, gaining their trust. Johnson was unimpressed with his men's acceptance of Roberts.

"So this Roberts, he's your unit's assassin is he?" Johnson snarled, startling his men by his angry outburst. They'd all been sitting inside, watching Steve train outside with two of his men. Looking up to see if his words had hit home, Johnson stared down the barrel of Ali's pistol. All the SAS present sat dead still, as Aaron, Cody and the FBI agents swiftly raised their weapons, pointing them at the other SAS soldiers who sat shocked.

"You've got no idea what that man's been through Captain. Say something like that again, and I'll kill you," Ali spat out, shaking with rage, before walking away. Even after Ali left it took several seconds for Aaron, Cody and the FBI men to lower their weapons and withdraw their anger at Johnson obvious.

"Did you see that men?" Johnson growled angrily jumping to his feet, looking around the room.

"No Sir we saw nothing," his corporal answered, as the other SAS soldiers got up and moved outside.

"What's going on corporal?" Johnson asked angrily, surprised by his men's reaction.

"We've all got family in London, Sir. These men are pros; they know what they're doing. No one cares what happens to these fucking terrorists Sir!" the Corporal told him, before walking out with the other men.

Johnson stood frozen with anger at his own men's action. Walking out the side door of the hangar, he reached into his pocket, taking out the orders handed to him. He'd been at his base to recruit the other two teams, for this raid when his commanding officer had called him in for an update. Present at the meeting was Ross Stuart, the CIA director. He seemed concerned about Ali's unit's ability to handle the situation. After Johnson had left the meeting, Stuart had handed him the message from his commander, wishing him luck. It was marked confidential, for his eyes only.

To Captain Johnson
On completion of the mission, terminate all members of Ali Mustaffer's unit. It was signed Captain Wolfe, his Commanding Officer.

This put Johnson in quite a bind, as his men now respected Ali's team more than they did him. He saw only one solution, as soon as the battle was finished, he himself would carry out the order, without his men knowing. Ripping the letter into pieces, Captain Johnson went to talk to his men, hoping to smooth the trouble over. Behind him Cody came out of the shadows, silently picked up the pieces, before meeting up with Ali.

"So someone doesn't like us," Ali said smiling as they finished reconstructing the letter. Passing it to Steve, he glanced at it before handing it on to Natasha.

"What are you going to do about the Captain?" Natasha asked Ali as she handed the note to Nigel.

"Nothing, we need his men, and I don't think they'd help us if we put a bullet in Johnson."

"Why are you so happy?" Steve asked surprised, he didn't feel like smiling.

"We knew this might happen. Now we know who it is and he stupidly hasn't told his men." Ali pointed out.

"Look I don't like the Captain either, but I don't want him killed for following orders. What do we do?" Nigel asked neutrally, watching Cody, who sat there silently, fingering his knife. Nigel had heard about Cody from the SAS soldiers involved at the warehouse. He sensed killing Johnson wouldn't worry him too much.

"I thought after this we could walk away," Aaron said sadly.

"There is also the third assassin called the Thistle. He could still be after Steve," Ali reminded him.

"He's been taken care of!" Cody said sheepishly from the corner putting his knife away.

"How do you know that?" Ali asked suspiciously.

"Because I'm the Thistle" Cody answered, as the room went deadly quiet.

"You took ten million to kill me?" Steve growled dangerously, swiftly drawing his weapon.

"Take it easy Steve, I had no intention of going after you, I just needed the money."

"You gave them information on me and the others, including our families!" Steve shouted angrily.

"I'm sorry about that Steve. I was trapped," Cody replied before explaining what had happened.

Cody had lost everything in the stock market crash. To make ends meet he had hired himself out as an assassin using 'The Thistle' as his cover name. After building up quite a reputation, he'd been approached by the CIA, for the hit on Steve. He'd panicked, knowing if he refused they wonder why. When the meeting was set up with the other assassins, he'd given up some information on their whereabouts and missions to show his commitment.

He told them nothing about their families. That information had come from the CIA, not him. He'd spent most of his time, tracking down the assassins in London, but Ali had beaten him to them. When he'd finished, the room lapsed into silence, all eyes were glued to Steve.

"We go back a long way Cody, but you crossed the line on this one," Steve replied, before putting his weapon away and walking outside.

"It's the truth, Aaron!" Cody said, Aaron, being his closest friend.

"I believe you, but if you needed money you should have asked us," Aaron replied sadly, as the group silently broke up, leaving Cody sitting alone. Ali, in the end, went to Steve, finding him on his own, sitting on a fallen tree.

"I can't believe he betrayed us!" Steve groaned, having trouble believing one of his closest friends had sold him out.

"He was trapped, Steve. I know what he did was wrong, but we weren't there."

"Do you think he's telling the truth?"

"I hope so Steve, I hate to think he ratted on us, giving up our families locations for money."

"Do you trust him?"

"With my life Steve. Remember he has already saved my life once in London. He could've done me in there, no one would've known," Ali confessed.

"What do you think we should do?"
"What we came here to do. So let's finish it!"

THE EXCHANGE

Brennan led sixty of Ahmed's men into the tree-lined area, bordering the spot where the plane would land. Standing out in the open, was Ahmed, and five unarmed men. Brennan and the men knew there'd be trouble, as they didn't have the money for the trade, so they moved into position expecting it. The plan was simple when Ahmed gave a prearranged signal, his men would surge forward seizing the two weapons, and disarming the Ukrainians. If the Ukrainians surrendered they would be let go, but if they resisted they would be killed. Ahmed's confidence had been overflowing at their meeting earlier that night, as he excitedly waited for their war to start.

"We will force them to follow the teaching of the Prophet. They will give up their evil ways accepting our beliefs, or face the consequences!" Ahmed screamed, his eyes blazing, as his followers shouted hysterically. Brennan found his enthusiasm dampened by his meeting with the old man. Sign or not, the old man was not a Muslim but had shown compassion for Brenan's beliefs. Surely God didn't want them to slaughter so many innocent people, as Ahmed's supposed vision suggested. The word 'supposed' stuck in Brennan's thoughts, as he lay behind an old oak tree watching his leader, who waited confidently for the Ukrainians to land.

"What do I do God? What do I do?" Brennan said softly, as the sound of a plane approached.

Near the hangar, Ali, Cody and Aaron, equipped with infrared goggles, watched the British Freedom Brigade forces take up position. The SAS, under Captain Johnson's command, had moved earlier that afternoon, taking up position outside the boundary fence. There they waited for the enemy to park their vehicles before taking up their final positions. The plan was to wait for the exchange to take place and take out the enemy forces, as they prepared to leave in their vehicles. They too believed the meet would not go well, although in case it did, Aaron had one SAS soldier near the end of the runway with a stinger, to make sure the Ukrainians didn't get away.

"Can you see Steve?" Ali whispered to Aaron, as he switched from his goggles to his sniper rifle, which was fitted with the same infrared system, but far more powerful.

"No I haven't seen him since the light started to go, but that's not unusual!" Aaron replied a slight smile on his lips.

"Yeah we might be getting on, but the basics we learned seemed to have stayed with us," Cody softly answered, which was met with silence. No matter how he tried Cody realised, admitting that he'd taken a contract on Steve, had opened a gulf between himself and his closest friends.

Money had always been his weakness, slipping through his fingers like water. The hundreds of thousands he'd made over the years while working for the yanks, he'd frittered away on get rich investments. Broke and desperate, he'd thought of asking his friends, but pride had stopped him. Turning to the only thing he knew, he'd become a gun for hire, getting a reputation for getting the job done. When the ten million dollar contract on Steve had arrived at his email site, plus the promise of a bonus, he had greedily accepted.

That same night after taking the contract, Cody had lain in bed, as his life had unravelled before his eyes. For the first time in his life that he could remember, he cried like a baby. He had no family, no girlfriend or wife. No one would grieve his passing, except his brothers in this unit, who he had betrayed. Since that night he'd tried to track down the hitmen after Steve, having Ali beat him to them. Now as Cody lay in the darkness watching the enemy prepare their trap, he had come to a decision. No matter what they thought of him, tonight he'd protect their backs and win back their trust.

Steve heard the plane circling above the runway, long before he saw it. At any other time, he would have laughed at the situation. Heavily camouflaged in a 'Gillis suit', borrowed from the SAS, Steve lay motionless not four metres from the six men standing on the side of the runway. He lay there waiting to kill these men who themselves had men waiting to kill their suppliers, while the SAS waited to kill who was left. On top of that, the SAS commander was also trying to kill him. And why was Steve doing this, to stop the first group killing other innocent people?

He, like most normal people, hated the word kill. Even his camouflaged suit name had been changed from a killer suit to Gillis, to get rid of the word 'kill'. Now here he was, right in the middle of all things, a killing ground.

'No matter what happens tonight, this is the last time I'll hold a weapon!' Steve promised himself, as he crawled slowly forward towards his targets.

Natasha and the FBI agents also heard the plane. Fear of the unknown gripped them all as they lay on the floor of the office area, in the pitch black waiting for the inevitable. Nigel at least felt slightly in control, having a radio supplied by Ali, giving him a rough outline of what was going on. As he heard information, he'd pass it along to the others, especially Natasha, who sounded uncharacteristically scared. Bill also felt a touch of fear though no one would know from his hardened shell. He missed Leone he realised and wanted to be back with her, not here risking everything.

Over the last couple of days, he had spent some time with Steve and had to admit, liked him. He'd always had trouble bonding with other men, who hadn't shared his experiences. Steve, on the other hand, had been through hell making him feel like a rookie by comparison. This was it for him he realised, 'when this is over I'm out' Bill told himself softly, as he fingered his weapon safety switch, hoping for once, not to have to use it.

The plane slowly circled the disused third runway, before swiftly descending and approaching the lights held by Ahmed's men. The twin-engine plane had seen better days as it thundered down the runway, guided only by the lights of surrounding buildings, belching smoke and the odd flame as the engines backfired. Coming to an unglamorous stop, the plane suddenly increased power turning full circle to face the way it had landed. Ahmed's group showed signs of nervousness, as they waited silently for the passenger to appear.

Time froze as if all present were holding their breath, as the door of the plane slowly opened and the portable stairs were deployed touching the ground with a small thump. A group of four armed men quickly climbed down the stairs taking up positions covering every direction, as their boss descended. Ahmed and his men slowly approached, as one of the Ukrainians guards swiftly checked them all for weapons.

"Allah be with you, my brothers!" Deros, the Ukrainians leader exclaimed, coming forward, embracing Ahmed.

"It is good to see my brother, how was your flight?" Ahmed asked smiling happily.

"Dangerous my friend, the infidel's air forces are everywhere. We were lucky not to have been forced down and searched several times. Luckily we have learned to avoid them," Deros admitted as he nervously watched the surrounding sky.

"No problems with the weapons?" Ahmed asked sweat starting to appear on his face.

"No, they are safe, did you bring the money?" he replied looking around seeing no cases.

"It is in the vehicle, my friend. We too have learned to be careful," Ahmed informed him turning to one of his men and pointing to the vehicles. This was the signal Brennan, and his men had been waiting for, as they all surged to their feet running towards the aircraft. Surprisingly the Ukrainians didn't open fire. Instead they raise their arms. Disarming them all, Brennan sent one of his men into the plane to get the pilot.

"I trusted you, my friend, we are brothers in the struggle against the disbelievers. Why have you deceived me?" Deros asked, glaring at Ahmed.

"We need the two bombs for our cause, God commanded us to take them!" Ahmed said out loud, as his men cheered.

"You deceive yourself and your men. God would not want our cause to suffer, to grant your so-called vision!" Deros laughed, having heard of Ahmed's vision.

Suppressing his rage, at first, Ahmed stood there as if turned to stone. Then, grabbing one of Brennan's men's weapons, he shot Deros in the head at point-blank range. Deros' men, who had at first followed orders, allowing Ahmed's men to disarm them, reacted instantly to their leader being shot. Greatly outnumbered, the Ukrainians exploded into life, attacking the men guarding them.

Unlike their English brothers, they had all seen action, using their skills to overpower Ahmed's untrained men. Disarming their guards, they then open fire on the confused Englishmen, spraying them with automatic fire.

Brennan's men, no matter how green, knew how to pull a trigger on their weapons. At point blank range, numbers counted as Deros men were one by one killed. Even so, before all the Ukrainians were dead, ten of Ahmed's group were also, with another six wounded. Brennan felt absolute shame at the shooting of the Ukrainians.

Standing, looking at the dead, he noticed Ahmed slowly getting to his feet. He had dived for cover after shooting Deros. Now he roared a battle cry, inciting his men to join in, overlooking his own cowardly actions. Rushing to the plane followed by several men, the two bombs were carried outside, along with two briefcases.

Opening one he found a transmitter for triggering one of the bombs. Jubilantly he held the device up for all his men to see, as he switched it on, powering up the transmitter.

"Shit no!" Aaron said out loud, startling Ali and Cody.

"What's wrong?" Ali asked watching the firefight with his goggles.

"One of those idiots just armed a bomb!" Aaron informed him sounding scared.

"Captain Johnson!" Ali said into his radio getting an immediate reply from him.

"What's up?" Johnson whispered back, as Ali brought him up to speed. After a couple of minutes of discussion, Ali and Johnson both decided it was best to move in and not wait for the enemy to approach their vehicles. Passing the word, Johnson and his men formed a skirmish line slowly moving forward towards the plane's location.

Brennan, seeing things were getting out of hand approached Ahmed asking him what was going on.

"We are ready my brother. Nothing can stop us!" Ahmed excitedly informed him.

"We must move from here Ahmed. The shots must have been heard by someone, the police could turn up at any moment."

"Let them, we can always set off the bomb," Ahmed laughed, before thinking closely on what Brennan had said. "You are right brother; here the people are few, while in London the effect will be much greater," Ahmed pointed out smiling.

Passing Brennan the triggering device, Ahmed gathered his men telling them to head for the vehicles. Standing there silently, Brennan looked down at the small transmitter he held in his hands. Repulsed by the evil he felt through the device, he made a decision.

Ahmed's men had just started to move towards their vehicles when the first bullets hit the jubilant group. Ahmed's men went down like bowling pins, as the SAS hosed the hapless men repeatedly. Diving to the ground Ahmed looked for Brennan for support, seeing his lifeless eyes staring back at him accusingly. Shaking with fear, Ahmed grabbed the transmitter from Brennan's hand and slowly crawled into the surrounding bushes.

The SAS were taking no chances, firing at anything that didn't have a hole in it, while all the time Steve motionless on the ground fired kill shots into the wounded survivors. He'd accounted for most of the key targets, even the one with the transmitter. Unfortunately the big mouthed speech giver, Steve presumed was the leader, had taken it from him.

When Ahmed had dropped to the ground, he'd luckily managed to land in a blind spot, which Steve couldn't see. With all the enemy soldiers down, Steve surged to his feet racing forward signalling with his headset radio to the SAS to cease-fire. Going from body to body he searched for the leader unable to locate him.

"All units, the enemy leader has slipped away, and he's got the detonator. Make sure no vehicles leave and start a sweep," Steve ordered as he continued to look for the target.

While this was going on, Ali ordered Nigel and his agents to secure the two bombs and if possible have Aaron look at the live one and try to disarm it. The night had become silent again, as the last enemy soldiers standing were cut down. A game of cat and mouse then started, as the SAS and Steve hunted the terrorist leader.

Ahmed lay motionless, scared shitless under a thick clump of undergrowth, watching dark shapes, slowly glide through the bushes around him. He knew he must keep moving, or the soldiers would kill him without mercy as they had his men. Holding the transmitter up, he stared at it realising that it held no power if you weren't prepared to sacrifice yourself. Ahmed had planned for one of his followers to detonate the bomb not himself, knowing the cause needed him alive, to continue to greatness. He knew he still had loyal men waiting for him at their hideout, they would carry the bomb gratefully, but he had to get there.

"I wish Brennan were still alive he'd know what to do!" Ahmed softly said to himself, as another dark shape drifted through the trees, making him fearfully turn to stone.

Natasha and Patrick sat huddled in the corner of one of the hangar offices, wondering what was happening. Nigel and the other agents had left, carrying Aaron, who still couldn't walk unaided. Although the SAS forces weapons were suppressed to cut down on noise, the terrorist weapons were not, making them sound a lot closer than the good guys. Peeking outside, Patrick saw the shape of the agents and Aaron racing down the runway, towards the aeroplane. In the distance, they could both hear the sound of sirens approaching, as the shooting died away and silence hung over the airport.

"I don't like being here, while the action is out there!" Natasha said out loud, startling Patrick.

"They told us to stay put Natasha."

"Well the shootings stopped, and those sirens tell me the local cops are coming. I think we should find out what's going on, that's our job remember," Natasha reminded him, knowing Patrick, who was a great researcher, would never be a true reporter. She knew he lacked the motivation to get out and take a chance to get the story, something that now had to be done.

"Okay, Okay, I get the point, but let's be careful shall we!" Patrick answered sounding none too happy. They'd walked about half the distance to the plane, when Patrick who was leading, saw a shape moving swiftly towards them. He was just about to call out when the figure raised a pistol.

"Get down Natasha!" Patrick screamed turning and pushing her backwards onto the ground, as two shots rang out. Patrick above her was catapulted from his feet. Too shocked to yell, Natasha scrambled out from under Patrick's body hearing him moan in agony. She was just about to turn him over and check his wounds when a hand grabbed her hair dragging her to her feet.

Ahmed had remained motionless for ten minutes, hoping to remain undetected, when he had heard the sound of distant sirens approaching. Realising he would soon be trapped; he took a chance and headed away from the group's vehicles. He knew that a hangar was in this direction, and hoped either to find some type of transport or a better place to hide. Fear made him move quickly as he hurried blindly forward, swapping the detonator for his pistol. Though sweating heavily, Ahmed felt confident he'd made the right decision, when he suddenly saw two shapes approaching him. Hearing the lead shadow yell a warning, Ahmed fired two shots knocking the first shadow onto the second. Rushing forward he was just about to finish the second shadow when he saw it was a woman and the thought of having a hostage came to him.

"Be silent, or you will die like your friend." a male voice hissed in her ear, pushing her back in the direction of the hangar. "Is there a vehicle in the hangar?" the voice whispered, his breath coming in gasps as he sucked in mouthfuls of air. Natasha, too scared to answer, worried sick about Patrick, was hit across the face, sending her onto the ground. "You have ten seconds to answer?" the voice chuckled enjoying having her at his mercy, as he shoved his pistol against the side of her head.

'I'm going to die no matter what I answer', she thought, as she looked up defiantly at her executioner.

"Go to hell, you arsehole!" Natasha spat out, as a shape rushed out of the darkness, smashing her attacker to the ground.

Steve had just met with Aaron, Nigel and his men when the shots rang out from towards the direction of the hangar. Realising the SAS was spread out towards the vehicle, and away from the hangar. Steve recalled them sending them towards the shots. Cody, who was also with the SAS watching Johnson, was the closest. He without hesitation charged back towards the hangar, knowing Natasha and Patrick weren't armed. Fear touched Steve too, as he too realised Natasha was defenceless.

Giving instructions to Aaron to disarm the bomb, and the FBI agents to cover him, he turned and ran blindly towards the hangar. Cody arrived there first, crash tackling Ahmed, ripping the pistol from his grip, as they both hit the ground hard. Rolling to his feet, Cody ran in, smashing his boot into the terrorists face, knocking him flat on his back. Looking up he gave Natasha a smile.

"You're safe now lassie!" was all Cody got out when he heard running feet. Turned swiftly preparing to fire, he was relieved to see

Steve rushing towards him. He was just about to say something funny when Johnson appeared behind Steve weapon raised.

"No!" Cody screamed running forward and colliding with Steve, sending them both to the ground, as a stream of bullets erupted around them.

Time seemed to slow, as Steve dazed and in shock, tried to move. Instinctively, he knew he'd been seriously hurt, as pain ripped through his body. Fighting to stay conscious, he realised something had fallen across his chest, pinning him to the ground. As his hands went to move whatever it was, they came away wet with blood. In great pain, he lifted his head and focusing, saw Cody's eyes staring at him.

Looking beyond Cody, Steve saw Johnson smiling, as he loaded a fresh magazine. With a cruel smile on his face, he lifted his weapon to fire, when his face changed showing both surprise and fear, as multiple weapons open fired on him, from the surrounding area. Johnson appeared to Steve to have been electrocuted as he danced and jerked wildly around, driven away from Steve by the impact of bullets. In the end, he tumbled face down into a small group of bushes.

"Shit, it's Captain Johnson!" one of the SAS men yelled to the others, as Johnson's men rushed in thinking they'd killed the last terrorist. When Johnson had opened up on Steve and Cody, the other SAS soldiers were just behind Cody. Hearing Cody scream and collide with Steve as shots ploughed into them, the soldiers had come to a conclusion, that the last terrorist was the one firing. They had all opened fired, as soon as their target offered them a clear shot when Johnson walked forward reloading into the open.

"That explains the surprised look," Steve said to himself as the soldiers gathered around checking the downed people. Steve coming to his senses yelled a warning!

"The target with the detonator is on the ground here somewhere, find him!" Steve shouted wincing with pain as the soldiers scanned the undergrowth coming to a tree where Ahmed sat propped against it.

"You have all failed infidels!" he shouted insanely through his broken teeth. "I will destroy you all!" he screamed pressing the button on the detonator. Many of the soldiers blinked, trying to think of something to say to God or to their friends, thinking their lives were over. Ahmed's too closed eyes as he embraced his fate smiling serenely.

Reality made his eyes fly open when he realised that the bomb had not gone off. Screaming in panic, he pressed the button again, as the SAS getting over the shock, fired into him till their ammo was gone.

"Shit looks like we did it again!" Cody said out loud coughing blood and trying to smile, as Steve cradled him in his arms.

"Yes my friend you saved us all this time," Steve replied hugging him, thinking his crash tackle had damaged the detonator.

"I never meant to cause you any harm Steve," Cody stuttered out through a wall of pain, as blood oozed out of the corner of his mouth.

"I know my friend. Just stay still, we'll fix you up," Steve answered tears in his eyes, making it hard to see. Aaron arrived diving down onto the ground next to Cody cutting open his shirt, his broken leg forgotten. One look at the wounds was enough for anyone to know Cody was doomed, but Aaron battled on, applying field dressings to what was left of Cody's stomach. Pushing a vial of morphine into his arm, Aaron moved away unable to face his friend. Natasha, supported by Ali took his place.

"You saved my life, thank you!" Natasha said sobbing, kissing Cody on the check, as Ali grabbed his hand.

"You'll be up in no time Cody, just hang on till the medics get here," Ali told him, his voice trembling as the group went silent.

"Shit I hope none of you plays poker, you haven't got the faces for bluffing!" Cody chuckled before he closed his eyes for the last time. Steve felt the life leave his friend, as he remembered the first man he had killed so many years ago had done.

Ali, Aaron and Steve sat silently with their friend unable to let him go, till Aaron unable to look at Cody, glanced at Steve's side seeing the blood.

"You're hit Steve!" he stammered out. Clearing his mind of his friend's death, he frantically cut Steve's clothing away locating two wounds. Natasha held Steve while Ali ordered the SAS soldiers to continue looking for enemy soldiers, before telling Nigel to have one of his men call an ambulance.

The police and emergency services arrived on the scene shortly afterwards, along with a large contingent of media, who'd been tipped off to the shooting. Natasha stayed by Steve's side as two medics worked on the two wounds he had, one in his left side and another in his upper left leg. The one in his side was severe; she could tell by the expressions on the faces of the medics who treated him.

While Natasha stayed with Steve, Ali and Aaron moved Cody out of view, covering him with their jackets. So engrossed was she that at first, she didn't realise Patrick was standing above her.

"Oh my God!" she screamed clutching her heart, startling everyone as she jumped up hugging him. "I thought you were dead!"

"Not yet, but I'm awfully sore," Patrick answered before explaining. Being a little scared about going out into the open, Patrick had put on a spare bulletproof vest the SAS had left behind. He was going to give it to Natasha but figured he'd be leading, so he'd worn it. When the terrorist had shot him, both bullets had hit him in the vest, propelling him backwards, knocking him unconscious.

"Well I'm glad you did put it on," Natasha replied, giving him another hug and kiss, before returning to Steve's side.

"How is he?" Patrick asked one of the medics.

"Better now, but he's lost a lot of blood," the medic answered neutrally, watching Steve as a stretcher arrived.

"You've got yourself quite a story Miss!" the other medic smiled recognising Natasha.

"Yes, we certainly have," Patrick answered distantly for her, wondering how much they could tell, as Natasha continued to hold Steve's hand.

CHARRING CROSS HOSPITAL
WEST LONDON

New York Times reporters scooped the whole story as pandemonium broke out at the story of what happened at that small airport in the western suburbs of London.

The story went that a group of FBI agents assigned to help Australian Federal police investigate links with a terrorist in Australia had stumbled onto a plot to detonate two bombs in London. With the help of a local Mosque in London, where the terrorists had once attended, they gained vital information about the terrorist cell in England.

Contacting the English SAS, the FBI with the help of the London police force had raided the cell's base in the docks area of London. Not finding the bombs, the SAS had found information on a concealed laptop, about the handover of the weapons from a Ukrainian terrorist group to their British counterparts. Seeing this was their last chance to intercept the weapons, the FBI agents and the SAS set up an ambush at the small airfield to the west of London, where the exchange would take place. In the firefight that followed, the entire terrorist cell was wiped-out along with the loss of Captain Johnson, and an innocent bystander named Cody Mactavish.

It appeared that during the firefight with the terrorists; their leader had secretly slipped away activating one of the bombs before he left. Captain Johnson, who had finally cornered the terrorist leader, had been fatally shot while trying to disarm him. Cody Mactavish, who had been studying for his pilot's licence in a disused hangar, had seen Johnson shot and had decided to help. Without any thought to his own safety, Cody had run in knocking the terrorist leader from his feet and inadvertently causing the terrorist to drop the detonator.

Still armed the terrorist had fatally shot Cody, before the other SAS soldiers arrived on the scene, killing him. In the firefight, all the terrorists had been killed, four other people were hurt, none seriously, including two SAS soldiers and a New York Times reporter, and her assistant, who were there helping the FBI with their investigation.

Captain Johnson and Cody became national heroes when the news broke. The Queen herself posthumously presented both

Captain Johnson and Cody, with the Victoria Cross Medal for bravery, before announcing a state funeral for them both. The SAS soldiers along with several London police officers received various medals for bravery, which they would personally receive from the Queen.

Also honoured was the spiritual leader of the Mosque, which had helped in stopping the attack on London. The Prime Minister himself would visit the Mosque to attend a prayer meeting for world peace. Nigel and his team were also presented with bravery medals, from England, Australia and their home country. The Vice President who would represent America at the funeral would award them after the service.

Steve was unaware of any of these happenings, as he lay in a coma, fighting for his life in hospital, guarded by Natasha, Ali and Aaron. His loss of blood had nearly killed him, and even if he recovered, doctors speculated that he mightn't be able to walk. Natasha had only smiled at their pessimistic views.

"You don't know Steve like we do!" Natasha replied smiling optimistically, as she watched over Steve, like a protective lioness with her cubs. Four days passed before Steve finally awoke. Looking down at his side he saw Natasha asleep in her chair beside him, her laptop on the bed near his feet still on.

"Do you ever stop working?" Steve croaked out, his lips dry as Natasha stirred. At first, she wondered what had awakened her when she looked at Steve's face seeing his eyes open. Too shocked to speak, she burst into tears, as she tried to pull herself together.

"Do I look that bad?' Steve asked softly, a small smile on his lips.

"I glad you think it's funny! You scared me half to death!" She answered angrily and crying at the same time. "And this is the last time you do anything like this if you expect me to come and live with you!" Natasha continued nervously wiping her eyes and adjusting her hair. Steve lay there staring at her, wondering why she wanted to live with a person like him. Signalling her to come closer, he raised his hand slowly and touched the side of her face lovingly before pulling her forward and kissing her on the lips.

"Shit, I thought you said he was on death's door!" Edward shouted down the hallway to Aaron and Ali, waving the others to come down to his room. Steve's whole family had travelled to London after Ali had sent them a message explaining what had happened.

Upon arriving that morning, the group rushed to the hospital and were greeted by Ali and Aaron who explained about the coma Steve was in. Edward seeing the fear in the eyes of the women, who loved Steve, volunteered to have a look first to help reassure them. Edward had to admit it was a gut-wrenching walk down the corridor, wondering how bad Steve would look, and worried for the others. As he slowly opened the door, he found. Instead, Natasha and Steve kissing.

Looking around surprised, Natasha ran to the door hugging Edward, as Steve's whole family came through the door followed by a stunned Ali and Aaron.

"I can't believe it!" Ali shouted above the noise to Edward. "An hour ago he was like a vegetable!" Ali was embarrassed after telling his family to expect the worst.

"Must have been the mouth to mouth he's been getting!" Edward laughed, as the others joined in.

Steve missed the funeral, he was still too sick to move, so Aaron volunteered to stay with him, while the others attended. Edward was part of the official group of dignities from Australia, including Shane. He and Shane had received bravery awards from their Prime Minister, who stood beside his men proudly, next to the British Prime Minister. Edward and Shane would later look back on this moment, as the high point of their careers.

On the other side of the British Prime Minister stood the Vice President of America, along with his President, who had secretly decided to attend. Guarding him today instead of his usual detail of Secret Service agents, stood Nigel and his team. This was the greatest honour these men would ever have, as they stood there proudly before the world, guarding their country's leaders.

The Queen arrived shortly before the service commenced, accompanied by her husband and family. She'd also brought a special guest, the spiritual leader of the London Mosque. At first, the crowd was silent. After getting over the shock, they cheered wildly at the Queen's gesture of friendship. Once inside the Cathedral, the service proceeded quickly as several friends of Captain Johnson, gave a brief rundown of his life, followed by his Commanding Officer, General Wolfe.

Cody had no family, so his Commanding Officer from when he was in the Army twenty years ago and still his friend Captain Ali Mustaffer retired, gave a brief description of his friend, describing him as the bravest man he had ever known, a man who always first to help another person in trouble.

After the service concluded the two fallen heroes were taken to a private plot belonging to Captain Johnson's family, escorted by his SAS team. The family had asked if Cody could be buried with their son as they had died in battle together. Everyone had agreed, Ali and the others thought it was what Cody would have wanted, to be part of a family.

At the reception held at Buckingham Palace later that day, Ali had sat with the Mosque's Mullah, or Cleric, to see how he was handling the situation.

"I don't like all the attention my brother, but if it brings some peace here it is a good thing," the Mullah smiled looking around amused.

"It is too bad, so many had to die, especially Brennan," Ali said softly for the Mullah's ears only.

"He was just as bad as Ahmed my followers tell me, why should he not die?"

"No, he was not like the others my friend. The reason why the bomb didn't go off was Brennan removed the batteries from the detonator," Ali explained secretively, before saying his goodbyes and moving away. The Mullah sat there for some time thinking about Brennan. He had known him as a hot head, one of the first to join Ahmed's group. Yet he had stopped this carnage, why the Cleric asked himself?

"God works in mysterious ways!" He said out loud smiling, as the people in hearing range clapped, before he headed home, feeling better for knowing.

General Wolfe silently took the thanks from his Queen and Prime Minister knowing the real heroes went unrewarded. Looking into the crowd, he saw Cody's supposedly retired Captain talking to the American FBI agent in charge of the operation. Breaking away from several other dignitaries, he made his way to Ali wanting to thank him.

"I know it's not much, but you have the SAS's thanks for your help," Wolfe thanked him, putting out his hand. At first, he saw confusion in Ali's and the FBI agent's eyes, before Ali returned the gesture, shaking his hand.

"General I must say I'm surprised after the letter you sent Captain Johnson," Ali replied still wondering what was going on, as Nigel moved away giving them privacy.

"What letter Captain?" Wolfe asked intrigued and a little surprised by the lack of respect for his gesture. Ali seeing the General knew nothing took him aside, explaining briefly what had happened.

"My God whoever sent that letter, supposedly from me; got two good men killed and could have killed thousands more," Wolfe exploded, as Ali signalled him to keep it down.

"Were you there the day Captain Johnson arrived for reinforcements?" Ali asked watching the crowd.

"Yes, the head of the CIA arrived to see how things were going. He even went down and talked to Johnson, before he left," Wolfe whispered, as a light went on in his brain. "He set it up, saying the message was from me!" Wolfe growled his anger evident, knowing he'd been had.

"We can't prove it General, let it go!" Ali answered thinking about what to do. The general seeing the worried look on Ali's face handed him a card, with his personal phone number on it. General Wolfe quickly looked around before he spoke.

"If you need any men, no questions asked, ring me," Wolfe told him before walking off, his meaning clear.

Ali looked at the card for several seconds before making a decision and approached the American President. Seeing Ali's face coming through the crowd, Nigel automatically placed himself between Ali and the President. The Secret Service agents, who were never far away, materialised right in front of Ali, barring his way.

The President, who remembered the last time he'd been held hostage by this man surprisingly waved to him, telling his men to relax.

"I suppose I should thank you, but I only say this makes us even," the President smiled as the Vice President approached.

"What's wrong Ali?" Vice President Baker asked coming straight to the point. Ali handed the message to the President before explaining.

"This letter got one of my men killed and an SAS officer. We're lucky thousands weren't killed because of this stupidity," Ali explained, his anger just held in check. Passing the letter to the Vice President who also read it, the group moved away from the watching crowd.

"Why would General Wolfe do this?" the President asked his mind racing.

"He didn't. Stuart was there that day and gave the message to Captain Johnson, who thought his Commander had given it to him."

"That would be hard to prove Ali?" Baker replied feeling exposed talking in the open to a supposed dead terrorist.

"He improvised that day not knowing if he'd run into Captain Johnson, it's in his own handwriting!" Ali smiled.

"We'll take care of it, Ali. You go home and retire no more violence!" Baker ordered as Ali nodded his acceptance moving away.

"That man scares me," the President admitted, as Ali was swallowed up by the crowd.

"Ali and his unit are no danger anymore Sir. The old Ali would have gone straight after Stuart without a second thought, for killing one of his men. This Ali's come to us to sort it out, rather than do it himself. They're a spent force Sir they've seen too much action," Baker said sadly, the President agreeing.

"What about that bastard Stuart, he was told to lay off! He could have got millions killed if that bomb had reached London!" the President growled looking around making sure no one was listening.

"He's not well, he needs a break. Maybe the same place his predecessor retired to," Baker suggested; referring to a mental institution the former CIA boss was confined in.

"Good idea. He knows too much to take him to trial, see that it's done!" the President answered smiling, as he moved off for more photo opportunities, with his famous FBI agents.

BANDYUP PRISON WESTERN AUSTRALIA

Morgan 'The Blade' lay in her cell, gazing at the ceiling. She'd been moved here after her arrest at Roberts' house to await trial. Bandyup was the only maximum-security women's prison in Western Australia. It contained the worst of society, who next to what Morgan was charged with, seemed acceptable. News of her crime had filtered through the prison system giving her notoriety amongst the inmates.

The guards saw her as trouble, watching her closely expecting at any moment for her to strike out at them. To their surprise, she seemed at peace with her situation, always polite to the guards and her fellow prisoners. Her appointed legal team found her easy to talk to her, believing her story of being forced to be a terrorist.

In Australia, she'd been charged with murder and attempted murder. The first was for killing Hussein; the second of attempted murder was for someone the Federal police refused to name. The second charge had been dropped after her legal team kicked up a stink at there being a charge without a victim who could testify.

Hussein's death Morgan told them was in self-defence after he'd raped her. In shock, she then had wandered onto the beach to be arrested near someone's house, who claimed she'd tried to kill him. Even the charges she was wanted for overseas were on fingerprints and one case with DNA, which only placed her at the scene. She had explained this by being forced by her captors in England, to accompany them on their missions. There she was forced to have sex with them while pretending to be one of their wives as cover for their operations.

To most people there she seemed broken by her treatment, even the physiatrist after examining her agreed that she was unbalanced by mistreatment from her youth.

Given extra freedom for her good behaviour by the guards, she used the gym continually keeping herself in shape. Being a women's prison most of the guards were women though there was a sprinkling of men, who found Morgan very desirable. To the female guard's amazement, she kept her distance from them never using her sexuality to her advantage. Impressed with her behaviour, both the guards and her legal team were convinced she was innocent. They all looked forward to her trial; most believed she'd get off.

When the story broke of the terrorist cell that held her captive in England, being killed in a shootout with the SAS and FBI, the guards brought her papers showing her what had happened. She broke down in tears, telling them how now she was at last free.

The day of her trial, two guards were sent from the courts to pick her up. They arrived at five in the morning for the three-hour drive to the Perth courthouse. There she'd be held till the trial was completed. Several guards were there when she left wishing her good luck as the courthouse guards handcuffed her, locking her in the rear of the van. One guard travelled in the rear with her his only weapon a baton, while the other drove.

"Look after her," one of the prison guards stated waving, as they started off, getting a 'will do' from the guard in the back of the van. As they drove towards the court, Robby Thompson couldn't believe his luck. The woman was beautiful, and it appeared well liked by the prison guards, meaning she was well behaved.

"That was quite a send-off," Robby told her, trying not to look at her long legs that now showed as she sat on the opposite bench to his.

"Yeah, the guards have been good to me, I hope if everything goes okay, to come back and visit someday on the right side of the bars," she smiled suddenly bending over in pain.

"Are you okay?" Robby asked seeing her strain against the cuffs.

"It's okay I've just got a cramp in my leg. I know you can't release the cuffs, but can you rub my left thigh?" she pleaded.

"No problem," he replied as leaning forward he massaged her leg from her knee to her dress, staying away from her panties.

"That's great thank you," she smiled sitting up, as Robby reluctantly stopped. "My name's Morgan, what's yours?" she asked trying to get comfortable as the van went over a bump making her fall sideways. Jumping to her, he pulled her up off the floor and back onto the seat, getting a good look at her breasts.

"My name's Robby," he said chuckling as she too laughed at their predicament. Hitting another bump, Robby was ready this time holding her to him, stopping her falling. 'This is ridiculous' Robby thought as he felt her breath on his neck, making a decision.

Reaching behind him he pulled his keys from his belt undoing her cuffs.

"I'm sure I can trust you Morgan and this way you can keep yourself upright". Robby smiled.

"Thank you, Robby, that's much better," Morgan purred rubbing her wrist, as a banging came from the front. Robby moving forward asked the driver what was wrong. He found the driver was just checking on him, warning him there were roadwork's to hang on. Moving back opposite Morgan he told her what the guard had said warning her.

"I'll sit next to you," Morgan replied sliding off her seat moving next to him. At the next series of bumps, Robby put his hand behind her steadying her, as she moved in close.

Robby knew she was on trial for murder and that she was supposedly dangerous, but not why. As they travelled along, he asked her what she'd done. Morgan told him how while being held captive her companion named Hussein had tried to rape her. She'd fought back killing him with his own knife. Unfortunately, he had friends and so now she was going to trial even though the guards all thought she'd get off. Robby was disgusted that it had got this far believing her, as the guards had.

"It worries me that I might go to jail, I'm still a virgin," she confided in him crying.

"I'm sure it will be okay," he answered pulling her to him hugging her. Tears flowed from her eyes down his neck as he held her to him, her hand resting on his thigh. Comforting her, he kissed her neck and hair trying to reassure her that someone cared. Before he knew what was happening she had straddled him her legs on either side of his, as she kissed him on the lips.

At first, the kiss was soft as if she wanted just to enjoy a person's love. Then the kiss became more urgent as both of them clutched each other as her hips worked their way back and forwards on his thighs. Breaking apart Robby found himself fully aroused as Morgan sat beside him watching him.

"I don't want to go to jail a virgin Robby, take me now Robby, so I've got something to remember," she begged pushing herself upon him she kissed him excitedly, thrusting her tongue into his mouth.

"Are you sure Morgan?" Robby asked breathing heavily, as she nodded yes. Past caring about his career, he swiftly unbuttoned Morgan's dress pulling it over her head.

"Hurry!" she implored, as standing in the limited room Robby swiftly stripped of his uniform, as before him Morgan removed her bra and panties.

Both stood holding onto the sides of the swaying van as they looked at each other's nakedness. Rushing forward Morgan kissed him before laying down on the bench opening herself to him. Robby excited beyond belief, jumped upon her entering her roughly holding her mouth as she screamed, muffling the noise.

Robby couldn't remember in his wildest dreams ever imagine making love like he was now. Thrusting repeatedly, Morgan drove him on encouraging him moaning for more. In the end finished he groaned in pleasure as she instructed him to lie down while she mounted him.

Eager to please he obeyed, as looking up he marvelled at her body as she rode him moaning above him. Completely spent Robby, as close to heaven as a man could be, lay exhausted. Morgan smiling at him grabbed his neck, ripping it sideways snapping his spinal cord and neck, killing him instantly.

Barry, the driver in front, listened to what was going on in the back with a great amount of envy. Even though Robby tried to stop Morgan from screaming Barry was well aware of what was going on. Robby and Barry weren't married, so Barry figured what no one knew wasn't going to hurt anyone. Morgan suddenly screaming made him jump.

"Robby, what's wrong?" Barry shouted as Morgan open the connecting hatch.

"I think Robby's had a heart attack," Morgan cried out. Barry pulling up looked back through the hatch to see Robby face down on the bench and Morgan standing naked next to him. Knowing how this would look, Barry drove off the main road onto a deserted side road. Pulling up, he ran back to the rear of the van opening the door with his gun in his hand. Morgan was crying bent over beside Robby, her naked backside facing Barry as he entered the van. Feeling for his pulse and finding none, Barry considered what to do.

"It's my fault! I asked him to make love as I might be going to jail. We were just getting started when he grabbed his chest," Morgan cried out, as Barry put away his gun hugging her.

"Help me get him dressed. Then I'll ring for help," Barry suggested as she willingly helped. Getting Barry's clothes back on wasn't easy, especially with Morgan's naked breast swaying in front of Barry as she helped. Finished, Barry decided to put Robby up front with him so he could secure Morgan in the back again as if that's the way it had happened. Once they'd moved the body to the passenger side, Barry walked back with the still naked Morgan, both resting leaning against the back door.

"Have you got any water?" Morgan asked as Barry asked her to move back into the van getting a cup of water for her from a bottle kept in the van for the prisoners. Sitting there watching Morgan drink, Barry's eyes were drawn to Morgan as she sat there silently.

"Best we keep this quiet miss. It could hurt his family," Barry said softly knowing he would get fired for this.

"Of course I will, and my name's Morgan," she smiled as she suddenly looked at herself as if realising for the first time she was naked. "God I'm so sorry," she said grabbing her dress covering herself.

"Well at least he died happy," Barry smiled trying to lift her spirits as he prepared to lock the door.

"Can you just sit with me for a few more minutes I'm so scared?" Morgan sobbed her dress slipping below her breast. Barry unable to look away hopped into the van closing the door.

"It won't hurt to sit here for awhile," he said, pulling her to him, holding her. The silence continued for several minutes, as Barry mesmerised, continued to watch the dress slide onto the floor revealing more and more of Morgan. Having had enough of looking, Barry started to undress.

"What are you doing?" Morgan asked sounding scared, as Barry dropped his pants to the floor stepping out of them.

"I'm just finishing what Robby started. I'm sure it won't hurt," he laughed, as Morgan sprang forward smashing her fist into his throat. Winded, unable to breathe Barry watched as Morgan pick up his pistol from his discarded pants.

"This won't hurt either!" she giggled, as placing his gun against his right eye, she pulled the trigger.

It was another two hours, before a major search by the police found the van. Morgan of course, was long gone.

FAREWELLING A FRIEND

The day after the funeral, Steve sat up in bed, looking through the papers Aaron had brought in showing the funeral. Captain Johnson and Cody's photo were on the front cover, both in their uniforms. Steve felt a great sadness for Cody, he'd come close to shooting him, when he admitted he was the Thistle, but then he'd turn around and given his life to save Steve's.

"I'm going to miss that big thug!" Steve admitted wiping his eyes.

"Yes I feel bad about the day he told us that he hadn't given you up, I didn't believe him," Aaron confessed. Aaron had been a closer to Cody than the others, and Steve wondered what Aaron would do now.

"Are you going to be okay?" Steve asked thinking Aaron could come back with him and Natasha, wondering if he should have checked with her first.

"Actually I've met someone Steve. She works on my vineyard as storeman of all things. I was going to tell you all, but this business came up," Aaron replied smiling sheepishly.

"I'm happy for you my friend. Bring her out to Australia when you can, I'd like to meet her," Steve answered happily.

"You won't have to wait that long, she's coming here tomorrow to meet you. I told her everything Steve," Aaron confessed wondering how Steve would take it.

"You did the right thing!" Steve said grabbing his friend's arm, as both went silent looking again at the paper.

"Hey isn't that one of your daughters with Agent Chambers?" Aaron asked smiling, seeing Steve focus on the picture of Lindsey hugging Nigel. The caption read 'Hero engaged to Aussie model'.

"Hey here's another one!" Aaron laughed, showing a picture of Patrick with Robin kissing passionately in a photo of the crowd. Steve looked at the photo; his protective fatherly emotions making him crush the paper while he was holding it.

"They're fine young men Steve; your girls have done well," Aaron added seeing the anger in Steve before he saw Steve relaxed smiling.

"God I've got a nerve being angry, I haven't exactly been a model parent have I?" Steve admitted letting go the paper.

"They love you Steve and understand what we've been through. Let them live their own lives," Aaron suggested, as Steve swung his feet over the side of the bed.

"If those boys are coming to ask me something, I'm not going to appear weak!" Steve grunted, trembling as he put weight on his legs as he made to stand.

"Shit Steve if you're worried about that, I could scare them with my knives," Aaron chuckled, gripping Steve's shoulder, and taking some of his weight, which was tricky considering Aaron still had plaster on his leg. At first, Aaron thought Steve would go face first onto the floor, but he was a tough bastard, and after standing upright he took several tentative steps, getting more confident with each one. After managing to walk around the room unaided, Steve collapsed back onto his bed sweating heavily and feeling exhausted.

"Are you happy now?" Aaron scoffed.

"Well, at least I can walk!" Steve smiled secretly relieved that he could.

Given the importance of the funeral, and the fact their President was there, Aaron gave Nigel and Patrick until lunchtime, to see the paper and realise they had to come and see Steve. So it was no surprise when at about one that day two silent young men, accompanied by two unusually quiet young women, appeared at the door. Hurrying forward Lindsey and Robin hugged their father smothering him with kisses, as their two boyfriends stood like silent sentinels behind them. After the show of affection was over, an unusual pause in conversation gripped the room.

"I'll be outside if you need me!" Aaron announced grim-faced, exiting the room. Steve stood up facing the young men, waiting. Nigel and Patrick had the impression that Steve was towering over them, as he stood there waiting for someone to say something. Patrick was the first to speak, as while the girls were hugging their father, he had seen the papers beside the bed, opened at the shot of him and Robin at the funeral.

"Mr Roberts, sorry I mean Steve; I'd like to marry Robin if that's okay?" Patrick stuttered out nervously, making the other three giggled, as Steve's face became stone.

"How are you going to support her? I'm not too sure that a reporter's life is very solid!" Steve shot back, seeing Robin give him a look that said 'what about your life'.

"I've been offered a job doing research for the New York Times in Australia; I'll be based in Sydney," Patrick replied a lot more confidently this time. Looking at his two daughters, he saw the pleading puppy look, and he knew he was cornered.

"Okay Patrick, but you'd better look after her!" Steve warned him, giving his best 'I'll kill you if you don't' look.

"I will Dad," Patrick laughed, seeing Steve's turn back to stone.

"I wouldn't push it Son!" Steve answered, before smiling at the effect he had on Patrick.

"What about you?" Steve asked looking at Nigel making him flinch.

"Look, Steve, I too want to marry Lindsey. In the meantime she's coming to live with me in New York. We'll marry sometime next year, rather than crowd Robin and Patrick's wedding," Nigel rushed out bravely, looking Steve right in the eye, as Lindsey grabbed his hand for support.

The young group stood there silently waiting for the explosion about them living together, but Steve instead wiped his eyes as tears started to fall. He remembered back to his time with Michelle, when they'd moved to Perth, living together until they too had married. Covering his embarrassment by wiping his nose, Steve carefully stepped forward offering his hand to both young men.

"Who am I to talk about how you all live your lives. You have my blessing," Steve said eyes misting up again.

After the rituals of promising they'd all do the right thing, the four excitedly hurried from the room to tell the others how it had gone? This left Steve sitting there alone, contemplating his life. As two laughing couples walked down the corridor, hand in hand, they passed Aaron and Ali sitting at the end of the corridor. Aaron cleaning his fingernails with a wicked looking Stiletto knife.

"We'll be watching you two!" Ali said flatly to Nigel and Patrick, whose smiling faces disappeared, as they continued on. Once they'd gone, Ali and Aaron got up and walked to Steve's room smiling.

The next day, Steve, Ali and Aaron, along with all their families and friends, met at Cody's grave saying goodbye to their friend. Everyone took his or her turn saying something funny or memorable about Cody, Natasha ending it by telling how he saved her life. In the end their friends and family drifted away, leaving just Steve, Ali and Aaron. They sat silently in contemplation, remembering better days.

"We really did shake the world up didn't we?" Aaron admitted softly, wiping his eyes.

"Yes, but I'd give anything to have Michelle, Sukai and Cody here with us now," Steve groaned, knowing their loss would never equal the good they had done.

"We must make the most of what we have now my friends. I'm sure our departed friends would want that," Ali murmured, as they all stood supporting each other leaving Cody to rest in peace.

They'd just reached their vehicles when Edward jumped from his car moving towards them. Steve tensed, as did Aaron and Ali sensing trouble. Edward seeing they knew something was wrong broke it to them.

"The woman named Morgan or 'The Blade' as you know her escaped from jail in Australia three days ago. They've just rung me on the off chance she may have escaped overseas and be coming back home to England," Edward told them.

"Could be nothing?" Aaron pointed out, as they all looked around, knowing they were all unarmed.

"Best we get moving anyway, just in case," Ali suggested getting agreement as they moved towards their cars.

One hundred metres above them on a small hill, Morgan trained her sniper rifle on Steve Roberts' head, as he moved towards his car. 'Once he stops at the car door he's mine,' she smiled keeping him in the crosshairs.

After she'd killed the two buffoons in the van, she'd hitched a ride in four-wheel drive driven by a pig hunter going shooting up north near Broome. He'd driven her north at great speed with the promise of an unforgettable night of wild sex. It had proved unforgettable for him, as she tossed his body out of the van driving into Broome. From there she flown to Sydney retrieving a spare passport, before travelling onto New Zealand, she'd changed her appearance, before boarding another plane for England.

Customs in England had been her only worry. Luckily the Australian's had moved too slowly, only notifying the Brits after all efforts to capture her in Australia had been exhausted. Her description arrived the day after she had returned. Finding her group had been decimated; she sought out anyone who remained, finding only one. He been sick on the night and hadn't gone with the others. Morgan could tell he'd been shaken by the destruction of the group, so after getting the location of a weapons cache, she killed him.

Now being the last of her group, she'd thought to kill the men responsible for their downfall. All three of the units remaining members were here, so after she finished with Roberts, she try for the others. Her excitement over the coming kills made her breathing erratic, so she lowered her weapon. Taking several deep breathes calming herself; she refocused on Roberts as he approached his car.

"Goodbye Steve," she giggled, as Steve Roberts stopped at his car door. A pistol fitted with a silencer, coming to rest on the side of her head, made her freeze.

"Take your hand off the trigger and put both your hands behind your back," a voice ordered with a slight accent that she couldn't recognise. Doing as she was told, she rolled slightly to the side to see her captor. He was a young man in his early twenties she guessed with blue eyes. The Gillis camouflaged suit he wore hid his other features.

"So what are you going to do with your prize?" she asked seductively, as he pulled the trigger. Looking around making sure no one had seen or heard the shot, the man slowly moved back into cover. He then met up with the other member of his team, who was also wearing a Gillis suit.

"How did it go?" she asked in French.

"The threat's been neutralised," her companion answered signalling for her to follow him. Standing slowly, the two pieces of vegetation ghosted through the trees, arriving at a small track. There sat a black Mercedes, carefully concealed under a large spreading willow tree. Swiftly changing out of their army gear the young couple tossed it into the boot, changing into casual clothing. Making sure everything looked normal they both jumped into the car, the young lady furiously brushing her blonde hair. Starting the car, the young man pulled his companion to him kissing her.

"Later," she smiled, as taking another looking around, they drove down the track reaching the main road. Following the properties boundary wall, they came to the main gate, entering. Driving up the tree-lined road, they came to a stop next to Steve Roberts' car making him look towards them.

"Peter!" Ali yelled as the young man jumped from the Mercedes. Approaching his father, he hugged him.

"Everyone, this is my son Peter and his girlfriend Marlies," Ali announced clearly pleased to see him. After introductions were carried out, the friends drove back to Ali's hotel celebrating retirement.

"What do you two do for a job?" Steve asked Peter and Marlies as they sat with Natasha.

"We're both in the army. Marlies is in the French paratroops, I'm in the Swiss Special Ops. We're both on holiday at the moment, so I thought we could stop in and check on Mum and Dad," Peter answered smiling.

"We're all glad you came. Come I'll introduce you to my family." Steve suggested, as everyone happily and finally, got to meet the friends of the unit members.

It was a good night, though Edward seemed on edge worried about Morgan.

"Relax Edward, it's behind us. She is not going to bother anyone again," Steve assured him, making Edward finally relax. By three in the morning, nearly everyone had departed, leaving Steve, Natasha, Ali and Julie sitting with Peter and Marlies. The women moved off to clean up, leaving Ali and Steve to walk Peter and Marlies out to their vehicle.

"Nice car," Steve said as Peter climbed behind the wheel Marlies hoping in on the passenger side.

"Yes he got it cheap, borrowing the money his dad," Ali laughed.

"Looks the same as the one Aaron saw parked up that track, on the other side of the property where Cody's buried," Steve pointed out, as Peter and Marlies turned to stone.

"She's dead I guess?" Ali asked looking at his son.

"Yes, how did you know?" Marlies said softly.

"Aaron was worried about us all being in one place unarmed. He and I drove past seeing your car there yesterday. We figured you were keeping watch, which seems to have paid off." Ali explained looking none too happy.

"I'm glad you were there Peter. It saved Aaron wobbling up that hill and having to do it. He would've missed out on paying his last respects to the rest of us," Steve smiled, seeing Ali in Peter.

"We'll talk about it later son and remember even a silenced pistol makes a noise, all three of us heard it even though no one else did," Ali warned his son.

Peter not knowing what to say drove away, leaving Steve and Ali standing silently in the driveway.

"You're full of shit Ali. There's no way we'd have heard that shot, even in our prime."

"He's too cocky. I was just bringing him down a peg or two," Ali smiled proud of his son.

"Let's go inside, and you can watch me drink to our retirement since you don't," Steve chuckled as they both walked inside feeling free.

Peter did not talk for ten minutes as he drove Marlies back to their hotel.

"That car was well hidden, how'd they know to look there?" Peter suddenly said thinking he'd somehow stuffed up.

"They must've been shit hot when they were young Peter," Marlies chuckled, moving closer to him. Since the skiing trip, the two had remained close, sharing the same interests. They'd both joined the army the same year, though Marlies was in her last year having decided to leave. At the moment they'd shared a place on the border between Switzerland and France.

"I just can't believe I was so easily spotted, let alone heard," Peter whispered as Marlies starting giggling.

"They were having you on Peter. I was watching through my scope. None of them saw or heard anything."

"Those old bastards!" Peter smiled, hugging Marlies as they both burst out laughing.

Ross Stuart relaxed in his office, happy with the world. He knew the President and Vice President suspected him of trying to get Ali and his unit, but they couldn't prove it.

'They'd have done something by now if they could!' he smirked, lighting a well-earned Cuban cigar blowing smoke towards the No Smoking sign. Going through his appointments for the day, he saw that Don Brooks the ex-head of the CIA had asked to see him, indicating he knew how to retrieve the ten million held in a Swiss bank account, the final payment for the hit on Roberts. Stuart knew he wanted something in return, so he intended to play ball until he had the money. Rapping his fingers on the desk, Stuart wondered what else he knew as pushing his intercom button; he called for his car and driver to meet him out front.

"Won't hurt to find out what else the nut job knows?' Stuart smiled. Grabbing his coat from the hat stand and walking confidently to the lift. Jumping into the back of his limo, Stuart told the driver where to go, seeing it wasn't his normal driver or security escort.

"Where is my usual driver and security escort?" Ross Stuart asked angrily, at not being told of the change.

"I'm sorry Sir, they've both got a day off under the new roster Sir, should be back tomorrow," the security escort informed him, sounding slightly afraid of Stuart, which of course he liked. Nodding his okay, the driver professionally drove out onto the highway heading to the asylum.

While the security escort updated their location and where they were going, Ross sat secretly impressed. These two new men were more professional than his usual team, going about their duties expertly. Pressing the screen button, he raised the glass wall between himself and the two men in front so he could work without being overheard. Sitting there feeling invincible, Ross smiled to himself, before starting to yawn.

Looking out the window, thinking of ways to ruin the President's re-election, Ross had trouble keeping his eyes open. A feeling of dead tiredness settled over him, as he found concentrating on his thoughts difficult. Shaking himself, fighting to stay awake, Ross slumped back into his seat wondering what was wrong.

"I shouldn't be tired," Ross muttered, his eyes fluttering, as he toppled sideways across the back seat. In one last effort to alert his men, he stumbled forward banging the glass-dividing wall several times with his hands. In the front seat, Allan and Ian looked back smiling as Stuart collapsed onto the floor.

"Have a good sleep Alice, you're going to Wonderland!" Ian chuckled as Allan cut the flow of gas to the back seat.

"Wake up Mr Stuart, it's time for your meds," a distant voice murmured, as Stuart tried to concentrate.

"What's going on?" Stuart grumbled trying to stand, finding his hands bound to his side.

"You know the routine Mr Stuart. If you don't take your meds, you don't get to play with the others," the voice cheerfully informed him, as his eyes focused on his surroundings. Two white uniformed men taking his silence for consent, put two tablets in his mouth followed by a cup of water forcing him to swallow.

"Do you know who you're manhandling?" Stuart yelled, suddenly realising his predicament.

"Let me guess, you're our President. You can't be the Vice President, he's black," one guard stated causing both guards to laugh.

"I'm Ross Stuart head of the CIA, release me immediately!" Ross screamed trying to stand and barge his way past the two guards. Instead, he became dizzy, collapsing back onto his bed.

"God now we got two of them!" the one guard laughed, as they both grabbed Ross, carrying him out into a large activities area. Seating him, they made sure he was comfortable before moving off to attend to their next patient. Focusing Ross looked across at the inmate sitting beside him, who looked familiar.

"You!" screamed Stuart trying to stand causing the guards to return. Settling him down again the guards stood watching him making sure he was okay.

"You two try to get along now," one guard smiled thinking they could leave now.

"Yeah, you've both got so much in common!" the other guard chuckled, as they walked off. Ross tried to work out what was going on, as the man's face next broke into a smile.

"Don Brooks, is that you?" Ross asked realising what was going on.

"Good morning Ross and welcome to Wonderland!" Don screamed laughing insanely, as the other inmates around them joined in. Stuart scared shitless, jumped to his feet, and ran groggily towards an entrance at the side of the room. Pounding on the steel door Ross looked through the glass section of the door, seeing John Wilson standing there smiling.

"Enjoy your holiday Ross!" John shouted through the thick pane of glass, before smiling and walking away.

"You can't do this; I'm the head of the CIA!" Ross shouted back, as the two guards in white arrived.

"Settle down Sir, or it's back to your room," one of the guards informed him, as they both walked him back to his chair.

"It's a setup! John Wilson from the FBI is out there!" Ross cried, looking across at Brooks seeing him sleeping soundly.

"Sure he is. We'll invite him in for lunch with the President later," the guard replied trying not to laugh, as they walked around the room, settling the other inmates down. Stuart sat there comatose, wondering how this could possibly have happened.

At the front door, John Wilson climbed into his limo, which was exactly the same as Stuart's. In the front seat sat Allan and Ian, who with a smile started up, heading out onto the highway.

"Good work men. That's two problems that can sit on ice for the next ten years," John growled, wishing they'd both faced trial.

"What happens when they get out?" Allan asked gladly the whole affair was over.

"Who cares no one will believe them, and we'll all be retired or someplace else. There might be some trouble, but I can sleep with that," John smiled.

"If you want to sleep boss, I can turn on the gas," Ian smiled.

"Don't even think about it agent!" John laughed, as they drove towards Washington.

EPILOGUE

In time Steve's family departed, leaving only Steve and Natasha. They spent the next six months in Europe with Aaron and his partner Petra, and Ali with his wife, Julie. They had a lot of catching up to do, promising from now on to keep in touch.

In the end, Steve took Natasha back to Perth where he finally caught up with John, his neighbour and his family. Another surprise was after contacting Dave to see how he was, Steve found out he was getting married to Susan.

He was taking her back to Ballina where she was taking up a position at the local hospital. He was also a bit upset with Steve for tossing the gun away he'd given him. Contacting Edward, Steve got him to ask his new boss Shane to smooth it over with the state cops, which helped. Both promised to keep in touch but no more shooting.

Natasha while there finally, sent in her report about chasing terrorists all over the world, ending in London. Her boss at first wasn't too impressed with letting the Roberts story go, but after the President invited him and his wife to a special night at the Whitehouse, explaining what had happened to Stuart, he decided to let it drop.

ONE YEAR ON

Hand in hand Steve walked along the sand with his new love beside him. He still jogged every morning, but today being special, he took Natasha for a walk in the sunshine. It was one year from the day Cody had died; it was also the day Steve had given up his old life. Happy and free he was at peace with himself enjoying every minute of it. Looking across he saw Natasha watching him, knowing what he was thinking.

"It's so peaceful here Steve, I don't think I'll ever leave unless I get a better offer," Natasha laughed, splashing Steve and pushing him over before running. Getting over the surprise attack, Steve raced her after, knowing she was trying to cheer him up. Chasing her into the surf, he pulled her bikini top off, laughing at her surprise. She then chased him pushing him under, before kissing him.

On the hill above the beach, two men watched the couple's antics through powerful binoculars.

"God they behave like teenagers!" one of them smiled.

"Yeah he's a lucky man," the other replied, as reaching for his radio he called their base, informing them the targets were still there.

THE END